I0640273

The Goat Woman

Mike Champagne

Copyright © 2016 Michael Champagne

All rights reserved.

ISBN-13:978-0-9984083-0-9

DEDICATION

For my Wife who is and always has been my encouragement and inspiration.

CONTENTS

ACKNOWLEDGMENTS

With gratitude to Rea Rosno, Mary Bloom, and Kathleen Moore who have worked with me to make sure this book arrived at its best.

PROLOGUE

What was this madness?...it was much too big! She didn't need it!
What the hell was wrong with her? As she watched the moving men
coming in and out, she could feel the pressure build behind her eyes.
What would she do in Massachusetts, in this little town? Yet, she felt
powerless to stop herself. It was as if something outside herself,
some...power had seized control, taken her over. Why had she bought
this house? Here she was moving in! All of Gram's things were being
unloaded. It was like a bad dream you couldn't wake up from. She
seemed powerless to yell, "Stop! Put it all back! Cancel it!"

CHAPTER 1

There was no psychiatrist. No, no, no, no, no—she didn't need that. This was *not* getting back to the office. What she needed was a break, time away, time to think. This was nothing more than some mid-life crisis, a "Petite Mal," an anomaly—something you get over...something you move past!

She knew Holmsford—maybe that was why. There was a connection. As a little girl, she had stayed with her grandparents...maybe. Maybe coming to Holmsford was the natural thing to do! It was the only place outside of New York where she felt any connection at all. It was the last place she remembered being happy. Coffee ice-cream after grocery shopping with Gram—at Lorraine's Coffee and Tea Emporium with its massive marble ice-cream fountain, sawdust on the floor and the smell of roasting coffee in the air. Shopping at Gray's Mercantile with Grandad. Neat rows of tools and hardware—bins of screws and nails and the smell of fresh cut lumber. Secure, carefree, protected...normal. Just a little girl with no particular agenda except for growing up. Nowhere she had to be; no one expecting anything of her, in charge of nothing and no one but herself.

As she stood in the middle of the huge living room piled with boxes and furniture retrieved from storage, she closed her eyes and pictured the old house...

Grandad called it a "Painted Lady," one of those absurd Victorian valentines with a square tower and little "balconies" on the upper stories, a big wrap-around porch across the front and side with a "cresting" of fancy wrought-iron work all around the roof. Queen Anne, that's what they called it. It was silly and ornate and Gram and Grandad were so proud of it! It was a "symbol of our family's standing in the town," Grandad always said. It had a little room at the top of its square tower with an oval window that looked out over the immaculate lawn. She would climb up there and pretend she was a queen in her castle tower looking for her knight. It stood outside of town on its own fifteen acres of land. It was the grandest house in the tiny town of Holmsford, but when Grandad had his accident, Gram Esther was forced to sell. Now a shopping mall stood where it had been.

When Gram Esther passed, Eve was given the key to a storage unit dutifully paid for by the estate lawyer while she was a minor, and later she continued to pay. A note had read:

> *"There's no money, Honey, but I kept everything I could in case you wanted it. Do whatever you need to. Love, Gram."*

This house could never be like that! It was a new place pretending to be old. This house was...empty. It had been left by its original owners after only three years—long before there could ever have been a soul to it.

But it was big all right. It was big enough to bring everything from the storage place and unpack it all, and try to find...something. There she stood reading Gram's short, little note wondering what her next move might be.

It had started with a sense of...distance. That was it!...It was as though she were far away from herself. She remembered all the usual office insanity, the "push and shove". People talking to her, but she didn't hear them. She couldn't focus on what they said. She took a meeting with Pete Gladstone, a client, and she couldn't remember it—any of it. She was aware of talking, making suggestions, joking with him, but it was as if she weren't in her own body. She panicked and told her secretary that she was feeling "ill"—ill! She had never been ill! She couldn't snap out of it, come to consciousness—whatever. She remembered driving to her apartment. She remembered calling to say that she would be out of the office "for a few days" and that she would maintain contact by phone and online. The next thing she remembered, she was driving past the town line into Holmsford and renting a room at the Holmsford Inn, a cheesy motel north of town. She remembered the real estate agent's office—signing the closing documents. Two days! That's all it had taken to upturn her entire self-image. The next thing she knew, she was making arrangements to have Gram's things delivered out of storage.

She didn't trust herself. She'd been away from the office for a full month! She monitored the accounts by computer and sent her recommendations and instructions every day, but Eve knew she was only holding open the door. She was Vice President of Accounts and Management in Novus and Gardner. She was a partner; she had control of the entire department. Nothing and no one escaped her attention. She ruled with an iron fist; no one—no man—tried to push her around. She was the "Dragon Lady," and that was all right with her. She had made her reputation by being uncompromising, demanding, and totally dedicated to the business...No, it was better for her to wrestle her demons here away from observing eyes. She knew the Board might begin to question her soon, but nobody under her would dare question her absence, except, perhaps, Jace.

Jace. Her indulgence, her...she didn't want to say "weakness." He came in as a hot-shot trader from Plunkett & Klein, but he had bold ideas and an uncanny intuition for stocks. In the first few months he had boosted their revenue by twenty percent, and he had made a move on every woman in the office. When he got to Eve, she had cut him dead. No "shave-tail" trader was going to use her to get ahead—no matter how insistent he was.

And he did insist! He charmed and canoodled and talked himself all around her. He was young, ten years younger. That was flattering. It amused her to see him turn himself inside out to try to seduce her. But Jace also worked like a devil! He was in before everyone and left as late as she did. He knew every twitch in the market almost before she did, and his recommendations were always on the money. It was during one of those late-nights-at-the-office. They had just scored big on an IPO. It had started with celebratory drinks and wound up in the bedroom of her co-op with the drapes opened to view the southern half of Manhattan.

He told her she was the first woman who could keep up with him. She didn't believe him, but she did enjoy him. He was glossy and totally self-involved, but he was also playful and funny, and he had stamina! There was no doubt that this was his "sport." Moreover, he was her inferior at the office. She had control; that made it somehow more exciting. Eve had cautioned him that if he ever tried to "trade" on it, he'd be out the door like yesterday's newspaper. She wouldn't tolerate office gossip. He could take it or leave it.

He took it—and she took him. He was the best—the only—diversion she had allowed herself in a very long time. She had it all…career…money…younger lover…control—What was it? What the hell was it! What was it that woke her in the night in a sweat? What was it that made her come here and buy this house? What was she trying to do? She was ambitious, self-made, accomplished…it was absurd! She was thirty-eight. She had no illusions about herself. What more could she ask for? She was disgusted with herself feeling the way she did, but she knew there was something …wrong. She couldn't risk going back and looking weak.

She felt like the house she had just bought, stylish…and empty. It was as if she hadn't lived long enough in herself to possess a soul either. She was exhausted thinking about it.

"What the hell do you want?" She said out loud to herself.

"Sorry, I didn't mean to disturb you or nothin'. I just wanted to know what you want us to do with the rest of the furniture. The truck's still half full." The moving man stood awkwardly on the raised step that made the living room "sunken," looking even taller than he actually was.

"No—not you...I was...talking to myself." Eve noticed that the man was handsome in a rough sort of way, Blonde, muscular...clearly proud of his body.

"You want to watch that. People'll think you're crazy..." He smiled at her in a frank and inviting way.

"Put all the beds and dressers upstairs—in fact, put it all up there. I'll sort it out later."

"...You got nice stuff...you know that?..." Now he had crossed the line. It was obvious that he wasn't talking about her furniture, but Eve chose to ignore his unblinking stare at her.

"...Just be sure you treat it with respect." She shot back with a level warning in her tone.

"Don't you worry. I got the touch...Never had no complaints..."

"OK, that was enough!" she thought. Time to put him in his place. "I hired you for work, not conversation. Put the rest upstairs and make sure you don't damage anything. Any damages come off your fee."

"No, Ma'am...my guys are good...and I'll give it my personal attention...You can count on it..." He turned and left, but Eve didn't like the defiance in his manner. It sounded like a threat. She was debating whether or not to report him to the company when she heard the Westminster Chimes from the front door clang. "God, that bell has to go!"

She put down her lists, which were clamped securely in a clipboard, and went curiously to the front door.

Standing there was a woman, about forty, dyed chestnut brown hair, in a designer jogging outfit and wearing an absurdly frilly kitchen apron—something out of a fifties sitcom—carrying a ring cake on a plate.

"Hi! I'm Marian—Marian Wainwright—from next door! Welcome to the neighborhood!..." She stood there for a moment with a wide grin pasted on her face and an expectant look.

Eve was dumbfounded for a moment. The woman had perfectly manicured hands and was made up as if she were expecting to go to a Broadway opening. It was nine a.m.! "Uh...thank you. Why don't you,"—before she could say "Come in," the woman had pushed past her into the hallway and handed her the cake.

"Well, I know it was clean! Junie was a maniac for clean, of course she's been gone a year, so—God, you have beautiful things! So many antiques!"

"My Grandmother—"

"So much furniture!" The woman went from piece to piece appraising Eve's furniture as Eve closed the front door.

"Thank you for the cake..."

"It's store-bought.—Sorry! I have a kitchen...somewhere in my house. I don't cook. I mean, why bother for one? I prefer to go out. Anyway, it's all on Harold. Let him pay! He wanted the divorce, now he can keep me in the style to which I want to become accustomed! That'll teach him to walk out! Oh, Honey, if you don't want the cake, just dump it. I can see you're good about your figure. It's only Sam's Club, but I wanted to make a good impression."

Eve couldn't help but smile. "I can manage some coffee. You want a piece? I'm Eve—"

"Truesdale! We know. We asked. I suppose I should have waited until you got settled, but why wait? I mean, what difference does it make? With all this furniture, you'll be a month just getting settled. Would you like me to help...or anything?" Marian's eyes were darting all around the room burning with curiosity about anything under a cover.

"...Why don't I make coffee...in here?...The kitchen?..." Eve held the door to the kitchen as Marian pried her eyes off the rest of Eve's belongings.

"Oh! Sure! Coffee...That'll be good..."

In the kitchen where practically nothing had been placed, Eve was finally able to catch the woman's whole attention. "Who's 'we'?"

"Huh?...Oh! Just the girls and me. Donna Cosgrave—she's the mock chateau across the street and Libby Fletcher, the ugly Second Empire Victorian with the Mansard Roof.—She likes it, but I think is looks like that house in *Psycho*—You know, the Bates Motel one?"

"Yes...I know the one you mean.—How do you like your coffee?"

"Black...It gives me the creeps, that house! Maybe that's why Libby drinks..." For a split second the woman seemed to be considering what she said.

"...She drinks?"

"Huh?" Suddenly the woman started from her brief hiatus.

"...Your friend...Libby, is it...she drinks?"

"You bet! Oh, honey, you'll meet her. Nothing against Libby, you understand, but she's got a real problem. But she's the best person—the one who will tell you what's what! Those people are hard to find, you know?"

"...Um hm,...I know....It's instant. I hope that's all right. I haven't had time to shop...or do much of anything."

"Totally understandable! I haven't been grocery shopping in three years! I think there might be a lemon in my crisper, but that's about the extent of my larder, so I completely understand. When you're single, you live light!—When did you get your divorce?"

"...Divorce?..."

"You mean, you're not divorced? Well, I'm an idiot! I just thought, big house...pricey antiques, must be a recent and hefty settlement. I was prepared to be sympathetic."

"...I'm not married. The furniture was my Grandmother's."

"So, you come by all this honestly?...I'm impressed! What is it you do, Evie?"

"Eve. Vice President of Accounts and Management at Novus and Gardner in New York."

"You work?...In New York?...Well, what are you doing here in Holmsford? Honey, if I was the Vice President of anything in New York City, trust me, I would not be living in this Podunk town!"

"...My family...are from here. I...came back. I suppose..."

"...So...You're going to commute?...to New York?"

"...I haven't decided...Who's June?"

"What?....Oh! Junie! Junie Hildebrande! This used to be her house. She and her husband Paul owned it before you....Poor Junie!"

"...Poor Junie?...Why 'Poor Junie?'"

"Oh, honey, didn't the real estate people tell you?—Junie disappeared! Just like that!" She snapped her fingers. "Over a year ago! Dinner on the stove, clothes in the closet...credit cards untouched! She just disappeared. We all thought it was Paul! I mean, wouldn't you? We all knew what he was like! He was fun, but Paul was cheating on her left and right! But it turns out he was in Chicago— with his secretary, of course! Such a cliché!—but it was a pretty good alibi. The Police assumed she walked out on him. There was no body, no evidence of foul play, but would you just walk out of your house one day—without the car, I might add—and leave your husband...if you were married, I mean? Who would do that? Why? We all knew he was planning to leave her, but he was clean! Nobody could pin it on him! When the year was up, he sold the house....I miss Junie...even though she was a maniac about cleaning! Lord, that girl was crazy about cleaning!"

"...Are you saying she was murdered?...Here?" Eve was beginning to feel a little strange.

"Nobody knows! I told you, she just disappeared! There was no trace of what happened to her! Anyway, we all locked our doors pretty tight after that. I mean, if there was someone...someone who did it...who's to say he wouldn't come back for one of us! The world's full of crazy people! It could have been anyone!"

"'Scuse me?..." The moving man was standing in the kitchen door leaning casually on the jamb. "We'll be done in about fifteen. You want to settle up?"

Eve saw that he was still carrying a chip on his shoulder, and she wasn't about to allow him any more opportunities.

"I'll write a check. If there are any damages..."

"You won't find a thing. I gave it my personal attention." The man was leering at Marion now who was smiling at him.

"...Do you hire out?...for small jobs, I mean?" Marian was obviously flirting with him and it made Eve uncomfortable after her first encounter with the man and especially after hearing about the previous owner of the house.

"...I...don't consider any job small. I can do whatever you want done..."

"Well, I might need some...moving. Just a few things." Marian was flushed and eyeing him.

"Let me give you my personal card. Dependin' on what you need, I could come by and... help you out..." He handed Marian a small card which she took from him with a coy smile.

"...I'll definitely give you a call."

"I guarantee my services..."

"Here you go." She cut into their little flirtation with cold purpose. "Now, we were having a conversation. You can just shut the door when you leave, and thank you." Eve was pointedly final.

"Yes, ma'am! Any time you need me. Just call...I like a challenge!" Once again Eve detected his attempt to intimidate her.

"I'll do just fine on my own. Goodbye."

The moving man snickered slightly and turned on his heel returning to the outer room.

"Um hm! I like 'em a little rough!...Don't you?"

"You know, Marian, I appreciate the visit, but I have an awful lot to do..."

Marian caught her meaning and got up immediately. "Of course, honey. I completely understand! You get yourself together. Maybe...maybe I'll come back later and take you out to dinner? How about that? You know I don't cook, but there's a really nice little place up the road...'Hell's Kitchen.' It's got nothing to do with New York, but the food's good. Why don't I pick you up and take you out? How would that be?"

"Thanks, Marian, but I need some time. You can see how much there is to do..."

"...Sure...sure! You just...I'll come back another time. I'll bring the girls! You'll like them! They're dying to meet you."

"Thanks, uh, for the cake!...Bye..."

Marian stood for a minute and then realized that there was nothing left to say. "OK, then. I'll be back..."

"I'm sure!—Oh, and Marian...?"

"Yes, Evie?"

"Eve—Don't call that guy. He's not everything you think he is."

"Maybe. It might be fun finding out!...See you!"

The woman left and Eve stood in the middle of her empty kitchen wondering what she had gotten into.

...It was then that she heard the screaming.

It was a distant, high-pitched, insistent screaming like the sound of a woman being attacked. It was coming from the rear of the house, but Marian had gone out the front. What was going on? Eve turned around and peered through her kitchen windows into her new back yard. All she could see were woods, but off in the distance there was some kind of corral or enclosure. The screaming seemed to be coming from there.

Quickly she ran out the back door and stood a moment on the brick patio that led from the kitchen and listened more attentively. Now that she was outside, the screaming was clearer. It was definitely coming from the corral area, and she picked up a hammer sitting on the weathered picnic table and jogged in the direction of the sound. As she got closer the sound increased, but she couldn't see anyone nearby. She gripped the hammer tightly in anticipation of trouble. She slowed now, keeping her senses alert for something unexpected. The screaming came intermittently, and at this moment there was nothing but silence.

She got closer to the corral structure. It was a simple wooden fence, but she still saw no one. She stopped and turned back to look at her strange new house when suddenly a loud scream directly in back of her caused her to whirl with the hammer raised above her head ready to swing!...And there it was...A small, tawny goat stood on its hind legs leaning on the fence with its forelegs and screaming at her with all its might. Its eyes rolled back in its head as it screamed seemingly for dear life. As it screamed, it seemed to clamber at her through the fence, as though pleading for help.

"What's going on with you, girl, huh?..." Eve reached out and scratched the animal between its huge ears, and immediately it was silent. It stayed on its hind legs hopping slightly like it wanted to get over the fence. "C'mon, now, you're all right!...Shh, shh, shh...settle down. You're a pretty thing, aren't you?...Quiet now. What's the matter, hm?..."

As she soothed the animal, it moaned back in its throat and struggled to get closer to her. This animal was in distress. It was evident that she was terrified and seeking something. Eve's petting and quiet reassurance was having an effect. The goat lowered its head and buried it into her stomach, taking in her soft tones and her touch. "Shh! Now...see, everything is all right. That's right, sweetie...nothing to be excited about...There you go—"

Suddenly the goat raised its head again and tensed. It let out an ear-splitting scream that caused Eve to pull back from the fence. Suddenly she saw a fist swing out from behind her and land squarely on the side of the goat's head, knocking it to the ground in the pen.

"Get off it!"

Eve turned quickly to see where the punch came from.

She was a tall woman, older, in her sixties perhaps and raw-boned. In her farm boots, tattered coat, and longish skirt, she stood close to six feet tall. A gristle of gray hair poked out of her kerchief, which she wore under a broad-brimmed hat. Her skin was rough and reddened by the elements and she carried a staff cut from some ancient sapling nearly as tall as herself. It was shiny with age and wear. She stood there after clouting the goat and stared at Eve.

"...I'm sorry...I—I heard the screaming—"

"They ain't pets, Missy. They're workin' animals. You can't tolerate their ways." The woman looked down at Eve's hands. "What's the hammer for?"

"I thought someone was in trouble."

"So, you come to help?..."

"Uh...yes. I've never heard anything like that before." Eve was still stunned at the sudden appearance of the old woman.

"They're beasts. They make noise...That gonna trouble ya?"

"...Uh...no. Actually, I like animals!...I just...didn't know..." Eve's words trailed off as she sensed the woman studying her. "Eve Truesdale. I just moved into the house."

"Eyah....Sometimes they stink—if the wind's wrong. That gonna bother ya?"

"Uh...no. Not now that I know—"

"Good. Last one didn't like 'em. Wanted me to clear 'em off. She's gone now." The woman stood there keeping a steady eye on her, and Eve suddenly felt the need to meet her stare and stand her ground. There was an awkward moment of silence between them. "...Truesdale..."

"Yes, Eve Truesdale—"

"I know who you are, Missy. I know your family. I keep to myself, and like it that way. See you do the same, and we'll git on right well." The old woman turned to leave and Eve could feel her anger rise at being dismissed so rudely. She couldn't stop herself from replying.

"No name?"

The woman turned it seemed to Eve a little surprised, "...Eh?"

"It's fine with me if you want to 'keep to yourself,' but if you know my family, you know we've been in this town since it was founded. I'm no stranger here, and I'm not 'summer people.' It's customary and right to give a proper introduction. That's the New England way. I've done that. How about you?" Eve leveled the woman in her gaze and stood her challenge to see what the old woman would do.

She cocked her head to the side and looked at Eve for a long moment, "...You gonna hit me with that hammer?..."

"Do I need to?..."

"...Maybe...might do me some good. Been on my own so long, I don't know my manners....Hetty...Hetty Livesey." The old woman thrust her hand out and Eve took it and shook. The woman's hand was rough from hard work and her grip was strong. There was nothing delicate about her.

"How do you do, Miss Livesey." Eve was still on her guard.

"Hetty's fine. Don't see the point of all that 'Miss and Mister'.... I'll make sure the beasts don't bother ya."

"They don't. The smell of a farm isn't going to put me off."

"Good, then..." They broke from the handshake. Eve could tell that the old woman was pondering something and then changed her mind. "...See ya." With that, the old woman turned and strode away, stopping once as if to turn back, but stopped herself and disappeared in the line of trees beyond the pens.

"Ok, then...I guess I'd better get on with...with whatever it is I'm doing here! Eve Truesdale, you have lost your mind!..."

***

CHAPTER 2

"Where'd you get all this stuff?"

"My Grandmother. I had it in storage. They had a big house a long time ago..."

"...It's...nice..." Jace stood in the middle of the living room trying to be encouraging. It was a miserable attempt, and Eve laughed.

"It's out of control! But give me a week and I'll have everything where it belongs." Eve looked at the disorganization around her and realized that this was at least a short-term goal—something to draw her away from the gnawing emptiness she was feeling.

"What about you?—Are you going to have *yourself* where you belong?...When are you coming back?...Why are you here?"

"Right down to business, huh?"

"C'mon, Eve, you know you've been away too long. What's going on?" Jace had put his arms around her, but it wasn't an embrace. It was to hold her from avoiding the subject.

"Right now...I'm here, and that's what I decided..." Eve knew she didn't sound convincing. She pulled away from him.

"Yeah, but why buy a house—do...all this? Aren't you coming back?"

"Of course I am! I just wanted to be here. I saw the house; I liked it."

"So you bought it? You bought a whole house; put all this stuff in it?...Why?"

"I don't answer to you, Jace. You work for me, remember? The only people I owe any explanations to are the Board, and they aren't complaining!"

"...Sorry...Boss Lady!...I didn't come here as an employee. It's the weekend. I'm on my own time." Jace sounded a little petulant.

"...So what did you come as?"...Eve looked him right in the eye, challenging him. She knew that Jace always had an agenda.

"Ok...I'm here as your...friend." It was clear that he was having trouble defining his identity with her.

"'Friend...' That's nice."

"Where have you been? It's been a month. I've been hungry for you!" He attempted to enfold her again, but she moved away.

"You make me sound like a steak dinner!...I know you, Jace—don't tell me you haven't had a few 'snacks' while you've been waiting."

"...OK....All right. Yeah, but I don't hide it with you! You *know* me! You don't whine and act all betrayed, like other women. When we're together...it's like a freight train!—There are no other women—none that count! I want that. I want what we have."

"'What we have?—What's that?" Eve chuckled a little to deflect her own confusion about their relationship.

"Passion! Pleasure!...An adult relationship. No illusions. We're like a couple of lions—working, making money, moving the earth! No...expectations—Just every day challenging each other and every night...exploding! You don't ask me for anything, and I don't ask you."

"You're asking me now. You want to know 'why' and 'when'..."

"I just want to know if you're coming back!"

"I never left! I'm in constant contact with you—with the office and with clients."

"Cell phones and computers. That doesn't cut it in the sack. I want some real contact..." He reached down along the line of her stomach, and, once again, Eve pulled away.

"Now you're sounding...I don't know...territorial?"

He reached into his pocket and pulled out a small box, opened it to reveal a glittering ring and handed it to her. "Marry me."

She wheeled around and looked at him and began to laugh, "...What?"

"Marry me. Let's make it real! I...I've been thinking about this for a while. There's nobody else like you. Nobody who gets me like you do."

"...You haven't thought this through!"

"Yes I have!" She turned and looked at him, handsome, self-assured. He was like a piece of hard candy in a glittering wrapper. Everything about him was exactly what she saw. He stood there smiling.

"You're my employee, and...you're too young for me."

"I'll get older! Everybody does."

"...So will I."

"...When it's over, it's over! What's wrong with that? No harm, no foul. If I get too old for you, you can kick me out!"

"We both know that's not the issue—"

"What! What's the 'issue?' You're ten years older than me—so what? I don't care, why should you? Who makes it to their golden wedding anymore? You're the only woman I can talk to!"

"Business, Jace! Do you realize that's all we talk about—when we do talk."

"What's wrong with that? That's who we are! We're great together!"

"We're obsessive!"

"We're successful! I know you want me, and I know you like it when we're together. You can't hide that! We'll be a team in the office and the bedroom. In two years we'll own Novus and Gardner. Hell, we'll own the whole Goddamn world!...And we'll keep it moving! C'mon, Eve, I know you want to!"

"...Sounds more like a merger than a marriage, Jace."

"...Tell me you don't want to 'merge' right now!" He flashed that boyish grin at her, and she knew he was right. It was flattering. She couldn't deny that. He was so sure, so definite...and she was feeling anything but sure.

"...I could use some help with all this furniture."

"...Are the beds in?..."He was still smiling at her.

"We could put one together. How are your mechanical skills?"

"I know everything there is to know about beds...."

***

18

CHAPTER 3

The weekend was thunderous and completely wasted. They made love and talked about clients, investments, office gossip, market trends. It was as if she really hadn't left the office. It energized her, and for the moment, she forgot the emptiness that had brought her to Holmsford and to this silly house. Jace filled her time and devoured her senses. She had no time to think, or doubt, or feel. It was an orgy of distraction.

When he left, the little box he had brought was sitting on a table in the largest bedroom, closed and set apart. They hadn't discussed his proposal. The way they left it—she would keep the box...consider it..."give it some time," but Jace bounded out to his car with the sure and certain step of a man who had just closed a major deal.

She watched him as he left. He was perfect. Young, handsome, confident...empty. That's what she knew. He was as empty as his proposal. It was everything she had lived, and she became aware suddenly that it was nothing that she wanted. Not anymore. But she had everything! What "more" was there?

She looked around the room filled with boxes and furniture in a jumble and she thought of Gram's note,

> *"... I kept everything I could in case you wanted it. Do whatever you need to. Love, Gram."*

"Oh, Gram, I don't know what I need, and I don't know what I want..."

She realized that nothing was going to move unless she did it, and she set in to the task of unpacking....

Everything weighed a ton! The antique furniture was solid and beautiful. Some pieces were easy, but the larger pieces had to be slid along on pieces of cloth or moving blankets—whatever she could find. Slowly the room was beginning to take shape. As she unwrapped each piece, she checked it for damage and wear. She waxed and polished it to renew its luster, and with each piece she remember the old house. She thought of Grandad and Gram and how good they had been together in that old house. Grandad had taken such pride in his garden and in keeping the old house "in good order." And Gram—Gram cleaned and cooked and partnered him in the garden. Sometimes they hardly spoke but worked together in perfect harmony. When they talked about their early years, about Ely, her father, their eyes would shine, and they would laugh...or tear up, but there was always an intimacy to it that made Eve feel...comforted.

It occurred to her as she set the room up, that that was part of what she was seeking—Comfort—that kind of Comfort, not convenience or physical satisfaction, or even independence, but the deep comfort of a bond with someone that goes beyond words. It startled her, this recognition. It was more than that, it was a kind of revelation! It was as if all this old furniture, the product of generations of her family so lovingly kept by her grandparents had touched her.

"...Thanks, Gram..." She couldn't help but say it out loud. For a moment she thought she heard her grandmother say in that prim and amused tone she often used, "You're very welcome!"

The sound of a truck pulling into her driveway roused her from her reverie, and she went to the window to spy the covered moving truck from two days previous come to a stop. On the side it read, "Demon Movers." The cab door opened, and a blonde, muscular man, the same man she had cut cold, hopped out onto the brick driveway. He brushed his shock of hair back with one hand as he strode up to the front door. Eve watched him as he approached.

She opened the front door almost as the man pressed the bell. The absurdly loud Westminster chimes were still clanging out, and the man jumped slightly not expecting so quick a response.

"...Huh—Well, I guess you were waitin' by the door?"

"Yes?" Eve stood with the front door braced by her knee...just in case.

"I was drivin'....Thought I'd check and make sure you were satisfied with...everythin'." He stared at her in that same aggravating, openly inviting way. The scent of a powerful after-shave wafted through the door on a slight breeze.

"Everything is fine." She was sure to use a final tone.

"You know...I take a personal interest in my customers...No damage or nothin'?" He smiled.

"Everything is fine. No damage."...

The man peered into the living room. "Looks like you're doin' all right!"...He pushed open the door as if she weighed nothing and walked into the hallway. "You moved a lot of stuff around!...You must'a had help, huh?..."

Eve could feel her anger spiking at the man's obvious contempt. "No, and I don't need any! Now, if you don't mind—"

"...No help?...All this stuff to move, and you got no one to...give you a hand!...You just...tell me what you want, and I'll do it for you?" His smile was more of a leer.

"Look, I'm going to pretend that you're really concerned about your work, OK? But I'm not buying what you're selling..." Eve stood her ground holding open the door for him to leave.

"Oh, naw!...You don't understand. I ain't sellin' nothin'! I'm givin' it away." The man spread his arms out and cocked his head to the side suggestively.

"...I'd like you to leave, please..."

"C'mon! I want to help you out!... I figure a woman alone...she could use some muscle...."

Eve leveled him with her eyes. "Do you really think that works? Do men like you really think that excites a woman?—"

The man wheeled on her as he was stepping to the door. In one fluid move he pulled the door away from her and slammed it as he grabbed her face with his other hand and drew it close to his, "What's the matter, bitch? I ain't good enough for you? I know your type—high 'n mighty, but you ain't no more than any other bitch!"

"Let Go!" Eve pushed herself away from him and squared off further in the hall. "You get out! GET OUT, OR I'LL CALL THE COPS!" She reached into her jeans for her cell phone, but he was on her. The cell phone flew across the hall and shattered against the far wall.

"Right now you're mine, bitch! You're gonna do what I say 'n you're gonna like it! Oh, yeah, you're gonna like it! So am I!"

With that he lunged at her and grabbed her by the arms. He spun her around like she was a rag doll and began to pull down on her sweat pants. With all her strength Eve freed her left arm and brought her elbow down into his groin. He let out a sharp, "Oof!" and let go for a minute, and she ran into the living room looking for her briefcase. That was where she had her gun.

21

"You like it rough, huh? Ok, honey, you got it! I'm gonna do you like you never been done!"

He was on her again almost before she knew it. He was surprisingly fast and agile, and he was strong! He pulled her down behind a sheet-draped sofa, and holding both her hands with one hand, he continued to pull her sweat pants down. Eve kept staring into his face.

"You don't want to do this. Would you want someone to do this to your sister or your mother?

"I ain't got a sister...and my ma was a bitch too!...shut up!" He pulled back his arm and slapped the back of his hand across her jaw.

It made her see stars, but she kept on talking. "Stop now, and go away, and nobody has to know. Go now!"

"Oh, sweetheart, I don't care who knows. Lonely lady customer asks me back for 'extra work,' happens all the time! Can I help it, if she likes it rough? Who's gonna think anythin' else? Now why don't you just relax and enjoy it?—"

There was an enormous "Crack!" and suddenly the man was sprawled out on the floor, gripping the side of his head.

"Stay down! Get up, and I'll split your skull, ya shit-faced bastard!...

"Ah!..You old bitch!...You old cunt!..."

"You all right, Missy?" Hetty stood there with her staff gripped midway and her eyes on the moving man. He was crouching on the floor holding his head.

"...Uh.... I-I'm all right." Eve got up from the floor. She was disoriented from the suddenness of the attack.

Blind rage took over and Eve attacked the man. "YOU BASTARD! YOU FUCKER! GODDAMN RAPIST!" With each phrase, she kicked the man with all the force she could manage. He stayed down protecting his head with his hands and moaning.

"—I'm calling the police!" Eve absent-mindedly went for her cell phone and then saw it sitting shattered on the hallway floor.

"You ain't doin' nothin'!" The man sprang to his feet and lunged at her, and Hetty launched another swing of her staff to the back of his head, and he went down again.

"I can handle this dung heap!" Hetty stood over the man calm and sure of herself.

Instinctively Eve went to her briefcase and retrieved her gun. She pulled the safety. "GET UP, YOU!"

The moving man rose painfully holding his head. A bloody bruise was forming on his right temple, and his right eye was bloody-red and swelling. He was having trouble seeing for the moment, and he was unsteady on his feet. Hetty circled him with her staff raised and ready.

"I'll get you, you Bitch!...You think I won't? So high and mighty! Think your shit don't stink! You wait! You too, you old cunt!..."

Hetty was almost as tall as the man and she lifted her left hand with her fingers splayed and swore at the man. A stream of expletives came out of her mouth as he backed away confused for a moment, and then he seemed to clear.

"That's what you got? A stick! Ha, ha, ha...! You wanna play, bitch?"

He made a quick move toward Hetty, and she countered him still spewing out words and spitting, it seemed, with every phrase. She moved back as the man moved toward her.

Eve struggled to understand what Hetty was saying. She couldn't quite get all the words; they were coming so fast.

"I'm gonna kill you, you crazy old bitch!"

Eve cocked the gun, and he froze for a moment assessing his position with the two women.

"HIT THE ROAD, YOU PIECE OF SHIT!" Eve barely recognized her own voice. The adrenaline rush was still pumping her, and she pulled the trigger. The bullet whizzed over the man's shoulder through the open door, and the man jumped backwards banging his shoulder heavily on the door jamb. For a moment Eve thought she had hit him, but then he righted himself.

"YOU'RE CRAZY! YOU'RE BOTH CRAZY BITCHES!

"You heard her!—Hit the road! That'll do you right good, you whorin', prick-ridden bastard!"

The man staggered out the door. Eve fired another warning shot, and he half hobbled and half ran to his truck. He pulled himself up painfully into the cab and slammed the door. The engine roared and raced, and the gears slammed noisily into place as the truck pulled out of the driveway and sped up the street away from the house.

Both women watched it pull out of sight.

"...Ain't much of a shot, are ya?" Hetty's voice was calm and steady.

"...I wasn't trying to kill him." Eve was still breathing hard.

"...Too bad."

Eve deflated, leaning on the stair bannister, and they both laughed together.

The older woman was the first to gain control, "Where's your hearth?"

"Through there." Both women went into the kitchen.

Instinctively and without being asked, Eve filled a teakettle from the sink faucet and put it on the stove. The flame sprouted and she turned to face Hetty who stood studying her.

"...I have to go to the police."

"What for?"

"He's got to be stopped. He'll do this again to some other woman!"

"No, he won't."

"Hetty, men like him—"

"He ain't gonna bother no one. 'Sides, I know 'em here. They're all men! They won't do nothin'!"

"But if he—"

"Did he hurt ya?" Her tone was challenging.

"You stopped him!" Eve was confused.

"Uh huh...So he done nothin'!"

"You're my witness—"

"...Huh!—Witness! They ain't gonna listen to me!"

"You got him with your stick! They'll see that!"

"He says a crazy old woman beat him. They put me in the jail, and he has a beer! No, Missy, I ain't no witness!"

"But—"

"He ain't gonna bother no one.—I can promise you that..."

"Hetty, I have to report this!"

"...Suit yourself...ya got cups?"

Eve reached into an open carton and fished out two cups wrapped in newspaper...."Here."

Hetty reached down to a pouch tied at her waist. She drew out a few dried leaves, and dropped them on one of the cups. She poured in hot water.

"What's that?" Eve watched as Hetty made the cup.

"Healin'. This'll take away the shakes. Cure them bruises your makin' too. Drink it all." The old woman put the cup in front of Eve, and she picked it up cradling its warmth in her cold hands.

"...Thank you."

"Eyah...It's the New England way. Might not talk much, but neighbors are there when you need 'em."

Eve lifted the cup to her mouth and took a long sip of the bitter tea. She turned again to express her thanks, but when she did, the old woman was gone. The back door was open and Hetty was nowhere in sight. Eve looked around curiously and closed the door.

"...And gone when you don't!..." Eve completed to herself.

She returned to her cup and sat and sipped it down. Before long, she let go of the twisted feeling in her gut. In a few minutes she would drive into town. In a few minutes she would file a report. For *this* moment she would just breathe. It was a close call. They had escaped. How did she know? Better not to wonder. You were lucky! Better to get busy. Better to put your house in order.

***

CHAPTER 4

"You mean she was here?...In your house?...The goat woman? My God!"

"Oh, for Christ sakes, Marian! She's not Adolf Hitler!—What's she like?" Libby Fletcher turned to Eve with frank interest, as she stood by the sink dosing her coffee from a small flask from her pocket.

"Junie hated her! She said she was—'Uncouth!'..She must smell to high heaven! Tending goats—can you imagine?" Marian was interested too.

Donna Cosgrave sat apart only half listening to the conversation. She was perched on a high stool leaning on the kitchen island stirring daintily and surreptitiously peering around the room at the furnishings and appointments which had finally been set out.

There was Gram Esther's antique coffee mill in the center of the round table with a silk flower arrangement in white and lilac, and all of Gram's copper pots had been polished and hung from a child's sleigh, which served as Eve's pot rack. The sleigh had been Grandad's decades ago, its ram's head runners curved gracefully up to the sleigh's seat, which held a lush Boston Fern, sending its long fronds over the island under a domed skylight. In the English Pine sideboard, all of Gram's Limoges china was spread out in all its glory with a collection of silver and pewter that had been part of 'the family pieces' Gram used with such pride and care. Some of them, she said, had been brought by the very first of the Truesdales when the town was founded.

"She doesn't smell, and she probably saved my life..." Eve sipped her coffee and surveyed the three women, who had decided it was time to invade and assess her acceptability. Marian had brought them without warning. They had arrived with another Sam's Club cake just after Eve had laid the last of the rugs on the first floor and arranged the downstairs furniture. The upstairs was still a total wreck. It had been strenuous, but the activity pushed away the shakes from her encounter with the moving man.

"Tell us about it, honey—the rape. How awful!" Marian was all too eager to hear about it as she moved closer, but she quickly adjusted as the other women frowned at her. "I mean...it must have been horrendous! You poor thing!"

"Actually there wasn't any rape. We...handled it. That was his intention, I'm sure, but... it didn't happen."

"You should've cut his balls off!" Libby tone was flat and definite as she slugged back a good swallow of 'coffee.'

"No need. Hetty got him good a couple of times with her staff—"

"Staff?—" Marian was listening hard.

"She carries a long kind of walking stick. It's pretty heavy. Suddenly she was there, and she swung it at him and beaned him pretty good! That gave me time to get my gun—"

"Gun! You have a gun!" Marian's eyes were wide with excitement.

"...For protection. I trained. I'm a pretty good shot..."

"Oh, my God—Oh my God! This woman!—She's a hero! She's a living, breathing hero! It's like Annie Oakley or...or...I don't know! I mean, who knew someone like this would be moving into our neighborhood!"

"Take a chill pill, Marian!—Did you shoot him?" Libby leaned forward intently for her answer.

"I shot *at* him."

"...Too bad." Libby poured a little more from her flask into her coffee cup.

"That was enough. He ran for the truck and left. But it was Hetty who got him off me. She hit him and circled around him cursing and brandishing that staff...She freaked him out!"

"You and the Goat Woman! —My God!—That's the same guy from the first day, right?

"That was him."

"Ugh! Why are all the cute guys such bastards!"

"For Christ's Sakes, Marian, Nobody's cute if he tries to rape you!" Libby barked her annoyance at Marian while she continued to study Eve.

It didn't bother Eve that Libby scrutinized her or that Marian talked compulsively, nor did she care that Donna Fletcher was "casing the joint." They were extending themselves to her. They were human contact, and she knew she needed that. There was something endearing about the effort they were making to include her in their sorority. Except for Gram, it occurred to her that she was a stranger to the company of women.

"You reported it..." Donna was leaning across the island fingering the Limoges cake plate Eve had used to serve the sodden 'flourless chocolate cake' Marian had chosen from the righteous 'ovens' of Sam's.

"Of course!...I went down and made my report..."

"He gave me his card! Told me to give him a call, if I needed anything! Can you imagine? Oh!" Marian was trying hard not to appear excited

"What did they tell you?" Libby kept her gaze on Eve.

"...They took the information, and told me they'd 'look into it.'"

"Well—That's outrageous! 'Look into it?'—What's there to look into? Arrest the bastard! Haul him in and charge him —I don't care how cute he is—he could have killed you!" Marian dramatized.

"Ha!—That's the Holmsford Police! Bunch of old Yankee boys sitting around the cracker barrel trading smutty stories! Goddamn town!" Libby seemed to toast her own judgment with another slug of coffee.

"I told them 'Demon Moving,' so they'd know where he works...."

"...You don't think you'll hear from 'em, do you?" Libby was looking right at her.

"...My word against his...it's been three days...Probably not. Anybody want a piece of Marian's cake?..."

"What about the Goat Woman, honey? She could back you up!"

"...I suppose...if it comes to that..." Eve reflected on Hetty's appearance trying to imagine the impression she would make in a courtroom.

"Suppose he comes back! My God, Evie, suppose that bastard comes back here. I mean, aren't you scared?" Marian was looking at her with an exaggerated look of dread.

"...If he does...I won't miss this time." Eve took the silver knife slicer out of Donna's appraising hand and expertly sliced up the glutinous pastry and began putting it onto the dainty dishes.

"But then they could prosecute you, couldn't they. I mean, if you killed him? Oh my God!"

"I made my report. If he comes back and I shoot him, I claim self-defense. Anyway, I don't think he will. We gave him a pretty good idea of what he could expect if he tried." Eve began to hand out the cake to each woman.

"You are so brave! I mean, I don't know what I'd do if I thought a rapist was coming for me!"

"Put on lipstick." Libby's dry delivery made Donna choke on a swallow of coffee. All of them burst into laughter including Eve.

"Oh! You are—Oh! I am not that desperate!" Marian feigned outrage as Donna continued to gag.

"—We all are!" Libby returned.

The laughter felt good. Eve was trying to remember the last time she had laughed.

"...So...what do you do, Eve? Marian says you run something or other?" Libby was getting down to it now. She wanted the vital statistics. Apparently Eve had passed the first acceptance hurdle.

"I'm the head of Investments at Novus and Gardner in New York. We're an investment Firm. Mid-sized."

"Jesus Christ, what are you doing here? I mean we're all stuck here, but you—you *do* something! What in the hell are you doing in Holmsford?"

"...My folks were from here...I spent summers here...as a kid...and then I lived here briefly...I don't know, I guess this is kind of where my roots are..." It was a question that Eve knew she couldn't really answer.

"Well I'm not stuck! I like it here!"

"Yeah, Marian we all know. You love it here because you got the house in the settlement and a running blank check from Stupid Harold. We've all heard it. Can we focus on Eve, please? We came here to see her!...Sorry, we all know each other too fucking well, I guess...."

"Are you commuting—to New York?" Donna was studying her silver fork as she cut tiny pieces from her cake slice and nibbled on them.

"Well, for now, I work from here. Telecommuting...at least while I get everything sorted out."

"...You've got enough antiques to make Sotheby's cry for mercy! You need a guard living here! Trust me, I know good from bad, and everything you own is worth a fortune!—That server is Hepplewhite. The chairs are Windsor—You know that, right?..."

"Donna's ex is in antiques. Domestic—international. He does it all!" Marian chimed in.

"Yeah...and he does *them* all too. Men—women...he...he's an equal-opportunity son-of-a-bitch! I caught him with local dealer named George on an antique Chesterfield. He tried to tell me it was an 'occupational hazard!'"

"She got half the business!" Marian was clearly proud.

"My interest is purely monetary, but I keep my eye on the business. He can have all the 'occupational hazards' he wants as long as my half comes rolling in!..."

"...Uh huh..." Eve looked around the room for a moment. She was taken by surprise. She hadn't really thought about Gram's furniture. It was just family stuff. It didn't occur to her that it had any real value outside of its connection to her family."...Uh...well, I'll insure everything...I suppose..."

"I would...I certainly would! I mean...it's amazing!"

"...I just got it out of storage."

"Storage! You had *this* in storage?!"

"Well, *I* didn't. My grandmother did..."

"It's a good thing I didn't know about it! I'd have robbed you blind!" Her statement was just a little too bald-faced to be less than true. Suddenly she smiled and giggled slightly. "—Just kidding!"

"...Does anyone want more coffee?" Eve poured out more coffee for the women and managed to put her own cake discreetly out of sight for later disposal.

"...So...Eve...you're not divorced?..." It was Libby who dropped *the* question. All three women stopped and watched Eve. She could feel them waiting for her to frame her answer.

"...Well... I thought I should get married first before I tried it." She could feel them relax.

"Oh, C'mon, Eve. I'm sure you've had lots of offers!" Libby's tone had that perfect blend of encouragement and patronage.

"I work with the biggest, ball-clanging, testosterone-driven, alpha males on the planet! I get propositions—lots of them...not too many proposals."

"So...Who was the BMW in the driveway all weekend?..." Marian looked at the other women with a conspiratorial nod.

"...He works for me."

"Oh, honey, he could work for me!...Kinda young, isn't he?" Marian nodded knowingly to the other women who chuckled with each other.

"He's... an employee..."

"To the workforce!" Libby toasted her right from her flask.

"Does he do odd jobs, Honey!" Marian laughed heartily and the other two women joined her.

"Well, I can see it's pointless for me to try to convince you—"

"Don't mind us. We're all jealous! You got yours, and you didn't need a lawyer!" Libby winked.

"Even if he's part time, I'd hate to think of you rattling around this place alone!—I think that's what drove Junie so crazy!" Marian continued with a little more thoughtfulness. There was a brief break in the mood.

"...June was crazy all by herself!" Libby's judgment was definite.

"She was our close friend!" Marian insisted.

"Compulsively cleaning, decorating, entertaining. She was like Martha Stewart on crack!—You couldn't wear shoes in the Goddamned house! If you came here—she had little color-coordinated slippers by the door! It was like coming in to a Japanese teahouse, for Christ's sakes!"

"She made the best banana bread I ever tasted!—Uh! It was to die for! And at Christmas time she threw the most amazing parties!" Marian added.

"Oh, God! Handmade canapés—little poopie-twirly things, and Santa Clause cookies, and Holiday dips, and drops and durdles—everything smelled of cinnamon and Good Cheer!—It was enough to make you want to join a terrorist organization." Libby took another slug of her 'coffee' to wash away the memory.

"I noticed *you* came! We all did! We were here all the time! We spent hours in this kitchen!" Marian couldn't help sounding self-righteous.

"We had to. She wouldn't let you go anywhere else in the house!"

"Not when she had just cleaned!" Marian defended.

"She always 'just cleaned.' You could do surgery on the basement floor!"

"You're just jealous! It wouldn't hurt you to clean up a little! The last time I was in your house there were dust bunnies rolling around like tumbleweed!"

"I dust—when it's necessary!" Libby added with an air of superiority.

"...It was Paul who drove her crazy...." Donna offered quietly.

"Paul...," Libby stopped to absorb the comment.

"...Poor Junie..." Marian fell silent as well.

"...um...Who is Paul?" Eve had waited as long as she could, but with all of them silent, she couldn't contain her curiosity.

"Oh! Paul was Junie's husband, Paul Hildebrande. You don't know about any of this! We're going on and on about Junie and...and you don't know! Junie and Paul owned this house!"

"Well, I figured that out, but—"

"It's so weird! So—unexplainable!...Junie disappeared. About a year and a half ago. Just—disappeared! Pfft!" Marian snapped her fingers to emphasize the fact.

"...Disappeared..." Eve was a little unnerved.

"I'm the one who phoned it in!" Marian claimed her place with a certain sense of importance. "Oh, honey, it was the strangest thing. I had just seen her about an hour before. She was making one of her casseroles to have it ready when Paul got back—I had gone home, but then I realized I left my ring on that sink top when I was helping her, so I came back. When I got in, that casserole was smoking in the oven! I turned it off, and I called for her...No answer! I looked all through the house—No Junie! That's when I called the police. Honey, they found nothing! Clothes in the closet, wallet still in her purse, keys in the key box, car in the garage—but no Junie. No sign of a struggle—no blood!—She just wasn't there! No trace at all!"

"Our crack police force didn't do a thing! All they'd say was 'She's not missing unless seventy-two hours go by.' Those fuckers wasted three days!" Libby was still angry.

"I called Paul's office—I mean right away! Junie was never away from the house like that! I knew he was somewhere and due in soon—That's why Junie was making the casserole. They told me he was coming into Boston from Chicago on the 8:30 flight. They got in touch with him, and he got here pretty quick. How could she disappear like that? What could have happened?" Marian was winding up again.

"They asked Paul to come down to the station...for questioning! But they wouldn't go looking for her! Figure that one out..." Libby shook her head as she took a long sip of her coffee.

"After three days, they went around. Talking to the neighbors. Nobody saw her. Nobody heard anything. Nothing turned up...It was just so awful!" Marian teared up and dug for a Kleenex in her pocket.

The three women were silent for a moment as Eve processed the story.

Finally, Donna spoke in a small, even voice, "There were *some* clothes missing..."

"Oh, those! That was nothing, Donna! Junie changed clothes to go to the bathroom! She had every closet in the house full of beautiful outfits. They were all still there! I tell you, Evie, that girl could dress! And she had the figure to go with it!"

"...I think she left him..." Donna was quietly insistent.

"Why?" Marian challenged. "You have a beautiful home which you keep perfectly, beautiful clothes, a husband like Paul Hildebrande—Oh, Evie, you should have seen this man! He was gorgeous!...and charming! That man could have had anybody!"

"...He did..." There was a distinct 'ping' in the air as Donna's statement landed in the middle of them. "C'mon, Marian, *you* know..." Donna's small voice seemed to carry a weight now. Eve could feel all three women retreat into themselves.

"...She's right, Marian, we *all* know. Paul Hildebrande was a hound dog! He was fun, but he was a real dog with women." Eve could see that Libby and Donna were dead serious.

"She never said a word about it! Never!" Marian wouldn't look at them. She was desperately trying to avoid eye contact.

"Why the hell do you think she did all that...Goddamn work—perfect house, perfect life...perfect Her! She knew. She had to! She was doing everything she could to hold onto him, but he was never hers—not really. ...We all *know* that!" The three of them absorbed the moment.

"...I think..." Donna finally broke the silence, "...she just...had enough. She took a few necessary things and some loose cash nobody knew about and...walked away....That's what makes me feel better...So, Eve!..." She got up from her perch on the stool and tried to break the atmosphere, "If you ever want to sell any of your beautiful things. You come to me. I'll get you the best price!"

"I don't plan on it, but I'll keep it in mind"

"...She hated that woman...the Goat Woman. Remember?" Marian was trying to revive herself.

"Oh God! She made us sign that stupid petition! It was like a crusade with her!—Your friend—the Goat Woman...?" When Libby picked up on that ridiculous title, it annoyed Eve. She wasn't sure why. "You know she keeps her goat pens on the edge of your property?"

"Well, yes. I went out to see them a few days ago. That's where I first met Hetty."

"June was on a Goddamn rampage to get her to move them. She went to the Town, to the Board of Health...She buttonholed a couple of Town Selectman and bent their ears about the smell and the 'danger to health.' She wouldn't let it go."

"They don't bother me. It's nice having a farm on the edge of my lot."

"I'm surprised you saw her! Nobody sees her much. Once in a while at the farmer's market. She sells her cheese or something. I don't know. Personally, I go to Sam's for what I want. Anyway, she lives in the middle of that big farm. The townies stay away from her.—You know, *this* place—Clover Terrace?—This used to be a farm! The whole thing...Ramsay Farm...then they built this development...Harold and I were one of the first to buy here, that's how I know."

"'Clover Terrace? I thought it was *Cloven* Terrace."

"That's the Goddamn Town again! They spelled it wrong! Bunch of Swamp-Yankee hicks!" Libby's disgust spilled over.

"Well, now, I actually asked about that. There's this little antique shop in town—'Dilla's." Marian offered.

"I've been in there." Donna joined, "It's a 'one-off' shop. Odds and ends. She only opens when she feels like it..."

"The little old lady who runs it is so sweet! And she knows everything about the town. Honey, I mean everything! I went in just to look around, you know, and she asked me where I was from, and when she found out I had moved in up here, she told me about how this was a farm and how it was sold to some developer and how when they named the development, the Town switched it up because of the history of the town."

"What history?" Eve was intrigued.

"Oh, honey, this place? Right where we live—was the place they brought witches to hang way back when! Didn't you know that? I mean, weren't you raised here?" Marian seemed surprised.

"I spent summers here, but...this is news to me...."

"Well it was right here! Town's very proud of its 'heritage,' but if you ask me, honey, I don't see much to be proud of, hanging a bunch of poor people out of some religious hysteria!"

"What else have they got? The whole Goddamn town's nothing but a bend in the road to Boston. Who would want to come here?" Libby drained her coffee cup.

"Do you run?" Donna interrupted.

"Huh?" Eve was still digesting things in her mind.

"Do you run? You know, jog?"

"Uh...well, yeah, I used to run in the park all the time."

"Good. I'll pick you up tomorrow morning at 8:00. We'll do a five-K. That ought to get you breathing! Thank God! June used to run with me, but these two—"

"Honey, if God wanted me to run, he never would've invented high heels!"

"The only way you'd get me to run is to tie Brad Pit naked on the trunk of car and drive real slow in front of me! C'mon, girls, we've kept Eve away from her work—We have, haven't we." Libby threw Eve a knowing glance.

"Well, I do have a few clients to call...some office things to do." It was true. This impromptu coffee klatch had pulled Eve away from the computer. But she was grateful for it. Now she had some 'friends.' That seemed so odd to think about. 'Friends.' It was an idea that she had

35

never considered much before coming to Holmsford, but now it seemed somehow important. And there was one friend to whom she owed some serious gratitude!

***

CHAPTER 5

"Marian, I don't *do* church!..."

Eve was annoyed by her doorbell ringing at 9:00 a.m. on a Sunday morning. Marian stood there in all her glory, full makeup, heels, and a designer dress.

"Oh, honey, you want to do this church.—Well, more accurately, you'll want to do this minister! I know *I* do!"

"Marian, it's early...and honestly, I'm not looking for a hook up with some clerical type!"

"I am! Evie, just come with me, please. He's new, he's a widower, and he's yummy! I want to get to him before anyone else does. C'mon, do a favor for a neighbor. I need a 'wing man!' Those church ladies are fierce!"

"What about Donna or Libby?"

"I'm not taking them over there! They'll try to steal him away!...You're safe. You've got your 'employee!' C'mon, Evie...be a pal!"

Eve swallowed hard and took a deep breath. "You want a lot for a Sam's Warehouse cake, Marian. Come in. Give me a couple of minutes to dress."

"Service is at 10:00, and, Evie?..."

"Yeah?" Eve was on her way up the stairs.

"Don't try to look too good, huh?..."

The little church in town was a perfect rendition of an old New England church. Painted white with its needle-sharp steeple standing proud above the village green. The pleasantly comforting bell rang calling in the small congregation, and its plain, neat interior had the spare dignity of a church built with the spiritual confidence of an earlier age.

Marian nodded demurely to people who obviously didn't recognize her but nodded back out of politeness touched with curiosity. She stood out from the other women. Her designer dress was splotched in oranges and hot pinks, and her accessories finished the impression of a woman looking for attention. Eve did her best to disappear at her side as they slipped into a pew close to the front.

The organ wheezed out a rendition of "Lead On, O King Eternal," and the 'new minister' entered and took the pulpit. Marian dug an elbow into Eve's ribs as he ascended, and Eve almost cried out in pain.

He wasn't 'all that' as far as Eve could see. He was tall, sandy-haired, kind of cross between Jimmy Stewart and Harrison Ford. Younger, of course. Perhaps about forty or forty-five. He had nice eyes, she gave him that, very blue and...truthful. She reflected that that must be a really good tool in his profession, but when he began his sermon, Eve turned off entirely.

He went on and on about 'traditional values,' and the 'proper balance' between men and women, which, as far as Eve could determine, meant to him that women should remain barefoot and pregnant and chained to a stove. What formulaic crap! How pedestrian! As he went on Eve turned off her brain and let her mind wander. She had no intention of listening to all his bullshit. Before she realized it, she was standing singing the closing hymn with the rest of the congregation, and she felt Marian's sharp elbow in her ribs again.

"OW! Marian, will you stop it!"

"Sorry, Evie, but this is it! Fellowship! In the downstairs hall. That's where I need you to fend off any competition while I make my move!"

"I don't know why you're so interested in this guy, Marian. He's pretty much 'run of the mill,' from what I heard."

"Honey, if that's 'run of the mill'—run me a few more! C'mon, grab some cake and coffee and run interference!"

In the downstairs hall quite a few of the congregation had gathered to socialize with the new minister. Most of the women were accompanied by their husbands, who stood aside drinking coffee while the women ingratiated themselves with the Reverend. Marian stood close waiting for her opening and nodding to Eve to clear the way for her.

Eve maneuvered herself to the front and managed to exchange a few pleasantries with the ladies when the minister came up to her.

"I don't think we've met. I'm Adam Singleton—the 'new minister.'—that seems to be my title right now. Reverend Thompson, the 'old minister' was here for forty-five years, so I guess I'll be 'new' for quite a while."

"Eve. Eve Truesdale. I'm...new here too."

"Oh...Well, I'll look forward to seeing you and Mr. Truesdale at church, then."

Eve looked at him and tried not to roll her eyes. "...Not married."

"...I guess that was obvious, huh?"

"Yes, Reverend, it was."

"I guess I'm a little out of practice. I haven't—"

"It's ok." Eve wanted to end this approach before it began. "I don't think I'll be coming very often, but you should meet my friend, Marian. She was very impressed by your...sermon."

Marian fluttered up to the man and took his hand.

"Hi, I'm Marian. Very pleased to meet you!"

"Didn't you like my sermon?" He was still focused on Eve even as he shook hands with Marian.

"...It was....very instructive. Thank you." Eve quickly retreated to the coffee urn as Marian consumed Singleton with flattery and questions. She positively drowned him in a tidal wave of chatter and charm making it obvious to anyone who watched that she was out to snag the minister.

At the coffee urn, Eve caught a few snide remarks from the congregation women as they watched Marian laugh and flirt with their minister.

"Who's she?"

"That's quite an outfit for church!"

And "Who does she think she's fooling?"

Finally, the church hall was emptying out and Marian was winding down. Singleton was patient and kind with her, and Eve admired his ability to listen to her without displaying any impatience. At last, she was standing alone by the coffee urn, and she heard Marian intone, "Of course! I'd love to" as Singleton ushered her toward the urn where Eve was standing.

"Evie! I'm going to organize the bake sale!"

"Congratulations. Sam's stock will probably go up."

"Thank you for introducing me to Marian, Ms. Truesdale. She's very enthusiastic. I'm sure she'll be very helpful at church."

Marian giggled, "Oh, Adam, there's so much I can do around here! I'm sure we could really get things going!"

"I'm sure." Singleton didn't catch Marian's obvious meaning. He was focused again on Eve.

"Um...everyone's gone. I think we should go too, Marian! Reverend Singleton must have a lot to do." Eve was trying not to get drawn in.

"Oh, of course! I've monopolized you, Adam. I'm so sorry! Well...c'mon Eve."

"Marian tells me you're a business woman. Investments?" Singleton wasn't giving up.

"...Uh, yes." Eve turned to face him.

"We could use a little advice with our finances. We're pretty much hand to mouth."

Eve stood looking at him without saying a word and trying not to be unpleasant.

"I realize that we're probably a small fish to you—" he was trying to open a conversation.

"...My firm only handles major corporate entities, I'm afraid."

"...Oh. Of course. I just thought—perhaps on a personal level—"

"Reverend... I don't think I can help you. I don't think I'll be joining your congregation."

He looked at Eve, and there was an amused glint in his eye that annoyed her even more. "...May I ask why?"

"Business considerations. I will be commuting extensively. Sunday will be my only day off."

He smiled and his eyes narrowed slightly, "That's not it. Why don't you tell me the real reason?"

"Sure. I don't think we'd get along. Judging by your sermon, you're still stuck in 1950 with regard to women, and I don't have the time or energy to deal with you."

"Eve!" Marian was shocked.

Singleton smiled and laughed, "You don't pull any punches, do you?"

"Look, Reverend—"

"Adam, please."

"OK, Adam…All that 'balance between men and women' is just code for trying to put us back in our places! I don't buy it. Donna Reed is dead and so is wearing cocktail dresses and pearls when you dust the furniture. The genie isn't going back into the bottle, and couching it in platitudes from the pulpit isn't going to wash!"

"That isn't want I meant! Ms. Truesdale—"

"Eve! If we're going to argue, call me Eve!"

"Fine. Eve. I wasn't suggesting that women should be submissive any more than I was that men should be dominant. If you listened to my sermon, I was talking about balance. Partnership! A relationship that recognizes each person for his and *her* strengths!"

"Here we go—And that means…?"

"That men and women each have—"

"Their own strengths!" Eve finished the phrase for him. "There it is! The age-old con! Women are nurturers and men are hunters! Therefore, women should be protected, which is code for 'controlled,' and men have to roam the world for the means to support them, which is code for….well, let's just say it doesn't mean 'control'—certainly not self-control."

Marian just stood there wide-eyed and dumbfounded as Singleton and Eve squared off.

"I wasn't implying that at all. Didn't you hear anything I said?"

"Frankly no. As soon as I heard the opening remarks, my brain went numb. Women have been hearing this for centuries! Why would I want to listen to this bullshit again?"

"Eve! Uh, Adam she just moved in. She's exhausted. I made her come with me—" Marian was desperately trying to quell the dispute, but both combatants ignored her.

"So you judged me without listening to what I had to say? That wasn't very fair, was it?"

"Don't talk to me about fair! I have the entire history of Women to back me up. 'Fair' isn't what men do with women!"

"And you think my sermon was some kind of sneak attack on the independence and equality of women? You think I'm that atavistic?"

"I know the cues when I hear them!"

"But you didn't hear them! You weren't even listening, remember? Rude, but maybe that's part of your charm."

"Oh, really? Sarcasm. That's what you have to offer as a defense? Not much to go on."

"Look—Eve, I like women! Quite a lot, as a matter of fact! I like working with them and I like them...in every way. I have no agenda to subjugate women. I just don't want to see them masculinize themselves in order to grab for some illusion of equality. Being a ball-breaker doesn't make a woman equal!"

"Nice talk for a 'reverend,' Adam!"

"That was rude, I'm sorry!"

"...Maybe that's 'part of *your* charm.'"...

The argument hung in the air for a brief moment until Singleton burst into laughter.

"....Th—that was good!" He managed when he caught his breath.

Marian hung between the two of them, mystified as to what had just transpired. She didn't know what to make of this entire interchange. She just knew this wasn't right! She had just cornered the new minister and hopefully charmed the pants off him, and now he was standing there completely absorbed in Eve. What was going on here?

Singleton's laughter annoyed Eve even more, but she managed to stifle the urge to slug him. "I don't think we're going to agree on anything. Marian, I think we should go."

Marian was grateful to leave as Eve pulled her by the arm.

"Hey! Hold on, now! You can't just turn tail and run. Not after that last zinger—or is that all you've got?" Singleton's tone was challenging.

Eve turned back and faced him again, "Oh, I've got plenty, 'Reverend,' but I don't like dueling with an unarmed man!"

"If you can't argue the case, argue the man, hmm? That's weak. Then, you really don't have anything else."

"If a woman is assertive, then she's a 'ball-breaker.' If she's ambitious and successful, she's a 'bitch.'—you 'old boys' seem to have us all neatly categorized. Why should I try to shake up your little men's club?"

"Because none of that is what I talked about. You're so busy making assumptions that you've done to men exactly what you accuse them of doing to you."

"Oh, please! Tell me men don't pigeonhole women! It's the 'Madonna and Whore' syndrome! If we do what you want—Madonna...saintly, nurturing, perfect, protected...controlled! If we don't do what you want—Whore...paid, available, used, discarded...controlled! I don't see much in either scenario that screams 'balance,' do you?"

"Frankly no. But I think you're the one stuck in 1950. I don't know what your experience with men is—"

"I work with a lot of men, Adam! I haven't seen much change in the model."

"Maybe that's because you're viewing us through the lens of your expectations instead of who we really are."

"Yeah well, if some guy slapped *you* on the ass and called *you* sweetie, how would you feel?"

"...Are we talking about football?" Singleton's amused smirk at her questions pushed her past her tolerance level.

"We're done here! Marian, you can stay if you want, but I have a few things I need to do." Eve headed to the church hall door and the stairs to the outside.

Singleton called out to her, "Ms. Truesdale!...Eve! Where's your sense of humor?..."

"It died—of boredom!..."

Eve mounted the steps and arrived at the church entrance. The man was ridiculous! She didn't have another minute to waste on him, the smug son-of-a-bitch! He was so much like the men in the office, full of themselves! The only difference was he wore a collar and they wore their egos! She walked down the side of the green, her heels clicking loudly and angrily on the pavement, running the conversation over in her mind and re-writing her comments to level Singleton and his absurd complacency!

Without realizing it, she had stopped halfway down the green and was standing in front of a small shop front with old-fashioned cabinet windows. Inside was an amazing assortment of curiosities, collectibles and antiques. The sign over the door read, "Dilla's," and she went in.

A little bell tinkled as the door opened and again when it closed. Inside the shop was a jumble of things everywhere you looked. There was a layer of dust over most of the merchandise, but the entire store had the feeling of welcome and familiarity. Old silk flowers peeking out of antique vases, and kerosene lamps from a hundred years ago lifted their smoky chimneys above dignified frosted globes. Children's toys not played with for decades sat hopeful, waiting for pudgy little hands to wind them up, and the scent of candles and hand-made soaps filled the store with a confusion of the aromas of flowers and spice.

"Can I help you, dear?" The voice came from behind a tall arrangement of dried flowers. It startled Eve who was still fuming from her 'conversation' with Singleton.

"What?—Oh, excuse me. I didn't see you!"

"Well, I'm not much to look at, dear, but if you're looking for something, you might need my help. I'm Dilla." The old woman stepped out from behind the arrangement and the counter. She was a tiny woman of perhaps eighty, still spry with a smile behind her bright brown eyes. Her voice was kind and had a warmth to it that made you feel as if you knew her.

"The owner...."

"Yes, dear. I decided it was a nice day to do a little business, so here I am. What can I do for you?"

"Well,...I don't know. I'm looking for something for someone I don't know very well. A kind of a 'thank you.'"

"Man or woman?"

"Woman, but I don't know her very well. I just came to town."

"You're Eve Truesdale!" The old woman lit up when she said this.

"Uh...Yes...how did you—"

"Oh, you wouldn't remember me, dear, but I know you! Your grandparents were friends of mine! Sam and Esther Truesdale's little Granddaughter!—I'm sorry about your Grandmother, dear!

"Uh...thank you. That was a long time ago."

"When you're my age, time seems all the same, I guess."

"I was sixteen."

After Sam's awful accident, she went downhill fast.

"...I remember..."

"What a man his age was doing on a roof!...He was so proud of that old house. They both were. Kept after it like it was a baby! Built when the Truesdales pretty much ran this town! They owned the mill, the old General Store. Proud as peacocks! Your Grandma, she was a Prescott! She was 'new people.' Her Great, great....whatever granddaddy only came over in 1720. Sam was a 'first family,' like me. I was a Peabody—before I married my husband. Anyway, dear, when Sam—your Grandad, was killed, Esther couldn't take care of that place anymore."

"No...she couldn't..."

"I remember you when you were just a tyke! Trailin' after your Grampa over at the Mercantile! Lord, that man thought the world of you! He'd talk about you all winter until you'd come for your stay."

"Two weeks every summer..."

"Like clockwork! The two of them would get so excited! Esther would go on about how big you were getting...how smart you were. Then that awful fire! Both your parents! I thought Sam and Esther would die of grief. Their only son!..."

"I try not to think about it—" Eve was trying to change the subject.

"Well, of course not! You've been through hell, haven't you, dear! Who would want to think of that?" The old woman couldn't help reviewing the past, but Eve could feel herself flushing with all the memories.

"Of course, they took you in! Sam and Esther Truesdale would never do anything else. Of course...it didn't last long, did it?"

"...Less than a year..."

"When those people from Boston—'Innovative Realty,'—some of John Marlin's cronies!...When they offered to buy the house, Esther jumped at it. It was robbery! They gave her hardly anything for that beautiful house and property. Nobody else wanted the place. Too big, I guess. Needed work...like most old things. And she needed the money...for you, dear....Then...she went too...I'm sorry, dear! Listen to me! Going on about things...I didn't mean to make you feel bad, dear."

"...It's all right. I survived." Eve's voice was quiet as she reviewed things.

"Of course you did! You're a Truesdale!...Anyhow, they tore it down like some old packing crate! That beautiful place! Put up that ugly mall! Well, that's all in the past, isn't it? You're here now, dear, and we're glad to have you! Welcome home! And you need a thank you gift. Who's it for?..."

"Huh?..." Eve started from her daydream, "I just bought a house in—"

"Cloven Terrace. Yes, dear, I know. That was another of Marlin's deals with those 'Innovative' people.—I wonder how much Marlin made on that?—You can't tell me he didn't get of piece of that pie! That man would sell the cemetery if he could hide the tombstones!—Says it's all about progress and the future, but it's not! I know that!—Holmsford's a very small town. There's not much that gets by me. I'm a town meeting member...and the Historical Society. That's me. There aren't too many people I don't know! I'm just glad to have a Truesdale back in town! You know, dear, you're the last Truesdale. Your family was one of the founding families of Holmsford!"

"Yes. You told me."

"I'm repeating myself, I guess—Yours, the Ramsay's—the Liveseys, the Marlins, the Peabodys...a handful of others. Precious few! 1660. That's when your people came here. The first settlers. Puritans. Good English stock!"

"Really?...Well, I guess I knew some of it...but—"

"Of course, you wouldn't know. You were just a teenager when the lawyers put you with that family in Boston. Esther had that put in her will. That you'd go to a family that would take care of you 'til you came of age. She never stopped worrying about you!"

"...I know..."

"Was that all right, dear?...Going to other people? Did they treat you right?"

"It...taught me a lot..."

"Well, that's good, dear! Now suppose you tell me who this 'thank you' gift is for."

"Hetty Livesey. She's the old woman who lives—"

"Oh...." Dilla's eyes widened at the mention of Hetty's name.

"Of course. You know her too."

"Well, yes, dear. Not well. I don't think anybody knows her well. Comes to the farmer's market every month or so and sells her cheeses.—Pretty good, too! She makes extra money that way. Anyways, she stays pretty much to herself up on that farm of hers. Uh...Can I ask why you need a 'thank you' gift for her?"

"She...helped me with...a difficult...move. I know she's eccentric, but I wanted to thank her."

"Hetty Livesey helped you move in?" The old woman was incredulous.

"Not exactly. There was something I needed a little help with, and she happened to be there at the right time. I thought I'd bring her something nice, but I have no idea what she might like."

"Well, dear, now that's a tough one! I don't know that *I* know. That farm of hers is the last large freehold in the town. It's practically unchanged since this town was founded. Her house is the last original structure left—most of the other homesteads were burned down by the Indians during King Philip's War. Hers is the only one they never touched."

"Uh...King Philip?" Eve was confused.

"Indian chief. Led an uprising around 1670 or so. Killed quite a few settlers before he was done. Holmsford wasn't more than a scattering of isolated farms. Easy pickings for the raiding parties. Just about everyone got burned out...except the Liveseys. She lives up there in that house—I don't even think she's got electricity!"

"...There must be something..." Eve gazed around the shop.

"You might try something pretty...feminine. She's hardly a soft type, but she wasn't always that way. Most women like something that makes them feel...girlish. How about some of these handmade soaps and a nice fluffy bath towel? That's a nice thing!"

"I guess....I wish I knew what she liked."

Dilla pulled a selection of scented soaps and grouped them in a small gift box along with a large white terrycloth towel. "As they say, 'it's the thought!'—You know, she used to be beautiful."

"Really? You knew her?" Eve turned to the old woman.

"I saw her now and then. I was married already. She was just a girl. She'd come to town once and while. Lord, the men went crazy! She was a beauty! My Mother used to say she was the spitting image of her grandmother—She got that farm from her grandmother. She'd been away —Boston is what I heard. She was tall for a girl, and she was striking! Red hair. She just about drove Billy Ramsay crazy! Billy Ramsay was the farmer that owned your 'Cloven Terrace' oh...about 45 years ago. When it came up for auction a few years ago, she wanted to buy it, but Marlin had his Innovative people outbid her. That man grabs for everything that's not tied down!"

"What happened to Billy Ramsay?"

"He left her. Disappeared! That's what I heard. One day he just lit out...left everything behind. Didn't surprise anybody. He wasn't much as a farmer...and he did like the women! There was no family left, so the farm went back to the town. Most folks figured he got what he wanted from Hetty and just...went on his way.—Anyway she went up there to live, and she's been there ever since."

"By herself?"

"Pretty much! Oh, I heard things. About some of the local boys trying to...'court' her. None of them got anywhere that I could see...except Billy. I heard she had a daughter; never saw her. I don't think anybody did. I think she was probably Billy's, but nobody could say for sure. Word is the daughter moved away. Died without coming back. I guess living up there with just Hetty wasn't much of a life. There's a granddaughter, but I've never seen her." Dilla tied the box with a ribbon from a galley of dusty ribbon rolls from behind the counter. "There you are, dear. I can't promise this'll be something she likes, but it's the best guess I could make."

"Thank you—"

"You call me Dilla, dear! Everybody does...and you're almost like family. Anytime you need something, you just come to me. Esther'd want me to help you."

"What do I owe you?"

"Nothing, dear!" Eve was about to protest, but the old woman continued, "Oh, don't worry about me! I don't need the money! At this point, I run the shop for fun! And I want to do something for Esther and Sam's beautiful Granddaughter! Makes me feel like they're still around! You want to pay me something? You pay me another visit! I'd like that just fine! I'd like to know how she likes her gift!...Guess I'm kinda nosy!"

"It's a deal." Eve thanked Dilla again and walked out into the town green. The sun was higher and the air was warm and clean. She had forgotten her annoyance with Singleton, and for the first time she felt as if this place might be good for her.

***

CHAPTER 6

The north road out of the town proper was little more than a paved cow path. Winding and treacherous, it took you under the overpass to I-95, which led into Boston. It wound upward to Cloven Terrace, which had been constructed as high on the hilltop property as its builders could manage-to give prospective residents a view of the town below. The town itself was a perfect gem of prim New England rectitude. Its grid of streets framed the town green. On one end of the green stood the Town Hall, where monthly town meetings were held as was the custom from the earliest days, and in the back of which was housed the police station. On the other end was St. Barnabas Church, which had originally been a small, square Puritan meeting house. Over the years, that doughty lot had been outnumbered by arriving groups from England, equally devout and equally eager to share in the wealth of the colonies. It was they who built the newer Episcopal Church, which graced the town green, while-the disgruntled remnants of the original colonists retreated to a smaller, poorer place on the outside of town. That spare, barren building was now closed and locked up tight, no doubt, by its own stingy resentment. The Puritans were long gone, and-it alone stood as a bleak testament to their religious resolve. It was opened on weekends—by appointment only—for those who wanted to view the Puritan God from an historical perspective.

As she drove back toward Cloven Terrace, Eve reflected that Singleton was the pastor of this intruder church. She pictured her forbearers casting him out of town, with a hostile tribe of Indians just waiting to take his scalp.

Up ahead, a cruiser sat across the roadway just in front of the overpass with its lights flashing! From behind it a plume of dark smoke rose furiously and the town's one fire engine was at the scene spraying a vehicle with water. A policeman, the very one to whom Eve had talked when she made her complaint, stood in the middle of the road waving his arms at her approaching car.

"...Go back! Turn around. Road's closed for now!"

Eve pulled up close to the man and rolled down her window, "What happened?"

"Road's closed, Miss—Oh...it's you."

"How am I going to get back home?"

"Well...You gotta turn around and take the other underpass over to the mall. But you can't come through here. Not now."

"That's five miles out of my way!"

"Don't make no difference, Miss. Nobody goin' through here till we get that fire out and pull out the wreck."

"What happened?..." Eve was unable to see over the fire truck clearly. The smoke was too thick to see the vehicle.

"...You don't need to know, Miss..." There was something in the policeman's tone that alerted Eve.

"What do you mean, 'I don't need to know?'" She demanded.

"...Somebody you know..."

"Oh, my God! Marian? Is it Marian Wainwright? She's my neighbor! Oh, God!"

"Take it easy, Miss. It ain't your neighbor..." The man seemed to delight in this grisly guessing game.

"Well...I don't know many people...!"

"It's Kenny Tierney." He said it with a finality that suggested she should know the man.

"Ke-Kenny Tierney?...uh..."

"He's the one you reported. You know—the one you claimed tried to rape ya?"

"Uh..." Eve tried to process what the man was saying. The word 'claimed' stuck in her ear having come with just a suggestion of accusation. "...You mean the moving man?"

"That's him. Hit the overpass doin' at least seventy."

"Is he—"

"We'll be scrapin' what's left of him off the cab of his truck for a while. Had a wife and three kids. Guess you won't need to come down and make no deposition now." There was a cruel smirk on the man's face.

Eve couldn't let herself answer this suggestion. She turned away from the man, rolled up her window and turned the car around. She drove to the next underpass with her hands shaking...Why should she feel guilty? *He* attacked her! This was Divine Retribution! Poetic justice! It didn't matter! The man was...gone. Gone! The incident was closed. It was best to put it out of mind. She knew how to do that...

***

CHAPTER 7

The morning was a cool one. Thank God for that! Eve had stopped to rub her calf. A painful charley horse had grabbed her and wouldn't let go. Wearing her earbuds, Donna had run on, unaware of Eve's predicament. Eve had discovered that Donna was only partly aware of other people's predicaments. She saw the world solely through the filter of her own needs. Everyone else was part of the set, and she was definitely the star of the movie! She was brutally honest. Eve had to give her that, and it was good to be running again. The running trail around Cloven Terrace was pretty in the mornings with the mist rising off the surrounding woods.

There were a few other runners, not many, but everyone nodded and managed a 'Good Morning,' as they jogged by. It was so much friendlier than her run in Central Park. She pulled herself just off the running path and was frantically rubbing her calf to release the muscle spasm when a voice from behind startled her.

"Need some help?" It was Singleton. He had on running shorts and a cutoff Harvard sweatshirt. He looked more like a frat boy than a minister and it took her a few seconds to register just who he was.

"...I'm fine. Just a charlie horse." Eve tried to look unfazed by the pain in her leg.

Singleton knelt down by her and quickly grabbed her leg and began to message the calf.

"No...I-I'm Ok, really...ow!" She had to admit that his deep kneading of the muscle was helping.

"You have to get into it. Otherwise it'll just tighten up more. It can be a real bitch!" He kept kneading, not looking up.

Eve relaxed and let him work on the twisted muscle until she could feel it begin to release. When it did, the pain subsided and Eve let out a sigh of relief and quickly pulled her leg back awkwardly. "You're a little out of your territory, aren't you, Reverend?"

Singleton sat down on a flat rock next to her. "I run here most mornings. I didn't know you did."

Eve looked away from his earnest eyes, "Just started...Harvard, huh..."

"Divinity school...I started in Med. My folks wanted a doctor. They got one, but not the kind they were hoping for."

"...So you were a privileged type. Full ride to Harvard. Daddy paid the fare..." Eve couldn't hide the edge in her voice.

"...How about you?" Singleton looked out over the path.

"...Stanford...Business all the way. I didn't have a ride...from anyone. Merit scholarships and a big, fat loan, which I paid off within two years of graduation. I made sure money and I were very good friends!"

"...Well, that must be nice..."

"It is! I make a lot of money for my clients and for me."

"...Most people have a love affair with money..."

"Oh, Reverend. You're not going to lecture me on money as 'the root of all evil,' are you? Besides, it's not the money I love, it's the not having it I hate."

"...Have dinner with me." Singleton blurted it out without thinking. It was a purely impulsive moment.

"...What?" Eve had been trying to put him off. This was not what she expected.

"Have dinner with me. Please. We got off on the wrong foot a few days ago, and I'd like to...repair your impression of me."

"I don't think you'd want to have dinner with me."

"I do! I...think you have the wrong idea about me...completely. I'd like the chance to correct that."

"Rev—Adam, I'm very busy with my work, with getting settled in my house—"

"It's just one evening! Or are you afraid to find out you might be wrong?"

"Are you that hungry, or are you just desperate not to eat alone?"

"I never eat alone!—I'm constantly asked out to dinner...gatherings, parties...and not a few 'intimate suppers' by female congregants with an eye to defrocking the minister for a night—if you're wondering."

"I wasn't! For that matter, I wasn't even curious! Maybe you should have a night *alone*..."

"*I* want to do the asking. I want to make an evening...that doesn't involve...obligation."

Eve blinked as she took this in. "...I don't know how to take that..."

"As an invitation to dinner. Just that. Just two people eating together...talking. That's all!"

He was looking at her again with that same earnest expression that she found so unsettling. "...I don't know how to take that either..."

"Take it for what it's worth...How about it?"

Eve looked at him. His blue eyes were looking straight at her. He wasn't calculating and he wasn't suggesting anything but what he was saying. She could tell he was completely serious. "...All right...dinner...talking."

Singleton held out his hand. "It's a deal." They shook hands!

"...This is a little like a closing." Eve reflected as they shook.

"It's an opening...I hope." Singleton bounded up from the rock and dusted himself off just as Donna was running back.

"Eve!...What's the holdup?..Eve!" She was waving and calling as she jogged toward them.

"Tomorrow...Seven-thirty. Casual...Are you all right with seafood?" He was re-tying his shoe in preparation for returning to his run.

"...Uh...sure—"Eve held her hand over her eyes to deflect the oblique morning sun.

"Good. See ya..." And Singleton was off before Donna could arrive.

Donna jogged up the hill to where Eve still sat looking a little puzzled about what had just transpired.

"What happened to you? Who was that?" She was looking after Singleton appreciatively.

"The new minister at Marion's church."

"No wonder she's all...Christian all of a sudden. With a butt like that he could save my soul. What did he want?"

"A date...I think."

"Is he as good coming as he is going?" Donna was still staring after Singleton.

"He's...all right, I guess. Not really my type...I'm not sure I have a type, for that matter..."

"So you're poaching the minister right out from under Marian's nose. I'll have to be careful of you."

"Relax. I don't even like the guy. He just...wanted to mend fences with me, I think. We had a little run-in at the parish house on Sunday. I objected to his antiquated ideas about women. He seems to want us to stay in our places. I sort of...put him in his."

"Well...I could think of a place to put him...."Donna was still looking appreciatively.

Eve sighed slightly looking at Donna, "...Ok..."

"It's easy to criticize. You have your 'employee.' We're three divorced women with few options.—Well, technically two divorced women— Libby's a widow."

"...I didn't know that. Her husband died?"

"That's why she drinks. Stan and her son Brad died in a boating accident. Fishing. She and Stan were talking about a divorce. He went off on a trip with their son...The boat capsized...the bodies were washed ashore two days later.—She doesn't drink because of Stan...But Brad...that got her."

"Well....that's...sad." Eve wasn't sure how to react to Donna's bloodless recounting of Libby's tragedy. There was no trace of empathy, just a simple stating of facts.

"As far as I'm concerned, if there's a loose guy available, and I like him...I have no commitments! Why not! I did that once—that whole 'cleave to me only' bit with Dennis! What did I get?—Half a business I have to watch like a hawk so my fucking ex-husband doesn't run away with the delivery boy....We did him, you know?...Paul Hildebrande? We all did him."

"Wh—what?" Eve was trying to focus on what Donna had just said.

"Oh, yeah, I know! Not very nice—June was our friend and...and all that! But Paul..., Paul was something else. A real swine...but what a swine. He knew women...knew what we liked...knew when to make his move. And let's face it, all three of us are lonely! I know that's not an excuse, but he had just about any woman he wanted. June had to know! She'd throw these parties, and you'd know he was screwing half the women in the place, and the other half...he'd get to. He used to slip over to my house when June did the grocery shopping. That's when he did his own 'shopping.' Libby doesn't admit to it, but I know she went with him. Marian was the last. I think that's why she's so emotional about June. She thinks she's the reason June took off like that...That's us. That's our little group...awful, huh?"

"...I don't know. I'm not one to judge." Eve was trying not to reveal how strange Donna's emotional disconnection seemed.

"Sure you are. You did the first day, but you didn't let us know it. That was...kind, I guess, or else it was just classy. Anyway, I liked it. C'mon, we've got 2K left, and I've gotta get my hair done...." Donna bounded up and put her earbuds back in before Eve could reply. She took off at an easy canter down the path and motioned for Eve to follow.

Eve rose carefully and brushed away the gravel from her running pants. "Who are these women, and what am I doing here?..."

Eve followed Donna down the running path back toward her "New Victorian," pondering what possible reasons she could have had for coming back to Holmsford.

***

CHAPTER 8

"Where the hell do I go?"...Eve talked to herself, finding herself on the edge of her property, clutching the wrapped present and realizing for the first time that she had no idea where Hetty's house might be on the property.

She found herself by the goat pens, and she turned in two different directions trying to decide which one seemed more promising. Suddenly behind her came a sudden and alarming scream. Eve jumped a little but quickly realized that it was coming from the pens. It was her little friend, the tawny goat. There she was on her hind legs focused on Eve and screaming as she had done that first time.

"Well, what are you doing out here all alone, huh, sweetie? Where are all your friends?..." Eve looked around the empty pen. She approached the fence and reached out to the animal to scratch behind its ears and between its horns. The animal seemed immediately soothed by her touch. She leaned her head into Eve's hand and made deep, guttering sounds in her throat as Eve stroked and scratched.

"There now!....That's better, huh....Now you're not so upset! Uh uh...now it's better, isn't it?..." Just then Eve caught sight of a pair of eyes in the shadows at the far end of the pen. The eyes were yellow and low. What was it...a bobcat?...A dog?

The little tawny goat continued to lean into her and enjoy the petting when the eyes suddenly popped up and sprang toward the two of them. As they did, Eve could make out finally that they were the eyes of another goat, black...larger than the little tawny female. The animal increased its speed and at the last minute put its head down, running into the little tawny goat with a force hard enough to produce a loud crack.

The little tawny goat grunted as she was butted right off the fence onto her side, stunned and disoriented. Quickly she clambered to her feet and began to scream again, trying to climb back up to the fence where Eve stood.

"You get away! Get! Get away from her!" Eve was almost shouting at the larger black goat, but it didn't even notice her. Again, the creature put its head down and ran at the tawny female, propelling her back into the penned area by at least ten feet.

Now the tawny goat screamed in sheer terror. She seemed to be pleading to Eve while the black goat butted her again and again, driving her toward the far side of the enclosure. Eve was frantically trying to scare the black intruder away. She finally resorted to throwing rocks at the creature, but it would not stop its onslaught.

Finally driving the little tawny goat to the far side of the enclosure, the black goat forced her into a corner and mounted her. Now Eve understood. He was in rut. It angered her to see how he brutalized and dominated her. All the while the little tawny goat screamed, her eyes rolling back in a plea toward Eve. Eve shouted, she threw rocks, but nothing she did would stop the black goat until he had accomplished his domination of the smaller female. Eve had even tried to get around to where the two goats were to beat him away with a stick, but that side of the compound was wet and muddy. The sucking mud had literally pulled off one of her shoes, and finally she had to quit.

"I'm sorry, sweetie!" She said half to herself and half to the little tawny goat. "They're all the same, you know. Not much subtlety! I'm sorry..."

She retrieved her muddy shoe and scraped away the accumulation of muck with a leaf. As she did so, she noticed a worn path on that side of the pen that led into the woods.

"That's got to be it...." She took off down the path in hopes of finding the house.

***

It was time. Hetty knew she had to take the rooster. A quick slit to the throat of the bird as it hung suspended and it was soon done. He was a big one. There was a lot of blood. That was a good thing. As it drained into the bowl beneath, she hummed a distant, long-forgotten chant and listened while it trickled out.

The large, red fowl fluttered only once under her expert hand and then poured out its life. When it was drained, she took the bowl out to the edge of the wood and poured out the blood, committing its strength to the four elements and thanked its spirit for its power.

Returning to the barn, she set about scalding the bird and gutting it. She had slit the fowl open and was reaching in with her strong hands to remove the entrails as she had seen her father do so many years before, as she had done for so many years now, when she heard the barn door creak open wide.

As she looked up quickly she could make out only an outline against the outdoor light. She squinted to try to discern who would dare to come here.

"Who are you?...She stood up straight, both hands dripping blood and guts as she demanded her answer. All she heard was an intake of breath.

"Tell me who you are, or I'll run this knife right up your middle!" In one fluid motion, she grabbed the gutting knife and held it out toward the shape. "...Well!"

"Hetty!...It's me...Eve Truesdale..." Eve was stifling a gag reflex from the sight of the blood on Hetty's hands and down the front of the canvas apron she wore.

"What do you want?..." Hetty was confused. Nobody came here! She was alone—always! Leastwise no one ever come up to the house like this! "I asked ya, what you wanted!"

Eve leaned for a moment against the barn door, trying to catch her breath. "I brought you a gift..." She was trying to recover.

"Gift?...What do you mean you brung me a gift?" Hetty stepped forward toward Eve, the knife still clutched in her bloody hand. Eve backed up a step, holding the gift box Dilla Merkle had tied with the dusty ribbon.

Hetty saw Eve recoil and look down at the knife and her hands and apron and then back at Eve. "Don't tell me you never saw a rooster slaughtered!"

"...N-no!...." With that Eve ran out into the door yard and threw up.

Hetty cursed softly, wiping the knife on her apron and putting it down on a barrelhead. She took off the apron and hung it on its iron hook near the slaughtering block. She doused her bloody hands with cold water from the bucket and wiped them with an empty grain sack, and she went out into the light.

Eve was leaning on the split log fence dry heaving. Hetty stood watching her for a moment unsure what to do. Finally she spoke,"...Are ya done?...."

"I-I think so...I wasn't expecting to see...I'm sorry!"

"A little puke don't bother me...You look pretty done in. C'mon on up to the step. I'll get ya something."

"I've been enough trouble—"

"I ain't askin'!" Hetty led the way to the house, a sturdy salt-box cape larger than Eve expected. It was as Dilla had told her, completely untouched. "The step" was a huge slab of granite that had been shaped and place tight up against the front door. It was large enough to place a chair on and served as a transition from the ground to the rough floor of the house. Hetty motioned for Eve to sit on a split oak chair by the door as Hetty went inside for a moment. She returned with an earthen mug full of an herbal tea of some kind. "Drink this. It's sweet. It'll settle your stomach."

Eve took the cup and took a tiny sip. It was sweet and it had a vaguely minty aroma. She took a large sip and settled back on the chair while Hetty squatted down on the granite step waiting.

After a moment, the liquid seemed to soothe her queasiness, and Eve let out a deep sigh. "Thank you. What is this?"

"Wicca weed. Grows 'round here. Good for the gut when it's twisted—or the heaves. Use it on my goats mostly."

Eve looked back down at the cup considering this last remark. "...Well...thank you..."

"How'd ya know how to find me?" Hetty wasn't looking at her straight on. She seemed to be keeping watch on the rest of the barn area.

"Path. I followed the goat path...through the woods."

"...Uh....That was good." Hetty seemed a little surprised by her ingenuity.

"I saw the little blonde goat again....alone in the pens with a brute of a black male."

"That's Old Billy. He does the job."

"Job?"

"If she don't kid, she don't give milk...What's that ya got?" Hetty was trying not to look at the box that Eve still clutched tightly to herself.

"Oh...here. I wasn't sure what to get you ...I hope you like it." Eve handed the box down to Hetty and the old woman took it awkwardly, not really knowing how to receive it. "She was screaming...the goat, I mean. She was terrified."

"Eyah...Nothin' for it. She'll get used to it. What for?"

"What?"

"What for? Why'd you bring me somethin'?"

"Hetty, you practically saved my life—"

"I did save your life—Ya can't shoot worth a damn."

"...I thought that called for something. A little show of appreciation."

Hetty looked away, absorbing this last remark and fingering the ribbon. "T'weren't much..."

"Open it." Eve could see the old woman wasn't used to gifts.

Hetty broke the ribbon and tore off the paper, letting it drop to the ground. She lifted the lid and reached inside, pulling out the white terrycloth towel. She gave a puzzled look and reached in again after the cakes of scented soaps. These she sniffed at. "...Lavender....bayberry...what's this one?...Lemon. Do ya eat 'em?"

"No, Hetty! They're soaps. For bathing!... And that's a bath sheet to dry yourself."

Hetty quickly put the cakes of soap back into the larger box and awkwardly folded the large bath towel onto her lap, "...Smell good enough to eat...glad ya told me." She looked away. Eve couldn't tell if she was embarrassed by the gift or annoyed by not knowing what the soaps were.

"...I should have brought you something else."

"You done fine...Just...not much of a fancy bather...I live simple..."

"It's beautiful! I was admiring it as I walked over here."

"...It's plain. Been this way since the beginnin'."

"It's so lush and green. Everything seems so...natural!" Eve realized as soon as she said it how stupid the remark was.

"...Everythin' in nature is good. Somethin' grows to cure whatever ails. Seasons wipe everythin' clean..." She stopped as if she had run out of words.

"...That man, the one you hit? He's dead...." Eve felt almost guilty bringing it up, but somehow she thought Hetty would want to know.

"...That so..." The old woman said this matter-of-factly, almost as if she already knew.

"I saw the wreck. On my way home yesterday..."

"Brung it on himself. You...sorry?" Hetty was looking straight out at the surrounding farm. They both were. It was as if the conversation needed only their voices, not their eyes.

"...No...At first, but...no."

"...You told him to 'hit the road'...guess he did."

"...He had a wife and three children... The policeman at the wreck, when he saw it was me...he told me. ...I'm sorry for his family."

"If he done that to you, guess what he mighta done to his own woman. Bad for a good. It evens out."

"I didn't think of that."

"Eveythin' comes 'round. The earth strikes even—all the opposites. Spring for winter, fall for summer, rain for sun ..."

"...Man for Woman?..."

"That's the one, ain't it? We ain't opposites lest we make it that way. Men are good for that. Makin' women to blame. They been doin' that since Adam. Don't like payin' for their own sins. There's power in us. I think they know it. Scares 'em. There's power in you...more'n ya think...if ya know where to look..." Hetty's voice was low and definite. It rolled with conviction like a prayer.

"...Maybe that's why I came..." Momentarily Eve was listening, reaching for herself. "What about...love...?"

"Not the same for us. For them, ain't no more'n a hunger to be fed. For us—it's life. We give life, and they use it on us. Trap us and train us. But we don't have to take the trap. We can turn it on 'em! Use it—like they use us. We can turn away…keep our power to ourselves."

"…But then…you're alone…"

"…Eyah…you are. But you got yourself. T'other way, you're still alone and he owns you…."

The old woman fell silent and they sat there for several minutes, just thinking. Around her Eve was aware of the sounds of life. The woods around the house and barn were alive with birds and birdsong, and the goats called softly to each other in the pen by the barn. The breeze in the trees made a pleasant "whooshing" that sounded like the whole earth breathing. Even the bees and beetles buzzing around sounded like affirmation.

The sweet wicca weed tea had settled her stomach and Eve was full of a feeling of well-being that she hadn't felt for months.

"Could…could I see your house?…"

"…My house?…nothin' to see there, Missy. Just a plain place…"

"It's very old…"

"It is. Built by them that came. Same as it was. I ain't changed it…."The old woman stood up clutching the bath towel Eve had given her and grabbed the box that contained the soaps, "C'mon, then…"

Hetty pushed open the stout wooden door on hand wrought strap hinges and beckoned Eve in.

It took a moment for Eve's eyes to adjust to the dim light. The lattice windows were small, making the interior seem dark. On the far wall, a huge stone fireplace contained the remnants of a fire that had been banked to preserve the coals for another lighting. Over it hung a bulbous iron pot on a crane. The floor of the main room was made of wide, rough-hewn planks worn smooth over the years and worn down in the spots where one would have stood and moved repeatedly—by the hearth, by the table and near a narrow winding staircase which led up to a loft-like second floor. There was a door that led to another room, which Eve supposed was Hetty's bedroom.

"…Oh, Hetty!…It's wonderful!"

"…I'm used to it."

"...It's like stepping back in time!"

Hanging from the low-slung ceiling beams were strung peppers and bunches of dried herbs of all varieties. Braids of garlic and onions hung near the table which Eve noticed could double as a bench when its top was lifted and pegged. The room was small but not stuffy. The herbs perfumed the room with a rich pleasant aroma that was indescribable and welcoming. A bucket of fresh water with a dipper stood by the hearth, ready for cooking, and a wooden bowl filled with fresh morning eggs was on the table. There was a rough loaf of bread peeking out from under a cloth and all of Hetty's cooking utensils hung in perfect order from an iron rod. The inside was swept clean and kept orderly.

"There's some that thinks it oughta be pulled down...."

"Oh, Hetty, no! This is...beautiful!" Eve moved around the room taking it all in.

Hetty watched her, and seemed to draw satisfaction from her appraisal. "Built by Giles Livesey. 1640. He was a learned man! He was a preacher, and a fair hand at buildin'. Finest house among the first ones built. Glass in the windas!—That was somethin' then!"

"Look at those cooking utensils!" Eve lifted a huge, long-handled iron spoon off the bar.

"They say them as eats with the devil should have a long spoon." Hetty chuckled at her own joke and at Eve's obvious delight with her house.

"Why is everything so big?"

"You don't want to be cookin' in that hearth without long handles. You get too close to them coals and you go up in flames. Many a woman's died like that."

"Really? Of course! You practically have to walk into the fire to cook!"

"Done it myself a coupla times...That's why I keep that bucket filled." Hetty pointed to the bucket with the dipper.

"it's a hard way to live."

"...Hard?"

"...No electricity...no running water...."

"Ain't hard if that's what you got." Hetty seemed to back up a little.

"I don't mean—"

"Nothin' hard about it.....I'm used to it. I didn't change nothing.' It's just the same as always! Like it was meant to be!"

"...What's this, Hetty?" Eve stopped by a small table in a very dim corner. On the table was a huge, ancient, leather bound book closed by a metal hasp.

"Keepin' Book." Hetty moved over to the table and looked at Eve tensely.

"The what?"

"Whatever wants writin' down ...Recipes, nostrums...things that happened, bits of learnin'..."

"Like a journal."

"Nothin' so grand...Missy, ya seen my house. I got quite a bit to do before nightfall..."

"I'm sorry, Hetty. I've said something—"

"I just have work to do, Missy. Thank ya...for the gift. That was...very fine." Hetty seemed to soften again.

"I'm glad you liked it. I should go. I've...got a date tonight."

"...Do ya."

"The local preacher...It ought to be interesting."

"...Be careful...A Man of 'God' will swallow you whole." There was something in Hetty's tone that made Eve stop.

"...As a matter of fact, I may just chew him up and spit him out myself."

"You just be careful..."

Eve wanted to reassure her, but she could tell that she wasn't going to succeed. "Hetty...why don't you come to my house for supper some night?"

"Oh, Missy—"

Before the old woman could continue with what Eve was sure would be a refusal she added, "I want to thank you properly. Give me a chance. Please! After all, you saved my life. I guess that makes you responsible for me now!"

Hetty was unnerved by that last comment, and she didn't seem to know what to say.

"Just name the day—I promise you, I won't give up until you agree!"

"...All right....Friday. Sundown...That do ya?"

"Friday it is...And, Hetty? If that preacher tries to swallow me...he'll choke!"

Hetty nodded sharply and humorlessly, less certain than Eve of her control of the situation. Eve let herself out the door and walked down the path to home.

Inside, Hetty watched her go through the window. "...Them as eats with the devil should have a long spoon..."

***

CHAPTER 9

"It hasn't been a very good deal for women, has it? I mean marriage—kids—then she's pretty much finished!"

"Really?—a 'deal?'—it's a choice—for men *and* women. Mutual comfort, protection, procreation..."

"Right! How 'mutual' is it when the woman is the one who has to carry the offspring, birth it, and then *she's* the one who winds up wiping its nose, it's dirty little hinie and pushing it through the next twenty years of maturation! Where's the mutuality in that?..."

Simpson's was a simple, out-of-the-way lobster shack tucked in one of Boston's little side streets. It was a neighborhood place, not a lot of atmosphere, but great seafood! It was a place the dockworkers used to come after their shifts, and not much had changed. They still spread the floor with sawdust, and the wait staff tended more to the brusque, but Eve liked it. She and Singleton ordered the "lobster Dinner" which came with not one, but two chicken lobsters apiece, drawn butter, potato, vegetable and a pitcher of draft house beer. The place was buzzing with locals. At the bar the TV blared a hockey game with all the attendant cheering and argument.   There was noise everywhere, and so their conversation simply converged with all others and disappeared to everyone but the two of them.

Eve noticed the jeans and cowboy boots—not to mention a tee under an open flannel shirt—and he had showed up in a truck! It was an old Ford battered but well-maintained. He had said nothing; he just smiled, but Eve caught the blush that flashed across his face as they got into the vehicle to drive here.

"You can't change biology!" he countered. "Women have the children; that doesn't mean they stop being individuals!"

"Oh yeah..." Eve was pointing at him with a lump of lobster tightly skewered on her fork, "That's what you men want us to think. Then comes the two o'clock feedings and you're all snoring up a storm!"

"'You men?'...What do you mean 'you men?' You make it sound like some kind of centrally-planned conspiracy!"

"Well, isn't it?"

"Men didn't invent childbirth!"

"No, your God did that. He's a man...isn't that what you've told us."

"What?"

"I believe it! He's got to be a man! Otherwise She would have had men having the babies!"

"Then we'd be women!"

"And you'd be better people!"

The two of them dissolved into laughter. They concentrated for a moment on their meals, enjoying the food, and, Eve had to admit, the company. Singleton wasn't what she thought. He was sharp, and he had a sense of humor. They had bandied back and forth all the way into Boston and all the way through the meal so far. It was a draw. He didn't talk business and he could disagree without being disagreeable. He listened before he debated; that was interesting! It occurred to her that for the first time talking to a man, she didn't feel she needed to watch her every word.

"So...marriage and family—not an interest then..." Singleton was still concentrating on his plate, but Eve could tell he was listening especially carefully.

"Oh, you're not going to do that, are you?..." She had to challenge him.

"Do what?" He looked up with that forthright, blue-eyed look of his.

"Check my biological clock! See if I'm getting desperate to pop out an offspring before it's too late?"

"You know, it's too bad you're not more outspoken!" They both laughed again.

Eve recovered herself, "OK...all right...If you really want to know. I'm not against either one."

"So...it's not off the table."

"It's not on the menu!—And it's getting pretty close to the end of dinner; I don't see it being served."

"Why not?"

"I work! Everything goes into that...I make my own way."

"You're loaded! You could stop." Singleton smiled.

"I am not 'loaded!'...I've made some money. I won't deny it..." Singleton kept smiling at her and she could feel her face burn. "All right, I'm loaded. I've made plenty of money! What's that got to do with it?"

"...I don't know!...I just think it's important to be honest with yourself."

"I am honest with myself!"

"...OK..." Singleton turned his attention to his dinner.

"...Look...I handle a lot of guys—Hell, I run 'em!...Hard-playing, two-fisted money-grubbers who want anything and everything they see. If I let my guard down...they'd have me for lunch! Most of them have wives and families. That doesn't stop them! They count on a woman being soft...emotional. I'm not! Not with them! I run 'em and, if I have to, I run over 'em! I know them; so I sure as hell am not going to marry one of them." Eve thought of Jace's ring still sitting in the box on her dresser. She had forgotten it until that moment.

"...I love a Romantic."

"I have a romantic side, but not there! Not where I work!"

"...You must love it...to put so much into it...." Singleton didn't look up. He just kept eating.

"Actually, I do! I love, the...the..."

"Challenge? Excitement? Control?" Now he was looking at her with those penetrating blue eyes.

"...I don't have to depend on anyone...."

"Uh huh..." He was still looking at her, "So...why *did* you come here? It sounds like where you were is exactly where you wanted to be."

"It was....It...is! I just...I don't know." Eve fell silent.

"...Something?..." Singleton leaned forward.

"I...had this little...spell. In the middle of a meeting. Nobody saw it! But it was there. I was going through the motions, but it was like I was outside of myself, watching. It never happened before, and it hasn't happened since, but I—needed to...think about it."

"Stress?"

"No! I live with stress. It's a constant in my business. This wasn't stress...I...I don't know why I'm telling you this."

"I could put on my collar," Singleton offered.

"If you do, I'm walking out of here."

"OK! I just thought—"

"Don't think! Just be pretty, and silent."

"...You think I'm pretty!"

"'Silent' was the operative word. 'Pretty' was just the camouflage."

"Drat!—So close!"

"Anyway!...I got in my car and just...left. I found myself here—I don't know why. The next thing I knew, I bought a house! This whole experience is like someone else's idea. For a while, I was afraid I was losing my mind...but, now...I'm thinking that maybe this is something I needed. Maybe I just had to get away from the bullpen and...breathe."

"...No one at your office knows?"

"They know, but they don't *know*. I've been working...all along. I keep up with my accounts and clients by phone and computer as well as the office, but...but I've got to get back there and...fix it."

"Fix what? Can't you have a house?"

"I've got one...a condo. Midtown. Beautiful view...to die for, really..."

"So?..."

"I'm a partner! Partners do not just waltz out of the office and stay gone for over a month to set up housekeeping in some country town in New England. I'm expected to be there driving the business, keeping the staff moving, juggling clients, keeping the money wheel spinning! Partners don't take side trips!"

"...But, if you need to—"

"I'm tougher than any of them, I don't 'need' to!...They'd just love to find a weakness—any excuse to strip away what I built and claim I was never what I am!"

"...You'd confirm their secret...expectations..."

"...That's pretty much it..."

"What are *your* expectations?" Singleton sat back and looked at her again with that disconcerting forthright expression on his face.

"Wh-what? What do you mean, 'What are *my* expectations?" Eve could feel herself getting annoyed with him.

"What do *you* want? What do *you* need?"

"I don't want anything! I don't need anything!"

"So, then what do you care what they think? Do what suits you. It sounds like any of *them* would. Why do you need to go on proving what you already know—what *they* already know. If you're doing your job, and you have the power—use it!"

"...They'll want to know. Where am I? What am I doing?"

"You do your work?"

"Yes!"

"You're a partner?"

"Yes!"

"Do they ever report to you about their...activities?"

"...No." Eve sat a little straighter in the booth. "...You think I don't need to...repair anything...to explain."

"Oh...they'll want you to. Because you're a woman. They're used to women explaining themselves.—It's a woman-thing. But if you don't..."

"That'll really scare them..."

"To death!....They'll ask you...to put you on the defensive. Don't answer. Just do what you do. Deliver the goods, and keep right on going. It'll drive them crazy!"

"...How do know this?..."

"...Word has it I'm a man."

"If they find out you're giving trade secrets away—"

"They'll drum me out of the corps!—I know. Say nothing!"

"Your secret's safe with me...Would you excuse me? I need to use the powder room."

Eve slid out of the booth and Singleton sipped on his beer. She was amazing, he reflected. Fierce, warm, smart, and real. She wasn't trying to please him. She wasn't helpless and...secondary—that was the only word he could think of. She was right there—even with him. Level. It was...exciting.

When she returned, she stood by the booth, "C'mon, I paid the tab. Let's go."

"You paid the tab?....As I recall I asked *you* out."

"I'm 'loaded,' remember?"

"...Ok..."

"...Don't worry. Just because I paid for dinner doesn't mean I'll expect you to put out?"

Singleton got up, slugging down the last of his beer, "That is no way to talk to your vicar!"

"You are not my vicar!"

"Sure I am—I just counseled you!"

"I don't have a church, and I most certainly do not have a Vicar!"

"We can negotiate this on the way back in the truck..."

They continued this way all the way back to Holmsford. It was the best time Eve could remember having.

*****

CHAPTER 10

"Board of Selectmen opens to the meeting members, the matter of locating an industrial park in Holmsford..."

John Marlin was happy. So few came to the town meetings that he was free to steer most business he wanted done through the process without too much dispute. This was another matter however. Jim Reedy at Innovative wanted a bigger bite of the town than he thought he could deliver. He would have to be clever. Delivering up the old Ramsay farm was easy enough. No family to object...only one other bidder—the old Goat Woman! What a joke! Marlin's cut was a tasty one—$250,000 off the top. Nobody had to know. A 'finder's fee' they called it. Innovative got six-hundred fifty acres overlooking the town for their development, and Marlin got richer. And the town was better off, Marlin reflected. All those nice expensive homes—potential for new taxes! Holmsford was the real winner! But now Reedy wanted more. What did Reedy know? He knew something; Marlin was sure of it, but how could he find out?

"Mr. Marlin!"

"Board recognizes Mrs. Merkle. Evening, Dilla, how are you?

"Fine, thank you! What the hell are you talkin' about, Johnny? What do you mean an 'industrial park?'"

"It's just a term, Dilla. It's a place where businesses locate all together. It'll mean jobs for the town!"

"What kinda jobs are you talking about?"

"Depends on the businesses that take out space in the park, Dilla. I have no way of knowing that now."

"Don't you think we oughta, Johnny?..."

"Business doesn't work like that, Dilla. We need this. Holmsford hasn't been anything more than a Boston Bedroom since the forties when the mill shut down."

"Right. And do you think any of those 'bedroom people' will care what happens to Holmsford. You're a Marlin, John. A first family. There's damn few of us left! We're the ones here tonight—most of us! At this meeting! Don't you think we ought to think about it before we invite businesses to town we don't know anything about?"

"Look, Dilla, the park is built, and different businesses rent space for offices, and...whatever."

"It's the 'whatever' we need to know! This town has a long history—"

"Dilla, we all know you're the head of the town historical society."

"I'm the whole damn society!"

"Yes, we know, Dilla. And we're very grateful for your work—"

"Stop patronizing me, Johnny Marlin! I know you since you were a squalling brat in your mother's arms. This is our town we're talking about, and you're not gonna sell it out from under us! Who's building this 'Industrial Park' to start with? It wouldn't be your Innovative people again, would it?"

"...Mr. Reedy did contact me—"

"Ha! I knew it! You pushed the sale of Ramsay farm past us and now what have we got? They went and built 30 god-awful McMansions up on that hill and there aren't but half of 'em sold, and it's been five years!"

"The tax revenues—"

"Don't cover the extra town services. You went and gave them an abatement for 10 years. That means no one's paying on those unsold monstrosities and the town still has to provide services for empty houses!"

"Real estate has had a setback—"

"Right!" Dilla interrupted, "And you're about to propose another big real estate deal! How smart is that?"

"We're talking about jobs, here! These businesses will bring additional employment to people right here in this town. Don't you want that?"

"That depends on what kind of jobs you're talking about! Half the town works out at that mall for minimum wage. That what you're talking about? Is that the kind of jobs you want to bring here?"

Marlin could tell he was losing the meeting members. Damn that old woman! He had to think of something, if he wanted to at least have the project discussed among the Board. He could manipulate that. A little money spent and he could get the votes he needed, but this open discussion had to be tabled before she did any further damage.

"I recommend we postpone further discussion in view of Mrs. Merkle's objections. All in favor?..."

"Hold on there, Johnny! I want to know just where you're planning to locate this 'Industrial Mall' of yours. We don't have any large tracts of town land left. How much land are we talking about, and just where are you planning to locate this thing?"

"We'll have to determine that once we have voted on the proposal, Dilla."

"Behind closed doors, you mean! The way you did the mall and that development!"

"The Board of Selectmen will review your ideas, Dilla, as well as any from other town meeting members then we will decide!"

"Don't get high-handed with me, Johnny! I'm old, but I'm not stupid. You've got some deal cooked up already, and you're not telling us the whole thing! Until you do, I'm recommending a 'no' vote."

"Duly noted. I move this meeting adjourned! All in favor?..."

The hands went up and John Marlin was grateful for an end to this stupid tradition! A 'Town Meeting'—it was medieval! The only members who came were the cranks and nut-jobs like Dilla Merkle. He knew what was good for the town! If he did himself some good along the way, what was wrong with that? But what was it that Jim Reedy knew? There had to be something...

***

CHAPTER 11

The insistent knocking on the door was loud enough to alarm her. Eve looked at the alarm clock by the bed—4:00 a.m.! "Who's that?" Eve said to herself as she squeezed on her slippers and threw a robe over herself. She got to the front door to see Marian frantically knocking on the door and peering through the side-lights. She seemed panicked.

"Marian! What's the matter?" Eve had flung open the door as soon as she saw who it was.

"Libby! It's Libby. You gotta come with me. I think she might have done something to herself. C'mon, Eve. I don't want to go over there myself!" Marian was already halfway down the sidewalk to the street.

"Wh-what do you mean? What are you talking about?" Eve found herself running to catch up to Marian.

"She called me! She's having one of her...things! We've got to get over there! C'mon!"

Whatever it was, Eve could tell that Marian was scared. They ran the half block to Libby's huge second-Empire. Marian was right, it did look like the Psycho house! The yard was straggly and the landscaping was poorly maintained. It was something you didn't notice from a car, but when you got close, you could see that there wasn't much attempt to maintain the place.

Marian fished into her pocket and produced a key.

"She gave me this......c'mon...." The two of them entered. The house was cluttered and not very clean. The furniture was good, but it was obvious that no one had vacuumed or dusted in some time. There were odd piles of newspaper in spots around the room. "Libby?....LIBBY!" Marian called out, staying close to Eve the entire time.

After a moment, they heard Libby's voice weakly from up the stairs, "Here...I'm up here..."

The two of them climbed the stairs slowly afraid of what they might find.

"Libby?..." Marian called again when they got to the top of the stairs."

"In here. I'm all right..." Eve could hear soft crying coming from one of the rooms down the hall.

As they entered the room Libby was sprawled out on the bed, face down and sobbing. The room itself was clean and organized in contrast to the rest of the house. It was like a set, Eve thought. It was obviously the room for a young boy. There were posters of rock bands on the walls and soccer trophies on the dresser. A laptop was open on a small desk as if waiting to be turned on. Around the room were pictures of a boy with Libby and a man. Some of them were of the boy and other teens, some were of the boy in mid-action on the soccer field. It was clear that this had been her son's room. Nothing had been moved. Although she might have neglected the rest of the house, Libby had kept this shrine clean and neat, awaiting the return of a son who would never come back.

Marian went right over to Libby, picked her up off the bed and held her and rocked her like a baby, all the time repeating, "It's all right. C'mon, Lib, it's Okay..."

Eve didn't quite know what to do, so she stood by in case Marian needed help. After a few moments, Libby seemed to stop and slowly repossess herself.

"I—I'm sorry...I tried..."

"It's all right, Libby. We were just worried. I'm glad you called me!"

Libby looked at Eve standing by the door. "You gotta think I'm Goddamn crazy!...I...probably am..."

"Are you all right, Libby?" Eve wasn't sure at this point what to think.

"Sure!...why not?...You can see I'm the fucking picture of mental health!—You don't know about any of this—Why should you?...This was...my son's room..."

"...Brad?" Eve remembered Donna's somewhat clinical bio of Libby's tragedy.

"They told you?" Libby shot an accusatory glance at Marian.

"It wasn't me!...It must have been Donna." Marian continued to hold onto Libby.

"That bitch can't keep her big mouth shut!" Libby sank a little again and fought off the tears. "It was...a year ago today...I just came in to straighten out and...I..."

"It's a nice room!" Eve tried to use a gentle tone.

"What a great kid he was!   He was, wasn't he, Marian?   Handsome, athletic—"

"I can see by the pictures." Eve was trying to reassure her.

"And he was smart! Not like his Goddamn father! He was a straight 'A' student! And kind!—He would've been somebody in the world!" At this Libby dissolved again.

The two women maneuvered her away from the room and brought her downstairs. They gravitated to the kitchen, which was in a deplorable state. The sink was loaded with dirty dishes and the counters were full of take-out cartons containing spoiled food, the whole room smelled sour and rotten. Without saying anything to one another, Marian and Eve set about to put things right. Marian set Libby on a kitchen chair as Eve rinsed out the coffee-maker's carafe. She had to use a utility sink off the kitchen in the laundry room because the piled dishes in the kitchen didn't allow enough room to use the faucet. She filled the carafe and returned to make the coffee. She found the coffee in the cupboard above the coffee maker.   Marian began to dump the empty containers into a half-full garbage bag sitting in the middle of the kitchen floor. All the while Libby kept talking.

"He always talked to me. Can you imagine that? A sixteen-year-old boy who actually talks to his mother? And not just grunts and shrugs—we had conversations! God knows that son-of-a-bitch father of his never talked to me! I think he saw that—he knew! He stepped in where Stanley didn't.   That boy was thinking about the future.   He wanted to be doctor...a pediatrician! Can you figure that? He loved little kids! Loved them!..."

Eve quickly emptied the sink of dirty dishes, carrying them to the utility sink, and swabbed it out to begin washing. Marian tied the now full garbage bag and took it and three other unsealed but full bags sitting along the wall to the back stoop. She opened a window to air out the kitchen. All the while, both women listened.

"...I knew Stan was seeing someone. I knew it! So what? I...I had...my moments too. I couldn't blame him altogether!...But I wasn't leaving him! I wasn't ever going to do that! Why did he have to tell me it was over? What? What was over? We were all right! We could've put it back together!   We needed to—for Brad!   He deserved that!..." Libby continued as Marian and Eve worked.

By the time the coffee was ready, Eve had washed half the dishes and stuffed the rest into the dishwasher, which was humming under its heavy load. Marian had soaped down all the counters. Eve found three clean mugs and poured out the coffees. The milk in the refrigerator had soured. Eve poured it out into the sink and found powdered creamer in one of the cupboards. She creamed all the coffees, and she and Marian sat at the table with Libby.

Libby took the cup, "Thanks..." She reached into her robe pocket for her flask and Marian took it out of her hand.

"Honey, that is one thing you do not need right now!"

"Just sit with us...have your coffee..."Eve sat down with the other two women and she listened as did Marian.

"He...he told me he was going to tell Brad...on the fishing trip. 'He's old enough to understand,' he said.—That bastard! He killed my son! He killed him! I hope he rots in hell!..."

"Libby, you don't mean that. You don't mean any of it...What happened, happened." Marian was soft and soothing in her tone. Eve could tell that she had suffered through this before with Libby.

"I did it too! It was my fault too. I could've stopped them. I could have told Brad myself. They didn't have to get on that fucking boat!"

"It's done now. It's not Stan's fault, and it's not yours! It was a terrible thing...but it's nobody's fault!"

"...Yes, it is. I'm stuck with it! He's dead, that prick, but I'm still stuck with it!..."

"Honey, do you think that's gonna bring anybody back?...You can't go on this way!...You know Brad would never want you to blame yourself! He loved you!"

"He did...didn't he!...He loved his Mom!..." Libby seemed to get some comfort from this.

"That's right, honey. He would never want you to go on like this!...I remember him saying, 'Mom, you are the strongest person I ever knew!'"

"You do? You remember that?" Libby was looking at Marian now.

"Of course I do. It was right after Junie...right after that. We were all falling apart, but you just held it together. You were like an anchor! Oh, honey, he admired you—we all did!"

"...You're right. I can't keep doing this!" She blew her nose and seemed to straighten up... "Both of you...I'm really sorry...I...just let things run away with me, I guess."

"Well...you got your kitchen cleaned!...Something good came out of this!" Marian pointed to the now empty counters.

"My house...You gotta think I'm a pig!" Libby was looking at Eve.

"No I don't!"

"Sure you do! Look at this fucking place! It's a sty! It's me. I've been so Goddamn crazy, I let it get this way—Not anymore! Marian, this is the last time you have to do this. I'm sorry I got you two out of bed so early...but thanks..."

"I had to get up anyway. I've got to drive in to New York today." Eve had decided that she had to show her face. If she left right away, she could be there by mid-morning.

"Honey, are you coming back tonight?"

"No. I need a couple of days in New York to...to take care of some business."

"You go—both of you. I did enough to screw you up for one day!" Libby got up from her chair. "As for me...I'm going to do some cleaning!...Go on! I'm fine! I'm a goddamn anchor, remember?"

"Are you sure?..." Eve was doubtful of Libby's quick return.

"Honey, I know this woman! She'll be fine. If she says she's fine—she's fine! C'mon, we're just in the way now." Marian guided Eve to the front door while Libby stood in the kitchen surveying the work that had to be done. At the front door Marian whispered to Eve, "It's OK. She'll be solid for at least a week."

The two of them left the house and were walking back.

"Are you sure about her? Shouldn't we call someone?" Eve was still doubtful.

"I've have been through this four times with her. She'll be an 'anchor' for at least a week—until the cleaning is done. Then she'll fall off the wagon again and get drunk as a sailor, and eventually we'll go 'round another time." Marian looked at Eve, "Thanks for coming with me. I thought this time...maybe she'd do it."

"You mean this is her...routine?"

"About every two or three months."

"She needs help!'" Eve stopped for a moment.

"Oh...honey, how do you help that? How do you take that kind of pain away?" Marian took Eve's arm, and they resumed walking as the sun was beginning to rise.

"...You handled her well. That bit about the son...."

"Brad?...Oh, honey, that boy was the sweetest young man you'd ever meet!..."

"He sounds like it!"

"Yes....Gay as a goose."

Eve stopped again, "Marian!"

"Well, honey, he was! Everybody knew it but Libby! Libby fussed over that boy until he had no choice but to be gay! Stan took him fishing as an antidote, I think. The soccer—he was captain of the team, you know...everything he did was to make his parents stop their cheating and fighting. Lord, if I lived in that house, I'd probably be gay too!"

Marian walked Eve to her house and then went on to her own. As Eve dressed for her trip back to the city, she thought about Libby, Donna, and Marion—wounded survivors. Then she thought about Singleton's description of marriage as a 'choice.' It didn't look like a good one.

***

CHAPTER 12

"Yeah, yeah...We've heard all that before! MassDOT plans a rail line to the Southcoast and nothing ever happens! I need to know, Fred! Is it really happening or not?" Jim Reedy was making sure. He had been buying up land all along the proposed corridor for Innovative. Dummy projects. Developments that paid back something, but could be "re-purposed" if the line ever went through. There had been a line, in the last century! But that had been allowed to deteriorate like most of the rail stock in the country. The growing population, the choked interstates—they all screamed for a high-speed rail line re-linking that part of the state. Whoever had solid tracts of land along that corridor would reap big money, and Reedy was going to make sure it was him. Fred Costa was his best source to the real information. Costa was on the MassDot Board and he was connected to the Governor's office. Anything that happened to hustle that development Costa reported directly to Reedy.

"I'm telling you, Jim. It's a sure thing! The governor's behind the bill, the first money's been earmarked. They'll announce next spring. All the towns along the way Cranberry, Holmsford, Littleford...all the way to New Bedford and then to Providence and the Cape. We're set up!"

"All right. I've got deals cooking. When this goes through,...they'll come to us because we'll have what they need."

"Go easy, Jim. If it's too obvious, they'll crucify us."

"Will you relax! I've been buying up parcels for years in anticipation. We're just...accelerating our interest in the region."

"They can't know I've told you anything!"

"Why would I tell them anything? And when this is done, Fred, you're going to do quite well. Quite well, indeed!"

"Yeah...OK...just make sure it looks...kosher."

"As a pickle, Fred, as a pickle!" Reedy chuckled as he ended the call. It was a blind cell phone. Untraceable. The phone would be destroyed by the end of the month. No hint of inside information would be detectable. Finally, all the campaign contributions, all the 'free' vacations and junkets for 'piss-ant' politicians were going to pay off. Innovative would control huge tracts of land right in the middle of the proposed rail line.

Businesses would be lining up and paying a premium to buy what he had been picking up at distress-sale prices for years! The future was looking good.

***

CHAPTER 13

The milkin' was good. The herd gave near fifty-five gallons in a day—give or take. The men come and took it fresh. They come in their truck. Inspected the cans and paid her and left her new cans for fillin'. They were the only ones Hetty saw regular. Not much was said, and they were done. That suited her fine.

She kept a few gallons each week for cheese makin'. The cheese brought in cash, and her cheese was special! Farm made...done with sea salt and herbs she picked herself. She aged it and took it to market. Most times it sold out in an hour. Less time with people. That suited her too.

She'd warmed the raw milk in the big kettle and used the buttermilk to start the curd when she heard the car. Grabbing her staff, she went out of the barn to confront the intruder.

The car stopped short, raising a small cloud of dust, and the door opened. A gray-haired fat man got out and stood smiling at Hetty.

"Miss Livesey, you probably don't remember me—"

"I know ya, Marlin. What do ya want?"

"That road could use paving, couldn't it? Must be difficult getting down to town when the weather's bad."

"I manage. I asked ya what ya wanted..."

"..Uh, ha...well, I wanted to come up and see you—"

"You done that, now what?"

"I wanted to come up here and see if we—the Town, that is—could maybe make things a little easier on you."

"That so..." Hetty didn't budge, holding her staff out in front of her and leaning on it slightly.

"..Uh, well, in view of your...maturity...and the...lack of amenities you're forced to live with—"

"Ya gonna talk all day, or are ya gonna come out with it? I got a batch of cheese workin' and you ain't makin' my work any easier keepin' me."

"All right...I came here to offer you a deal, Miss Livesey."

"A deal, huh...what kind o' deal?"

"Well, now, it occurs to us that you have quite a lot of acreage up here that you have to maintain, and we'd like to offer you the chance to perhaps sell—"

"No." Hetty's answer was flat and plain.

"We can offer a good market price!—it'll relieve you of so much responsibility—"

"No. I ain't sellin'."

"Now, just listen, Miss Livesey, You wouldn't have to leave your farm. Nothing like that. You could keep the acres you need...for your goats, but the rest would be—"

Hetty took a step toward Marlin and he took a step back. She was several inches taller than he, and despite her age, it was clear that she was capable of giving him a good drubbing. "You come at me before with that Board o' Health complaint...with that Hildebrande woman."

"That was none of my doing, Miss Livesey. The woman had a legitimate complaint. Your goats were causing her physical harm!"

"Didn't go nowhere then, nor will this! I ain't interested! Not now...nor never."

"Actually you would be helping the town, Miss Livesey! Think of that."

"Eyah...You think on this. The town ain't give me one thought in all these years I been up here. It ain't done a thing for me, and that suits me fine. Me and mine been here from the beginnin', and here we stay. Now you can turn ya'self 'round and don't look back."

"You're not getting any younger, Ms. Livesey—"

"Neither are you, Marlin! What ya want with all this land, huh? What you gonna do with it, eh? I know! Ya lookin' for money. Everybody knows that."

"This is not for my personal gain, Miss Livesey!"

"It ain't, huh? Well, then you won't mind my sayin' no. When I'm gone—since you're so interested in my gettin' old—my granddaughter will be takin' my place! She won't be sellin' neither. Now get!"

"Miss Livesey!—"

"I said, git!" Hetty took another step forward and raised her staff, ready to swing.

Marlin jumped back and opened the driver's-side door to create a shield between him and Hetty.

"You're going to have to deal with us! This is about jobs for the town, Miss Livesey! You can't stand in the way of progress."

"And you can't stand in the way of this here stick of mine...or do you want to try, Marlin?"

"I'll be back! There are other ways to handle this. Think about that!"

"And you think about this, Marlin!" Hetty swung the staff and knocked off the mirror as Marlin ducked back inside. The car engine roared and Marlin slammed it into reverse just in time to dodge another impact from Hetty's heavy walking staff. He pulled around, splaying gravel and turf as he did, and sped out of sight.

"Not now...nor never..." Hetty muttered as she watched the car pull out of sight down the unpaved farm road.

***

CHAPTER 14

It was ridiculous! He was behaving like a sex-crazed high school kid! Here he was in the middle of a Rotary meeting, and all he could think about was the previous evening. She was challenging, intelligent...independent...and all he could think about was having her! He knew he was blushing. Thank God the other men didn't know what was on his mind! He was the town minister! This was a meeting to talk about ways to improve the town; He was a walking erection! Every time Singleton thought about Eve, his body would react. He tried to push it out of his mind, but his thoughts kept wandering to their evening together. It wasn't even that kind of a date! Sex wasn't the objective...and yet he knew it was.

Ever since he had seen her at the fellowship meeting, he wanted her. He hadn't felt this chemistry since Caroline died. Eve wasn't Caroline...but there was something about her that...had...awakened him. It was weird! She was...one-of-a-kind—maybe that was it. She was unique.

Caroline was unique...When she died, he crashed pretty hard. She had been assistant the to the head curator at the Boston Art Museum. She was...galvanizing! People just loved her! Anywhere they went, she knew people—people knew her. It was magic!...And then she had a pain one day...ovarian cancer...advanced. Two months. He couldn't leave the apartment for weeks. When he finally found his courage, he asked to be sent somewhere...quiet to 'restore his soul.'

Eve didn't look at all like her, God knows she didn't have Caroline's charm, but there was this...ferocity—yes! That was it. She was ferocious, keen and penetrating. She had that, and there was also something essentially feminine about her. Underneath all that assertiveness, there was still warmth and vulnerability. Caroline was like that. When she took something on, she took no prisoners. When she took him on, there was total commitment! He had no doubts. She loved completely, and she demanded the same from him. She made him a better man. He could feel that same energy in Eve. He wasn't sure his soul had been restored, but this woman...this woman had certainly reawakened his libido!

"...What do you think, Adam?..."

"Well....I think it bears...consideration..." Good cover! He hadn't been listening at all. Charlie Metcalf was looking straight at him, expecting more of an answer, he could tell. Charlie was Chairman of the Rotary Committee and a Town Selectman. He was a good-natured 'old fella,' and Adam liked him. He was the sort of older man who reminded everyone of a favorite uncle. He was jovial, sincere, and always appeared interested in what you had to say. Somehow, you didn't want to disappoint Charlie.

"...Really?...I thought you didn't like the idea. After all, we don't know that much about it, do we?"

"Well..." Singleton was grappling for a way to find out what had just been discussed, "What exactly *do* we know?"

"We're both on the Board, Adam. All we know is what Marlin told us. Those Innovative people want to buy more town land and develop that 'Industrial Park,' but, hell, we don't know what kind of 'Industry' we're talking about. They say it'll mean jobs, but how do we know? And suppose it's some kind of chemical plant or waste disposal site they want to put in there—I mean, do we want that in Holmsford?"

"...We could draw up some kind of sales contract limiting the kind of businesses that can go in. Call the shots. If Innovative wants to do this, they ought to realize that the town has to have some constraints on the kind of activities that go on within the town limits."

"Marlin told us they don't like interference. They want a nice clean deal. He's got Fry, Bolling, and Carter in his pocket. You know that, Adam. There's just you and me right now."

"He doesn't want to look bad, Charlie. If there's one thing John Marlin likes, it's his reputation. He won't want us and the Rotary to come out against the deal."

"...We need jobs here, Adam. You know that...Holmsford hasn't been much for decades. Not since the old Truesdale textile mill closed!"

"If we give them a blank check, Charlie...they'll own us."

The old man thought for a moment, and then he nodded, seeming to understand something.

"I move we delay our support until we get more information from Marlin. All those in favor?..."

Singleton was relieved. He had to conduct himself more like an adult—like a minister! This preoccupation with....fantasy...had to stop!...

***

CHAPTER 15

"So... how are you, Eve?" Harold Gardner had asked her to 'come in' just as Eve was headed to her own office. She knew is wasn't so much an invitation as a command. Gardner was a founding partner in the firm and on the Board. He kept a light touch, but you didn't refuse him if he invited you in.

Eve loosened her silk scarf and put her computer bag down by the chair as she sat. "I'm fine, Harold. How are you?"

"...We haven't been seeing you lately..." Gardner left it open, expecting her to explain her absence, but Eve decided to wait.

"...No. I've been out of the office."

"...Is everything all right?" It was another expectational opening.

"Absolutely. You saw the report I sent on 'Allied,' and I snagged two more accounts out of Boston—'Hancock' and 'Mayerly'."

"Very impressive! The Hancock account will be important, I think...I can see you've been working..."

"Of course, Harold. You know I don't let up." Eve had decided that she wasn't going to offer any explanation for her absence. She would let her work speak for her.

"No. You certainly don't! Your department continues to turn out solid results!...Is that what you were doing up in that area? Fielding new clients...for Novus and Gardner?"

"...Jace has been assisting me in some of the paperwork...but with modern communications—"

"I never will get used to all these computers and fancy phones!.." Gardner slipped into his non-threatening "grandfatherly tone."

Eve had seen him do it often in difficult conversations with younger subordinates. So what was so 'difficult' about this conversation? Was he planning to try to fire her? He couldn't do that ; she was a partner! But he could suggest a buyout...Eve held her emotions in check. She refused to panic.

"Harold, you're the most adaptable person I know! It's a little late to pretend that you're a Luddite."

"I'm not saying I'm *against* all this technology. I just remember when it was important to look a person in the eye. All this screen and text...it's dehumanizing!"

"...This is the first time in ten years I've been away from the office, Harold." She forced herself to level her eyes on his. He looked away. No, he wasn't going to fire her! So, what did he want?

"So you realize how important your...presence is to us. You are a fixture here, Eve. It's not the same office without you." Now he was massaging her.

"Harold, haven't you always said no one is indispensable—including you? Besides I haven't been away at all! I've been working constantly. The only change is that I haven't been here physically. Are you telling me the office stopped running while I was away?"

"No. I'm just saying that we missed you."

"...Thank you, Harold..." Nope. He hadn't gotten to it yet...

"You keep us on our toes! Remind us of why we're here..."

"I'm sure some of the staff was grateful for my absence!"

"Well, I was not! You're my protégé, Eve. I brought you up to partner. It's...important to me that you're happy with us."

So that was it! He was afraid she was leaving! The old boy thought she was planning to leave the firm, take her accounts elsewhere, or else go out on her own! "Harold, I'm not leaving Novus and Gardner. You can relax!"

The older man seem to exhale, "Well, now I didn't think you were! I told the Board you were exploring the market! And look what you brought us! Two major new clients in just a month! It's wonderful! But you know the Board...very cautious men!"

"Harold, you know me. I'm not saying I would never leave or form my own firm—but if I did, I would tell you straight out! I don't believe in dancing around things."

The old man's eyes turned steely again, "OK...what were you doing all that time?"

"You know—working."

"We like having you here. You caused us a great deal of anxiety."

"I'm a partner—"

"Limited partner." the old man countered.

"Right...so I'm 'limiting' my time on site!...I'll be spending more time away."

"May I ask why?" Now he was beginning to sound distinctly parental, and Eve was beginning to feel her anger rising.

"It's none of your business, Harold." Eve got up from her chair to leave.

"Now wait a minute, young lady!—"

"'Young lady'—really, Harold? I'm not your daughter, and I'm not your wife. You don't own me, and as you've just told me, you don't want me leaving here, so don't give me a reason to consider that."

"You seem to have an exaggerated idea of who you are, Eve!" Now he was in full bluster.

"And you don't? Look, Harold, let's not make this a war. I'm very grateful to you and this firm. I'm happy here. I have no immediate plans to go to another firm or branch out on my own. I'm quite content to fatten the firm for some time to come...but don't make the mistake of treating me like a first-year analyst. I know my worth. *You* know my worth. I'll be here a lot of the time, but not as much as I used to."

"Why can't you just explain to me—"

"I told you, Harold...with respect...it's none of your business!"

The old man sat back in his chair and looked at her. "You don't give me much to hang my hat on!"

"You've got a coat rack for that, Harold. I still love you. Now I have work to do."

***

CHAPTER 16

Dilla's was open.

Driving back, Eve reflected on the past two days in New York. She felt a deep sense of satisfaction that since her brief meeting with Harold, nobody questioned her about her absence. Only her assistant asked, "How was your trip?" Eve had been careful just to say, "Fine!" and offer nothing to the office rumor mill.

Apparently, only Jace knew about the house in Holmsford.

Jace! He kept pressuring her to come to the apartment. He was very clear about what he wanted, but Eve avoided the topic. Somehow taking advantage of his all-too-ready needs just didn't seem right. She found herself noticing how obvious he was and how shallow his conversation seemed. Everything revolved around the office, their sex life and the new car he wanted. It was all one-sided. The pronoun 'I' was the only one he seemed to use, and she was beginning to feel like a prop in play about Jace Brillig.

As she opened the door, the little bell rang and a little puff of dust rose up from an antique table by the door.

"Well, you did come back! How nice!" Dilla's voice came from behind the dried flower arrangement as before, and the old woman scuttled around the end of the counter to welcome Eve. "I've been open all day, and you're my only customer!"

"Hi, Dilla. Since I was driving through town I thought I'd stop by....I wanted to bring you this..." Eve reached into her bag and took out a small, elegantly wrapped box and handed it to the old woman.

"...Well...now what did you go and do that for?!" The old woman's eyes brightened, seeing the gold wrapping-paper and the lamé bow.

"You were so nice to help me with that gift...this is just a little thank you..."

Dilla tore open the paper and inhaled as she saw the box, "'Compel!'...Oh, my dear, that's way too much. This is fifty dollars an ounce! That old towel and the soaps were nowhere near that kind of value!"

"Weren't you the one who said, 'it's the thought?' Besides, I wasn't trying to pay you; I'm thanking you for making me feel...a little like I used to with Gram." Eve could feel a little catch in her throat.

Dilla looked at her and instinctively reached up with a solid hug, "There! That comes directly from Esther! My goodness. On the TV commercials it says it 'Compels a man to notice!'—You suppose that's true?"

"There's only one way to find out...." Eve smiled as the old woman opened the box and extracted the little crystal atomizer. She sprayed a tiny bit in the air and sniffed.

"Mmm...lovely! C'mon, dear, I'm past being noticed, but you aren't!" They each sampled the perfume and giggled like a pair of schoolgirls. "Now, tell me, how did it go with the Livesey woman?"

"It went well, I think. She's...there's much more to her than meets the eye."

"Did she like the gift?"

"...I think she was more pleased about the *idea* of a gift. I don't think she's gotten too many of those. In actual fact, she didn't really know what the soaps were for. I had to explain."

"Really? But she was pleased?..."

"She showed me her house!"

"She did? What's it like? Is it still...intact?"

"Perfectly. It's like stepping into another century! She still cooks on the original hearth. She uses herbal remedies...there's something...very...primal about it. I can see why you'd want to preserve it. It's beautiful in its own particular way. I can't quite describe it...."

"...Well, that's something, isn't it? You know, it's the only original house left in the whole county! The only one!"

"So you said....something about the Indian raids—"

"King Philip's War! The Wampanoags rose up against the Puritan colonists. Burned them out...all except the Livesey house. It was the only one they left. I did some reading after I saw you. I went back into the town's historical accounts. Seems that Giles Livesey, the original settler, and his wife Rebecca managed to stay on the right side of the natives while the rest of the town were all for wiping out the whole tribe!...Made for some bad blood between 'em."

"What do you mean?"

"The record's just bits and pieces. But a few years later, Giles and Rebecca were hanged...as witches."

"No! You're not serious!"

"Sure am. That's what they did when they didn't like you. Everybody knows what happened later on in Salem, but here in Holmsford...we were ahead of the crowd. It could have been anything...land dispute, personal misunderstanding...These were simple, superstitious folks living on the edge of nowhere. I guess you can see the devil in anything if you're scared enough."

"We're quite a breed, aren't we..."

"Well, I don't judge, dear. I just try to understand what went on. I'm glad you gave her the gift. Sounds as though you made a friend."

"I don't know about that, but she's coming to my house for dinner tonight."

"...I don't think I've ever heard of that woman going anywhere, never mind to someone's house for dinner!"

"I kind of bullied her into it. I realized the soaps and towel might have looked like...like a criticism...You know, a suggestion that maybe she needed to bathe."

"Lord! I didn't think of that!"

"I know, Dilla!...Don't worry. I told her that I wanted to give her dinner to make it a proper thank you for her help. She agreed."

"...Well, I'll be!...Now, dear, you've just gotta come back and tell me about it! I don't think I can stand it waiting to hear how it went. You will, won't you?..." The old woman looked hopefully at Eve.

"Every detail!..."

Eve quickly made her goodbye to Dilla. It was already late in the afternoon. She had to get back and start this dinner for this reluctant guest. She wanted everything to be perfect. How odd, when she thought about it, that her first dinner guest in her own home in Holmsford should be "The Goat Woman!"

She was just unlocking the car when she heard a voice behind her.

"Eve!...You're back!" It was Adam Singleton.

"Adam! Yes. I was in New York for a couple of days. Face time."

"How did it go?" Singleton stood there staring at her smiling. He was trying not to show how glad he was to see her, but he knew he was a miserable failure.

"...I didn't explain." She smiled triumphantly. Seeing Singleton standing in his black coat and collar with his blue eyes staring at her made her feel oddly giddy.

"...Well, this calls for a celebration! Simpsons?—This time I'll pay!"

"Oh, Adam...I can't!"

"Why not?"

"I've got a dinner guest tonight."

"Oh..." Singleton's face fell and it pleased Eve to see that he was honestly disappointed.

"A woman I know. It's kind of a debt of gratitude."

"Oh..." Singleton's smile returned.

"We argued all evening. You sure you want to take me on again?" Eve's eyes flashed a challenge.

"Maybe this time I'll win..." Singleton could feel himself blush.

"What about your flock? Don't you have obligations, Reverend?"

"I'll be 'counseling' one of them!"

"Ho, ho...You are so deluded! I am not now, nor will I ever be one of your 'flock!'"

"Don't be disrespectful to your vicar!"

"Reverend, you are just begging for trouble!"

"OK!...when?..." He was trying to be casual, but he felt again like he did the first time he asked a girl out!

"Tomorrow's Saturday night—'date night...'" Eve enjoyed seeing him blush again.

"7:00 o'clock...Be prepared for salvation...."

As she drove home, Eve couldn't help but smile. Singleton was something she had never expected. Perhaps this was the reason she had come here. Some things were beginning to fall into place.

***

CHAPTER 17

When the doorbell rang, Eve had just finished setting the table. She had kept the meal simple—a roasted chicken, baked potatoes, vegetables, and a salad. She had uncorked a good bottle of wine, and there was a "Juniors" cheesecake in the fridge. She didn't want to overdo the dinner. Her brief view of Hetty's beautiful and unadorned house and basic lifestyle told her that fancy cuisine wouldn't be right.

She didn't dress up because she was sure Hetty wouldn't, and she wanted her guest to be as comfortable as possible.

She opened the door and there was Hetty, standing awkwardly, leaning slightly on her staff and trying hard not to look out of place.

"...It's sundown..."

"Hetty, I'm so glad you came!" Eve beckoned her in and the old woman stepped across the threshold as if she were entering a foreign land.

"...Said I'd come." She sounded almost defensive.

"I know, and I knew you would! I'm—I'm just so glad that you did. Come in!..." Eve encouraged the woman to enter more fully.

Hetty looked around at the house that had been so carefully arranged. It didn't look at all like the place it was when she had burst in and defended Eve. "You fixed it up some..."

"Do you like it? You know, putting this place together really helped take my mind off...off that awful experience..." Eve watched her guest walk slowly into the living room and stand looking at everything.

"...Grand..." Hetty's tone was flat, factual.

"It's too big for me, I know, but...but I bought it. I had all this furniture from my family." Eve stood expectantly.

"...Truedales always been proud..." Once again it was more a statement of fact than judgment.

"...Well, everything fits...and I'm getting used to the place..."

"...Eyah...are we eatin'?" It was a simple question, and it took Eve out of herself.

"Yes! Of course. Come on in to the dining room. I have everything set up!—I hope you like chicken."

"...It'll do." Hetty followed Eve into the dining room, noting everything with curiosity and a kind of reverence. She was like a visitor in a museum, afraid to touch anything.

Eve poured out two glasses of the wine she had chilled into fine crystal glasses and handed one to Hetty, who took it with elaborate delicateness, studying it closely.

"...What is it?" Hetty peered around the glass trying to be careful.

"It's wine, Hetty! I picked up a good bottle! After all, you're my first real dinner guest since I've been in Holmsford."

"...That so?...Wine...eh? The glass is like a ladyslipper..." Hetty gently touched the etched wine glass with her other rough hand.

"It's crystal. For the occasion!" Eve was encouraging her and took a sip from her own glass.

Seeing her do this, Hetty took a tentative sip of the wine and swallowed carefully.

"Well?...do you like it?" Eve could see that the whole idea of wine before dinner was foreign to the old woman.

"...Ya won't get drunk on it..." Hetty took another larger taste of the wine.

"Well, it's not to get drunk on, Hetty. It's an aperitif."

"...A what?"

"An aperitif. Something to help the appetite..."

"Missy, once ya milk forty goats, ya hungry...cat piss or not!"

Eve couldn't help but laugh out loud at Hetty's candor.

"...Sorry. I ain't much for fancy things." The old woman seemed a little embarrassed.

"No, Hetty! I just didn't think about the day you might have had. You're right! After all that work, I'll bet you're hungry. Let's sit down and eat...." The old woman seemed to relax a little even as she sat at the table set with Eve's Limoges and silver service...."Does it really taste like cat piss to you?"

"... A little. Now, if you had some apple jack as I make...you'd know ya had somethin'!" Hetty sat with her hands in her lap looking at the table and unsure what to expect.

"I'll bet I would. Let me get our dinner."

Eve sprang into the kitchen and returned with the whole chicken and a platter with the vegetables and a huge bowl of salad. It was much more food than two people could eat, but she wanted to present a full table.

Hetty seemed to view the meal with satisfaction. Even before Eve could sit, the old woman reached across to the platter, and with one expert swipe she cleaved the chicken in two. She used the carving fork to slap half the chicken onto Eve's plate, the other onto her own. Over this, she ladled a huge portion of vegetables and salad, and topped the mess with a steaming baked potato.

"Ya want to sit an' eat, Missy. You need to add some flesh! Ya too thin." Hetty fell on her meal and ate with total concentration.

Eve was mystified at Hetty's appetite. The old woman worked her way through the mountain of food with an efficiency that was epic. Eve managed to get through a leg and a thigh and had put down her fork, but Hetty kept right on eating noisily until her plate was completely empty. When she had finished, she belched loudly.

"That was good eatin', Missy. I didn't think you'd be much of a cook, but ya done all right."

"Thank you, Hetty. I'm glad you enjoyed it...I have dessert—If you'd like..."

"...I won't say no..." The old woman sat looking comfortable.

"...All right...I'll get it." Eve took their plates out to the kitchen and retrieved the cheesecake from its carton. She placed in on a cake plate and placed the silver cake slicer next to it. As she returned to the table, Hetty was still sitting with her hands in her lap, waiting patiently. "I hope you like cheesecake."

"...What is it...you say...?" The old woman looked curious at the small thick disk sat in front of her.

"It's a cheesecake, Hetty. From New York...." Hetty looked up slightly confused.

"...Is it a savoury?..." Hetty was still looking doubtful.

"It's sweet. It's very rich though You won't want much after a big meal."

Hetty had reached across and cut the small cake in half as she had done with the chicken and plopped the half onto a waiting dessert plate. The portion was too large for the plate and it hung precariously over the edges of the plate. She plunged in her fork eagerly encouraged by the earlier meal, and shoved a huge bite into her mouth. Almost immediately her eyes lit up and she looked with pleasant surprise at Eve.

"Howja make this, Missy?"

"I didn't, Hetty. I bought it. Do you like it?"

"it's...tolerable good..." Without saying more Hetty polished off the half cake in only a few bites. Eve was so amazed at the speed with which she ate that she hadn't even tried to cut a piece from the remaining half for herself.

"Ain't you eatin' none?" Hetty pointed to the cake with end of her knife.

"I don't think I can...but you can have it..." Eve could tell that the old woman wanted it.

"...Uh..No...I guess I'm done too..." Hetty eyed the remaining cake longingly.

"Well, I'll box it up and you can take it home with you, Hetty."

"Oh...no. I—I guess I had my fill of it.." Her tone was hesitant.

"It'll only go to waste if you leave it here, Hetty. I won't eat it."

"...Fine, then, Missy. I'll help you with it." The old woman sat looking around at the room again now that she was no longer hungry. "You...live fine, Missy."

"All this?...It is nice, isn't it? I didn't buy any of it. It was my family's. My Grandmother saved it for me...I miss her."

"...Eyah...family's important...You ain't like the Truesdales, are ya?" The old woman was looking at Eve critically for the first time.

"...Really...how do you—" Eve was puzzled by this remark.

"Stiff-backed lot—the Truesdales. Holier than thou. Proud as peacocks. 'Pride goeth before the fall!'"...The old woman seemed to look into the distance.

"What do you mean, Hetty?

"Don't mean nothin'...I'm just sayin,' you ain't like 'em..."

"How would you know what they were like?"

"Folks know. Your people and my people...they were the first 'round here."

"Are you saying that my family has a bad reputation in Holmsford?"

"Far from it, Missy! Far from it! They was high up! Righteous people..."

"Then why do you say they were 'proud' and 'stiffbacked?'"

"Don't mean nothin' by it, Missy. It's just...they done a lot 'round here. You're the last one, ya know."

"I guess I am...but why would you say those things about my family?"

"It ain't nothin'...Long time ago...your family an' my family...It weren't so good."

"What do you mean? How do you know that?"

"...It's in the Keepin' Book..." The old woman trailed off and stopped talking.

"...You mean Giles and Rebecca?"

Suddenly Hetty looked at Eve sharply as if she had just been slapped, "What do you know about them!"

"N-nothing, really. Just about what happened to them."

"How do you know!"

"Dilla told me."

"The Hessian woman?"

"The what?"

"The old woman who married that Hessian man. Has a store in town on the green."

"Dilla Merkle. She's the town's historian. She told me about your ancestors being hanged as witches."

"A lie! They weren't no witches! It was Truesdale! He done it!—*Your* man!"

"Hetty—I don't know what you're talking about!"

The old woman stopped for a moment and seemed to pull herself back, "'Course ya don't!...but that's the way of it, ain't it. Folks talk. Old lies die hard...or they make history out of 'em."

Eve pulled her chair closer. "Hetty if you know something about my family, I'd really like to know! I've never known much. I was just sixteen when my Grandmother died. Younger than that when my parents went. I wasn't interested then, but I am now! I really want to know...!"

"It's an old story...nothin' to trouble with." Hetty seemed to be shutting it away, but Eve was fascinated.

"Dilla couldn't tell me anything about my family. Just that they were one of the first. And all she knew was about Rebecca and Giles. C'mon, Hetty, what do you know?"

The old woman looked at her and seemed to soften, "It's writ in the Keepin' Book..about the hangin' and...the trouble."

"What trouble, Hetty?...

"...There was two ministers...Giles Livesey and Josiah Truesdale. Friends they was and leaders. They brought the first settlers when they come. But your man, Truesdale, didn't like sharin' the pulpit with mine. Giles Livesey was a learned man. Read Latin and Greek. Studied medicine. Truesdale could barely write his name. Wife died of the croup that first winter. Turned him sour and close. He decided Livesey was too big for himself with all his learnin' and led the others to suspect him of bein' unrighteous and full of pride. Didn't take much for that ignorant bunch to come over out of envy! Ya see, Livesey had some money. Of his own. Enough to buy his land and not be in thrall to the Company for his transport. Livesey left the Church to Truesdale. Stayed away and kept to his farm. Built it up and got to know the tribes. He traded with 'em, and when they was sick, him and Rebecca healed 'em with the learnin' he had of plants and herbs. When the trouble started between the settlers and the tribes, Livesey went between and smoothed it over. Kept the peace. People started lookin' to him again as a leader. Truesdale called him out...Him and Rebecca. 'Witches!' he said, knowin' that if they confessed, they'd lose their land. Neither one did. They hanged 'em.

Right on this here hill! In an old storm oak." The old woman stopped and looked at Eve, "...That enough?"

"...That's in your Keeping Book?"...

"Eyah...that and recipes and farm things and such... Things ya don't want to forget..."

"What happened to the land?...They must have had children."

"One. A daughter, Mahetibel."

"Were you named for Her?"

"...I guess."

"...What a story!"

"Ain't a story. It happened. Some say hate stays in the blood—passes to the next of kin, but...*you* ain't like that." The old woman looked frankly at Eve.

"How could he turn on his friend like that?"

"Jealous...prideful. Easy enough."

"...They were men, I suppose."

"Ya don't think a woman would do as much, Missy?"

"We're not like that."

"'Course we are! Worse even! Ain't no one more vengeful than a woman when she's hurt!—-And women have power, Missy—like I told ya..." The old woman looked at Eve expectantly.

"...I think we're better than that..." Eve was surprised at the old woman's vehemence.

"Are we?...It's a thing that feeds ya...that power. It's big...hard to control...*You* know your power—some of it."

"...'Some of it?' Hetty, I don't—"

"There's no man here. You ain't waitin' for one, dyin' for one! Not like that lot you talk to."

"The girls?—Hetty, you don't even know them!—"

"Don't need ta. Weak!...Nobody there. They see through a man's eyes—how he looks at 'em...if he wants 'em. If a man ain't lookin' at 'em,—they ain't alive!"

"They're not perfect..." Eve began to defend her new-found friends.

"Nobody there! Don't trust in 'em, Missy; don't rely on 'em. They'll pull on ya. Most will...but...you're different..."

"Hetty, I—"

"Ya know your own mind. That's the beginnin' of it.—If ya don't throw yourself away..." Hetty trailed off still looking at Eve, who sat completely puzzled by this sudden burst of judgment.

"...Being alone, Hetty..."

"That's the price! The price of power, Missy." The old woman challenged her. Her eyes were hot with conviction. "We can have men! All we want...but we can't keep 'em! As soon as we do, they start to thinkin' of us like we was theirs to play with, to own, to use...to leave. We're done then."

"Hetty, we were made male and female—"

"A rib! A second thought. Made to bear. Take the blame! That Wretched God made us to serve men! But we didn't!...We pushed Adam to take from the tree—stand up on his own two feet! And for that He blamed us! We made His man better, and He made us the goat! Damn Him!—But we don't have to let it be! Not if we don't serve Him! Not if we serve ourselves!...That's the power, Missy! That's the real power!"

"...You've...given this quite a lot of thought!..." Eve was a little unsettled by the old woman's intensity.

"...More than you know...I—I want ta beg a favor of ya..." Hetty's tone changed suddenly, and she dropped the burning look in her eyes.

"All right."

"Not so fast, Missy—it ain't an easy favor."

"What do you need, Hetty?" Eve was still stunned by the sudden change in the old woman's demeanor.

"I got a...a granddaughter...Mirabel. I got to...go away for a bit, and she's comin' to take care of the place while I'm gone. I wonder, would ya...teach her?..."

"Teach her...what, Hetty?" Eve was confused by Hetty's sudden supplication.

"She's young! Been...been workin'...'round another farm...for quite a while—"

"If she's been on her own, Hetty, she can probably teach me a few things!" Eve tried to smile.

"No! She ain't...educated. She's...rough...like me. I couldn't send her nowhere...to learn. You know. You have the power, but you ain't...coarse an' bitter like me."

"Hetty, you're not—"

"Don't shine me, Missy. I know who I am. I ain't fit for this new world, but *you* are! Could she come to ya...to get some...smoothin' down? Would ya do that, Missy?" The old woman looked at her with the first real vulnerability Eve had seen in her.

"I don't know what I have to teach her, Hetty. I'll be gone three or four days a week...."

"That'll do. Whatever time ya got. Can she come? Will you let her? Teach her to have...manners...talk to people. Get on with things?"

"...I don't know that I'm much of a mentor, but...if it means that much to you..."

The old woman didn't stay long. The dinner was strange, Eve thought, but she was glad to be able to do something for Hetty that the old woman wanted so much. She seemed truly grateful. It was a side of Hetty that Eve hadn't expected. Unguarded...intense...in need. As she closed the front door, Eve was satisfied with herself. She had been able to return a kindness to someone who, from the looks of it, had been friendless for a very long time.

***

CHAPTER 18

"...You don't want to hear all that...." Singleton played with the food in his plate, not looking up at her. Simpson's was in full swing. A small live band was playing pop tunes, and they weren't half bad. Singleton was back in jeans with boots, and Eve realized that this was really an expression of the man he was.

"C'mon, cowboy...give a little. A girl likes to know more about her—"

"Pastor?" Singleton looked up with a half playful smile.

"Friend!" Eve shot back. "How does Harvard translate to a battered truck and a small town church?"

Singleton chuckled slightly. "...I'm...hiding out...I think."

"...Ok...I sense a little mystery...Hiding out from what?"

"...I...thought coming to Holmsford would be good for my soul." She noticed that he wasn't being playful now.

"...And has it been?..."

"I think that's what I'm hiding from. My soul! If it finds me,...I don't know that it will accept me back. I'm still...angry, I think. Maybe a little less, but I don't want him to find me yet..."

"...No...see, you can't put a prologue like that out there and just leave it! C'mon, cowboy, spill your guts! I have a lobster fork and I know how to use it!"

Singleton looked up and smiled shyly..."This is not something I should be talking about on a date with a beautiful woman."

"...Well, when she shows up, we won't tell her, will we?" Eve lifted her eyebrows in expectation.

"...You do know you're beautiful, don't you?..." Singleton looked at her with his blue-eyed earnestness, and Eve wavered for a split second.

"No. You're not going to divert me with flattery. I'm going in for the kill. Talk! What are you so angry about that you think your soul won't have you back?"

Singleton drew into himself and then looked up again, "...Caroline."

Eve struggled with the name for a moment and then put it together, "...Your wife..."

Singleton nodded. "Now you know why this...is perhaps the worst conversation for me to have right here with you. The last thing a woman wants to hear is about a man's late wife!"

"Why?" Eve challenged, "You think I don't have a strong enough ego to stand up to it?—You don't think much of me, do you?"

"I think way too much of you, as a matter of fact—way too much!"

"Oh...Well, that's...interesting—but it's beside the point! What is it about Caroline that's making you so...angry?" Eve softened her tone when she saw him lower his eyes again.

"...I can't...forgive God. Isn't that ludicrous? A minister who can't forgive God?"

"For what, Adam? For taking her away?"

"...Yeah..." Singleton's voice was husky now, "...We were perfect. Caroline was. She was assistant to the head curator at the Boston Museum and an artist, you know? Just beginning to make a little name for herself. And her ambition for her art was...contagious. It fed me; made me a better man. I was in line for a prestigious post in Boston. We were planning a family...in fact, we thought she was pregnant. It turned out to be ovarian cancer..."

"...I'm sorry, Adam. I'm really sorry..." Eve reached across the table and took his arm, but he pulled away.

"Yeah...well, you now see before you a complete fraud. I minister to a congregation, and I can't forgive my God. I'm pathetic."

"You're the second person in the space of twenty-four hours who has told me that they have a beef with God. You know, if He's that aggravating, there must be something to Him!"

"...Well, I guess I've ruined this date." Singleton leaned back in his chair looking around the restaurant trying to avoid eye-contact with her.

"Who says?" Eve reached across and grabbed his shirt pulling him forward to face her, "An attractive, moral man dealing with an intense internal struggle...very sexy!...I know a dozen women who would love to cure you of your dilemma."

Singleton chuckled and looked at her again..."Maybe you could introduce me."

"Not on your life!...You're *my* date."

She held onto his shirt, and as he looked at her, his smile faded to a different look.

"...I have to warn you...I've already paid the bill."

Eve held onto the shirt and looked at him frankly"...Does that mean you expect me to 'put out?'"

"...I can only hope..."

✳✳✳

CHAPTER 19

"Half the stores on the green are empty, Charlie! You remember what the town was like when we were kids. There was the Mercantile and Lorraine's—God, remember Lorraine's? I can still almost taste the coffee ice cream they made! And that big old coffee grinder at the front of the store...Now...nothing! There's Dilla's, if you can still call that a business—she only opens when she feels like it. You've got Carney's sporting goods, the bakery, the bike shop, this place and two or three other stores that have been half-a-dozen different things in the past five years! I'm tellin' you, Charlie, Holmsford's dying if we don't do something!"

"Let me remind you, Jack, all that started when they built that mall on the old Truesdale property. That was *your* big idea. It killed all the Mom and Pop operations in town! Before that, we were holding our own!"

The Puritan House Coffee Shoppe on the green was full early every morning. It was the only really 'going business' in town. Just about everyone dropped in for their coffee or a quick breakfast especially on a Sunday morning. Church-goers came by after services, retired folks made their way there and greeted each other to avoid another solitary morning in their own houses. The working folks usually stopped in for a quick bite before starting their shifts at the mall or in the few businesses that did offer employment. The Puritan offered clean surroundings, big portions and low prices—everything a poor town could ask for in an eatery.

"Is that what we want, Charlie—just to 'hold our own?' Is that looking out for Holmsford? All right, maybe the mall had an impact, but who could have known that? And there are a lot of folks working there now, Charlie! A lot!"

"C'mon, Jack—people come to the mall, shop, and pass the town right by! Nobody comes to town except for townies! We want people coming to town! We want traffic in town where businesses can make some money. People can earn a living!"

"This industrial park will do that, Charlie! Big companies will come—real industry! We're talking jobs here, the kind of jobs that'll make Holmsford a prosperous town again!"

"How do we know that? Are your Innovative people guaranteeing that? Can they produce a list of companies that will locate in this park?"

"How can they do that before it's built? Be reasonable, Charlie! Nobody can know that until they have the property ready and we have the permit packages and tax structures in place for them to offer to prospective clients! That's business, Charlie, you know that!"

"...We want guarantees..." Charlie Metcalf stared down into his coffee cup. He was determined not to be sold again. He knew that Jack Marlin was a smooth talker. He always had been. Even way back when they were in high school together, Jackie always had the big ideas and Charlie always got blamed for the trouble that came after. Like when they set up that drag strip out on route two. Nobody knew about it—except they did. The cops caught up with them as Charlie was in the middle, setting up the races, and Jackie was nowhere in sight at the hearing. He never came forward to admit it was his idea. Charlie was left facing the judge alone, and it was his family who paid the fine. That was 'big time' back then! Charlie was lucky his dad had 'connections' or he would have had a permanent mark against him. God, that was awful! His dad always referred to that incident whenever Charlie did something even a little off center! It made his stomach churn every time he thought of it.

"What guarantees? Charlie, you can't encumber this deal and expect Innovative to make the investment!"

"...If you want the *entire* Board to vote on this venture, they're going to have to give us complete oversight on who's building in the park and what industries will be considered for location there." Metcalf wouldn't look up from his cup. He could still feel his stomach churning.

"...You're gonna queer this whole deal, you know. It's gonna disappear, Charlie!"

"Then...it'll have to disappear. The Rotary won't stand behind it unless we get that. Without them, you don't have the town behind you."

"...It'll be your fault, Charlie!"

Finally Metcalf looked up from his cup. His face was deep red and his eyes were blazing, "Don't tell me that, Jack! Don't put this on me! This is *your* big idea. Just like the Mall and that big development up on Ramsay farm. I backed you both times, and I took the heat! Not this time! You want it?—you *get* the guarantees, or there's no deal!"

"...Man...and I thought you loved this town, Charlie. I thought you cared about keeping Holmsford alive..."

"Guarantees or no deal." Metcalf fixed his gaze directly on his old friend. He wasn't giving in.

Marlin pretended for the moment that the whole idea was dead. He looked down defeated, took a deep breath and looked away. He waited to see his friend waver, but Metcalf stood firm.

It didn't really matter to Marlin. If he could deliver the Board's approval without restrictions—that was a feather in his cap. He knew Reedy would reward him with a bonus. If not, he still got his cut. Restrictions could be gotten around. Reedy's lawyers were experts at inserting subtle loopholes in the wording. Innovative would get what it wanted, and Marlin would get what he wanted. Screw Charlie Metcalf and his stupid Rotary! He'd save Holmsford in spite of that bunch of self-important little reactionaries, and he'd make sure he got his as well!

"...I'll take it to 'em, Charlie, but I don't think they'll buy it. I think you pretty much sealed Holmsford's fate. Nobody else is offering this town this kind of deal. Take a good look out that window, Charlie. It may be the last time you see anyone on that green. Holmsford will just be an exit sign on the highway."

"...That's the chance we have to take, Jack."

"Ok, ok!...I'll do what I can. It's a shame, though..." Good. He could see the worry behind Metcalf's eyes. He needed that. If he was going to pull this off, he needed Charlie to believe that the town would have to respond to Innovative's "extraordinary" flexibility with strong measures of its own.

***

CHAPTER 20

"...Every summer for two weeks while my parents had some 'alone time.'" Eve had nestled herself on Singleton's chest. The Best Western on Route 95 was as good as any, and it was far enough away from Homlsford not to compromise his position in town...although he didn't seem concerned about that. The choice had been hers.

"God, they were wonderful! They lived in this big old house on the outside of town. My family used to be pretty big, I guess. They owned the old mill—when Holmsford was a real going concern. They built this big place. My grandfather was the last one of the Truesdales to live in it. Very house proud...both of them. Grandad would keep it just so. Did all the repairs by himself—by then he had to. The money was pretty much gone. They kept that place like a shrine! I loved that old house!..

"One summer when I was fourteen...there was a fire in the hotel my parents were in. They didn't make it...I stayed with Gram and Grandad. The following summer Grandad fell from the roof. He died pretty much on the spot. It was an awful shock to Gram. She tried, but her health was failing. By then I was fifteen nearly sixteen. She made arrangements to have a 'good' family in Boston board me...make sure I went to school. She sold the old house, went to live in a nursing home...and then she died.

"My parents had left nothing. Gram and Grandad left next to nothing. What was left in the way of money went to pay for my board, but the family I lived with claimed it wasn't enough. I became their au pair to pay the difference. So when I wasn't in school—they did that much anyway—made sure I went to school—when I wasn't there, I was taking care of their two wretched brats.

"After a while, the man of the house got to thinking that I should be providing more than just child-care services. I dodged him pretty well, but I knew the end was coming. I doubled down on my studies, got a scholarship—Stanford Business—it was enough. When my host dad tried to make himself my high school graduation gift, I gave him a swift kick in the groin and left.

"Stanford got me some prestigious internships, one of them led to Novus and Gardner...I was the hardest working analyst they had ever seen...One-hundred hour weeks, no breaks, no mistakes—no fooling!...."

Singleton let her finish and let the silence stay for a little while, "...And she lived happily ever after?"

"She lived her own way...ever after."

"...Good for her...."

"Really?..." Eve sat up in the bed looking at Singleton stretched out with a content look. His blue eyes had a softer look to them. "Isn't this where you tell me how I'm not complete without a man—*you* in particular?"

Singleton laughed quietly, "...Oh, you're complete, believe me. You're a whole woman!"

"That's just sexual satisfaction!" She slapped him playfully on the stomach.

"Uh, huh....but it's true." He drew her down on him again and held her. "You're as certain of who you are as anyone I've ever known. I wouldn't dream of telling you what you need."

Eve took that in and thought for a moment as she listened to his heart beat, "...Well, lately...maybe I'm not so sure..."

"You seemed pretty sure to me!"

"Stop!...I'm serious..." Eve sat back up. "I came here without an inkling of what I was doing. My whole life was in New York. My work. I never thought about Holmsford! I sure as hell never thought about buying a house here! And now I have a house—neighbors...and...this...What is this, Adam? What am I doing?"

"...Changing..."

"Changing!"

"Maybe..."

"...No...no...how can I change everything I've built? Everything I created for myself? I have a life in New York. I'm a partner at Novus and Gardner. I run my department—I'm damn good at it! Better than anyone! This...whole thing...is some kind of...aberration...an anomaly!"

"...Are you unhappy...right now?" Singleton's eyes took on that earnest look that always unsettled her.

"Of course not!...This...feels right..."

"Good...I don't want to be an 'anomaly.'"

"That's just it! This feels right...and all the rest of it...doesn't. Not anymore. That's crazy! It doesn't make any sense!"

"...Then just let it be. Everything happens for a reason. Just wait and see what that might be..."

He reached up and brushed the hair from her forehead, and she looked down at him. His blue eyes were soft again, and she felt an overwhelming surge of desire well up in her. "...Are you talking as my...pastor?..."

Singleton chuckled and pulled her down beside him, "That's not quite the role I had in mind right now..."

***

CHAPTER 21

As Eve entered, the Puritan was in full swing. There hadn't been time for breakfast; Adam had to be ready for services at nine. He swung the pickup around the back of the church, and by agreement Eve went off to the coffee shop for something to eat while Adam tried to pull his thoughts together.

"Eve!.....Evie! Yoohoo!" Marian, Donna and Libby were sitting at a booth at the far end of the restaurant.

Eve steeled herself as she walked over. The last thing she wanted right now was Marian's constant chatter, but she couldn't avoid them. "Hi! How is everyone?" She said this last looking at Libby.

"I'm fine!" Libby returned, knowing full well what Eve wanted to know. "See?...goddamn coffee—without the garnish! My house is clean and I'm making dinner tonight—you're invited!"

"...Really?...dinner...Well, I guess...what's the occasion?"

"Oh, c'mon—my Goddamn survival! You and Marian pulled me out of that hole I was in. It's the least I can do. Nothing fancy...just the four of us. That all right?"

"Ok....good. What can I bring?"

"A bottle of Scotch! Just kidding!...Nothing! Just come. Roast beef, Yorkshire pudding..and...I don't know...something!" Libby looked much better. Her color was more natural and her eyes were clearer.

"...You know, I saw the two of you!" Marian pursed her lips as she made this pronouncement.

"...Uh...Marian...I—" Eve was thinking quickly about how to soften her sudden relationship with Singleton.

"Don't try to deny it! I saw you both You better tell me all about it!" Marian's brows were knitted and she looked grim. Eve glanced quickly at Donna who quietly studied her coffee without looking up.

"You know, we haven't been friends long enough that you should start keeping secrets from me. Remember, I live right next door. There's not too much that goes on that I don't know about!"

"All right, Marian..." Eve took a deep breath.

"Since when does the Goat Woman come to your house like—like a person! I saw her. She rang your doorbell and everything! C'mon, Evie, what's going on?"

It took Eve a moment to regain her balance, "Well...she is a person, Marian!"

"What was she doing there? I nearly fell out of my house when I saw her—with that funny hat and the long dress with boots, no less...and that stick she carries! What did she want from you?" The other two women were fixed on Eve out of curiosity as well.

"Dinner." was all Eve could think of at that moment.

"Dinner? What do you mean 'dinner?'"

"I invited her to dinner! After all, she practically saved my life, remember?"

"...And she came?" Marian was incredulous.

"Yes, she came! We...had a very nice dinner. She's a lonely old woman, and I wanted to do something for her."

"What's she like?" Libby's tone was almost mysterious.

"...Uh...practical...down-to-earth. She's got a granddaughter."

"*That* has a granddaughter?" Marian couldn't help laughing.

"Why not? I understand she used to be quite beautiful!...Anyway, she asked me to...I don't know...mentor the girl." This was where Eve was confused herself. What exactly had she agreed to?

"...So, you're gonna teach her about...investing...?" Libby and Marian were staring at her doubtfully while Donna seemed to be somewhere else altogether.

"No!...She...she wants me to give her a little...polish, I guess. You know, teach her about...things. How to dress...how to talk...girlie things. The girl works on another farm somewhere. She's been pretty much sheltered is the feeling I get....The old woman wasn't very talkative. I don't know! I don't know why I agreed! What makes me such an expert?"

"Oh, honey! You are perfect for it...because you have us! You leave her to me! I'll take her shopping!" Marian's eyes lit up with enthusiasm.

"No. Now, I don't think it calls for—" Eve didn't want Marian to wind them up.

"I'll teach her how to drink—"

"Libby, I don't think—"

"Not like that! Jesus, what do you think!—I mean, if she's a farm girl, she needs to know about....how to do it. Not get caught up and all that shit! Jesus Christ, Eve!"

"That wasn't—"

"I can teach her about men..." Donna quietly joined in.

"Oh, honey, we can all do that!" Marian blurted out and she and Libby both laughed.

"I mean...which ones...to avoid. How old is she, Eve?"

"....Uh...I don't know! She didn't say. I guess she's got to be old enough to be out working." Eve was beginning to realize how little information Hetty had related, and how this was beginning to get out of hand.

"All right, ladies. We have a project!" Marian lifted her cup in salute.

"Wait a minute!" Eve objected. "I don't know anything about this girl. Not really. I'm going to take this very slowly. Right now, I don't even know when she's going to show up."

"...Well...honey...if you don't want us to help..." Marian put on a show of being hurt, while the other two women watched in silent complicity.

"I didn't say that. I also didn't say that I was going pull a Cinderella makeover on this girl. I don't know her! The smart thing to do is to get acquainted and just see what it is that she might...need."

Marian looked at Eve for a second and then she broke, "...Well, of course you're right, honey! We don't know anything. We just have to wait and see. But already this little girl is one lucky duck! She's got a whole team of experts ready to step in and teach her ...everything!"

Marian went on about clothes and makeup, filling the booth with her chatter and ideas as the other women commented and bantered. It appeared to give them a focus and meaning to their morning. Meanwhile, Eve thought about Adam. Why did she feel so...different? She wasn't some school girl! She wasn't some little virgin experiencing her first man!

She had never told any man about herself...not like that,...yet she knew instinctively it was safe. She knew that he took her confidences as private...inviolable. His touch was deeply familiar even though they had spent only one night together. She could still feel him...It was natural...like breathing. It occurred to her that this must be what love is. The realization of this fact completely surprised her, and she found herself laughing out loud.

"Honey? Eve, did I say something funny?" She came to and realized that the three other women were staring at her."

"...Uh...I'm sorry, Marian. It just occurred to me how good it is—that you all want to help."

"Oh, honey, you know you can rely on us! We'll have fun—won't we, girls!"...

Finally, the booth broke up. Eve picked up the check over the other women's objections and walked to the register to pay. Her thoughts were still wrapped around Singleton and this new-found feeling. As she signed the slip, she heard a voice behind her.

"Uh...Ms. Truesdale?...Are you Ms. Truesdale?"

As Eve turned she saw a man in his fifties, a little paunchy but neatly "be-suited," standing holding his hat cocked in one hand in an old-fashioned gesture of deference.

"Yes? That's me."

The man smiled warmly and offered his hand. "How do you do? I'm John Marlin, Chairman of the Holmsford Board of Selectmen. You were pointed out to me, and I wanted to introduce myself. I believe you're our newest arrival here in Holmsford, although I understand your family is from here?"

Eve took this in and smiled and firmly shook Marlin's hand. "How do you do, Mr. Marlin. Yes. As a matter of fact this isn't my first time living in Holmsford. I spent some time here as a girl.

"Well, that must have been very recent. You're still, if I may say, very much a girl!—certainly from my perspective!"

Oh, the old boy was laying it on thick, thought Eve. He must want something.

"...Thank you! Nice to meet you." Eve handed the slip and the pen back to the cashier.

"...How are you finding things out on Cloven Terrace?"

"I'm still settling in, but...everything is fine, thank you."

"No...complaints. No...nuisances or...conditions we should address?"

"No...nothing I can think of."

"Because we're very anxious to...have the entire development filled soon. We want to be very sure that everyone who moves in up there is completely happy with Holmsford."

"...If you're looking for my vote, Mr. Marlin, it's a little early for electioneering!" Eve decided to poke at him a little. His manner was just a little too ulterior.

"No, no, of course! Town elections are still two years off! Not at all!...I was just remembering that the family who owned your house previously had a few...concerns."

"...What is it you want, Mr. Marlin?" Eve was done with the dance.

"I can see you get right down to it! Very good! I like that!"

"Good. So tell me what it is you're trying to find out." Eve dropped her tone to the timber she used at the office.

"Well, the previous owner of your house had lodged several serious environmental complaints."

"'Environmental Complaints'—that does sound serious!"

"It was. Yes, quite serious!" She could see him wait to see the concern grow in her, but she wouldn't give him that.

"...Suppose you tell me about them..."

"Well...you know that your property...as a matter of fact, the entire development was built on what had been a farm...a very old homestead...abandoned by the owner some years before. The property had reverted to the town and we sold it to put the land to some positive use..."

"Yes, I had heard that. Ramsay farm, wasn't it?"

"Oh!—you know! Very good. Well, then I'm sure you have realized that your property sits adjacent to the last working farm in town. The Livesey homestead."

"Yes. And...?"

"Well, we became aware that the farm's livestock pens sit right on your property line. The previous owner found that the air pollution from the animals...was detrimental to her health."

"...You mean June Hildebrand, the woman who disappeared?"

"Yes! She was very adamant that we do something about the pens."

"....Um hum...and is she still complaining?"

"Ha, ha...I see you have a...sharp sense of humor! No, of course not! But I wanted you to feel free to ...to renew that complaint if you felt a similar...effect upon your health."

Eve laughed slightly, puzzled at Marlin's elaborate approach. "I don't know why she was upset by a few goats near her property, Mr. Marlin, but they don't bother me in the least. In fact I think they're charming. I've been up to the pens petting them several times. I like animals."

"Oh, you have?" Marlin seemed surprised. "Oh...then you have no objections to the livestock so near your beautiful home?"

"I'm a city girl, Mr. Marlin. I like a little taste of the country, and Ms. Livesey's goats don't bother me in the least."

"Oh...well, that's good then. That's very good....And Ms. Livesey...doesn't object to your...petting her goats?"

"No. Not at all. As a matter of fact, we've become friends."

"...Friends?...Really?...Well,...good   then.   Friends.   That certainly...smooths things over...."

"I'm glad I could put your mind at rest."

"Yes!....uh, that's very good. Very relieving!...Surprising...pleasantly surprising! I like to be proactive about this sort of thing."

"...Is there anything else, Mr. Marlin?" The man stood there processing the information for a moment.

"No. No, nothing else. I guess I should say welcome back to Holmsford. It's a pleasure to have you here as one of our own again! Please, enjoy the rest of your Sunday morning!"

"I will, thank you." Marlin moved away quickly as he placed the hat on his head and went out the door.

"What the hell was that?" Eve muttered to herself as returned her credit card to her wallet and prepared to leave.

***

CHAPTER 22

"I'm going to need a key..." Jace was sitting with his feet sticking out of the passenger side of his car as Eve got out of hers. He handed her a thick file and then gracefully slithered out without a rumple to his jacket. "Harold wants you to look at the new proposal for Hancock before you come in tomorrow." He followed her up the walk to the front door as Eve took out her key.

"So you're my keeper, huh? Harold sent you up here to see what I was doing." She opened the door and walked inside with Jace right on her heels.

"He doesn't know you're up here. I told him I'd drop it off to your apartment. I mean, why would anybody volunteer to deliver a file four hours up the highway to Massachusetts?—I told him nada!"

Eve opened the envelope. "Why *did* you drive all the way up here? You know I'll be in tomorrow."

"Why do you think?..." Jace slipped an arm around her waist and pulled her against him and kissed her neck.

"Jace...I'm reading..." He released her puzzled.

"C'mon, Eve!...It's been over two weeks!...Don't you want to reward me for my conscientiousness?" He reached for her again but she evaded him.

"Abstinence makes the heart grow fonder!"

"It's not my heart that's been missing you," he offered as she moved toward the kitchen.

"That's what I meant, Jace....I can see why Harold wanted me to look at this. We can't work with these figures. We're going to re-do it. You want some coffee?"

"...I thought I could drive you back in the morning...."

Eve set up the coffee maker and started it as she went over the folder. "No. I'll take my car. That way I can get back here when I'm ready."

"I could bring you back."

125

"That's not necessary." Eve was still reviewing the contents of the folder and making margin notes.

"That way, I could...stay a few days...maybe."

Eve looked up from the folder, "Why?..."

"Two weeks, Eve! Hello!...Remember me...your fiancé?"

Finally Eve looked up from the folder and fixed him in her sight. "Jace, you're not my fiancé."

"Sure I am! I proposed, remember? Gave you a ring?...We sleep together...when I can get your attention..."

"...It was a very...interesting proposal, Jace. And the ring is beautiful—"

"It ought to be—I spent half my bonus on it!"

"It is! Beautiful!...And you'll get it back. You are not my fiancé."

"Are you...breaking up with me? Really? Eve!...Look at this! This is all yours!"

He turned around slowly and Eve had to laugh, "I'm putting you in perspective, Jace. You are definitely *not* all mine. You made that perfectly clear in your proposal."

"All right. I'll give you an 'exclusive.' How about that? I won't if you won't—now, that's fair!"

"Jace..." Eve kissed him on the cheek, "Haven't I taught you: never promise what you can't deliver."

"I can be just as faithful as the next fella!" His tone was slightly petulant.

"My point exactly. Now let's get to work. We need to re-do all the numbers again..."

"OK...but I'm still your fiancé. I'm not letting you turn this down. This is a prime machine!"

"Fine, Jace...now let's review the projections. I think we're overly optimistic there..."

As the morning drew on the two of them reworked the proposal and buried their personal relationship in the business at hand. By mid-afternoon, Eve remembered the dinner party at Libby's. She realized that she had agreed to go.

"What about the rest of the figures? Harold's going to want the whole picture...."

"You can handle the rest. I have a dinner party I promised to go to."

"Dinner? Where?"

"In the neighborhood—You re not invited! It's strictly a girls' night!"

"'Girls night'—naw, that's not you!"

"...Well...it is here, I guess...I don't know. I promised I'd go. Take the guest room. There's food in the fridge. Fix yourself something. I don't know when I'll be back." With that Eve went upstairs to change for the 'party' at Libby's. It was four-thirty. The day had flown by, filled with the proposal. In the morning they would leave early—Jace in his car, she in hers, and head back to New York. Tonight she was 'neighbor' Eve...friend of three women she hardly knew. Resident of Cloven Terrace in the town of Holmsford...Who the hell *was* she, she wondered?..

***

After six, the battered pickup pulled into the drive and stopped behind the sleek BMW. Singleton hopped out of the cab, still wearing his collar. Services went long and the "fellowship" lasted until only thirty minutes before. All he could think of was getting back to Eve. He had been more than usually eloquent after their night together. The euphoric feeling he had had kept him lifted the entire day. He had an abundance of patience for even the most tedious of the complaints of his congregation, and he greeted everyone afterward with warmth he hadn't felt in years. It was Eve!

She was his inspiration. Thinking about her filled him with a sense of comfort he had missed since Caroline's death. But it was different with Eve. She wasn't Caroline, and he didn't want to compare her to Caroline! Eve was her own particular connection for him. He was comfortable with it. This wasn't loneliness or...deprivation. It was honest feeling...a communion! That was it! She was like a missing piece he didn't know he was missing. She completed him. He caught himself smiling in anticipation as he hurried up the walkway. He had to see her again that day. He just needed to reconfirm his own happiness.

He pressed the bell and waited like a kid eager for a much-anticipated movie to start. Finally he heard footsteps on the other side of the door. It opened.

Jace stood there in a bathrobe, fresh from a shower. His hair glistened, and he looked like a GQ model ready for a photo shoot. Singleton was struck dumb for a moment.

"...Yeah...can I help you?" Jace leaned against the door jamb.

"...Uh...I guess I'm at the wrong house. I'm looking for Eve Truesdale?..."

"No, you're at the right place! She's not here. Dinner party, or something..." Jace smiled.

Singleton just stood there for a moment not sure what to say or do.

"...Was there something you needed, Reverend?"

"....Uh...no...no. I...didn't see her at services, and I...wanted to see if she was all right."

"You know, that's really nice! That's the thing about these small towns. We don't have that in the city! That kind of Brotherly Love. Jesus, I could be murdered on the floor of my apartment in New York and lie there until I stink up the place before anyone would notice. You know what I mean, Reverend?"

"...Uh...yeah...yes, I suppose that's true....Uh...are you...related to Ms. Truesdale?"

"Oh—sorry!" Jace offered his hand to Singleton. "Jace Brillig. Eve's my fiancée...."

"....Pleased to meet you." Singleton shook his hand and forced a smile to his face.

"...And you are?..."

"....Reverend Singleton..." Singleton could feel the blood draining out of his head.

"....I'll tell her you came by." Jace was at his charming best.

"No!...No need. I was...in the neighborhood.....I can see she's...taken care of."

"You don't have to worry about Eve. She's one tough lady. Trust me, she knows how to take care of herself!"...

"....Well....that's fine, then...nice to meet you Mr....."

"Jace! Jace Brillig. I work with Eve—in New York."

"...That's very...convenient. Just...don't worry about it....I'll see her...next time. Thanks." Singleton managed to get away before the smile fell off his face. As he got into the truck he could feel his hands shaking.

***

CHAPTER 23

"Marian, I'm not Betty fucking Crocker, for Christ's sakes!...."

Libby was responding to Marian's overly-enthusiastic response to the meal she had served.

"Well, I don't cook! If it doesn't come frozen, canned, or pre-prepared, it doesn't come into my house!...I gave up worrying about all that when Harold left. I'm thinking of turning the whole kitchen into a planter."

"It was a great meal, Libby. Thank you." Eve was impressed. The meal was expertly done and the table was beautifully set. In fact, the entire house was spotless, in contrast to the mess she had seen when she and Marian had come that earlier morning. "The house looks great too."

"There's not one Goddamn nook or cranny I didn't scrub! That's what I've been doing...cleaning. It's good for the soul, you know—cleaning. It wears you out...keeps you moving...makes you focus on right now...."

"Oh, honey, if you're done here, you can come and do mine! I could use a good clean out. I never seem to have the time!"

"Jesus Christ, Marian, does everything have to be about you?" Libby flashed at Marian, something she seemed to be avoiding through the meal. Without the liquor, she was more impatient with Marian's non-stop, self-centered monologue.

"...Well, you don't have to be so...harsh! Honey, you know I'm there for you. We all are. Didn't I come over here to help you? Haven't I always come over—Every time you have one of your...spells!"

"Right, Marian...I can always count on you. You're always there, Goddamn it...full of your fucking tea and sympathy!"

"...I don't think you appreciate how hard it is! Every time coming here—expecting to find you...I don't know...lying in a pool of blood or hanging from a rafter!"

"I don't have fucking rafters, Marian!" Libby threw down a serving spoon she had been holding and it landed on a vegetable dish cleaving it in two.

"Well, you might just as well have! You're so busy 'mourning!' You think you're the only one who's lost someone—who's alone?"

"Marian, you've had too much wine—" Eve was trying to defuse the two women.

"I am sick and tired of taking your abuse! I have been a good friend to you, Libby! You think it's fun getting a suicide call from you?"

"I think you love it! I think it gets you off thinking that you're the 'sane' one, the 'grounded one.' My God, you're a walking *Cosmopolitan* magazine...full of pop-psych and fucking attitude!"

"SO DON'T CALL ME! The next time, do whatever it is you're going to do, and lose my number! I don't need to come here! I don't need to put myself through all that crap you dish out! Thank God Eve was here this time. I almost didn't come! I almost let you do it!"

"Marian—" Eve reached out to Marian, but she pulled away carried on by the moment.

"How long, Libby? How long are you going to mourn that son-of-a-bitch husband and that queer son of yours, huh?"

Eve found herself inhaling at this last comment. She was frozen in her seat, and she happened to look across at Donna who was still eating calmly at her place. She looked up at Eve and subtly raised her hand to signal 'wait.'

"You goddamn bitch! You fucking whore!...Did you know that Harold planned the whole thing? Did you know that, Marian? Well, he did! You think you got the best of him? You got the house, you got the alimony...but he got free! Free of you! He laughed about it at June's last Christmas party. He knew you'd be bitter and vindictive, so he put most of the company's assets in a shell corporation. What you got? That was just a fraction of what you should have gotten!"

"Liar! I stripped him! I took him to the cleaners!"

"He had it worked out two years before he told you he was leaving. He told Stan, and Stan told me...Where do you think he is now, huh? He's shacked up with that twenty-something secretary in a condo near Beacon Hill...Dinners out...trips to Baja...Does that sound 'stripped' to you?"

"I DID DAMAGE! I hurt him!...He—He recovered, the bastard! He's always been good at business!"

"I think he's a fucking genius!"

Marian's lip quivered and she tried to come back, but her face shattered and she dissolved into tears collapsing back onto her chair.

"...Oh, God! He played me!....He...he...took everything. What have I got? Nothing! An empty house...I shop for bargains at Sam's Club! What kind of a life is that? I get my hair done...my nails...who cares?...No one!...He got a life and I got...the shell! Goddamn you, Harold! I HOPE YOU ROT IN HELL YOU...YOU SACK OF SHIT!" She was weeping inconsolably now, and Eve sat there wondering how to pick up the pieces.

Suddenly Libby went over to Marian and took her into her arms.

"...C'mon, shithead!...You can't listen to me! What do I know? I'm...an alcoholic! I'll say anything!..."

"Oh....Oh....You're right! I'm an idiot!...No wonder he left me! I'm boring! I'm not even young anymore!"

"Yeah...well, none of us is. Jesus! Why are men so obsessed with babysitters and cheerleaders? Once a woman's jiggle turns into a full-blown flap, they're out the goddamn door!....What do those balding, beer-gutted, lying mother-fuckers think they're going to find out there?....We keep their houses, have their children and shore up their sagging egos every goddamn day, and what do we get...huh? Left!...Don't you worry, baby, five'll get you ten she's fucking the pool boy while old Harold struts off to the office every morning, thinking he's cock of the walk!...There's only one of us at this table with any sense! Eve! The pool-boy works for her!"

Eve was about to object when Donna caught her eye and raised her hand again to tell her to wait it out.

"...I did everything right!—I always looked good! You saw me! I always keep myself up!..." Marian seemed to be winding down as Libby continued to comfort her.

It was a revelation to Eve how the two women savaged each other and then reconnected almost seamlessly. She found herself staring with her mouth half open. Finally Donna leaned across to her and whispered, "All clear. This is their act. You get used to it..."

"All right, everybody have some cake. So what if we get fat! Who's gonna care!" Marian pulled a tissue from somewhere and dabbed at her eyes while Libby sliced huge pieces off the cake and distributed them. "So when does the pool-boy come back, Eve? We'd all like to meet him!"

"He's...not...he's my colleague!"

"I thought he was your fucking employee! You give him a promotion?" Donna laughed huskily and Marian joined in.

"His name is Jace Brillig, and he's a key member of my department. That makes him *both* my employee and my colleague.

"Oh, honey, we're just having fun with you! If you say he's just an employee—or colleague!—whatever position you have him in—well, we'll just go along with that!"

Eve pulled back. She realized that she could only get in deeper by engaging.

"...I know a couple of 'pool boys'...if you two are interested..." Donna, as usual, was quiet and clear.

Marian and Libby looked at each other.

"Are you two going to go on playing The Suicide Game or—are you going to take care of business?...if you want that kind of...attention...you can get it...I do...You want the number?...

***

CHAPTER 24

The doorbell rang again. Jace had managed to don a pair of lounging pants and was sitting shirtless on the sofa going over the figures on the proposal in preparation for the morning meeting in New York.

"What now?..." He got up clutching a spreadsheet and went to the door.

As he opened the door he was looking down at the sheet and trying to absorb one of his calculations. He had put the folder in his mouth to free up one hand to turn the knob. There he stood bare-chested in lounging pajamas with a file folder gripped between his teeth, "Yeph?" He managed as he looked up at the stranger in the doorway.

"..I'm Mirabel.." She stood in the doorway, tall, in jeans with red hair tied in a single plait down her back. Her eyes were a light blue, widely spaced, and liquid. They seemed to radiate a light from within. Her skin was creamy white and slightly flushed. Her lips were exquisitely shaped and generous. About her there was a radiance that forced him to stand silently and stare at her.

"...Who are you?" She looked right into his eyes and demanded his identity. It was more of a command than a question, and Jace could only stand there for a full moment taking her in. He wanted to speak but seemed to lack the breath to do it.

The girl walked past him into the hallway as if she owned the house and turned to him, waiting for his account of himself.

"Uh...Jace. I'm Jace Brillig...Uh—*Who* did you say you were?" She seemed to give off a subtle perfume that filled his head and dulled his senses.

"Mirabel...I'm here for Eve."

"She's...out. Was she expecting you...?"

"...She knew I'd come.—I'm here now."

"...I...don't know when she'll be back..." Jace was still off balance looking at her. She was every fantasy of a woman he had ever had. He couldn't quite believe she was real.

"...I'll wait." Mirabel settled in a side chair in the hallway by the stairs and continued to look at Jace. "...You gonna just stand there?"

"Look...Miss—"

"Mirabel."

"...Mirabel. I don't know when she'll be back...Maybe you could come back later?"

"...I'll wait..." She continued to look at him with that same unnerving directness. "You oughta put on some clothes."

"Huh?....Uh, these are...lounging pants. For comfort."

"...You her man?"

"...Huh?...uh, we work together...in New York."

"...You're pretty enough."

"...Excuse me?..."

"To be her man. You're...handsome." She continued to look at him and Jace could feel his neck burn. He chuckled nervously.

"You don't play, do you?"

"What for? You come to the door half-naked. I gotta think you want it to be seen."

"...Ok...Look, Mirabel, I don't know who you are or why you're here, but Eve isn't. I think it would be better if you went...somewhere and came back when she was home."

"Why?"

"...This isn't my house; it's Eve's."

"What do you think I'm gonna do?..."

Suddenly the sound of a key entering the front lock could be heard. Eve pushed in and was confronted with the two of them facing off in the front hallway—Jace clutching reams of papers, bare-chested in his lounging pants, and Mirabel sitting quietly in the side chair, completely in command of the situation.

"...What have we got here?" Eve dropped her keys in a small bowl by the door where they lived when she was in the house. She removed a light lilac shawl she had worn to keep off the evening damp and hung it on one of a row of decorative hooks by the door.

"This is Mirabel. She says you're expecting her?" Jace deferred to Eve.

"You're Mirabel! Hello!" Eve went to the girl as she rose from the chair, uncertain how to greet Eve. The girl offered to shake Eve's hand, but Eve reached out and hugged her. "Your Grandmother didn't tell me you were gorgeous!"

The girl awkwardly allowed the hug and seemed suddenly uncertain where before, with Jace, she had been completely at ease. "...I don't want to trouble ya..."

"Don't be silly. I told your Grandmother I'd be happy to see you and help you out in any way I could!—Jace, this is Mirabel Livesey, Hetty Livesey's granddaughter."

"We met. She thinks I'm 'pretty.'" Jace grinned boyishly. Eve's return served to ease the tension that had been building between him and Mirabel.

"You are, Jace. You are!—Watch out for him, Mirabel; he's completely corruptible! He has no conscience when it comes to women!"

"That's a nice way to talk about your fiancé!" Jace pretended to be hurt.

"We've had this conversation. Don't pay any attention. What can I get for you? Are you hungry?" Eve turned her full attention onto the girl who continued to be slightly confused.

"I et. I come to see you."

"How long will you be here, dear?" Eve searched the young woman's face and figure, "My God, you *are* beautiful."

"Don't know. I come when she needs me. A few days maybe...maybe longer."

"Where did she go? Are you sure I can't get you something? Jace, don't you have to finish those figures for tomorrow?" Eve clearly wanted Jace out of the way. He had hung there with them smiling and completely intruding in the moment.

"..I guess I can take a hint! Pleasure to meet you, Mirabel. I'll be in the parlor...if I'm needed. Salaam!"

Mirabel watched him bow elaborately and leave. "...He...your man?"

"He thinks he is. .Where did your Grandmother go, Mirabel?"

She returned her attention to Eve after Jace had retreated to the living room,

"She had business. When she calls me, I come."

"Good for you! Most girls your age wouldn't help out like that."

"...Most girls ain't...like me. I've come to see ya. I should go."

"You just got here! Mira—can I call you Mira?—"

"..If ya like..."

"Stay, and we'll talk! I want to know what it is I can do for you. I didn't get much information from your Grandmother."

The girl turned and looked at Eve, "...I don't rightly know. I guess I could use a little learnin' about...most things. Hetty can't give me that."

"You're a young girl. You could probably teach *me* about what goes on these days. How old are you, dear?"

The girl paused and looked away for a moment, "...How old do you think?" It was a simple question. There was no attitude in it, and it surprised Eve.

"Well...I guess—what?—twenty-two or three?..."

"That's it. Twenty-three."

"Well, I'm sure you know more about your generation than me! I'm an old lady compared to you!"

"I...been workin'...on a farm. No time for funnin' or goin' places."

"...What about a boyfriend?..."

"...No."

"Don't you go anywhere? Clubs...dancing...going around with friends?"

The girl nodded 'no'. "...Guess that's why she asked ya..."

"No offence, Mira, but...what about school?"

"...I'm smart enough. I learn fast."

"I'm sure, but what about...college...career plans...?"

"I'll run the farm. When Hetty's done, it'll be me."

"...Don't you want something bigger...something more exciting than...tending goats."

"It's good work...We been there from the beginning; I can't leave it."

"Family tradition is a wonderful thing, Mira, but...it's a big world out there! Don't you want to go out and be a part of it?"

The girl lowered her eyes for a moment,"...Don't know..." She lifted them again and looked at Eve directly, "How 'bout you?..."

Eve frowned, puzzled at the question. "...I have to go to New York in the morning for a couple of days. How about we get together on Wednesday. I'll...I'll take you shopping...In Boston! How would that be?"

"You don't need to do that, Miss—Eve."

"Just Eve—and I want to. I think it's a good way to bring you out to the world! There's nothing like a shopping spree to give you a taste of the wide world. What do you say?"

The girl lowered her eyes again. "...I don't have that kinda money, Miss—Eve."

"It's on me! My idea—my credit card! C'mon, Mira, we'll have some fun!..."

"...Hetty said you was good...I'll go." Mira's eyes seemed to dance with the anticipation of the trip. There was a little fear and a lot of excitement evident in her body.

"What about now? You'll stay here tonight, of course!" Eve found herself fond of the girl even after such a brief meeting. There was something so innocent and unspoiled about her that Eve wanted to protect her.

"I've got the milkin' in the morning.—"

"Now, I know your Grandmother's house is beautiful, but it doesn't have indoor plumbing. I have a spa tub upstairs just crying out for some young girl to have a bubble bath!"

"I don't think—"

"And there's a guest room with a memory foam mattress just waiting for someone to use it. C'mon, I have this great big house! What good is it, if I can't entertain guests?—You can get up as early as you like and tend the goats! Tonight you can live it up!"

The girl looked at Eve in a way that made Eve feel as though she were some strange creature never before seen. It was an incredulous look, like someone who could not absorb what was being said. The girl hung in the air for a moment, seeming to wrestle with a thousand objections to the plan, but finally she turned her focus back on Eve, "I'll...stay."

"Great! Now you come with me and we'll get you settled in!"

Eve took Mirabel to the far side of the house. There were five bedrooms in the house. Eve had her room toward the front. Jace had put his things in the room next to hers, and she knew she'd have to make it clear to him that they would not be sharing a bed. Not now. Not since Adam, though she wasn't planning to divulge anything about Adam to anyone just now.

She guessed that Mirabel probably had nothing to wear to bed and she produced a pale green nightgown she had bought and not yet worn. It would be short on the girl, but not enough to matter. She filled the tub for her and threw in bath salts, talking all the time about things she thought Mirabel would like. A new toothbrush and a supply of shampoos and toiletries in the third-floor bath's medicine cabinet were made available to the girl, who watched everything closely and seemed to be studying the entire procedure as if there would be a test following the experience.

"If you need anything, just holler!—The towels are in the linen closet."

"...You...are good...really...good." The girl seemed to be at a loss for anything more to day.

"Mira!...it's just a bath. It's just a night out of the farm. It's nothing! I'm happy to have you!...You get up when you need to, and just go about your chores. Tell you what, I'll give you a key. You can come in, have a bath...watch television...whatever you want! I'll be back on Wednesday. Then, we'll have some real fun, eh!" Eve quickly hugged the girl, who received this contact with a little more ease than the first hug. Then she left.

***

The house was quiet. It wasn't like the farm, with the sounds of the goats in the pens and the marsh peepers by the pond. All the natural sounds she knew were completely muffled by the fabric of this house. It was fine, she had to admit, but it wasn't what she was used to. All that sound...that natural music was like a lullaby. Here, as soft as the bed was and how comfortable she felt, there was nothing to tie you to Life...you couldn't feel the earth move around you. The thunderous quiet had kept her awake.

Then she heard the tiny creak on the stairs, the soft but audible moving of the floor boards under someone's foot. Even though the room was dark, there was enough light from the street below to cast a faint glow in the room, and Mira could see quite clearly around her.

She sat up as the sound drew near to her door. Finally, the door swung open. Standing in the doorway Jace was looking straight at her.

"...Eve's asleep..." His voice was husky and, he looked at her knowing she understood.

"...You need to go." Her tone was hushed and flat. There was no fear in her and no complicity.

"Is that what you want?..." He made one step inside the room.

"Sometimes you don't get what you want." She stared straight at him.

"....She won't know...She doesn't care..." He came to the side of the bed and ran his hand down the side of her face to her throat and then her breast.

She grabbed his hand and held it tightly squeezing enough to be a warning, "I'll know...so will you. That's reason enough. Now git!"

"You don't know what I can do..."

"You don't know what *I* can do! You best leave..." She held his hand in her tight grip waiting to see if he would press any further.

"...Ok..." He stepped back from the bed and she let go. "...We can wait..."

He turned around and left as quietly as he had come. Mira stayed sitting on the bed. He was pretty.

***

CHAPTER 25

"Gentlemen, I believe I can guarantee you that your entire town will be revitalized by this project. Mr. Marlin has informed me of your concerns regarding the types of industries that will populate the Industrial Park, and I can understand your anxiety about disturbing the character of your beautiful town. I can assure you that no industry will be allowed in that would in any way disrupt the peaceful and normal lifestyle of Holmsford. In addition, my company will take pains to locate several retail operations on your town green—with your approval, of course—which will help to restore the vitality of the downtown area. You, as a group, would be able to select from a list of likely enterprises just what kinds of businesses would be a good fit in the town proper, and we will encourage the management level staff who come to the park to settle in the development on the bluff above the town which I have come to find out is another one of your concerns."

Jim Reedy was in rare form. Marlin knew he was good, but this magnanimous approach was beyond what he was expecting. When he told Reedy about Metcalf and his objections to the deal, all Reedy would say was, "Set up a meeting with them all! I'm coming down there." Innovative had booked the Radisson outside of town for the meeting. A guest chef had been flown in and the dinner had been unbelievably sumptuous—steaks, lobsters...anything the guests wanted. The bar was open before the meeting started to insure that all the guests were properly lubricated before Reedy began his presentation.

Charlie Metcalf stood up, "Mr. Reedy!"

"Mr. Metcalf, you have a question?"

"I do!...What do *you* get out of all this? It's a very...slick presentation. We saw the model...the slides and renderings...Why are you doing this?"

"I thought you loved your town, Mr. Metcalf. Don't you want it to flourish?"

"Sure do! We all do—right, fellas?" There was a rumble of assent from the assembled businessmen. Like Charlie, some were in the Rotary Club. "It's just—when a fella baits the hook real well, you gotta wonder what he's trying to catch!...What are you after, Mr. Reedy?"

"I can see I'm talking to experience! Very good! What Innovative wants, Mr. Metcalf is success! Over the years we have invested heavily in this part of the state. We view it as an under-realized resource. Towns like Holmsford have been ignored by Boston for decades...but we see that changing. We're betting that with key investments—like the ones we have already made and the one that we're proposing—the entire region will begin to wake up economically. New businesses will locate right here in Holmsford—high tech, medical research...financial. Towns like Holmsford offer them room to work and a way to avoid the congestion of an old city like Boston, and yet they're within striking distance of the metropolitan center. We think it's inevitable, and we want to be in on the change. We want to accelerate that change, and, of course, benefit from it."

"Uh, huh. Sounds terrific..." Charlie Metcalf remained standing, "But you'll excuse me if I say it doesn't sound like it's likely to preserve the town we know and love. Holmsford's been here for nearly four-hundred years. Sounds a lot like we're being swallowed up by a lot of hoopla!" Once again the men in the room voiced their agreement.

"That town green of yours, Mr. Metcalf, is the very soul of your town. It's the picture of small-town New England!—That's the draw! That's what we *have* to preserve—that, and all that it represents! The very character of Holmsford is what we are dedicated to preserving. That's why businesses and people will want to come here. They can work and live in the way their grandparents and great-grandparents did and still be in the twenty-first century! We don't want to change you, Mr. Metcalf—we want to join you!"

There was spontaneous applause from the group of businessmen. Marlin watched from the back of the room. Reedy was good! Whatever he was really planning, even Marlin was excited by that little speech. It was inspiring...But was that it? Was Innovative just looking for regional development—long term, marginal profits? Marlin wasn't buying it...even though the rest of them seemed to be swayed. It was just Charlie. He was still standing, waiting for the applause to die down.

"...What about those businesses, Mr. Reedy?...You gonna give us final say on who comes into that Industrial Park of yours, or not?" This was it. This was the deal-breaker for Metcalf, but Marlin knew Reedy was waiting for it.

Reedy waited for the question to sink in with the rest of the gathering. He kept his face serious and, perhaps, even a little grim until the room was perfectly silent. Finally he smiled broadly and warmly, "Absolutely!

No business will be allowed to locate in Holmsford Industrial Park without the express approval of the town's Board of Selectmen! That, gentlemen, I guarantee!"

The room burst into applause again. Some of the men stood up and clapped Charlie Metcalf on the back. He had faced down the 'big interest' from the city and gotten what all of them were there to secure. Holmsford would not be bullied by outside interests into become just another suburb of Boston. Holmsford would stay Holmsford, but now the town would have a renewed future! They were the men who had succeeded in providing a continuation for a proud heritage! They all felt like heroes. Jim Reedy smiled.

He gestured toward Marlin, who approached him while the rest of the room congratulated itself. "Now you let them know individually that we're looking for five hundred contiguous acres for the project. Plant the seed...."

***

CHAPTER 26

"Sweet thing...There you go..." Eve had brought a carrot down to the pens. The little tawny goat was there again. She screamed when she saw Eve and ran for the fence. Eve fed her the carrot which she chewed greedily and then buried her little head into Eve's stomach as Eve stroked and comforted her. "C'mon, girl, it's not that bad....See?...I'm here. You're fine!..." The little goat moaned and nuzzled seeking as much comfort as Eve could give.

A clang of tin sounded as Mirabel came around the side of the shed inside the pen. She carried a galvanized bucket full of grain for the animals inside. She was wearing jeans and a plaid man's shirt and old boots, much the same as Hetty had worn. As she turned the corner, she spotted Eve. Suddenly the little goat picked up its head and turned. As soon as it saw Mirabel, it bucked away from Eve again screaming and ran to the far side of the pen. The force of the movement nearly knocked Eve over.

"You're back...." Mirabel emptied the bucket into a shallow trough set up for the goats. The rest of the animals ran over and began to eat greedily...all but the little tawny goat, who stayed on the far side of the pen cowering against that part of the fence and screaming.

"...What's wrong with her?" Eve gripped the fence and looked apprehensively at the frightened animal.

"She don't like me..."

"She was fine a minute ago."

"You brung her a carrot. Spoiled! She wants that from me too...but she ain't gonna git it. Quiet, you!" The little goat fell silent but stayed at the far side of the pen. Mirabel's hair seemed to light up in the sunlight, and Eve thought how remarkable she looked. No makeup, no fancy clothes— just natural good health and real beauty. Mirabel stopped for a moment, noticing Eve staring at her. "Somethin' wrong?"

"...Nothing but pure envy! Twenty-three—I won't see that again. You're breathtaking, you know that?"

The girl lowered her eyes for a moment and seemed to be embarrassed, "I don't try to be..."

"You don't have to...not at twenty-three!...Is she going to be all right? I didn't know I shouldn't give her things."

"..She's fallow...The rest of 'em ain't—just her.   She'll have to kid...otherwise..."

"'Otherwise?'" Eve was alarmed at the suggestion.

"...Nothin'....Just takes time for some of 'em...She'll come 'round....I'm done with the milkin'..."

"Perfect!...C'mon up to the house. You can shower and change...I...hope you don't mind, my neighbors...some of the women I know here want to come along. I made the mistake of telling them I was taking you shopping."

The girl took in the information and seemed to take a moment to consider the situation, "...They won't like me."

"Of course, they will!...Look, Mira, they're just a bunch of women my age. They don't work. They have nothing but time on their hands and they all want to meet you and...help out."

"...Help out?"

"OK, this is 'Girl 101' older women need to feel needed. They like nothing better than a chance to...fashion young women—like you—into something they wanted to be."

"...That what you're doin'?..."   Mirabel looked straight at Eve with a penetrating stare.

"No...Mira. I just want to help you with...whatever you need. You'll be whoever you are—I don't know who that is...but I think you do."

"...Then why do we need 'em?"

"...We don't...but I think *they* need *us*. Help me out here. They want to feel useful, and...it'll be fun! You'll find out a lot just by listening and watching. Besides, they have plenty of money between them, and I wouldn't be surprised if they insist on buying you things!"

The girl seemed to contemplate this for a moment. She looked down at the ground and then off into the woods. Finally, she turned to Eve, "We'd best get started..."

***

"...Are you ready to order?..." The young waiter had taken the orders of the other women and now he stood by Mirabel. He was subtle; Eve appreciated that, but it was clear that he was trying to get the girl's attention. He wasn't' daunted by the circle of dueñas surrounding her.

Durgin Park was busy, but they had gotten a table. All morning they had shopped. They were loaded down with bags and boxes—Nordstrom's, Saks,—all the high end stores—all of it for Mirabel. They had fussed over her like a life-sized doll, and, to her credit, Mirabel let them. Eve quietly fended off the more invasive questions and suggestions, and there had been no need for the girl to talk much. Once they set eyes on Mira, they were enchanted. Her features, her figure, her coloring—the women admired, envied and indulged. They joked and talked and the steady looks the girl got from every man they passed did not go unnoticed.

The handsome young waiter stood staring at Mirabel with an intensity that taking an order did not require. "Do you know what you want, Miss...?"

Mira seemed unaware. She was looking at the menu and frowning so hard she had not looked up at the boy. Finally, she looked up at him and caught his intensity. "...Uh...There's so much...What do you think is good?"

The young waiter was almost speechless once she had looked right at him. For a moment, he seemed to be lost for words."...Well...that depends on what you want?..."

She looked right into his eyes and seemed to sense his discomfort, "...Don't want to trouble you." Her voice was soft and sympathetic, which seemed to make him even more stupid than before.

"Um...well, everything is good...The lobster is good...pretty much anything you order...is good."

"Lobster then...is that all right?" She asked the table and the girls quickly chorused their approval. Mirabel handed her menu back to the young waiter, who was still transfixed by her.

"You go to school, young man?" Marian led the fray.

"Um, yes, Ma'am. BU."

"College man!...Handsome and smart! What are you studying, honey?"

"Pre-med. I'm a junior, actually..." He hadn't taken his eyes off the girl. "One more year.."

"Then Med school, I suppose…" As she continued the other women were looking him over like he was a prize bull on the auction block.

"…Uh…yes. Med school…"

"Are you working your way through?" Libby elbowed Donna who watched curiously. The young man kept settling on Mirabel.

"Kinda. My Dad's a physician…neurologist. He…wants me to contribute. He says a man can't start too soon to pay his own way."

"Good for him! He a good Dad?" Libby was smiling at him in anticipation.

The young man nodded slowly still looking at Mirabel, "…He's…great. He's the reason I chose pre-med."

"I bet your Mom's proud of you!" Libby hung on this.

"She's…the best! She keeps my Dad and me right on track! Strong lady!"

"That's the Goddamn ticket!—pardon my French!…But a strong mother! Good for you! Good for you! You're gonna be great! You're gonna be Goddamned successful! You hear that, girls?"

"…All that study doesn't leave much time for fun, though, does it?…" Donna cut in quietly.

The young man caught her meaning and turned to her reflexively, "Oh…I have fun!" He turned back again to Mirabel who was still looking at him, "I…find time…to have fun."

"…Uh…maybe you should put our orders in?" Eve saw the other wait staff sending resentful glances toward their table.

"…Huh…Right! Sorry….I'll get them in right away". The young man pulled himself away taking Mirabel's menu and quietly dropping a small piece of paper into her lap as he left. The other women didn't notice; Mirabel picked it up and slipped it into her pocket without saying anything. Eve observed her but said nothing.

"…You could have him on a bed of lettuce, if you want him!" Donna was again quiet.

"…Uh…beg pardon?" Mirabel knotted her eyebrows and looked at Donna.

"He's yours! He was yours at 'Are you ready to order?'—I can think of couple of orders I could give him!'" Donna smiled slightly and the other women giggled.

"Oh, honey, a doctor!—Well, not yet" Marian's eyes were gleaming....."And he is handsome! I'll bet he's got lots of girls!"

"...Why would I want him then?" Mira's eyes fixed on Marian.

"Honey, A doctor! You would never have to worry!"

"...Worry?...About what?"

"About your security! Oh, honey, we've got to teach you! With your looks, you...could have any man. Any! And they're all gonna want you, sweetie, I mean, if you don't know that by now...But you want to pick a man who's going to keep you in style! You want someone who's going to give you the best things in life. A doctor...and a handsome one at that!"

"She'd have to wait ...until he makes some real money..." Donna weighed in, "He's straight—I can tell you that. But he doesn't have anything—not yet. Now, you find an older guy?...Established...a little bored. You let him show you the world, and you can have a dozen juniors like young Dr. Kildare there, just to play with."

"What the fuck are you telling her, Donna? You want her to...sell herself? Put herself out like some fucking merchandise for sale?"

"...That's what we all did..."

"We were all married, for Christ's sakes!" Libby was beginning to get loud and Marian shushed her to bring her voice down.

"...Uh huh...we sure were...." Donna retreated smiling slightly to herself.

"You know, I love this place! It's a little loud, but it's fun!...I think we did pretty well this morning, don't you?" Eve was hoping to divert the conversation.

"Just because you...'get around' doesn't mean *she* wants to. Christ, Donna, she's a baby!" Libby seemed to be calming.

"Did you see the men this morning? Everywhere we went!—All eyes were on you, Honey! I don't know what it is you have, but if I could bottle it...I'd have a new man right now!" Marian impulsively reached out and took Mirabel's hand. After a second the girl retracted it.

"...That what you want?" The girl focused for the moment entirely on Marian.

"Honey, sweetie pie...If I could....well, there's no point, is there? I'm at that age...All the men worth having are already married—

"Or gay..." Donna chimed in.

"And the rest are chasing their youth in little red sports cars..."

"Christ!—Let it go, Marian! We're here to have some fun! Let's show this girl how we women keep going! Who the fuck cares about Goddamn men or the past! It's over! Let's have today!"

"Here, here!" Eve raised her glass, "To today!"

The women picked up their drinks and raised them smiling. "TODAY!" Their choral toast silenced the restaurant and from other tables other women raised their glasses and echoed the call. There were scattered giggles from around the room as women joined in.

Marian, Donna, Libby and Eve looked at each other in pleasure and surprise and laughed out loud.

"Oh, this is fun! Honey, you are just the best time I've had in a long time! I hope your Grandmaw appreciates you, honey!"

Mirabel didn't smile, but she looked curiously at the women around her. "..Bein' young's not everythin'...

"Not while you're there, honey...!" Marian's tone turned just a little sour for the moment.

"Christ, sometimes you can't wait for it to be over! You keep thinking when the fuck is somebody gonna take me seriously!?"

"....That doesn't happen..." Donna seemed to be thinking hard.

"Who the fuck cares!" Libby raised her glass, now filled with diet coke and again and they all did the same, but quietly this time.

"...What...if you could...be young?..." Mirabel was still studying the women.

"I think the point is, Mira...We move along. Right now, we're all in Boston together, shopping, and you...you have a young admirer, and I think we're all a little jealous!...But it's fun to watch!" Eve was relieved that the girls weren't 'at' each other again.

"*You're* not..." Mira looked at Eve.

"...I'm happy for you."

"Of course you are; you've got that employee...colleague—whatever the fuck you call him. What is he—30?" Libby kept sipping on her coke.

"...And the minister." Donna added in quietly.

"What!" Marian turned to Eve. "What does she mean 'the minister?'"

Eve looked at Donna who only smiled back coyly, "...We've..had a couple of dates. That's all."

"Adam Singleton!?...You didn't even like him! You yelled at him when you met him!" Marian protested.

"I didn't yell at him. I disagreed with him."

"...Why didn't you tell me! I've been pushing cake at Fellowship for nothing!—How in the hell did you get from that display of bitchy uppitiness to—dating!"

"Marian, I didn't expect it! He was running when Donna and I were, and he stopped and...asked me out. I don't know why."

"I've been working on him for weeks!" Marian was completely nonplussed.

"Somebody want to clue me the fuck in. Who's this minister?" Libby had been trying to follow the track.

"Marian's been trying to get the new Minister at her church, but Eve snagged him..." Donna was brief and complete.

"I didn't snag him!...He...asked me out."

"And you *went!*" Marian could help sounding resentful.

"I didn't think it would amount to anything!"

"And it *did?*" Marian sounded even more resentful.

"...Uh...well, I don't know..." Eve was reluctant to irritate Marian any more with the real feeling she had for Adam. It was better to downplay her involvement—if it really was an involvement. Eve couldn't think straight every time she thought of him.

"...I bring him cake and help out and shower him with attention, and you come along and insult him, and it's *you* he asks out!"

"...I'm sorry, Marian....I didn't plan it..."

"I'm not taking you anywhere again! I find a man; none of you get to know!"

"I didn't know one fucking thing!" Libby protested.

"He's got a nice ass..." Donna shared with Libby. Eve glared at her for even mentioning Adam let alone letting the cat out of the bag.

"Men! They're like a furry sub-species! Who knows what attracts them!" Marian sipped on her cocktail and tried to put away her resentment.

"...Dominion..." Mirabel said it quietly, almost under her breath.

"...What, honey?" Marian hardly paid attention as she sipped her drink trying to forget Eve's betrayal.

"Dominion...That's what...Hetty says. They can't get it?..It eats at 'em." The girl surveyed the other women at the table as they looked at her."...No offense, sweetie, but I don't think your Grandmaw is exactly an expert!...Do-dom—"

"Dominion...It means power...control..." Eve offered looking at Mira a little puzzled.

"...Don't know...but she says 'long as we need 'em—they got us. When we don't need 'em—we got them."

"Well, honey, I'm not that old! I'm not ready to give up on men just yet!"

"Me neither! I'm a little down, but not Goddamn out! 'Us' and 'Them'— Why the fuck does it always have to be that?"

"...It is, though...Look at us...."

"For Christ's sakes, Donna, we all know you're not done with the 'battle of the sexes!'"

Donna smiled and lifted her glass again adding slyly, "...Here's to 'mercenaries!'"

The three women laughed and joined the toast. Eve lifted her glass in token support, but she couldn't help removing herself a little. She felt herself observing from the outside. Why was that? What was it she had missed?...She looked across at Mira and she could see the girl also observing from some strange, reserved distance. Why were they both so removed?

***

CHAPTER 27

"All right, members of the Rotary, come to order!...Adam, sorry you weren't with us the other night. You missed quite a feed!" Charlie Metcalf was relieved to see Singleton at the meeting. The younger man added a sense of promise to these meetings. Almost everyone else was ten to twenty years older. Most of them were getting close to retirement. Even though he was forty, Singleton was looked upon as a representative of the 'younger generation.'

Singleton smiled, but he remained quiet as the meeting came together. He refused to let his personal feelings show, yet all he could think about was Eve's fiancé.

...He felt like an idiot! He should have known a woman like Eve would have someone. What was he thinking? She was beautiful, brilliant...accomplished. And the guy...he was...young!—That was a surprise. Why? Why should it be a surprise? She was so...smart. What could they have in common?—Maybe that was the point. After all, what did he know? What did he really know about women?...Not much! He had misjudged the whole situation. And she could have anyone she wanted. He had no claim on her! If she wanted...a younger man... A middle-aged minister might be...interesting...He realized he was probably flattering himself...but a young "Turk" like that...Why didn't she tell him? Had he sent the wrong signals? Was he so anxious to have her that he let her think all he wanted was a fling? Was she really a woman who...would...? Did he let his attraction for her get the best of his common sense?...God, men are stupid!...

John Marlin was there, glad-handing everyone and reminding them of the 'terrific victory' they had achieved with Jim Reedy and Innovative. It made Metcalf a little nervous to see Marlin so relaxed. That was the way he always seemed when he got his way.

"OK, now you know what this meeting's about. Mr. Reedy outlined for us exactly what Innovative was prepared to do for the privilege of building that Industrial Park in Town..."

"They gave us the damn store!" Wally Fry shouted out.

"All because of you, Charlie!—You played 'em good!" That was Esau Carter. Charlie remembered how drunk he got at the open bar.

"Now, now..." Metcalf was trying to calm the men down and get the meeting started.

John Marlin stood up, "Way to go, Charlie!" He led the applause, and all the men joined in laughing and joking. They felt confident and flush after the 'face-to-face' with Reedy, and they wanted to vent.

"OK...OK!...Now, I'm not so sure, it's all that it's cracked up to be. Let's not forget that Innovative doesn't have the best track record with us."

"C'mon, Charlie, you squeezed 'em. You got 'em to give us everything we wanted!" Marlin was still leading the celebration and the group burst into another round of applause.

"All right...Now...I know Reedy promised us the moon. He gave us everything we came there to get. But I'm not so sure we've got a deal."

"Stop being modest, Charlie!" Marlin was still pushing the group.

"No modesty about it, Jack...They can promise us anything they like, that doesn't mean we're gonna get it! We're all experienced businessmen. Until it's signed, sealed and delivered, we've got nothing. And even then, the devil is in the details!...For one thing, we've got to look at what we're promising them to get this project here."

"Not much, far as I can see!" Marlin was still goading the boys along.

"Jack, please! First off, they want 500 acres..."

"We're not giving it to 'em, Charlie! They'll pay fair market for it. What's the problem?" Wally Fry was getting caught up.

"Nothin'! Nothin' except we don't have 500 acres to sell them. Not contiguous—all together. Oh, we've got plenty of acreage, all right, but it's in bits and pieces. 30 acres here, 100 acres there...but it's all split up. The deal specifically calls for 500 contiguous acres. How do we deal with that?"

The men were suddenly sobered by this realization. They looked at each other for answers that none of them had.

"There's no deal if we can't deliver..." Metcalf leveled his gaze at the assembly of men.

The mood in the room became somber as the realization hit home that the town couldn't deliver what Innovative wanted.

"So, what do we do, let Holmsford just...dissolve! Christ, Charlie!" That was Carter again, but the rest of the men began to voice their objections.

"Look, we've gotta look at what we've got! They want a big parcel—we don't have one...." The buzz circulated for a moment, then Adam raised his hand.

"The chair recognizes Reverend Singleton! Adam, what do you think?" Charlie Metcalf was relieved. He needed a calmer voice, and he was hoping that Singleton had a solution.

"...Uh...look..." Singleton stood shaking off his constant review of his experience at Eve's house and faced the men. "You seem to have a deal on the table that's the one you want, but you don't have goods to offer...at least not the ones the other...party wants. The obvious choice is to think about another way to get the goods. Are there any parcels of size close together?"

"Well...I don't know. Anybody know about that? What about you, Jack? You're Chairman of the Board of Selectmen. Are there any clusters of parcels close together?"

Marlin sat there for a moment thinking about the question. This isn't the way he wanted things to go. How could he divert this line of thinking?..."Uh....well, maybe. I'd have to check with the town clerk. We might have a few fairly close together, but I don't see how that helps us."

"Suppose you offer to buy up a few parcels in between and connect the dots, so to speak?"

"I don't know if I can get the Board of Selectmen to go for that!" Marlin was vamping, trying to think of a way around this idea of Singleton's

"Come on, Jack, you've got the whole Board here! We got the votes to swing it!" Wally Fry was on the Board. He and Esau Carter were in Marlin's pocket. Singleton could tell neither man had any idea that Marlin was stalling. But why was he?

"All right, suppose we vote it. Fine. Now we've got to go out and deal with the landowners, offer 'em deals...dicker with 'em. How long do you think that'll take? How long do you expect Innovative to wait for you to have the parcel they need?—You'll lose 'em!"

"You don't know until you try, Mr. Marlin. When you explain to those land owners that the future of the town might be at stake—"

"They'll smell blood!" Marlin cut in on Singleton. "Reverend Singleton, with all due respect, you don't know the small town Yankee mentality. If it's worth something, ask for more; if it's in the public interest—double it! The last time small town Yankees did something for their fellow man, was firin' the shot heard 'round the world. After that it was 'every man for himself!'"

A grim silence followed. Every man there was a small-town Yankee, and every one of them knew the truth in Marlin's judgement. "There is one thing we could do..."

"What's that, Jack?" Charlie Metcalf was drawn in now.

"Eminent domain! We can do that. Fix a price—a fair one and buy the land on the basis of the common good."

"Can we do that?..." Esau Carter sounded doubtful.

"We can. It's in the town charter and it's the law! If the Board of Selectmen deems it necessary for the good of the town, we can buy the land at the price we set as fair market value.

"That's not going to make us very popular with folks." Wally Fry was worried.

"Nope, it's not," Marlin added with finality. "That's why we don't want to be doing it with a whole gaggle of small free holders. We'll lose too many votes. They could contest us in court...delay us...maybe long enough to queer the deal."

"So we're right back where we started then," Charlie was frustrated.

"Not quite!...There is one parcel of land...pretty far out of town...big enough to hold the Industrial park and held by one owner...." Marlin looked around the room at the hopeful faces.

"...Who's got five hundred acres?...There's nobody around with that much land!" Joe Southworth waved his arms at Marlin in dismissal.

"Wrong, Joe. There's one...the Goat Woman."

"The Livesey place? Jack, that's the last original homestead left in town! It's been there since the town was founded! It's the last link we have to our local history!" Metcalf was alarmed.

"...You want history or a future?" Marlin let the question sit on the air as he watched the faces in the room.

"There's gotta be another way!" Metcalf was still objecting but the other men in the room sat in silence, thinking over the choice.

"I hear you, Charlie. But the Board's gotta take the good of the Town into consideration. The Town's gotta be our prime interest. As it is, it'll take a little time to schedule a Town Meeting and present the plan..." Marlin put the pressure on them now. It went better than he expected. He knew all along the Livesey property was what Innovative wanted. Together with the old Ramsay farm, now "Cloven Terrace," it gave them control of over a thousand acres just outside of town. He calculated his premium for delivering the property. He knew Reedy would be generous.

The meeting went on for over an hour. Charlie Metcalf maintained that there had to be another way, and he was hoping that someone would think of some other way to give Innovative what it wanted and not put them in the position of taking the last original farm away from an old woman whose family helped to found the town. He knew Fry and Carter were in Marlin's pocket. As Town Selectmen, they would vote any way Marlin wanted, and Jack Marlin was just a little too anxious to get on with this decision.

For Singleton, the meeting remained pretty much a blur as had everything else since he met Eve's Fiancé. He couldn't get the image out of his mind of that glossy, young man in lounging pajamas standing in Eve's doorway.

***

CHAPTER 28

"You made out like a bandit! Look at this haul!"

It was the following morning. Eve, Mirabel and the 'girls' had shopped the entire afternoon, followed by a dinner at the Copper Pot, one of the best places in Boston. They had returned exhausted and she had dropped each off at her house with a chorus of laughter and promises to "do it again soon." Mirabel smiled and nodded and kept as silent as she could. That night the both of them had collapsed into their beds exhausted.

The girl had just come in from her morning chores with the goats. She had on her jeans and boots and her hair was tied at the back to keep it out of the way. As she entered she saw Eve surveying the boxes of clothing the women had bought and admiring the collection.

"...More than I need." The girl seemed a little embarrassed by such bounty.

"Of course it is, Mira! That's the fun of it!" Eve picked up a simple flowing dress in a colorful print and a pair of matching shoes. "Here! Put these on."

"...I smell like a goat!" Mirabel pulled back a little from the offered clothes.

"Run up and take a shower, and then put these on. We're going out!"

"...We been out."

"That was yesterday!—Mira, It's Sunday! We're going out for breakfast...and I'm going to introduce you to my fella!"

"...The minister..."

"Reverend Adam Singleton!—At least I think he's my fella...Mirabel, you have no idea!" Eve couldn't help but smile when she said his name. She couldn't understand this feeling, but it had taken her over.

"...What about...Jace...?"

158

Eve stopped for a moment and looked at Mirabel. "Jace...is Jace. I hope I don't shock you, Mira. We...had an...arrangement, but it wasn't anything....real. Not really."

Mirabel took this in as she looked at Eve, "...He said you wouldn't care..."

"Huh?...He said what?..."

"...I just wondered..."

"Don't worry about Jace. He won't miss a step without me."

"...You know that...? It don't rankle ya'?"

"'Rankle me?'—Mira, men like Jace...are all about...the hunt. There's always another woman...As long as you know that...you don't get hooked. Now, c'mon, get cleaned up. I'm hungry!" Eve thrust the dress and shoes into the girl's arms.

Mirabel went up the stairs to 'her room.' She moved quickly and managed to re-emerge thirty minutes later in the dress looking perfect. Her hair was combed out and hung long down her back like a shower of rose gold. She hadn't used any of the makeup Eve had provided her, and Eve, looking at her, realized that the girl certainly didn't need it. In the dress and shoes that had made her even taller, she was stunning!

Eve had also dressed and the two of them stepped out to the car.

"...Those...women yesterday...you like 'em." Eve was making her way down Cloven Drive to the highway that led into town and the Puritan House. She had planned an early breakfast there, and then she would take Mirabel to services to meet Adam.

"Don't you? All those gifts! They were pretty generous to you!"

"......They were...guess I owe 'em."

"What?—no! Mira, the girls...are who they are...They've had a rougher time than you can imagine."

The girl looked at her without any expression, just taking in the comment.

They've experienced rejection...abandonment.—That sort of thing leaves its scars; I don't expect someone your age to understand. If they're a little...extreme...so what? They're....fun, in a weird dysfunctional way. I've spent most of my time in the company of men. I've missed that feeling of...sisterhood...."

"..They ain't *your* sisters..." Mirabel said this almost too quietly for Eve to hear.

Eve frowned at this and turned her head momentarily to see the girl looking straight ahead, without any expression on her face. "You have to take people the way you find them, Mira...You can't judge them."

The girl said nothing. She took in Eve's comment and then looked out the window thinking. Finally she said, "...That's what most do?"

It had been a few moments and Eve had been lost in her own thoughts, "...Most do what, Mira?..."

"...Judge." The girl was looking at her now and Eve managed to look over at the girl and saw a serious question in her eyes.

"...I suppose that's true...but it's not the best of who we are...is it?"

The girl took in the comment and looked out at the passing scenery as Eve continued to drive toward the Puritan house. "...Are you going to call him?..."

Mirabel turned this time to look at Eve, sincerely puzzled,"...Do what?"

"The boy—that handsome young waiter! Mira, I saw him drop his number in your lap!—Are you going to call him?"

"...What for?" It was an honest question; there was no trace of cynicism.

"He was interested! He wanted to take you out, that's why he gave you his number!...He seemed like a nice boy."

"...He was." Mirabel faced forward

"...So....why not?..." Eve was trying to get the girl to open up.

"...Don't need to."

"Mira, you might find that you like him."

"...Don't need to...and he sure as hell don't need to see me!" The girl seemed resolute now.

"Mira, what kind of a thing is that to say? He was practically falling over himself to get your attention. What harm is there to having a date with a nice young man?"

"...Let him have his nice girls. I'm not for him."

"Mira, *you're* a nice girl, and beautiful! Why shouldn't he want you?" Eve was nonplussed by what she judged to be the girl's negative opinion of herself.

"...I farm goats. What's he?—a doctor soon enough? He don't need to see me."

"But if he wants—"

"'Wants' easy; havin's hard! He'd find havin' me much more than he reckoned. No need to do that to him. Like you said, he's a nice boy." That seemed to put a lid on the conversation. Eve retreated wondering how to penetrate the girl's finality.

They had arrived at the town green. Eve parked the car and the two women entered the restaurant. As usual it was buzzing with Sunday Morning. They were earlier than most of the younger crowd. Most of the booths were occupied by gray heads. A waitress showed them to a rear booth, and as they passed, the restaurant grew quiet. Every head turned to view them as they passed through. It was eerie how all eyes were on them. Once they sat, the chatter resumed, but Eve could see some of the older customers turning and taking long looks at Mirabel. The women were suspicious and the men...the men were...more than a little appreciative.

"Remind me not to make an entrance with you!..." Eve whispered to Mirabel over her menu.

"...Don't know what they got to look at..." Mirabel seemed nervous at all the eyes on them.

"...Mira...it's you! They see how beautiful you look!"

"...It ain't good..." The girl retreated behind her menu hiding from the prying looks of the other customers.

"We'll order, and they'll stop. Small town...you're someone new. Mira, they stared at me the first time I came here too!..." With that Eve began to look over her menu.

But the staring didn't stop. Eve was oblivious, but Mirabel kept peeking over the menu. She was growing more agitated as the older patrons kept casting their looks at the two women in the booth. Finally, one old man rose painfully and made a show of walking casually past. It was obvious that he dropped his cane on purpose by their booth. When he bent down to pick it up, he pointedly reached out to steady himself on their table putting his hand directly on Mirabel's. As he hoisted himself up, he gave her his best seductive smile.

The girl pulled her hand back sharply, "Get off!" she snarled at him.

The old man seemed stricken by her rebuke and painfully shambled away trying not to be embarrassed.

"Mira!...He didn't mean anything! He's just....remembering, I think!"

"I don't like it!...Can we go? This...ain't a good place!" The girl looked panicky and agitated.

"Well...all right. But this is the only place open! We'll miss breakfast."

"I..ain't hungry. Can we go?..."

Mirabel stood and Eve reluctantly followed her. Once again all eyes were on them as they left the restaurant. Even Eve noticed with some disquiet the odd looks and the hushed conversations. It wasn't the same as the first time she had been there and sat with the girls. The day she met Marlin at the cash register. This was...a different feeling.

Once out on the sidewalk, Mirabel seemed to calm down, and the morning was soft and fresh.

"Well, it's too early for services....I know! Let's go around and see Dilla! I want you to meet her. She's the closest thing I have to a relative in town. She and my Granny were friends."

Although the sign hadn't been turned around to "Open," Dilla's shop door was unlocked. Eve knocked gently and poked her head in. The old woman was sitting at a small table in the rear of the shop by a window, sipping a cup of coffee.

"Who's that? Not open yet!" Dilla's tone was annoyed as she peered through the shop. Suddenly she recognized who it was, "—Eve! Eve, come in, dear! How nice! I was just wondering about you!...Come on, come on!...I've got some coffee, you want some?" The old woman stood and went behind the counter for the coffee pot. "Sit down, dear! Oh, this is so nice!..."

Eve slipped inside the door, followed by Mirabel. The little bell tinkled loudly startling the girl and Eve giggled. "I've brought a friend with me," She called out to the old woman, who was still behind the counter completely hidden by the merchandize piled upon it.

"Really! Well, who have you brought me? A customer, I hope. I haven't sold a thing in two we—" 'Dilla stopped in mid-sentence as she came around the counter carrying a coffee pot and a plate with pastries. She seemed to freeze for a moment when she saw Mirabel. "...My God!..." It took her a moment to come to herself. "...Oh, child, I'm so sorry, but you...did give me a turn! You are the very image of your Grandmother! It's uncanny!"

Eve was a little surprised at Dilla's reaction. "...So...I guess you know who this is!..."

"It couldn't be anyone else! The hair, the eyes....Child, I saw your grandmother a few times years ago; I was married then. And you...are a perfect likeness!"

"This is Mirabel Livesey..." Eve added, a little pointlessly.

"Mirabel!...What a lovely name! And what a lovely girl! It takes my breath away! You know, dear, a lot of us girls were more than a little jealous of your grandmother. She was the most beautiful girl...made the rest of us look like little field mice!"

"She didn't come to town much."

"A good thing! None of us would have kept our husbands! Well, now sit, both of you. I have some pastry! I'm glad you came; I might have eaten these all myself. Pour yourself some coffee. Go on!...Consider this your own private restaurant!" Dilla watched at the two younger women fixed themselves cups of coffee and helped themselves to some of the pastry. Her eyes kept moving to Mirabel. "How is your grandmother, dear?"

"...She does fine..." Mirabel's tone was quiet and respectful, but she sat bolt upright in her chair.

"Hetty is away on some kind of business, and Mira is taking care of the animals for her. She's been staying with me for a few days."

"I could stay at the farm."

"Of course you could!" Eve leaned into Dilla, "I'm afraid I've seduced her with a memory foam mattress and a spa tub!"

"I don't recall seeing you in town before, dear."

"No call to. When Hetty needs me, I come. I stay there."

"I see....Well, I'm so glad Eve brought you here! Are you staying long, dear?"

"Long as Hetty needs me." The girl still sat upright, sipping her coffee.

"...Do you know—I have the last of two of this town's founding families sitting right here in my shop. Eve here is the last of the Truesdales, and you, dear, after Hetty of course, are the last of the Liveseys!"

"...That so..." The girl continued to sip her coffee.

"Yes, dear. I'm the town Historical Society. It's my job to know these things."

"I know something about that that you don't know, Dilla!" Eve said proudly.

"What, dear? About what?"

"As a matter of fact, our two families were at odds, so to speak, when the town was founded. Did you know that?"

"How do you know that?" Dilla frowned a little and turned her attention to Eve.

"It's a story Hetty told me. Her ancestor and my ancestor were rival pastors!"

"Rival pastors, really? There's no record of that!"

"There is! Hetty has it in her 'Keeping Book'."

"'Keeping Book?'..." Dilla turned to Mirabel with a confused look. The girl looked slightly nervous.

"...Don't know nothin' about that. Hetty's one for her stories." She drew a long sip of coffee.

"Your grandmother is straight on with the truth! If she tells you something—it's gospel!" Eve couldn't help but add this.

"Well, I'd like to know that story! Do you think your grandmother would tell it to me, dear? If it's written down, would she let me read it?" Dilla was excited, thinking some new tidbit about the town might come to light.

The girl emerged from her cup and looked at the two other women, "...You'd have to ask her. I don't have nothin' to do with that."

"I'll ask her—the next time I see her!" Eve added.

"She don't like pryin' eyes," the girl warned.

"It's just sharing, Mira. Dilla has all sorts of old records going way back to the founding of the town. I would think Hetty would be honored to add something to the lore of Holmsford!"

"...Don't think so." The girl grew quiet again.

"Well, if she doesn't, she doesn't. I wouldn't want to upset her...So why are you two all gussied up? You look like a couple of *Vogue* models?"

"I'm taking Mira to St. Barnabas."

"She wants me to see her man," Mira blurted out.

"'Her man?'—Adam Singleton?" Dilla fixed her gaze on Eve who couldn't help smiling.

"...We've...seen each other a couple of times..."

"Ohhh....Eve! I'm so excited for you! He's a lovely man!" Dilla grabbed Eve's hand and squeezed it.

"I don't know if it's anything! I just...He made the first move—but I..."

"Oh, my God, you're in love, Eve." Dilla looked seriously at the younger woman. She could see the fumbling behind her eyes. "...And it's the first time!"

"No!...Now, it's not anything, not that I know about!" Eve couldn't look the old woman in the eye.

"Don't deny it! I've lived long enough to know love when I see it, and it's written all over you!"

"...Dilla! I'm hardly a blushing little virgin! We barely know each other. We're just seeing each other, that's all."

"Don't tell me!—I can see it. Mirabel what do you think?"

The girl had been looking on during the exchange between the two women and a soft smile had crept over her face that betrayed recognition. "...She's done for!"

"Mira, that's not true!" Eve kept protesting.

"You are. Ya done for..." Suddenly her eyes darkened and the soft smile disappeared, "He better treat you right."

"Now, come on, you two. I don't even know for sure how he feels! It's all too quick!"

"I knew my husband two weeks before I married him! We were married for forty-three years, and if he walked through that door today—I'd marry him again!...Adam Singleton!—I never figured you for a church-going type."

"I'm not! That's the ridiculous part of all this. I am not a Believer!...I don't see how this can work out!" Eve couldn't help but laugh.

"You're not going to let a little thing like God get in your way, are you dear? Besides, I have a feeling this....new development in your life, might make you see things differently!" Dilla was laughing too.

"Oh, no! Not me!...I'll take the man, but the Cloth is not part of the deal!"

"Well, don't fret, dear, they're all pretty much the same when the Cloth comes off!"

"Dilla!—Say it isn't so!" The two women were laughing together.

"...They take everything you are." The girl said this in a low tone, but its intensity cut through the laughter. The girl was sitting holding her cup, her eyes far away.

"...What, dear?..." Dilla looked at the girl.

Mirabel seemed to come back to them, "That's what Hetty says. Holy men...they're the worst..."

"Oh, dear, men are men! There are good ones and bad ones. I think Eve's found herself a really good one!...I am; I'm so happy for you. I really hope this works out. You deserve the best!"

"...Thank you, Dilla!...I...that's very kind....As a matter of fact, we'd better get going. Services start in five minutes. This time—whatever he preaches—I'm not going to argue with him!"

"Just be you, dear. He'll love you for that!"...

***

"I met him at Sam's Club! Can you believe it? I didn't think anything about it at the time! He asked me if the cinnamon rolls were any good, and I recommended them...and we talked. He gave me his number, but I didn't think...anyway when we got home yesterday I thought, "What the hell!' and I called him and invited him to come with me to Fellowship— And he came! Eve—He's a doctor! An Oncologist at Mass General! He's divorced. He's lovely, and I am going to make him all mine!—You're still interested in Adam Singleton, aren't you?" Marian flashed a suspicious look at Eve.

"Don't worry, Marian, I'm not interested in your new 'find.'" Eve couldn't help but chuckle at Marion's territorial declaration.

"We're going out for brunch later! Oh, my God, oh my God! I can't believe it! He's so...sweet! I'm in love already—but I'm not going to blow it. I'm going to take it slow. I'm going to build a good, solid relationship before I pounce on him!"

The two woman observed the man. He was balding, fiftyish, but trim with a kind face. He was impeccably dressed in a blue blazer and tan slacks. The tan on his face read as someone who perhaps spent time on the water—in a boat, Eve guessed. He was standing by the coffee urn sipping from a paper cup and talking to Mira, who listened attentively but made very few comments. There were several other men and boys by the coffee urn subtly eyeing Mirabel, but maintaining a polite waiting distance until she had finished her conversation with the good doctor.

Several women stood in a clutch on the side of the hall watching the men and obviously disgusted by their attention to the girl. Adam had been buttonholed at the far end of the hall by a young couple and was engaged in an intense conversation. Whatever they were discussing, it was clear that no one should interrupt, and so no one did.

Adam's sermon, the part that Eve actually listened to, was the old saw about the prostitute who was about to be stoned, and how Jesus had told the crowd to throw their rocks if they were without sin...Eve hadn't really been able to listen; she just kept looking at him and thinking about how he was unlike any other man she had ever met. She couldn't help but smile during the entire sermon. That man up there...she was in love with him! *She* was—Eve Truesdale—the Dragon Lady of Novus and Gardner! She was totally, stupidly in love. How...unlikely!

"OK, that's enough time spent with the beautiful girl! Time for me to reign him in. C'mon, Eve, I'll introduce you, but argue with him and I'll claw your eyes out!" Marian was only half joking.

"I will be as agreeable as a lamb!" Eve followed her to the coffee urn.

"Dr. Nelson Whittaker, this is Eve Truesdale, my neighbor."

"Eve." Whittaker offered his hand and smiled.

"Nelson, Marian tells me it was cinnamon buns that got you here!"

"That was just a cover! She's a flashy lady—I like flashy!" The man smiled pleasantly and gave his full attention to Marian, which made her absolutely twitter with delight.

"It's true, I have an eye for style!....Speaking of which, Mirabel, I was right; those colors are perfect on you!"

Mirabel smiled slightly and looked away coyly.

"This young lady belongs in a magazine! I was just telling her that her coloring is very unusual, and the skin tones...she's an amazing specimen!" Whittaker was doing his best to be charming, and it was working, Eve decided.

"'Specimen!' Nelson, I am going to have to teach you how to talk to women. 'Specimen' is not a compliment!"

"I just meant that the combination of her eyes and hair color are near perfection...and look at her skin—not a freckle! Very unusual."

"It sounds like you're ready to put her in a jar! Now you come on with me! You can save all those clinical compliments for me!"

"I guess I have to pay off with brunch now." He smiled fondly at Marian, and it made Eve glad to see her with an appreciative man. At least on the surface, he seemed a good match for her, and Eve was hopeful for her. The two of them headed outside the church hall.

The young couple was finally showing signs of releasing Adam. "Mira, would you mind waiting here for another minute? I want to rescue Adam before he gets waylaid by another needy congregant."

As Eve walked away, the small clutch of men at the urn were jockeying for position. A boy of perhaps seventeen was a little faster than the rest, and he boldly walked right up to Mirabel.

"Hey..." The boy stood there, feet spread apart, striking his best mating pose.

Mirabel nodded and said nothing, but there was a tiny smile at the corners of her mouth and her eyes flashed with mischief.

"...You from out of town?..." The boy was searching for things to say.

Mirabel let him twist. She nodded again.

"You know, I got a car. You wanna go for a ride?"

"...A 'ride?'" Mira raised an eyebrow and looked directly into his eyes.

"W-well we could stop somewhere. If you want..." The boy came closer to her with an attitude of conspiracy. "I got a bottle of whiskey in the trunk."

"...That so?..." Mira looked up; across the room was a small group of girls. Among them one, a petite blonde, was watching the two of them, nearly in tears. She looked closely at the girl; the signs were unmistakable. "Sonny boy, that little girl over there...the blonde one—who's she to you?"

The boy looked over at the girls and quickly dismissed them. "Uh...nobody. They're just girls from church."

"Uh, huh...how old are ya?..." Now Mira was nailing him with her eyes, and he couldn't look away.

"Seventeen! Look, I know what I'm doing. I'm not some kid. I been around!"

"Ya might want to talk to that little girl. I think she's got some...mighty important things to say to ya." Mirabel was trying to push him off, but the boy wouldn't relent.

"Look, you don't wanna pass me up. I got moves!" With that the boy grabbed Mirabel's arm

Mirabel looked down at the boy's hand gripping her and then she looked deeply into his eyes. She spoke quietly but deliberately, "Sonny boy, one night with me and your little prick would fall off! Now get off, or I'll be talkin' to that lady in the hat over there. She might like to know how her little darlin' gets on with women!"

The boy cringed as though he had been hit, and slunk away. Mirabel watched him go and continued to smile.

"Mira! This is Adam—Reverend Singleton—after all it is Sunday, and this *is* church Fellowship." Eve led Adam over by his arm but he hung slightly back.

"Mira—Is it OK if I call you Mira?—" The minister nodded halfway to a little bow and Mira focused on him, looking him in the eye.

"It's my name...."

For the moment Adam was caught by the frankness of her stare, "...I-I noticed the Glazer boy talking to you. He didn't say anything...inappropriate, did he?"

"...Just...bein' a boy."

"He's our 'wild child.' I've spoken to his mother, but she thinks her son can do no wrong."

"...She'll find out soon enough." Mirabel looked over at the blonde girl sitting miserably by herself in a metal folding chair.

"How's that?..." Adam cocked his head as if he hadn't heard correctly.

"...He weren't no trouble. Just a young buck smellin' himself." Mirabel could see the man cloud behind his eyes."—Sorry...guess I been too long in the barnyard."

"...No, I get it. It actually fits" Singleton was still struck by the depth of her eyes. She was...beautiful. It was disturbing, but he could feel himself responding to her.

Mirabel smiled again, that small, knowing smile; she turned her full gaze back on the minister. "...Once men get the hunger...It don't go away...does it, Reverend?"

"...Well...I'm...glad he didn't bother you..." Singleton pulled his thoughts away from her. She was...compelling; it was difficult, but he wouldn't let himself continue.

The girl lowered her eyes as if in modesty and the smile on her face broadened slightly. She stepped back slightly.

"You were a long time with that couple! I was jealous!" Eve's eyes glittered with mischief.

"I am the minister..." He couldn't help but sound a little officious.

"...Why don't you come out tonight? I'll fix dinner."

"No....uh...I have a few things to attend to—I'll call you."

"...OK... I have to be in New York tomorrow...When I get back?"

"...Sure. Eve, I've got to ...talk to people." There was so much Singleton wanted to say to her, but not now. He couldn't face it now. He already felt ridiculous; he couldn't let that be seen by those around him. "I—I'll call you." He pulled away and immediately began to talk to some of the other members of the congregation. He forced himself to be jovial, upbeat...concerned with them. It was a good way to bury his feelings.

Eve watched him circulating among the other people. She felt admiration for his devotion. "Mira, that man is definitely...special."

The girl watched along with her as Singleton mingled with the other people in the hall. "Hetty don't think much of holy men..."

"...What do you think, Mira?"

The girl watched Singleton for a long moment before answering, "...He's a strong one...don't know if he's good..."

"Oh, he's good, Mira...he's very good!"

***

CHAPTER 29

"We're not paying for that load of crap! Half of it's fake!" Donna was livid. Dennis, her ex-husband, stood there with a bemused smile on his face.

"What difference does it make? It'll sell. *I* can sell it!"

"We're not going to start selling phony antiques to the trade! We didn't build this business on fakes.—Our marriage, maybe, but not our business."

"You bitch!"

"Bitch, back at you! Send it back!"

"It's already sold! Back Bay Design wants it!..."

"Do they know most of it's repro? Did you tell them?"

"Of course not! Those dizzy queens wouldn't know shit from Sheraton! As long as it looks expensive. They'll mark it up and sell it to their clients and everybody wins!"

"Until someone figures it out. Then it comes back to us!—Call them. Tell them!"

"I'm sorry, you must have mistaken me for someone who listens to you!" The man pursed his lips and folded his arms.

"Fine..." Donna marched to the large desk in the office and began to pick up the receiver.

"What are you doing?" Dennis rushed to the table and pulled the receiver out of her hand.

"Give me the phone!"

"Go home, Donna! Stop playing business woman—"

"So *you* can?...Give me that phone, Dennis!" Donna lunged at the phone and grabbed it out of his hand. In reflex, the man pushed her away and she lost her balance, falling over a tufted footstool and knocking a small pile of silver trays to the floor with a terrible crash. As she fell, she grazed her forehead on one of the trays and opened up a shallow but nasty scratch that immediately began to gush blood. She rolled over on the floor dazed for a moment wiping the blood that was beginning to drip down her right eye. "You son-of-a bitch!"

Hearing the crash, the driver of the shipment rushed into the office, "Hey!" He moved on Dennis without any hesitation and landed a roundhouse right on his jaw. The antiques dealer went down like a sack of rocks. The driver sprung over to Donna and lifted her off the floor, "You all right, miss? You want me to call an ambulance?"

Donna looked at the driver. He was about thirty-five, working-class, but decent looking, and strong. He held her like a child without any hint of strain. She indicated her ex-husband in a heap on the floor, "...Maybe for him..."

***

CHAPTER 30

"Close the door, Jace..." It had been a hectic morning. Clients were ringing up wanting to talk about the market's volatility. They were all worried about something. It seemed nobody was happy about anything, and Eve had spent most of her time calming them down, answering questions and, eventually, recommending new things. It was always her strategy with nervous clients to deflect and redirect. If you kept them focused on future payout, they became less focused on short-term losses.

"What's up, boss-lady?..."

Eve eyed him as she rounded her desk to put a little distance between the two of them. It wasn't as though she was worried about his spontaneous amorous advances—not at the office, anyway. Jace was always careful about that. He seemed to regard that arena as sacrosanct. He knew his boundaries there. Finally she handed him the small box.

"I want to give this back to you..." She didn't want to look at him but she forced herself to face him squarely.

"...I told you I didn't want this back. Keep it. I'll wear you down, you know. I was serious, Eve, you're the only woman I want. You get me! All the others....it's just entertainment."

"Jace, I might 'get' you, but that's not what I want. Not anymore. That doesn't mean I don't care about you, and it doesn't mean I don't want you around—as a colleague, but we can't keep...doing what we've been doing. It's not good for either one of us."

"It's good for me!"

"Jace...please...."

"...Ok....You'll come around!"

"...That's Jace Brillig!..." Eve was relieved when he put the box in his pocket.

"What about Novus and Gardner...?" He sat on the arm of the leather sofa folding his arms.

"'What about Novus and Gardner?'...What do you mean?"

"Well, are we still going to shake them up, you and me?" He cocked his head like a dog listening for his cue.

"You still want to own the place, huh?"

"Every last pencil and paper clip!...*We* can do it!"

Eve smiled at his outrageous self-assurance, "...Sure! Why not?"

"See?..." Jace got up from the sofa arm and swaggered toward the door, "You're not done with me yet!" He pushed open the door and walked down the hall looking as if he had just come from any other business meeting.

As she watched him go, Eve felt a pang of conscience. She had used him—but it was mutual. What was she thinking? Was she thinking?....She was glad it was over, and now she had Adam. It made her smile to think how comfortable that made her feel. She had never felt like this—better late than never. Just three days and she'd be back in Holmsford...

***

CHAPTER 31

They sat in a small clutch of folding chairs in the dingy basement meeting room. Some were veterans, and some, like Libby, were first-timers. They were mostly a pretty ratty lot. Libby was the only person there who was well-groomed and 'professional' looking. It made her uncomfortable to stand out so much in the group. She could feel some of them looking at her wondering who she was.

It surprised her to see so many women—at least half the group were women. In a far corner, a young man of perhaps nineteen or twenty sat fidgeting and miserable. Libby recognized the symptoms—he needed a drink! So did she, but she was determined! This time it ended. No more false starts! She would put the 'genie' back in the bottle and there he would stay! That's why she had come all the way to Boston—away from Holmsford—somewhere where there was distance between her and the crushing grief. Somewhere where she could fight.

Finally, the group leader came to a small wooden podium and began, "Hi, I'm Steve."

"Hi, Steve..." The group responded perfunctorily.

"...And I'm an alcoholic..." The middle-aged man told his story, and before long the group seemed to coalesce into a single organism. The ritual was powerful, and soon Libby began to feel less ashamed of being among them. They all shared the same demon. They were all there to defeat him. She began to feel a sense of 'safety in numbers.' There were two 'new members' who took the podium next, a plain woman with greasy hair who Libby was surprised to find out was a computer programmer. She had begun as a 'social drinker' and quickly became addicted to alcohol. She had been drinking secretly for nearly two years until the alcohol had overtaken her discretion. She came to work rolling drunk one morning, and she was fired on the spot. She hadn't worked in six months, and her savings were gone. The next was a young father of two, a delivery driver. Driving drunk had landed him in court and he had been sent here on probation as the last stop before jail.

Finally, the leader came back to the podium and said, "Anyone else?" Libby could feel him looking at her. It was now or never. She closed her eyes, and she could hear her son, Brad, say, "Mom, you're the strongest woman I know!" She took a deep breath and rose from her seat. To her surprise, there was a small encouraging round of applause. She set herself in motion and walked to the platform, taking her place looking out at the sad little group.

"Uh...Oh, fuck!" She sank for a moment, but not a person flinched. They waited patiently for her to recover. "Uh...I'm...Libby."

"Hello, Libby!"

"...Hi....and...I'm...I'm an alcoholic..."

***

CHAPTER 32

"Sit down, Jace..." Harold Gardner shut the door to his office as Jace entered. The old man moved heavily. His tone was friendly enough, but Jace was alert to any changes in his voice. Gardner did not bring you in to his office unless he had a definite agenda. The old man lumbered to his chair and sat.

"So, Jace, how are things going? You feel you're moving ahead here in the company?" Gardner sounded decidedly avuncular.

"Our department is the most productive in the firm. I think we're doing well."

"That's not what I asked you, Jace. I want to know if you feel *you're* going somewhere, *personally*." Gardner was regarding him with that steely stare of his. Jace did his best to be casual.

"...Are you unhappy with my performance, Mr. Gardner?"

"Not at all! Relax, Jace, I have no complaints about the work you're doing. In fact, I've been hearing about how much you contribute to the department. You're Eve's 'right hand man!'—I believe that's what I was told. She relies on you for quite a lot of support." Gardner smiled his cold smile and kept his gaze on the younger man.

"...We work well together. Ms. Truesdale, is...amazing with clients. The best I've seen." Jace was trying to be careful. He could sense Gardner was digging.

"And your expertise is in values—isn't that right? I understand your trading record is pretty 'amazing' all by itself."

"Thanks. I usually consult with Eve—Ms. Truesdale—but I'm doing all right."

"More than 'all right!' More than 'all right!'...You satisfied with that?" Gardner stopped smiling when he asked this.

"The bonus was...generous this year," Jace sidestepped waiting to see where the old man was going.

"Chicken shit!"

"...I'm sorry?"

"C'mon, Brillig, 400K ain't bad, but in the scheme of things that's chicken shit! You want to spend your career as Eve Truesdale's errand boy, or do you want to make some real money?" Gardner had fixed his eye on Jace and he was measuring the moment.

"...Actually, I expect to take over the place in a few years." Jace decided to test the water. It would either be taken as a joke or...he'd be out the door.

The old man flushed deep red and his bushy eyebrows knitted deeply. Finally, he expelled what seemed to be a yowl that resolved into a wheezing belly laugh, "Ha, ha, ha!...So, you do have balls!"

"...I'm serious. Three—maybe four years, I could do it." Jace decided to push it just as far as the old man could take it.

Gardner held his smile and this steely eyes narrowed as they looked into Jace's, "Good!...That's what I'm looking for!....How would you like to run that department instead of assisting?"

It was Jace's turn. He burst into laughter and then suddenly stopped when he saw that Gardner wasn't laughing..."What are you talking about?..."

***

CHAPTER 33

The ride home was good. It had become almost a ritual. As Eve drove out of New York, she could feel the tension leaving her body as the distance from the city increased. She would leave at eight o'clock, and the drive would take her only three and a half hours. A little classical music and she was able to breathe. This drive seemed all the sweeter because she spent most of it thinking about Adam.

It was odd how all this had come about—her move, the house, her new-found friendships with women she would never have met before. If she thought about it, she hadn't ever had women friends. Just Gram—and she was a parent, not a friend. That one night with Adam was the greatest surprise. She was no stranger to men. Jace was just a less-likely liaison in a small but instructive series of relationships. None of them had fazed her. No one had caught her up, changed her direction, or reached her in any deep way. She had thought it was the way of life. Men and Women...collided. That was the only way to think of it. Sometimes they enjoyed the company, and ultimately they either disengaged and went on—or married. But why—she had no clue.

Now she did. Adam's touch—she felt it! She knew it. She knew she was his ...home! That was it! She was his home, and it made her feel the same towards him. She had never felt that from a man. It wasn't just sex. It wasn't just passion. This deep acceptance of one another was there that first time. It was as if they had always been together. It made her smile every time she thought of it. The revelation that something like this could happen to her at this stage of life...Not that she was old! She didn't feel old—and certainly not now! She felt a pang of sadness that she might have missed this—that she had lived this long without feeling this.

What to do?...When one has an epiphany?..How do you proceed?

She texted him: "Home tonight. Call me. See you tomorrow?"

As she pulled into the drive at Cloven Terrace, lights were on in her house, and she was suddenly reminded that Mira was staying with her. She really hadn't given it a thought all week. It was strange to see her own house lit up and so alive! There was something...warm about it. It was the first time she had any feeling for the place. Lit up like this and with the sense that there was somebody home, it made her feel for the first time a connection to what having a "home" really meant.

As she walked up the drive, she heard music playing, and she paused. It amused her to know that Mira was doing something for her own pleasure—that she had an inner life. She stopped and listened at the door:

> Every breath you take
> Every move you make
> Every bond you break
> Every step you take
> I'll be watching you
>
> Every single day
> Every word you say
> Every game you play
> Every night you stay
> I'll be watching you...

She put her key in the lock and turned it, and almost instantly the music stopped as she entered. Mira stood at the far side of the hall in her jeans and boots. She had an apron tied in front of her and she seemed a little embarrassed.

"...Didn't know when you'd be back..." The girl was wiping her hands on the apron.

"Listen to your music, Mira! I told you to make yourself at home!"

"..Oh..no. I was ...just...I made supper. I guess you're hungry."

"You did?...That is so nice!—have you eaten?"

"...Thought I'd wait...'til you got here. It ain't much...just a stew. It's ready, if you want it."

"I am starving! C'mon, Mira let's have a feast!"

The two of them sat at the dining room table. A huge blue tureen stood in the middle with the most heavenly aroma coming from it. On a cutting board next to it, sat a fresh loaf of peasant bread still hot from the oven.

"My God! You baked bread?" Eve couldn't believe how wonderful it smelled.

"Eyah....Hetty says bread is like handwritin,' everybody's got their own! Mine's not much, I guess, but it's hot." The girl took the bread knife and cut a chunk of the bread and put it steaming on the small bread plate by

Eve's side. She had set the table just as Eve would. Everything was perfect, down to the candles and a freshly washed and ironed table cloth. "...That there's goat butter. I made it."

She pushed a small chilled crock toward Eve, who eagerly slathered a dollop onto the bread and took a deep bite....

"...Mira, this is...wonderful! I've never—this is delicious! I've never had goat butter!..."

"Takes a bit 'o doin'...Thought you might like it.—You want some stew?"

"Please!" The girl began to ladle out a generous portion of stew upon the delicate plates. "Wait, Mira!....." Eve rose and went quickly to the kitchen. In a moment she returned with a chilled bottle of wine. "I've had this in the cooler for over a week. It's a good, crisp wine...Let's have some..." She opened the bottle and poured two glasses. She lifted her glass, and, mimicking her, Mira raised hers. Eve lightly clinked the glasses, "To...being home!"

Mira nodded and sipped quickly at her glass before putting it down.

The two women fell upon the meal and ate almost in silence. Finally Eve slowed and sat back satisfied.

"That...was incredible! Mira, you're a wonderful cook!"

"...Just a stew. Not much to it."

Eve looked at the girl for a moment, "...I tell you a boy likes you—you say he'd better stay away. Someone tells you you're beautiful—you look away....I tell you you're a good cook—you say it's 'not much'. What's that, Mira?"

The girl looked down at her plate to avoid making eye contact. "Don't know what you mean."

"...I think you do. It's not modesty, is it? You *know* your gifts." Eve scrutinized the girl. She sat quietly with her eyes down.

"...The world goes on. Nobody needs to see me...."

"Everybody does see you, Mira! How could they not? Look at you; you're a perfect beauty!"

The girl shook her head without lifting her eyes, "...I don't reckon..."

"You're as close as it comes! I've seen how men react to you! Don't tell me you don't notice that!"

"...That's when the trouble comes..." The girl finally looked up and stared at Eve.

"Don't tell me you don't feel good when you're admired."

"They look; then they want to touch! You're some kinda vittles to be chewed up and spit out if the taste ain't right.

"...You're too young to think this way—"

"Young...all the...feelin's. The wants and needs pullin' ya this way an' that! For what? Comes down to the same thing. Most times It don't go well."

"...It's a long life alone, Mira..."

"It's longer spent twistin' yourself into somethin' you ain't. *You* know that. I see you! You don't make yourself into nothin' for nobody! You make your own way."

"Mira...I think you have a greater opinion of me than I deserve..."

"You don't ask for nothin' an' you don't take nothin'. You give...more'n you get! An' you don't let nothin' get to ya! I see."....

"Looks good, doesn't it? I'm in charge! I run a major department in an investment firm. I court and soothe clients. I make a lot of money—and I'm completely isolated from people. Oh, I see people—-every day, but, until just recently, I've never been touched...not really...not by anyone. Don't you go by me, Mira."

"...I could go by worse...I'll get the plates..." The girl rose and cleared their plates. The small smile lingered in her eyes as she took them out to the kitchen.

Eve sipped her wine worriedly. "...Some mentor I am!..." She poured herself another glass of wine, as Mirabel returned from the kitchen carrying a small cake.

"...Dessert?...You made a dessert too?"

"Spices and some flour. You had everythin'....Hetty wants you to come to supper." The girl cut the cake in two halves and put one on her own plate, leaving the other for Eve.

"Hetty?—She's back?"

The girl stuffed a huge forkful of cake into her mouth, "...Not yet..soon...got some things to talk to ya about."

"When?..." Eve lifted the cake onto her dessert dish and sampled a small bite. The ginger and other spices filled her nose and mouth. "This is....this is...heavenly!..."

"Next week...a-Friday...if you'll come."

"Of course! We can tell her all about the things we've done!"

"...Eyah...we can..."

"...She's done with her business?.."

"Don't know...didn't talk about that..."

"...Friday...what time?"

"...Sundown...thereabouts..."

"...Of course...after chores."

"Hetty's a good one for work..." The girl smiled again and put another chunk of cake in her mouth.

Eve did the same and the two enjoyed the taste together. "...I called my grandmother 'Gram.'"

"...We're past that, Hetty an' me." It was a flat statement. There was no emotion behind it, just a fact.

"...So you're close then."

"...You could say. You gonna finish that?"

The girl had her fork poised over Eve's piece of cake ready to pounce. "Oh, no! This is *my* cake, and I'm going to savor it!" Eve pulled the plate away from the raised fork.

"The way you was goin' at it, I thought maybe you didn't want it!" The girl tried again with the fork laughing as she did.

"You get away! Just because I didn't wolf it down, doesn't mean I don't like it. Sometimes it's better if you take your time!" Eve lifted the plate away from Mirabel's reach altogether.

The girl smiled with her fork still raised, "...Eyah....That's so...but then you might lose it!" Mirabel made another stab for the cake, and Eve rose with her little plate holding it ahead of her as the two dodged around the dining table laughing.

***

CHAPTER 34

"I've got the votes in my pocket."

"Nothing's done until it's done!...I want this thing tied up by the fifteenth. If your friends don't deliver, don't expect anything from me, Marlin. I pay for results!"

"Have I ever let you down? Whatever you wanted, you got! I did that! Me. I'm telling you those guys couldn't wipe their own asses without my say so! I'm gonna save that Goddamn town in spite of all of 'em!"

"Fine...If that's what you need to think. But I want that land in my pocket by deadline or the deal's off, you hear me?"

The little lounge was nearly empty. It was too early for lunch. Marlin and Reedy sat in a rear booth with steaming cups of coffee in the dim light. It was an anonymous little place picked out by Reedy to insure that no one would know either man. Marlin had trouble finding it in the cluster of fast-food places and strip mall stores just off 95. Reedy was there ahead of him waiting impatiently.

"I hear you....So what's the hurry? Why by the fifteenth?—You never cared about the time it took before. What's the rush?"

"Just get the vote done, Marlin. That's all you need to do. You deliver that parcel on time, and I'll make your last bonus look like a waiter's tip!"

"Look, Jim, I don't mind...using my influence on your behalf if it's good for the town. But I don't want to do anything to hurt Holmsford! I live there too, you know. I have...a certain position to maintain—"

"And you do it well, Jack! You do a great job! 'Chairman of the Board of Selectmen,' I know how much that means to you. Why would we invest so much in Holmsford, if we were planning to do anything that would devalue that and the other holdings we have in the town? This project has certain time constraints, that's all. If Holmsford doesn't feel it can respond for whatever reason, we can always go to a neighboring town and make inquiries."

"No! That...that's not necessary, Jim. I said I would deliver. That land will be available to you by the fifteenth. I guarantee it!"

"I want it *closed* by the fifteenth, not just 'available.'"

"All right...fine...closed....I've got it covered."

***

CHAPTER 35

"Where are you goin'?" The man lay on the bed spread-eagled and naked. He was spent and sleepy and grabbed Donna's hand as she slipped by getting dressed.

"Out. I'm late..." She pulled against him gently. "Len, I promised the girls I'd be there."

"Un-promise 'em. Gimme a minute, and I can go again..." He pulled her down on the bed and began to cover her with his body.

"Lenny! You're gonna mess up my hair!...Let me go!" Donna pushed her way out of bed and went to the mirror to survey the damage.

The man rolled to his side with his head propped on his hand to admire her as she primped, "I'm crazy about you. Stay here and I'll prove it to you!"

"I'm having dinner with my girlfriends. I promised them."

"...How do I know you ain't goin' out to meet some other guy?..."

"...I guess you have to take my word." Donna primped in front of the mirror, repairing the damage his clumsy caresses had made.

"That faggot you married didn't know what he was missin'. If he did...he wouldn't be no faggot no more! Woman, you're killin' me!"

"Come back tomorrow, and I'll finish you off." She continued to review her reflection in the mirror.

"Just try an' keep me away!" The man landed a resounding slap on her rear and Donna stiffened and turned to him.

"Don't!" It was a warning clear and definite, but the man didn't see that. He was too full of satisfaction to catch the steely gleam in her eye as she walked out the door.

***

"Don't you fucking say anything, Marian! Don't you criticize and don't tell me what to do!"

"I didn't say anything!" Marian sat at the table trying her best to look hurt.

"The hell you didn't. He's not Charlie Manson, for Christ's sakes!"

"I'm just saying, you don't know this boy. You don't know anything about him! Asking him to stay with you...It's..it's just not wise, Libby!"

The four of them sat around Libby's vast dining table again. Libby had made another huge dinner and summoned them all for one of their soirees.

"He's a kid, for Christ's sakes! Jonas' parents threw him out! Just like that! I mean what kind of parent does that to a kid? And he's a great kid. He's kind, he's sensitive...likes to cook—that casserole? He made it! He even helped me pick out this dress! Tell me, he's some kind of psychopath!"

"...Honey...he's also into drugs—"

"Not anymore!—I told you that!"

"How do you know that? Libby, he's homeless!...AND...he's an alcoholic!"

"...So am I, Marian...does that make me—Godzilla? I wasn't' going to leave him in Boston to roam the streets. He's only nineteen fucking years old! All I did was offer him a room for a while—until he can get on his feet. You should see!—Neat as a pin! Keeps his room better than I keep mine! We go to meetings together—support each other! Eve! Tell her it's all right!"

"...Well...Libby..." Eve wasn't expecting to referee, "...I think Marian's just concerned for you. It's...a little risky, but if your instincts are telling you it's all right,...go with it. I'm proud of you going to the meetings! That's the big news here!"

"There, you carping crone! See? Eve thinks it's fine! And what the hell did *you* have to say about my going to AA? Huh? Nothing!"

"You know I think it's wonderful! I said so! Why do you always twist my words? Libby, this is the biggest thing you've done for yourself since—since forever! Applause! Applause!...OK?"

"...OK...it's insincere, but it's better than Goddamn criticism."

"Insincere? Insincere! I like that! I give you encouragement and support...and...and support...and what do you give me? Huh? Nothing but hostility! You haven't even asked about Nelson! Not once!" Marian was getting that tight-lipped look she got when Libby was really getting under her skin.

"OK. I knew it would come to that...you got yourself a doctor! Congratulations! You fulfilled a lifetime dream. You went out and got yourself a Goddamn doctor! Whoooopeeeee!"

"You should see the size of his boat!" Marian was holding her pride in behind a tightly held smile.

"Is that a new word for it?" Libby chuckled.

"...I'm not even going to entertain your jealousy!...50 feet! It's got a stateroom! He took me sailing on it. It was a dream!...Of course I did get a little seasick."

"Ha! That must have turned him on!" Libby countered.

"He didn't care at all! He held my head. He fed me saltines. He's the nicest man I ever met!...We sailed out to the Elizabeth Islands...it was...wonderful! Best of all, I've lost another five pounds! Nelson doesn't care—he likes me...zaftig, but the weight is just peeling off me! I'm going to look like a fashion model just for him!...and what about you, Eve? How's the good Reverend Singleton?"

Eve was tongue-tied for a moment, "...Fine!...Uh,...I haven't seen him yet...We texted."

"...There's a Romantic!" Libby's tone was acerbic. "I'm glad I'm not part of this whole Goddamn social network thing! Nobody talks! Whatever happened to talking?"

"He had a Chamber of Commerce meeting and then...something at the Church. I'll catch him after services tomorrow...." Eve was disappointed, but she reasoned that Adam had responsibilities. He was a figure in the town just as she held a position in the firm. It was his job. She wasn't going to put any pressure on him.

"But it's Saturday night! Date night!—or doesn't his religion allow him to go out on dates?" Libby was probing.

"Oh...we've had dates. A few...When do you see Nelson again, Marian?"

"What I want to know is..." Libby cut in, "How big is the Reverend's 'boat'?—or haven't you 'floated' it yet?"

"Libby!—"Marian acted shocked but couldn't help laughing.

"C'mon, Eve, give! How is the Reverend in 'lay' terms?" Libby was pressing now, and Eve was beginning to become annoyed.

"...Oh, I'll bet he's a man of *deep* convictions!" Marian giggled to herself as the other women around the table applauded.

"Halleluja!" Libby shouted as the others laughed. Eve smiled, but she didn't like this adolescent speculation about Adam and her.

"Where's Mirabel? Why didn't she come with you tonight?" Marian interrupted.

"I asked her! I told her she was invited, but she said she had chores to do. Hetty's coming back; she said there were some things she wanted to finish."

"Is Mirabel going away?" Marian seemed alarmed.

"I don't think so...I..I don't see why she should." This was something that hadn't occurred to Eve. It somehow vaguely alarmed her.

"Didn't you say she worked somewhere else on a farm? Won't she have to go back if Hetty's home? I don't want her to go. She's our good luck charm!"

"Good luck charm? What the fuck are you talking about, Marian?" Libby shot at Marian.

"Well, she is! Look what's happened to us. You have Jonas staying with you; you're going to AA. Eve has her the Hot Reverend, and *I* have Nelson—Wonderful Nelson! All since Mirabel came. Doesn't that qualify her as a good luck charm?"

"...Eve had Singleton *before* she showed up." Donna pointed out.

"Oh...all right! But I like her! Don't you? She's so...Well, she reminds me of myself!"

"Let's face it, Marian, none of us was ever that pretty! Jesus Christ, if I had her looks—let's just say I'd have a lot more to show for myself!"

All the women murmured agreement.

"...I...have someone new." As usual Donna waited for a lull in the conversation to drop in.

"Christ, you have someone new every other day, Donna. It's a wonder your charge card doesn't wear out!"

Donna was unfazed by Libby's crass remark. "No. I mean I *have* someone. Not...like that. I have a guy."

"You mean a relationship? Really? Donna!" Marian reached across the table to her, but Donna pulled away.

Eve noticed a small, soft smile on Donna's face. She wasn't sure if it was her imagination, but Donna seemed somehow...a little shy. Even her tone was different. The edge was missing and there was an uncertainty behind her eyes for the first time since Eve had met her.

"...What's he like, Donna?" Eve watched her as she wrestled with the reveal of this new thing.

"...Just a guy, really....Name's Lenny...Lenny Stoller. He...helped me out...with something. He's a driver for one of our carriers."

"...A truck driver...?" Marian asked quietly, but the implication was plain.

"Yes, Marian...*just* a truck driver. He's rough around the edges. Not much education...and he's *all* man! He...he's completely mine...if I want him. All he sees is me."

"....Donna...you sound...unsure." Eve was quiet with this observation.

"...Yeah...well, this is a first for me. Guess I'm waiting for the other shoe to drop."

"Don't doubt it—enjoy it. So what if he's a truck driver! What difference does it make?" Eve could see feeling peeking out of Donna's eyes like a little girl half hiding in the bushes.

"...Maybe your friend *is* something of a good luck charm. Who knows..." Donna retreated again.

"To Mirabel! Our Good Luck Charm!" Marian raised her glass, and the other women raised theirs in response.

"...I didn't think about her leaving...." Eve was unsettled at the thought that Mira might go away, but she wasn't sure why. *"I'll ask Hetty,.."* She thought, remembering the dinner she was having with the old woman on Friday. Then she began to wonder why she needed to. After all, wasn't Mira an independent young woman?...Wasn't she? It was odd that she looked at Mira as a kind of dependent child, not really a woman by herself.

Why was it so difficult to think of the girl as anything but some kind of satellite around the old woman? It was odd, but then everything was...odd since she had come to Holmsford.

***

CHAPTER 36

She was there, at the back of the church. Adam was aware of her as soon as he entered the sanctuary. He could feel his neck burn. The choir finished "Lead on, Oh King Eternal" and he had to mount the pulpit and deliver his sermon. He knew he had to face this, but he had hoped that she might not be there...at least not just now.

He launched into his sermon almost as if he were on automatic. The back of his brain could only think of Eve. He wanted to touch her; hold her, and at the same time he wanted to scream at her, *"How could you do this?"*...Or was he really screaming at himself?

Mostly, he felt like a fool. He had pushed this. He had made the first move. He was hardly an innocent! He had let his own desire draw him into thinking that a woman like her would settle on a small-town Minister. Maybe she was curious. He flattered himself that he was an 'interesting diversion,' but what could he really offer her compared to the life she led?...He was trying to be 'modern' about it all, but every time he saw the image of the young man, bare-chested standing in her doorway, he felt a deep flush of anger and shame. It was all he could do to stifle his embarrassment. He had to try to extract himself from this...stupid mistake without laying the blame on Eve. He had to preserve some of his dignity ....he hoped.

> "...and so we have to forgive. Forgiveness is what allows us to live in the world. We forgive each other, and we must forgive ourselves...for our mistakes, our failings and weaknesses...and after forgiveness will come a greater understanding of God's plan. God bless...."

Singleton stepped briskly off the pulpit and headed to the little dressing room off the sanctuary. He was sweating and shaking, "Stupid! Stupid! Stupid!" he muttered to himself as he removed his outer vestments. Instead of heading to the back of the Church to greet congregants as he usually did, he paused in the little room to catch his breath and find his courage. Most of the congregation would go to the basement for Fellowship. He prayed for a gaggle of anxious congregants with pressing problems, so that he could avoid a lengthy scene with Eve. He didn't think he could handle that.

The church hall was full of the usual people. Both coffee urns were being drained, but most of his flock seemed happily engaged in small talk. He made his way around the room greeting everyone, and trying to avoid getting to Eve, who stood patiently to the side, waiting by herself with a paper coffee cup and smiling in his direction.

"So sorry....A little warm for me....just took a moment to get some air...Nice to see you!...How's that arm?—all healed now?...Yes, very warm today...needed a little air....A little shorter than usual—are you complaining?...You're looking well!" He managed to avoid her until he could swallow his pride and actually speak to her.

"...I forgive you..." Eve offered her hand with a demure handshake being aware of the room full of people.

"Huh?..." Singleton barely heard the remark as his eyes found hers. She smiled and her eyes seemed to dance and sparkle, and he could feel himself lose it for a moment.

"...For not calling me! Oh, I know I can't compete with the likes of your...flock, but I do need to see my...pastor." She held on to his hand and squeezed it meaningfully. "How about brunch? We'll drive out somewhere."

"...Uh...I can't..." Adam gently pulled his hand from hers. "I..I have some church business to do. Eve, it's Sunday. I have to work."

"I know that!—So take a little break. Nobody's going to begrudge you a little time to...eat. Adam, I've been waiting all week to see you!"

"...This is what I do, Eve. I know it's not much on the surface, but...it's all I have."

"What?...What are you talking about?" Eve stepped back slightly and looked at him. He was avoiding eye contact and he seemed...embarrassed.

"Eve... I owe you an apology."

"...What?"

"I...I can't do this. It was foolish of me to...begin a relationship that obviously has no future. "

Eve could feel herself pull inside. She couldn't believe was hearing this.

"...Look, I'm not what you need. You make decisions involving millions of dollars. I...coach Little League baseball. I can't even get the parish books to balance!..."

He was standing there avoiding her eyes. What was happening? This wasn't the sly, subtle Adam Singleton who challenged her right from the start. This wasn't the gentle, insinuating man who exuded sexual interest with every counterpoint. Even arguing with him had been like making love! When they had finally gone to bed, it was as if their bodies had come to a fine and deeply satisfying agreement...a meeting of mind and body... A slick coating of anxiety was forming at the back of her throat as she watched him twist himself in front of her. Had she misread everything? Had she made all the same mistakes women make? Did she build up an Adam Singleton in her mind that didn't really exist?...How could she be so stupid? How could she be so...needy!?...

"Don't...do this..." She was still half inside her head trying to swim out of this cold-water pool in which she was suddenly immersed.

"You don't need me."

"You're going to tell me what I need?.."

"...C'mon, Eve..."

"That's for *me* to decide. If I tell you you're the man I *want*—that you're the *only* man I want—"

"You can't say that." Singleton seemed to challenge her in that second and then looked away, "...You can't say that..."

Eve looked at him unable to pull herself out. "...Maybe you're right...I guess...I let myself be carried away. I'm sorry!" Eve put down her cup on a nearby chair and quickly walked away.

As she did, Singleton called out to her, "Eve!....please...."

***

CHAPTER 37

It had to be done. The doe didn't kid. It remained terrified and fallow, and, worst of all, it had fixed on Eve, screaming for attention every time she came near. The beast had never settled in the pens. Once they were gotten, usually they forgot...settled in, became what they are,...but not this one!

Mirabel entered the pen, and the little tawny doe raced to the far side of the pen trying to bury itself in the rest of the herd. Mirabel waded through the tangle of other goats who scattered as she drew near. She succeeded in cornering the doe by the fence and slipped the noose over its head as it squirmed and screamed desperately.

"Settle down, you! No use fightin' You done this yourself! If ya' can't be useful one way, another'll do!—Come on!"

She half dragged the animal from the pen as it screamed and screamed. She was sure the beast knew its fate, the way it fought so.

Finally, they were at the barn. Quickly she tied the back legs together and hoisted it over the beam head down over a galvanized washtub underneath. The knives had been sharpened and hot water waited for her to wash up when it was done. There was always so much blood.

Quickly Mirabel seized the killing knife. She faced east and muttered the prayer to the Spirit of Life offering the life of the goat and expressing sorrow for the need to release it. In one deft move, she plunged the knife deeply into the animal's neck severing the carotid artery. The beast shuddered and let out a short, weak scream...and then hung loose on the line.

Expertly Mirabel gutted and bled it, letting the offal fall into the washtub. She sliced the pelt around the neck and hoofs, then along the four legs and tore down the skin like a sock inverting on a foot. It would be hung on the barn to dry, then softened and tanned. It was a beautiful color. She reckoned it would make a fine pair of slippers or a hat. It would sell. The meat would serve a fine meal, though more than two could eat. Some of it would be smoked and hung. One of the haunches would be roasted for Friday's meal. That had to be done right.

She went about the butchering almost without thinking. In less than an hour the beast had been knackered and quartered. The choicest cut went to the kitchen to be prepared. The rest she hung on the hooks in the small smokehouse. She'd banked the woodchips and they were smoldering in readiness. Nothing would be wasted.

The blood and offal she would take to the four corners of the property and offer it to the spirits as she had been taught.

She returned to the barn and washed thoroughly. The bloody apron was hung by the beam, and she was careful to clean the area completely. It was forbidden to leave any fragment behind. She changed her clothes and put all the stained items in the boiling pot outside to be washed clean and fresh with lye soap. These would be hung in the healing sun to remove any trace of the goat's terror.

Once all this had been done, the sun was high, and it was time to see to the meal that was to be prepared.

She stopped and carefully picked the right herbs in the dooryard before entering the house. Some of these were ones few knew about, herbs that had been cultivated from the time of the Founding. Some were traditional...sage, rosemary, parsley...but the others were herbs used by the tribes long ago and told to her family. Each one had a power and a healing. Each one had an aroma and a taste.

Once she had a fistful of the greens, she entered the house and placed them on the dry sink. The goat haunch lay soaking in a pot of cold well-water with a cloth atop it to keep the flies away. She removed the cloth and seized the meat, working it between her fingers to remove any taint of blood or dirt. She rinsed it the prescribed three times with fresh water and then dried it with the cloth, making sure that it was ready for preparation.

With a small hatchet, she chopped away the hoof at the ankle joint. Next she placed the haunch in the dry box to be salted and seasoned with the herbs. She quickly chopped the herbs she had collected and mixed them with coarse salt and pepper in a large bowl. She smeared this mixture liberally all over the meat, making sure it was covered thoroughly. She tied it inside a fresh cloth with a string and hung it by the massive fireplace to be spitted later. It would age over the day and be ready for roasting the following day for the evening meal. The seasoning would prevent it from turning while she worked to prepare the rest of the meal.

Once again she cleaned the space, making sure that no speck of meat or grease would touch the other dishes to be prepared. Vegetables would be collected and done at the last moment. Bread would be made two to three hours before so that it was still warm at table. But the honey tarts could be done now. They would need time to soak in the honey and raisins she would prepare next....

All this Mirabel did knowing that Hetty would want this to be perfect. It had been many years since a stranger had eaten at their table. There must be the best of everything—the best that they could offer. Nothing must be forgotten.

***

CHAPTER 38

The week had been miserable. After her scene with Adam, Eve had withdrawn from everyone. Normally she would have gone to Dilla's for a visit, but she couldn't bring herself to inflict her disappointment on the old woman. She had done this to herself! She still couldn't believe how easily she had let herself be sucked into believing she was in love. Was she really that lonely? Was she just a cliché, a woman approaching middle-age and making a last-ditch effort at 'pairing?'

She couldn't go to the the 'Girls.' They would, of course, commiserate, and bash all men, and invite her into their Victim's Club. She wouldn't do that! She would never let herself. There was no one to call, no one to speak to. Mirabel was staying at the farm and had left a note. In any event, she certainly wouldn't reveal her stupidity to her! She scorned herself—that was the only term that seemed to fit. She despised her rush into Singleton's arms. How could she be so...taken, and so quickly? Where was the 'Dragon Lady' of Novus and Gardner? Gone! Cut down by a 'St. George' of a country preacher. Fire out!....Idiot!

After her orgy of self-loathing, Eve realized that she had to do something. Sitting in her house and running over the scene again and again was driving her crazy. She packed a bag and headed for New York by mid-afternoon. At least if she worked, she could put some of the embarrassment behind her.

She drove her department, checking and re-checking with clients, reviewing accounts, and immersing herself in micro-managing every part of the business. The Dragon Lady was back. Even Jace cut a wide berth, sensing it better to avoid anything even close to casual conversation.

At the weekly meeting Harold Gardner sat at the end of the polished conference table taking reports and asking questions. When he got to Eve, she reported with cut and dried precision and delivered her view of her department without a wasted word.

Gardner paused and looked at her, "Well...that's something we haven't seen in a while!..."

"...I beg your pardon?..." Eve was surprised by the halt in the meeting.

"The 'Eve Truesdale Report.' Well done! Haven't seen that from you lately."

"...Harold, I always make a full report. You know that." Eve felt a flash of suppressed anger at the suggestion that she hadn't been doing her usual work.

"Of course you do. Of course you do! It's just...the style. That clipped, military delivery...That's the old Eve Truesdale."

"Harold, I don't know what you mean. I'm just reporting the department's business. If you're suggesting—"

"Don't get your garters in a twist, Eve! I'm just happy to see that you're returning to...to your usual format. Does this mean that you're back to a fuller schedule here at the office?"

Eve could feel her anger rising, but she managed to keep it down. The old boy was trying to embarrass her in front of the other partners. She knew he didn't like her being out of the office, but this was outrageous!

"As a matter of fact, Harold, I'll be out an extra day this week. I have a lead on some new accounts that I want to follow up on." It was a lie, but she wouldn't give him the satisfaction of thinking he could manipulate her in such an obvious way.

"Oh!...new accounts! Well, that's important....And the coverage here?"

"Jace is more than capable of taking the lead while I'm out. As usual I'll monitor the department's activities online and be in constant contact."

"...I see. Well, if that's everything, I move we end the meeting..." The partners rushed off. Most of them avoided Eve who lingered behind. Gardner was joking with one of men. It was locker-room banter and the two men broke into raucous laughter. Finally the other man left and it was only Gardner and Eve in the room.

"Harold, if you have any complaints with my work, have the guts to tell me to my face privately, instead of staging a ridiculous show like you just did." She was fuming and trying not to let her anger overwhelm her good sense.

"I'm sorry, Eve, did I embarrass you?" Garner was feigning surprise and not doing a good job of it.

"You know you did! I am doing the same work I always do. If you don't like the sound of my reports—"

"But I do! I thought I made that clear. Today's report was just like the old Eve would make—all fact and no nonsense."

"...Meaning my recent reports haven't been...satisfactory?"

"Not at all! Your reports are always very complete. It was simply a matter of style. You know, Eve, as a partner, you have a certain responsibility to...to reflect full dedication to the firm."

"Harold, I've told you I'm spending less time at the office. That is not a reflection of my dedication! I have earned this consideration, and I'm taking it."

Gardner looked at her for a long moment and then he exhaled, "Of course, you have, Eve. You do what you need to. Novus and Gardner will...adjust..."

"Thank you, Harold. I hope this is the last time we have to talk about this. I don't like having to confront you.—I'm...I'm quite fond of the firm...and you."

"Why, Eve...That's almost romantic!" Gardner smiled and his eyes danced slightly.

"Don't get carried away, Harold!" Eve laughed and Gardner joined her. There was something hollow in the sound of his laughter...

The ride back on Thursday was equally miserable. It rained heavily, and the visibility on the road was poor. It took Eve nearly an extra hour to get back to Holmsford.

She was determined to get back. In spite of Adam, she had made friends here. She had bought a house; she wasn't going to let one stupid mistake drive her away. It no longer mattered why she came back to Holmsford, or how she felt about Adam; it was a point of pride. She would be in charge of her life.

She pulled into the driveway and the house was dark. Mira must still be at the farm. Stepping out of the car she put her foot down in a puddle collecting there and the cold water penetrated her shoe. *"Perfect!"* she thought. She trudged up the walk with her left foot squishing the whole way and fumbled with the key in the lock. Finally, the door opened and she tossed her briefcase on the floor by the door, dropped her keys in the bowl on the little table by the hall tree, and went right upstairs to her bed.

She didn't even bother with pajamas; she just pulled off her wet things and collapsed exhausted.

***

CHAPTER 39

"We'll move it!"

"You can't do that, Jack! You can't just march into an old woman's home and tell her you're picking it up and moving it to another location—'Oh, and by the way, we're taking the lion's share of your property.'" Charlie Metcalf was nervously stirring his coffee as the two men hunched over their table in the Puritan House.

"We're not 'taking' her property, Charlie! We're buying it! At a good price too, I might add. The old girl won't have to keep goats anymore. With what she'll make on the sale she can live in style! It's not good for someone her age to live in an old shack, anyway. Charlie, we're improving her life!"

"The Livesey home is the only original farmhouse left in town, Jack! It's the only one for several towns around! Do you know how rare that is? The Historical Society with have a shit fit if you so much as mention touching it!"

"You mean Dilla Merkel? What's she gonna do? Besides we're not gonna destroy it; we're gonna preserve it! We'll move it away from the proposed Industrial Park and she'll have fifty *original* acres left. It she wants to go on living in that tumble-down hovel without electricity and running water, that's up to her! We'll make sure that every board and shingle are completely restored!...Reedy gave me his word."

"...It's not right, Jack. What kind of a town do we have if we sell out its history?" Metcalf was still stirring his coffee.

Marlin reached over and grabbed his hand, "What kind of a town do we have if we don't get some business in here, Charlie? You know we're dying. We're nothing but an off-ramp on the way to Boston! If we don't do something, Holmsford will be nothing but a road sign. You know I'm right."

"...I can't support you on this, Jack. I'm against it." Metcalf pushed Marlin's hand away and dropped the spoon. He looked directly at the man across the table.

Marlin sat back and smiled, "That's too bad, Charlie. You know I already have the votes. The Board of Selectmen will vote for eminent domain. Reedy will supply the funds. It's a done deal."

"You're a real son-of-a-bitch, you know that Jack?"

"Maybe. But I'm the son-of-a-bitch that's going to revitalize this town! With or without your support, Charlie!"

***

CHAPTER 40

"Well,...I'll be!...There it is! I knew I had it!"

It had been bothering her for days, ever since Eve and the girl had come to her shop. It was breathtaking! The girl was exactly the image of her grandmother! It was uncanny. At the back of her mind was the memory of something...a picture! She remembered a picture taken at a farmer's market decades ago. She and Rudy had opened the shop. Here it was tucked in an old paper album now yellowed with age.

In the foreground was Rudy, her Rudy! Handsome and young and standing next to a ridiculous pumpkin nearly the size of a chair. To the side was a stall and sitting behind the stall was a young Hetty Livesey. To her left stood Billy Ramsay.

"My God, you were a handsome devil, Billy!"...She had forgotten what a good looking young man he was, a shock of black curly hair and a smile that just begged for trouble. Hetty sat behind the stall seemingly lost in thought. She was beautiful! The black and white photo didn't do her justice, but it did capture the likeness. It was almost as if Mirabel were sitting there. What a striking couple the two of them made!...

Looking at the picture brought back a flood of old memories. She recalled when Billy took off. No warning. He simply walked away...from his farm...from Hetty...from everything. Folks went out to his farm; there was no one there. Hetty was questioned about him. She didn't know where he had gone. Some folks thought that Hetty had killed him and buried him somewhere. They knew how he was with women. It didn't go anywhere. There was no trace. The Ramsay farm went to the town for taxes eventually. Hetty stayed to herself for years. Every once and a while she'd come to town to the farmers market to sell goat's milk and cheese, but largely she was forgotten. Dilla was busy with her job, the shop, and her husband. She had been pregnant twice. She lost the babies both times; eventually they gave up on having children. Rudy had said, "Never mind, we'll have good times instead!" and they had. They had such good times! They came to an end when Rudy got sick, pancreatic cancer. It was a miserable death. She tended him until the end. It hadn't lasted long, but he was in such pain. When he died after four months, she was almost relieved. At least he wouldn't suffer any longer, and she could carry her own pain more easily than she could bear his.

There had been rumors of a child—that Hetty had a baby by Billy, a girl. Some said that they had caught sight of a young girl at the farm. By then Hetty was getting older, and she had a reputation for an irascible manner. When anyone asked about the girl, all she would say was, "She's off to school." Nobody bothered much. It was as if the Livesey place was not a part of this earth. It was there, all right, but nobody went there. Nobody thought about the woman or the child who was or wasn't there.

There were always rumors if one listened to them. Some said that the girl had gone off and left Hetty flat. That she had been living a wild life somewhere and had a baby and then died of some horrible disease. Ridiculous stories. Dilla paid very little attention to them. Apparently, some of it was true. Mirabel was here. She was Hetty's granddaughter. It would be hard to deny that, looking at this photograph!

Dilla put the photo in an envelope and put it on the counter to show to Eve when she visited again. She thought both she and the girl would be interested in seeing a picture of Hetty as a young woman. She doubted that Hetty collected such memorabilia, and it would be good for the girl to see that old people were young once too.

***

CHAPTER 41

"It's a foregone conclusion!"

"I don't understand, Charlie. What's a 'foregone conclusion?'"

"The Board of Selectmen will vote for eminent domain."

"I won't."

"Adam, you know he's got Fry, Carter and Bolling. Marlin's got them all in his pocket. If he wants it, they'll vote for it. They'll take the old woman's property....I-I just don't like it, Adam." Metcalf had come to St Barnabas right after his morning 'meeting' with John Marlin.

Singleton was in jeans and work shirt painting the rear wall of the Church. Since his breakup with Eve, he needed something to keep him busy. He had to try to take his mind off Eve Truesdale! He was more miserable than ever. All he could think of was how disappointed she looked and how angry he felt at being such a fool, and, yet, he knew it was for the best. If they had continued, he'd only be fooling himself. She was engaged to a much younger man; why would she choose a poor country minister over this month's Playgirl foldout? It was better to end it than to let himself get any further into the relationship....further in? In his heart, he knew he had already committed. She was his perfect mate. He had never been surer of anything, but what of that? He had been wrong! She wasn't serious. That was the part that deviled him. He was so sure she was a different person. To go with him if she already had someone—what was the point unless she was just...having fun. It hurt his head to think of her in that way.

It was a new world. He hadn't dated for years, not since he and Caroline met. He supposed things had changed. Attitudes were different. People were different. He was out of touch. For him, intimacy was not a casual thing; it was a pledge. That expression of love was not merely physical. He had made the mistake that Eve felt the same. Then he reminded himself that she had told him she was not a 'believer.' It all made the most painful sense. He had misjudged the entire affair. His strong physical attraction had led him down the garden path, and he was angry with himself for being such a typical male, for thinking with his lower brain first.

"...I thought we would approach small landowners and offer them fair market value for their land."

"That was the idea. But Jack Marlin isn't willing to wait for that. Reedy wants an answer right away. It stinks out loud, Adam. I know Jack Marlin; he never does anything out of pure altruism. There's something in it for him, or he wouldn't be so hell-bent on this thing."

"...What do you want to do, Charlie?"

"...Don't you know the granddaughter?" Charlie seemed almost reluctant to mention this.

"I've met her...She came to fellowship one Sunday with...with Eve Truesdale...but I can't say that I know her."

"...Right...but the Truesdale woman...you know her, right? And she knows the Granddaughter and the old woman?" Metcalf was trying to be diplomatic.

"Charlie..."

"Oh, for Pete's sake, Adam, it's a small town! What do you want me to say? I don't care who you go out with! I just think the Goat Woman ought to know what's being planned for her. She should at least have some warning."

Adam was a little surprised that it appeared to be common knowledge that he and Eve had been dating. They had been careful to be discreet. Apparently for no reason! He wondered how long it would be before people realized that they had broken off...

"I'll...uh...see about...relaying the information, Charlie." Singleton threw the brush he was holding into a bucket of water. The sun was beginning to heat up, and it was time to finish for the morning anyway.

"...Thanks, Adam. I just think it's wrong to blindside an old woman and take her farm to give to some corporation just because someone says there might be jobs. Don't get me wrong, I love Holmsford, and I don't want anything bad to happen to this town, but I don't want to see anything bad happen *in* this town either." Having accomplished his mission, Charlie Metcalf nodded to Singleton and awkwardly walked off toward the green.

"...Okay...." Singleton muttered to himself now that he was alone, "...What do I do?...."

***

CHAPTER 42

It was sundown, Friday afternoon. Eve had spent the day drifting around the house doing small chores in between bouts on the computer monitoring the activity of her department. Nothing helped. Thoughts of Singleton always returned. It tortured her to the point of making her angry with herself. She couldn't put him out of her mind!

But now it was finally sundown. She would have a dinner at Hetty's. Instinctively she knew this must be important for the old woman. She didn't know what to expect, but she wanted to approach it with the proper importance. She dressed nicely, but casually, because she knew that Hetty would not be dressed any differently than she usually was. She also had brought a small gift from New York—a silk shawl from a small boutique on Fifth Avenue. It was woven in shades of blue and green jewel tones. She wrapped it in a red foil wrapper with a big red bow. She knew this would heighten the old woman's pleasure in the gift. She had also bought a good bottle of wine to go with the dinner even though she didn't know what to expect of the meal.

With the rapid ending of the light, Eve headed out the back door toward Hetty's farm.

The goat pens were empty. Fireflies were gathering and beginning to flash in the twilight. In the swath of woods between the pens and Hetty's house, night creatures were beginning to stir and rustle in the undergrowth. An owl hooted sitting in a pine tree, and the path, deep in pine needles and leaves, was soft underfoot and full of a potpourri of woodland scents. She took her time making her way, enjoying the magic of dusk with all its healing smells and sounds. The moon was nearly full and rising quickly, lighting the way as the sunlight grew dimmer. As she walked, Eve began to feel her tension and anger subside. There was still sadness—that was deep, but the reactive emotions were letting go. The sorrow would be something she would have for a while.

Finally, she emerged in the clearing around Hetty's homestead. There was a warm yellow light from a lantern in the window. The barn was closed, and the soft sounds of the animals inside made Eve feel as if she had stepped out of time into a long-gone era. The house sat prim and erect with its weathered face proudly bearing up to the night. The cottage garden with its neat crop of herbs and vegetables was well-tended and orderly, as was the rest of the farm. Eve noticed how carefully kept everything was—with what—love—everything had been maintained.

As she mounted the stone step to the front door, it sprang open so quickly that it took her breath away. There stood Hetty staring straight at her. It almost made her jump back.

"Been expectin' ya, Missy...Come in!" The old woman stepped back and let her enter.

As Eve stepped through the door, the aromas of cooking were strong and warm and wonderful. The hearth seethed and bubbled with pots full of food. It looked as if there was enough food for a dozen people! On the small rough table a crisp clean white cloth had been laid. On it were two pewter plates with dinnerware and pewter goblets. Two split willow chairs had been drawn up to accommodate the two of them. Tallow candles were lit all around the room and the atmosphere was snug and welcoming.

"Hetty! This is wonderful! It smells so good in here!"

"...Well...it's what it is. I done what I could..." The old woman tried not to exhibit any pride.

"Where is Mirabel? I thought she'd be eating with us." Eve looked around and saw no evidence of the girl.

"...Oh...she...mentioned somethin' 'bout a young doctor...up in Boston?...You know somethin' 'bout that?..."

"Really? She called him? Oh, Hetty, that's wonderful! I didn't think she'd do it!—He's not a doctor—yet. He's a waiter...in a restaurant...studying to be a doctor."

The old woman kept staring...

"He was fascinated by her! You know how beautiful she is—He couldn't take his eyes off her, well, nobody can, really...but he gave her his number. But I never thought she'd call. She didn't seem interested!" Eve was delighted as she tried to explain.

Hetty seemed to take in the information, and when Eve was finished, she simply nodded, "...Eyah...You want to sit?..."

"What's wrong with me? Here, I brought this to go with dinner..." Eve handed Hetty the bottle of wine, "...And this is for you!" She gave the old woman the brightly wrapped package.

The old woman took the red-wrapped shawl, with her eyes wide and absently put the wine bottle aside on the table. She sat at the table with package in her lap staring at it with its red bow sitting upright in the firelight.

"...Missy...it ain't for you to be givin' to me...I oughta be givin' to you....the favor you done me..." all the while her eyes never left the package.

"Open it! It's not much, just something I thought you might like..."

The old woman tore into the package like a child at Christmas. The paper fell to the floor as did the red ribbon, and she pulled out the shawl with her eyes gleaming. She held it to the light and smoothed her hand over it, feeling the fabric and studying the varying color. She was completely concentrated and silent.

"...It's a shawl...it's silk...I thought...for nights when it gets chilly..." Eve couldn't tell what the old woman was thinking as she examined and re-examined the shawl. It was as if she was memorizing every thread, but Eve tried to give her the time. A long moment passed before the old woman spoke.

"...Blue sky...green sea...it's all there..." The old woman seemed to be talking to herself as much as to Eve.

"...I liked the colors...I hoped you would too..." Eve waited expectantly for a reply.

Suddenly the old woman quickly and lovingly folded the shawl and picked the red wrapping from the floor, folding it inside with the bright red ribbon on top. She placed it gently on a shelf and smoothed her apron.

"...Time we et...You set yourself here, Missy, I'll get the vittles."

"...Let me help, Hetty. Just tell me what I can do."

"...You can...open that bottle...if you've a mind ta. Don't want you in this here hearth. You'll get burned. I know my way 'round this..."

Eve had remembered to slip a small wine opener in her pocket before leaving the house. She figured Hetty wouldn't have one, so she set about opening the wine and pouring it. Hetty pulled a huge, pungent-smelling roast off the spit and set it on a huge platter. From the pots around the hearth she ladled potatoes, peas, carrots, corn and sliced cooked onion in a broth. These she arranged around the joint of meat and brought it to the table. The effect was a bounteous meal. Under several cloths which she removed were sliced fresh tomatoes and cucumbers, melon, apples, pears, and a scattering of berries. Under one of the cloths was a crock of goat cheese and a crock of butter, and under a third was a loaf of fresh warm bread.

"Hetty! How much do you think I can eat?...This is...amazing! It's a feast!...But there's just the two of us!" Eve's eyes were still taking in the field of food that lay before them.

The old woman took her seat opposite Eve and looked at her, "...Ain't we enough?..." It was a kind of challenge and Eve had to smile.

"...Of course we are!...I propose a toast!" Eve lifted her goblet and Hetty followed suit. "To women! We are always 'enough!'"

The two women took long drinks and then Hetty fell upon the roast, carving thick slabs of the seasoned meat for each of them. She served up the vegetables with equal generosity, and both of them had full plates facing them. Eve reached for the bread knife...

"Shall I...?"

Hetty nodded, and Eve started to slice thick pieces off the loaf for each of them.

"You know....this is just like Mira's bread. The same loaf...."

"...Eyah...she got it from me..." That was all that was said. The two of them ate for a full thirty minutes without speaking a word.

Eve was astonished at how much she ate! She emptied her plate and took more. Hetty too ate hugely, and as the two ate, they gradually emptied the wine bottle. Finally, Eve reached for it to pour and found it drained.

"...Hold up, Missy, that ain't no drink for this supper..." Hetty got up from the table and went to the corner of the room near a window. There were several crocks and storage vessels in a group. From behind she drew a brown gallon jug which she brought to the table. "Now, this here..." She spoke as she poured from the jug into their goblets, "...is my own apple jack. Best to take it with a little well water....." She added a dollop of water from a pitcher on the table. "To...the power o' women..."

"To the power!" Eve clinked her goblet with Hetty's and laughed. "Hetty, I don't think I've ever eaten so much in my life!

"...If ya hungry, ya should eat till you're full."

"If I ate like this every day, I'd weigh three hundred pounds!"

"...If that's what fills ya."

"Hetty! No woman wants to weigh three hundred pounds!...I want you to know, I've...enjoyed having Mirabel."

"...She...ain't been a burden?..."

"Hetty!—no! She's smart, intuitive...beautiful!...Is she going away?"

"I need her now...There's things I need her for."

"...Have you...considered sending her to school?..."

"...She's been to school!"

"College, I mean. Hetty, it's a different world from when you were young. Girls now...have to have college just to survive!"

"...She'll survive."

"She's so beautiful, Hetty! I mean it's arresting! Everyone looks!—The men are all...drawn to her. I've seen it!"

"...She don't care about that."

"But, Hetty, she's young!"

"Young's just a turn o' mind, Missy! Comes and goes in a minute. As for looks?—Ain't important.—A woman's beautiful if she knows she is."

"There's a world of women out there that would disagree with you, Hetty!"

"Let 'em! Always pamperin' and posturin'. Lookin' for someone to see 'em—men mostly. When she's by herself...that's who a woman is!

"You don't want her to be alone, do you, Hetty?"

"...She won't be, not if she don't want to be..." Hetty poured more of the apple jack into their goblets.

"...Why do you want her to spend time with me? If she went to college, she'd...have a wider perspective on the world!" Eve took a long sip from the apple jack. It was warm and fruity but not cloying. She had never tasted anything quite like it.

"...I want her to see things...through *your* eyes." The old woman focused on Eve.

Eve looked at her for a minute and turned away. "...That might not be a smart idea, Hetty..."

"Eyah?...Why's that?"

"...Because I haven't been so smart! Oh, I've made a lot of money. I'm a partner in a company in New York. I run a department full of...difficult men, but it turns out I *am* by myself,...and I don't much like it."

"...You got a man...A preacher...she told me."

"...I don't have him. Not anymore—I'm beginning to think I never had him."

"She said—"

"I didn't tell her. I didn't tell anyone...because I was too embarrassed! I was so sure! It seemed so right for the first time!...But I was wrong. In the end...he didn't want me."

"That's *his* lookout!" The old woman was instantly defensive.

"*I* did this, Hetty! I went for it.—I...gave myself to him! Once we had gotten to know each other, he decided...it wasn't right." Eve reached inside and held herself steady. She was not going to let herself fall apart.

"...There's ways, Missy...to get your own back. There's ways...to get even...When a man hurts ya..." Hetty's voice was quiet and even and waiting.

"No, Hetty! Why would I want to do that? I love Adam! I can say that. My feelings for him haven't changed. I can't blame him for not being able to deal with...what I've become. I've spent my entire adult life making sure I was insulated from people. I don't *need* anyone. Adam is a man who needs to be needed. I should have seen it coming."

"...There's ways to keep him..." Once again, Hetty's voice was low and even.

"If I've lost him, I've lost him. I'd best get over it. We're neither one of us likely to change much. We just...don't match up. Adam was right to...end it."

The old woman held Eve in her eyes for along moment then broke her gaze and poured out more liquor from the jug into their goblets.

"...That's why, Missy!" She announced almost ceremonially. She was more expansive now.

"'That's why' what, Hetty?"

"That's why I want her to see things through your eyes! Ya don't blame and ya don't complain!—Ya get on! Don't think *I* learned that proper! Somebody does me a wrong, it sticks in my craw! I don't turn a cheek to nobody! I get 'em!"

"Hetty!" Eve couldn't help but chuckle.

"Well, I do! If it was me, he better watch himself!"

"I can't say I didn't feel like that—at first! But...no. It was as much my fault as his. We both...were mistaken. I know that now."

"...You sure ain't like no Truesdale I ever knew..." Hetty took a reflective pull on her goblet.

"...How many have you known?..." Eve could feel the old woman loosening up.

"More than I care to, Missy!"

"...My Gramps was a Truesdale..."

"He had his edges! A damn sight too proud of the Truesdale name, the Truesdale money—even though it was pretty nigh gone. All made by the blood of others! He was too blind to see it....Died takin' care of that grand place 'o his...all gotten by Truesdale greed!

"...Oh..." Eve pulled back a little.

"Not you, Missy! You ain't like that! You...give without wantin' nothin'. You stand on your own—like me. Too many don't. Weak! Always needin'...Not you, not me."

"...Maybe that's the problem..." Eve was still thinking of Adam, but the old Woman reached across and put her hand on Eve's, a gesture that was strange and important for her.

"...You want to know 'bout the Truesdales an' the Liveseys?" Hetty pulled back and looked at Eve.

"You told me...the rival preachers...remember?"

"Eyah...That part, but there's more to it...if ya want to know...." Hetty refilled their goblets.

"...Yes...of course...," Eve took her goblet and held it.

"Truesdale weren't so much jealous of Livesey for the pulpit. He were a hungry one! A lot o' men are like that. Nothin's enough! Livesey had a daughter...you remember my sayin'?"

"Mahetibel?"

"...Eyah... Mahetibel. Marryin' age by that time. Truesdale's wife was dead. He had four young'uns' by her and a farm to keep. He come after Livesey's daughter. That was the real rift between 'em. Livesey knew the kind 'o man he was, and he told Truesdale to look elsewhere. There was no elsewhere! Every woman was spoke for...except for Mahetibel. Truesdale kept after him. He wouldn't wait 'til more women came; he wanted Mahetibel. He come courtin' her in sly ways...when Livesey was away from the farm, tryin' to make his way with her."

"Did she like him?..."

"What did *she* know! He was a minister! Had a house and a parish like her Pa. He was a man comin' for her. That was all she saw. He promised her things. Things her way. The life of a woman instead of the daughter in a household."

"Was he handsome?"

"...Some would say... Didn't take long before Livesey saw what Truesdale's game was. He was angry. He forbid Truesdale from his property—left the church. He let it be known that he wanted no part of anythin' Truesdale was party to."

"What about Mahetibel?..."

"What could she do? She begged! She cried for him....She thought Truesdale was her love...Giles and Rebecca were fixed on it, no daughter of theirs would marry a man like Truesdale."

"...Why didn't she just go to him?"

"Not so simple, Missy. Giles Livesey was still a leader. Folks followed him. Respected him. He was an educated man, a healer. If he said a thing,...most listened to him! His leavin' the church was a blow! The colony was split.

"Long about that time there was trouble with the tribes. Without Livesey to hold him back, Truesdale was dealin' double with 'em, takin' more than he was givin'—treatin' them like animals. To show he was the leader, he was pushin' 'em to be Christian. The Chiefs refused to trade no more. That put the settlers in a real fix. The goods the tribe traded kept

216

many goin' when food was short. Without it, some would starve. In spite, Truesdale sent the tribe blankets—blankets that come from a house with the pox. It spread through the tribe like a fire! Truesdale told the Chiefs that God was punishing them for not being Christian.

"The Chiefs turned to Giles. He and Rebecca went to the village and nursed the tribe. He used all his skills. Mahetibel went with 'em. She saw with her own eyes the misery Truesdale had wrought, and that cured her of any love she felt for him! When it was over, half the tribe was dead. There was great anger among 'em! The Chiefs were preparin' a war party, but Giles spoke up for the colony. Hadn't he come to them? Hadn't he worked to heal 'em? They couldn't blame the colonists for a fever. This he did knowin' that Truesdale was the one.

"Truesdale worried that word would come back to the parish of what he done. He knew Livesey would tell. He called him out! 'Livesey was a witch!' he cried. 'Him and his woman tended the savages. They were in league with the devil, bent on killin' good Christians! Didn't he leave the church? Didn't he foreswear his duty to the colony? He and his wife must die!'

"Fear was high. It was known Livesey was a man of learning. Truesdale turned that on him. 'Those books,' he said, 'were the tools of the devil. Who else could read 'em? They was writ in the language of the devil!'

"Sure enough, when they busted into the house, Livesey's books were mostly in Latin...and Greek. Giles and Rebecca were dragged out on the spot...and hanged."

"My God, Hetty! How do you know all this?"

"It's writ...in the Keepin' Book. I read it...oft times..." the old woman was deep in the story.

"It ain't all...The two of 'em were offered mercy—if they confessed. Knowin' their land would be taken if they did, they refused. They died so that Mahetibel would keep the land. She watched as they hoisted the two of them into that tree."

"My God, Hetty!"

"Truesdale was not done. After a time he come again to the farm. The girl was alone, cuttin' flax. He offered himself like before, but she knew now. She spit on him! For what he done, she reviled him, told him that she'd sooner marry a savage than him...

"'You won't think that once you been broken, girl' He came for her. She fought him. She weren't no weak thing. She cut him pretty good with a scythe she was holdin', but he caught her a blow to the jaw that stunned her....Afterwards he told her she'd either come to him, or he would tell how she consorted with the Devil. How she lay with savages and was a witch and should be hanged like Giles and Rebecca."

"...What did she do?" Eve sipped on her drink totally taken in.

"...Some...say she...got over it. Got on...."

"Did she marry him?"

"No, Missy. She never married."

"But she must have! There was a Livesey line."

"Eyah...must have been. I'm here!..."

"So, what did she do. Who did she marry?"

"...No record o' that. Not in the Keepin' Book."

"Then how...do you know she never married?"

"...I guess I don't...I guess I want to think she done what some folks said about her."

Eve waited while Hetty took another long drink from her goblet. "What, Hetty!—You can't leave me hanging here!"

The old woman came out of her goblet and took a long breath, "...Some said, she did what Truesdale said she did."

"...What, went to him? Married that bastard?"

"...I mean...danced in the moonlight...with the spirits of the Earth—what some call Satan. Gave herself to him. Ate the fruit from the Forbidden Tree and was forever freed of the power o' Men....I like to think it..."

"...Oh......Oh....ha, ha, ha...Hetty...If that were only true!" By now the room was fuzzy and Eve found herself having to think hard to stop from slurring her words.

"...I like to think on it."

"...You know...'freed from the power of men'...that's...jus...jus...not going to happen. They're everywhere!...And we're jus....jus so stupid. You're right, Hetty! We're weak! We give up ourselves to 'em! Always...tryin' to...to please 'em. Stay young...be appealing! Stupid!" Eve felt a little as if she were floating. It was a pleasant sensation and it made her feel for the moment...light and free.

"I told ya..." by now the old woman was also floating, "A woman has power. Young's just a turn 'o mind!"

"Hetty!...no matter how hard I think...I am not gonna be eighteen again. Ain't gonna happen." Eve wagged her finger for emphasis.

"You're wrong, Missy! I can prove it!...If she's willin'...if she's ready...a woman can be any age she wants to be!"

"Nope, nope, nope...That's not goin' to happen, Hetty! It's....impossible!" Eve was half laughing in her drunken state.

"All right!....I'll show you—but you can't tell no one!...It's just between us...you promise, Missy? Just us!..." The old woman unbuttoned the long sleeve of her left arm and pulled it up almost to her shoulder revealing the corded tendons and mottled skin beneath. Her hand was calloused and gnarled from years of hard work. The veins stood out like blue lumps under the creped skin. Her nails were jagged and yellowed and the knuckles were reddened and slightly swollen.

The old woman stood and muttered something under her breath and passed her right hand across the top of the length of the arm while Eve sat watching and giggling.

"Quiet, Missy!...I got to...pray...Quiet..."

Again the old woman muttered under her breath, but this time Eve managed to be silent. As the old woman moved her right hand over her left hand and arm, it changed!

The nails once yellowed and jagged were smooth and round and pink as if they had been freshly manicured. The skin on the back of the hand plumped and the veins disappeared. Likewise as she moved her right hand upward, the mottled skin took on an even, healthy glow and the corded tendons seemed to sink back down into the tissues of the arm. She passed the hand to the shoulder, and Eve could see an arm that was perfect, youthful...renewed!

Eve blinked trying to focus. Obviously, the apple jack was affecting her vision!. She looked again, and then pulled away slightly and chuckled, not trusting what she saw, "...That's...that's a good trick!...How do you do that?....That's...that's very good!..."

"...Go on, Missy, feel it. It ain't no trick. That's power! That's the power we all have! Feel it!" Both of them were reeling slightly.

"No, no, no...That's all right. It is. It's a really....really good trick. I applaud you!" Eve tried to applaud, but had trouble getting her hands to meet.

"...All right...Missy...I'm...gonna show you...what...nobody...ever sees. Just you! Just you, but you can't tell!...You can't..."

"Sh!..No! Not me! I can't tell now!...Ha, ha, ha...how could I tell?" Eve was giggling stupidly and she could barely see.

The old woman muttered under her breath again and passed her hand across her face....

The transformation was astounding! The skin was smooth, the eyes were clear and a beautiful shade of light blue. The hair went from a dull gray-auburn, to a rich vibrant red. The lips filled out and the wrinkles disappeared from around the eyes. For a moment Eve stared. She knotted her brows trying to focus, trying to see clearly...Was that Mirabel? What was she doing here? How did she get here?...What was...going on?...

In a sudden moment of clarity Eve screamed and stood up. She seemed to become aware of the reality of what she had seen happen. She knocked over her chair as she backed away.

"Missy!....No...now Missy...it ain't a bad thing...every woman has...the power..." Hetty tried to get up to catch her by the arm, but Eve was quicker than she. She backed away, shaking her head in disbelief, and, at the same time, trying to get her vision to clear.

"....I....I think I better go home! I...drank too much...I-I'm sorry..." Eve bolted for the door and was through it before Hetty could find her balance.

The old woman followed her through the door and stood on the entrance stone holding on to the frame of the door to steady herself. Her appearance was normal now.

"Eve!....Missy!...Don't go!...Don't run...You need me...Don't go away!..."

Eve crashed through the woods in the direction of home. The moon had set, and the woods were dark. The sounds of the night creatures no longer sounded comforting. They were distinctly threatening. Eve ran and stumbled as fast as she could in the direction of home. At one point, she stumbled into a bank of briers and was scratched mercilessly. She managed to extricate herself and continue.

Finally, twenty minutes later she was standing at her front door. Somehow, she had circled the house and had come to the front rather than the back door. It was locked. Of course, she had locked it! She pounded on it as though someone would answer. She was breathless and sweating, and for a moment she couldn't remember how she had gotten there. Hugging the contour of the house, she made her way to the back door, which she knew was unlocked. She let herself in and locked it behind her!

She stumbled up the stairs to her room and locked that door behind her as well. She could feel her stomach begin to heave and she made it to the bathroom just in time to release a wave of vomit into the bowl. She threw up again and again until there was nothing left in her stomach. She flushed the toilet and instinctively reached for the glass, which she filled and drank.

She staggered to her bed and collapsed confused, exhausted and with a monstrous pain forming at the back of her eyes. Unconsciousness overtook her, and she slept without dreaming.

***

CHAPTER 43

"Jonas!—c'mon, I don't want to be late!" Libby called up the stairs.

"...Right there!" the young man's voice was light and clear, and Libby felt warm just to hear another voice in the vast, empty house.

She looked around satisfied. Ever since that awful night...she had turned it around! Her house was in order! *She* had put it that way! Now, with Jonas here, she had better focus. They had found each other—two needy people. They kept each other on track...clean!

"I'm gonna get in that friggin' car and take off without you!" Even though she used her "annoyed" tone, she couldn't be angry with him. He had been so good. He cooked with her, helped clean, and they talked! He told her about his family, how their 'Christian' beliefs made him an 'abomination.' They had thrown him away! At fourteen he was out on the streets trying to stay alive! He did...what he had to do. Drugs blocked the shame and the pain. Alcohol was a side-effect. Poor kid!...Goddamn family!

Jonas came bounding down the stairs. He was slight, but handsome. He looked much younger than twenty, and in the chinos, crisp plaid shirt, and penny loafers Libby had bought him, he looked so much like her Brad. His long hair was combed back and his face was open and empty of all the...ugliness he had seen and done.

"What's the rush, Libs? The donuts are always stale anyway!"

"Right! I go to friggin' Boston to eat Goddamn stale donuts!—Neither one of us is so fucking great we can afford to miss a meeting!"

"You, are! You're like a rock!—Once you decide, nothin's gonna shake you, Libs." He leaned over and gave her a peck on the cheek.

"What the hell was taking you so long?"

"Checkin' my look! I don't know if this 'clean boy' style's gonna get me a trick..."

"It better get you a *job*! If you went to Goddamn school, it'd be a lot easier!" Libby reached up and pushed a stray strand of hair back into place.

"C'mon, Libs. Can't make money in school!"

"Get a job!—Anything...flipping burgers, for Christ's sakes! Get something legit, and *then* we get you into school!"

"I'm not flippin' burgers! All that grease?..What for? In twenty minutes I can make more'n I'd get in a week in a chump job like that!"

"You'll take what you can get! And you'll go to night school and get a diploma! What do you want to do, burn out at twenty-fucking-five? It's a miracle you don't have HIV right now!"

"I'm lucky! I've always been lucky!"

"Right! So lucky you spent the last six years strung out, drunk, and dodging the cops every two minutes!—That sound lucky to you?"

"...Lucky enough to find you, Libs!"

"Get in the fucking car, smart boy! Practice being straight!"

The young man bounded out the door. Libby locked the front door thinking how lucky *she* was. She was dry...for nearly a month, and she wasn't alone anymore.

She had Jonas...for now. Someone to...care about, to bully,...to love. That *was* lucky!

***

CHAPTER 44

The pounding in her head drummed forward insistently, making her come to consciousness. It felt as if her eyes were pushing out of her skull!

"Jesus!..." Eve pulled herself up painfully from the bed. Why was she still dressed? How did she get here? What had happened?

In a fog she staggered to the bathroom. There were towels all over the floor and the bathmat was rumpled and stained with vomit.

When she looked in the mirror, she was gray! There were dark circles under her eyes and her blouse was striped with dried blood! Quickly she took off the blouse and looked at her arms. They were covered with deep scratches. What had happened? How did they get there? The pounding came back worse than before, then she realized it wasn't just in her head. Someone was pounding on her front door!

She ran to the window and opened it looking down.

"Jace?...What...What are you doing here? It's seven o'clock in the morning!"

"Don't I know it!...C'mon, Eve, let me in, will you. I need coffee!"

"...Uh....I'm not dressed..."

"Eve, we've seen each other naked! Open the damn door!"

"I'll be right down...uh...just a minute..." Trying to pull her thoughts into a straight line, Eve rushed to the bathroom. She grabbed a facecloth and doused it with rubbing alcohol and rubbed it over her arms. The pain seared through her like knives, and she inhaled deeply. The pain behind her eyes was still pushing against her brain. She quickly fished in the medicine cabinet for Tylenol. She took four and downed them with water. What to do about her arms? She grabbed a dressing gown from the back of the door and slipped it over her. The long sleeves would hide the scratches for now.

She held onto the handrail as she limped down the stairs to the front door. When she opened, Jace was standing there with a big grin on his face which instantly faded.

"Jesus, you look like shit!..."

"Good morning to you, too, Jace...Come in..."

"What happened to you?"

"...Well....I'm not sure...I went to dinner...I...ate food...I had some apple jack..."

"Apple jack?...you mean hard cider?"

"...I guess...."

"Where'd you get apple jack?"

"I think it got me!...Hetty's...She made it..."

"Moonshine!...You drank moonshine!"

"...No...apple jack. *That* I remember!"

"Nope. I don't care what you call it, you drank some real dyed-in-the-wool moonshine! I *know* that look!...The 'Dragon Lady's' destroyed!...bad, huh?"

"...If you shot me in the head right now...I couldn't feel any worse!" Eve leaned against the stair bannister and held her head.

"Kitchen! I'll make the coffee—extra strong. Then you'll go upstairs and take a cold shower..." Jace led her to the kitchen and made her sit while he fed the coffee maker a load of ground coffee and filled the reservoir. "You got any eggs?"

"I don't want to eat!" Eve was hunched over the table.

"Not for you—for me! I didn't stop for breakfast. I'm starved!" He went to the fridge and began to take out eggs and bacon and bring them to the counter.

"...Why are you here, Jace?' Eve managed to croak out the question as she rested her head on the cool surface of the table.

"...It's Saturday...I figured I'd bring a few things out to check with you....see how you're doing...you know..." He lifted an iron frying pan from the pot rack and placed in on the stove. As it hit the stovetop Eve winced.

Eve pulled herself upright, "Uh, uh...no...that's not it....I'm not that far gone...Why are you here?"

"...I told you; I wanted to see how you were doing....see about...us." Jace was distracting himself by putting bacon in the frypan.

"Jace....I'm not up for this right now!...You know there is no 'us.' I thought I made that clear. Not personally, anyway..."

"...That's the theory!" Jace cracked two eggs into the pan.

"That's a fact, Jace!...Please...make yourself breakfast...ugh...the smell of bacon!—I'm going up to take a shower and...try to freshen up. Then you can show me whatever you brought...Right now...." Without finishing her thought, Eve pulled herself to her feet and dragged herself up the stairs.

Jace kept himself busy in the kitchen. Suddenly the bacon on the pan spit and splattered.

"Shit!..." There was a spreading grease stain on his shirt. Jace quickly tore off the shirt and doused the spot with cold water trying to remove it. The doorbell rang. Jace threw the shirt in the sink and went to the front door.

"Yes?...." Singleton was standing in the door way wearing ripped jeans and an old work shirt stained with white paint. It took Jace a minute to place him. "Oh, how are you....Reverend—"

"Singleton!....Fine, thank you..." Adam could feel himself flush deeply as he saw the same scene that had haunted him before repeated. There he was, the Playgirl Stud sans shirt, standing proprietarily in Eve's front door. "...Is Eve here?"

"In the shower...uh, you look different, Reverend."

Adam looked down at his attire, "...Uh...painting the church..."

"*You* do that? I thought you had people to do it for you."

"The Catholics do that. Could you...ask Eve to give me a call as soon as she's...free. It's important. I was hoping to talk to her personally, but...."

"....Oh, sure, Reverend! I'll tell her as soon as she's out. You sure you don't want to stay? I'm making some breakfast!"

"Thanks...I've already eaten. You won't forget to tell her?"

"Count on it. Could you excuse me, Reverend? Eggs! Don't want 'em to burn!" Jace ran off to the kitchen.

Adam stood there for a moment looking after the younger man as he ran through the swinging door into the kitchen. He tried his best to set aside his feelings. He was here to convey a message...nothing more. Whatever Eve did...that was her prerogative. Quietly he pulled the front door closed and walked away.

***

The hot water of the shower had reopened the scratches and made them bleed again. Eve decided it was best to let them bleed clean and then reapply the alcohol, which she did. As before, the slashing pain made her draw in a deep breath, but this time it faded quickly. She had let the water run over her for a good long time. It felt good...soothing. The Tylenol had pushed the headache back to a point where it was mostly a pressure.

She had thrown the blouse away. The blood had dried in the silk. She knew it was ruined. She put the towels and the bathmat into the laundry for washing, and she made her bed. The act of creating order helped her to gather her mind.

What had happened? She remembered going to Hetty's. She remembered a huge meal and the aromas of cooking...and she remembered tasting the apple jack. The rest of it was 'bits and pieces.'...She knew Hetty had told her some things...some things about...family and she remember seeing Mira...but not really...It hurt her head to keep thinking about it, so she stopped.

Somewhat refreshed she began to descend the staircase. She knew she would have to deal with Jace. He had to know that their relationship was only business now. She wouldn't allow it to be anything else any longer. She knew she had only been fooling herself. As she got nearly the whole way down the stairs, the doorbell rang.

Eve stepped to the door and opened it. Mira stood there looking at her, searchingly.

"...Hetty sent me...Said you might be feelin'...poorly." The girl seemed tentative, uncertain. Her manner was subdued, and she looked at Eve almost pleadingly.

"...Mira...as a matter of fact...Your grandmother and I...drank a bit last night!..."

"...She's...right sorry for that...She woke up feelin' poorly herself.....She thought you might want this..." The girl handed Eve a green bottle with a cork in it.

"...What is it?" Eve took the bottle and looked at it suspiciously.

"Nothin' bad!...She'd never send you nothin' bad!" The girl was anxious to set Eve at ease.

"...uh...come in, Mira. I'm sorry...I just....I'm not myself right now."

"Who's that—? Mirabel....nice to see you again!" Jace was still shirtless, and he shifted his weight as he took an appreciative look at the girl in the light of the doorway.

"..Mornin'...I come to bring Eve the cure."

"Cure?..." Eve took the bottle and looked at it more seriously, "Cure for a hangover?—Where's your shirt?" Eve noticed Jace's naked torso.

"...Cooking accident. If your grandmother has a cure for a hangover, she'll be rich. I could handle the IPO!"

"...Come again?..."

"Ignore him, Mira, he's just being a smartass. Jace, go put on your shirt; we've all seen it before!"

"...And yet you still look!" Jace returned through the swinging door.

"This is...supposed to take away the hangover?" Eve looked quizzically at the green bottle.

"Drink it down. Don't taste good, but it'll fix you up."

"...What's in it?" Eve was still studying the bottle.

"...Herbs...nostrums...things that drive out the vapors!...Hetty says there somethin' in nature that cures anything in the body....She'd never hurt you!"

"...Of course not, Mira!...I-I know that..." still, in the back of her mind, there was something niggling at Eve. There was some gnawing misgiving that she couldn't name. It hadn't been there before, but the green bottle was like a trigger for it. "I'll...I'll have it later."

"Got to be now!—If you want it to work. Sooner, rather than later!" The girl was insistent.

"...But I've just taken aspirin..." Eve was feeling her anxiety.

"This'll work better!...Hetty says" Mirabel looked at the bottle, then at Eve. It was clear that she was expecting Eve to take it immediately.

"...Actually, I feel much better already. I don't think I need this.—Do you want some coffee?" Eve put the bottle on the hall table.

"You need to take that fresh. Loses its strength fast. You drink it now!"

"Mira!...I'm not going to drink this. I don't need it. I appreciate Hetty's concern, but I'm a big girl, I can handle my own hangover...But tell her I'm...I'm touched that she's concerned."

"...She don't want you...feelin' bad 'cause of somethin' she done..." The girl seemed subdued suddenly.

"...I told you, I'm feeling much better. Mira, I don't blame Hetty! We drank too much of her...apple jack. I had no idea it was that...potent, but I'm fine! She can come by herself and check on me, if she wants to!"

"...You don't bear her no...hard feelin's?" The girl was still nervous and doubtful.

"Of course not!...Come on in. There's some coffee in the kitchen. I'll get you a cup."

"...You...want me to come in?..."

"Yes!—What is wrong with you? You know my house as well as your own. Come on in and have a cup of coffee with me, silly girl!"

The two of them went into the kitchen. Jace was seated at the table finishing up a plate of bacon and eggs. He had put on his shirt, which now sported a massive stain on the front.

"...Well, that shirt's a loss!" Eve noticed as she poured out two cups of coffee for Mira and herself. "Now, what did you need me to see, Jace?"

"...It's...it'll take a while..." He was more serious now that it was business.

"...All right...Why don't you settle into a motel, and you can come back later—now that you've eaten—and we can discuss whatever it is."

"...I can't stay here?" Jace was a little surprised.

"No, Jace. You can't stay here. There's a very nice motel about ten minutes from here. I've stayed there myself. It's clean and comfortable. When you've checked in, you can come back."

Jace held his breath for a minute looking at both women as the realization that he was just there for business dawned on him. "...Ok....Ok. I'll do that. I'll just...go check in." He got up from his chair obviously annoyed and pushed through the swinging door. As he did so he turned back for a moment, "Oh, the minister was here—Reverend...Singleton, is it? He wants you to see him. He says it's important. See you...later." With that Jace was out the door.

The two women could hear his BMW revving up and driving away.

***

CHAPTER 45

"Stop! Nelson!—You beast! You think just because you have me out on this boat, you can...just have your way with me!"

"...You had your way with me! It's only fair!"

The two of them had anchored off one of the smaller islands and spent the better part of the afternoon below decks because Marian couldn't take the sun. Dramamine patches behind both ears had stopped the nausea, but the sun was something Marian wouldn't tolerate.

"I don't know why I let you talk me into this sail. I'm a terrible sailor!"

"But you're a helluva crew!" Nelson nuzzled her and let his hands roam over her body. Marian giggled with pleasure at his touch.

"Now you stop that!" Marian rolled over and applied coconut oil on her arms. "The sun is going to turn me into an old wallet! Just look at my skin!"

"I'd rather feel it!"

"Dr. Whittaker!—please! I am a lady!"

"Don't I know it!" Nelson Whittaker rolled over on the bed deeply satisfied. Marian was just the thing he had been missing. She was fun-loving, flashy...and she devoted her entire attention to him. Best of all she wasn't a twenty-something girl out for whatever he could buy her. He'd tried that—A couple of nurses at the hospital...a girl at a bar. After the sex, there was nothing to talk about. They were...empty. They had nothing in common with him. Oh, they'd listen politely when he talked about his practice, but he could tell behind the fixed smiles and open eyes there was...nothing. They didn't have a clue!

Marian would listen, ask questions...respond! They had seen the same movies, remembered the same national events...been to some of the same places. Most important, Marian knew how to treat him.

It didn't bother him that she introduced him as her *"boyfriend, the noted oncologist, Doctor Nelson Whittaker of Massachusetts General."* He could see some roll their eyes slightly, but he didn't care. In fact, it made him feel important. He was a quiet, middle-aged man with no particular romantic qualities, but in Marian's eyes he was a Superman! He was a movie star! He was the center of her world, and that was exactly where he wanted to be.

***

CHAPTER 46

The milking and the feeding were done. The animals were settling into the pens. It was time to start the cheese-making. Mirabel kept a steady work pace driving out the anxiety she felt about Eve. Had Hetty somehow queered the thing? Why was Eve so reluctant to take the cure she had brought over? What was she afraid of?...The work took her mind off these worries some of the time.

She heard the roar of the motor, and, for a moment, she thought it might be the collection truck come for the tank of goat's milk, but this engine was too smooth!...She looked up and shaded her eyes from the late morning sun to see a sleek tan car churning up dust as it came up the dirt road.

It was Jace, Eve's Jace! The BMW moved up the road, leaving a billowing cloud behind it. Finally, it skidded to a halt just in front of the barn. The goats bleated and skittered in the pen at the abrupt braking of the car.

Jace waved as he brought the car to a stop and hopped out. He had changed his clothes and was freshly groomed. His black, shiny hair was combed with a crown of curls falling forward. Confidence radiated from behind his sunglasses and steady grin as he walked slowly up to her.

"...What is it ya want?..." Mirabel looked him square in the face.

"...That's what I came to ask you..." He stopped quite close to her and stared directly at her.

Mirabel turned away and picked up a large bucket, "Nothin' you got..."

"I don't believe that..." He didn't move.

Mirabel turned back to him shading her eyes with one hand, "You're Eve's. I don't do that."

"...She turned me away. You saw her..."

"...I don't bed a man my friend has. It ain't right."

"Eve doesn't own me! In fact, pretty soon...I might...own her."

Mirabel cocked her head, "...How's that?..."

"Eve's been...a little too full of herself lately. Pissed off the wrong people...They don't like that. I came up to...tell her I was taking over the department. They're buying out her partnership. It's a done deal. No hard feelings."

"They won't do that."

"It's done. She has to sign...it's in the partnership agreement. Don't worry, she has plenty of money. She doesn't have to work."

"...She wants to work!"

"Fine...She can work...for me...but I don't think she'll want that, do you?..."

"You...try to stop it?...help her out?"

"I helped her out...in every way. She didn't want that, so now I'm helping myself. I'm going to make a lot of money, Mirabel! Eve was good—but I'm better!"

"You sure 'o that?"

"I'm the best...A girl like you should...have the best."

Mirabel put down the bucket, "...pretty damn sure of yourself, ain't ya?"

"I've never had any complaints!..."

"...What do you want with a farm girl who don't know nothin' and ain't been nowhere?.."

"I got a feeling you know more than you let on...besides...I can take you places...show you things..." He walked toward the car and opened the passenger door. "How about it?"

Mirabel looked at him and drew into herself, "...You are...pretty."

The milk bucket lay overturned in the empty barnyard as the tan BMW sped away, raising a cloud of dust behind it.

***

CHAPTER 47

He looked up instinctively, and she was there, standing at the back of the church.

"...I thought maybe you'd call..." He could feel the floor fall away from his feet.

"...You came out to the house. If it was that important, I thought I should come to you..."

There was an awkward silence between them.

"Oh...right. Good...." Adam came closer to her tentatively, "Um...I got word about something the Board of Selectmen are planning."

"...OK..." Eve looked confused.

"They're planning to take Hetty Livesey's farm and sell it to Innovative for an industrial park."

"What?" Eve reached out to Singleton and put a hand on his arm reflexively. "Adam, they can't do that!"

Singleton looked down at her hand and she gently pulled it away. "Apparently they can. They're claiming the right of eminent domain. The industrial park would be a conduit for much-needed jobs in town...At least, that's what they'll claim."

"That can't be right! She's been there—her family has been there since the founding of the town!"

For a moment Eve had a flash of...something from the previous night. Hetty telling her a story about...Mahetibel...some land...something...She put her hand to her head as a stab of pain hit her temple.

"..What? Eve, what is it?" Adam could see her lose focus for a moment.

"Huh?...uh, that farm is the only original homestead for miles around! Why would they want to take that particular parcel of land?"

"I told you everything I know."

"That would kill Hetty! She loves that farm. She's spent her whole life there! There must be people in town who would object!"

"...I'm sure there are. But people need jobs, Eve..."

"Dilla! She's a Town Meeting Member. She'll know what to do."

"If the Board of Selectmen vote it through...There's not much anyone can do."

"That's a private firm. You can't just take someone's land and sell it out from under them to give to a private concern!" Eve was getting angry.

"If it's in the public interest—"

"How is selling off the town's heritage in the public interest?"

"Who's going to speak for her? She hasn't been very civic-minded. Nobody ever sees her except on market days once and while. Nobody knows her..."

"Adam, *I* know her! There's got to be a law—something!"

"...I don't know. I just wanted to tell you....I knew you'd be concerned." He stood there wanting to reach out and hold her, but he couldn't.

She looked at him. She wanted him to take her up into his arms, but he didn't. "...Thanks, Adam...I-I'll warn her. There's got to be some way to stop them."

"...If you need me...."

"Let me work on this. There's always a way...there's got to be!"

"...OK...I'm here..." They parted as awkwardly as the meeting started, both wanting to touch and both refusing to give in to that impulse. Finally, Eve backed away and turned out the rear door of the church.

"Shit!" As the door slammed behind her, Adam was angry that he couldn't think of something he could do to help her.

**

CHAPTER 48

"Marlin! That man has more turns than a corkscrew! You can bet your life he's gettin' something outa this!" It was Saturday and Dilla's was open.

"My firm has a strategic partnership with a good law firm in Boston. I'm going to call them up and ask them to take a look at Innovative."

"Why them, dear? It's Marlin doin' this! He's done it before. He did it to your Grandpa's parcel and then the old Ramsay place...and every time, oh, 'it's gonna be the best for the town!'—Like hell! He's the one they oughta investigate!"

"You've got to follow the money, Dilla. That's the ticket! Every time it's been Innovative buying the land. Why? What do they want with it? Why do they want so much of it?—That's what I want to know."

"...Does she know? Hetty, I mean?"

"She's just back...I had dinner with her last night. She invited me."

"At her place?—If that don't beat the drum! You mean...she cooked for you?"

"Did she! I never saw so much food! It was...wonderful...and we drank some...concoction of hers...apple jack?...Strong stuff!"

"What did she make?" Dilla was avidly curious.

"I only remember the quantity...it was delicious. I remember that!—She's an amazing cook! But once I drank her brew...I-I won't be doing that again!"

"...She must think a lot of you, dear. You're the only one I ever heard of breaking bread at Hetty Livesey's table!" Dilla reflected on the idea that Hetty Livesey would actually invite a person...to her inner sanctum...!—"Oh! I found something! Where is it? Where did I put that?..."

The old woman looked about the shop aimlessly for a moment until her memory sharpened, "I know!..." She went to the counter, and there was the envelope containing the old photo she had found earlier. "Here it is!"

She handed Eve the envelope and Eve pulled the picture out.

"Is this your husband?"

"That's him! That's Rudy! But that's not why I put this aside. Here, dear—" Dilla handed her a magnifying glass. "Look to the right...in the stall."

Eve moved her eye to the stall in the background. The magnifying glass caught the image of young Hetty, sitting, and next to her stood a handsome young man in overalls. "Oh...!" Eve let out a short cry and dropped the magnifying glass.

"It kind of takes your breath away, doesn't it?" Dilla picked up the glass.

"It's...it's..." There was something...something hanging on the edge of her memory. It made her headache come back.

"It's somethin', isn't it? I thought that the day you came in with her, dear. Of course, I didn't trust my own memory. You have to be a certain age to remember her young like that. Now you can see for yourself! That boy is Billy Ramsay! Standing next to her. Now he was quite a rake in his day, I can tell you!"

Eve only half-heard Dilla's gossip—something about how Billy Ramsay cheated on Hetty with every woman in town—except Dilla, of course. While she spoke, Eve's mind flashed back to the previous night. She remembered Hetty...and...Mirabel...but, Mirabel wasn't there. It was just Hetty and she...she shook her head to clear it. The image wouldn't go away. She took the glass from Dilla again and studied the photo.

"Is something wrong, dear?" The old woman noticed Eve's sudden intensity.

"...Dilla—When was Mirabel born?" Eve was still studying the photo.

"Well, I don't know, dear. She wasn't born here. The mother had her elsewhere."

"Oh. What about *her* mother, Hetty's daughter?"

"...I don't know, not exactly. It must be forty-five years or more. People talked about it. I never saw her. Hetty's always kept pretty much to herself out there."

"There would be a record of it, wouldn't there? In the town hall, I mean?" Eve was still looking at the picture. Her eyes were glued to it.

"...Not really, dear."

Eve looked up suddenly from the picture, "What? Why not?"

"There was a fire, dear!—a little after that time. I remember that night! I was working in the Clerk's office back then. What a mess! The records of the town—most of 'em burned. There isn't a single older resident of Holmsford with an original birth certificate on file. The younger people have 'em. Those are on file. Not the older ones. Mine's gone too."

"How do people get an ID—a social security card..."

"Some people had their own copies...the rest...we know 'em, so we just issued a new one! It was the only thing to do."

"...What was her name?"

"Whose name, dear?"

"Hetty's daughter. What was her name?"

"...Well, you got me there!...I never saw the girl. Heard about her, but I never saw her....All I know is she...went off and left Hetty....That's what they said. Why, dear?"

"...Nothing. I..I must still be hung over..." Eve was trying to push away the bizarre anxiety she was feeling. There was that...aggravating 'something' hanging just out of her view, like a name you're trying to remember but just won't come to you!

"....How're you and Adam Singleton getting on?" Dilla smiled expectantly.

Eve looked down for a moment. "...I'm afraid that didn't go anywhere. He...pretty much dumped me."

"I don't believe that! Adam Singleton?...He's a good man!"

"...He's the best man I ever met...but he doesn't want me, and I have to agree with him. We don't...fit together. It's too late; we're on very different paths. It would never work."

"Horseshit!—I'm sorry, dear, but you young people have the stupidest ideas about things! I never saw a better match than you and Adam Singleton! Why, you two are like peas and carrots!"

"Dilla, you're probably the only person in town who would refer to us as 'young people.'"

"Are you gonna stand there and tell me that thirty-eight is old? Because if you are, I'm throwin' you out of my shop for being too stupid to breathe! What's Adam?—Forty? You're tellin' me that the two of you haven't got enough bend between the two of you to reach for each other."

"We're too...different, Dilla! I have my career in New York; he has his parish here—"

"What do you think love is—surrender? Raise up the white flag and become a prisoner? Eve, love is two strong people standing together because that's what they want! The two of you are about as strong as they come! You're all 'can do, and get out of my way' and he's all steady thought and 'how can I help you?' If you can't make something of that, you're not the girl I took you for!"

"...It takes two, Dilla. He made it clear."

The old woman sighed, "...Well...that's just...horseshit! That's all. I don't buy a bit of it!..."

***

CHAPTER 49

"... I ain't good enough for ya?"

"I don't want to get married, Lenny. I *was* married; I don't want to do it again."

"To a faggot! You married a fuckin' faggot! I ain't no fag—Look, I know I don't have no fancy degrees or nothin'. I drive a truck. Is it that? I ain't educated?"

"...No. I gave myself away before; I'm never doing that again!"

"What, you think I'm some kinda stud—use 'im and move on? Cause nobody treats me that way, lady! Nobody! I'm offerin' what I never gave no girl before!"

"...I know. I like that. I...just don't want to get married."

"That don't make sense, I'm offering you my whole life here!"

"I'm just turning down the ring—not you. No rings...no strings! Let's just enjoy this for what it is...for as long as it is."

Donna leaned over in the bed and kissed him deeply. He responded with his whole body, and she molded herself to him.

"..I ain't givin' up!" He pulled up and looked at her eye-to-eye.

"...I know."

***

CHAPTER 50

"Did you hear me?..."

"...Eyah...I heard ya, Missy!..." They were out in the goat pen by the barn. Hetty was busy putting out grain for the animals and filling the water troughs. Eve had gotten right into the pen with her.

"I made a call to Boston. To Robinson and Grinnell, they're a pretty strong firm—strategic partners of ours. I asked them to look into Innovative. There's something fishy about their interest in so much land in Holmsford."

Hetty stopped for a moment and looked at Eve, "...You done that for me?..."

"They have no right to try to take it away—Ow!" A small, black buck butted her leg, nearly knocking her off balance."

"Here you!—Pretty Boy—get off there!" Hetty gave the animal a rough push. It stood off a short distance staring at Eve and bleating loudly. "Sorry, Missy! He's a new one."

Eve rubbed her upper thigh, "He's a strong one!—I didn't think you named your animals."

"Not the does. Too many of 'em, but I only got two bucks, Old Billy and this here new one. Called him Pretty Boy on account of them black curls over his eyes."

Eve looked around the pens, "...Where this little blonde one? The female who always comes to me?"

"...Gone." Hetty went back to her feeding.

"Gone? Gone where?"

"..Didn't kid. This here's a workin' farm, Missy. If an animal don't work, gets replaced...."

"...We're going to stop this thing, Hetty! I'm not going to let them do this to you!" Eve was focusing on her purpose.

As she finished feeding the goats, Hetty led Eve out of the pen and tied the gate with a loop of rope.

"...That so?"

"Not if I can help it!"

"That's...more'n anybody ever done for me, Missy....Means somethin'..." The old woman didn't look at her directly.

"...Robinson and Grinnell are—"

"Don't need 'em!" Hetty interrupted before Eve could explain what the law firm could do for them.

"I'm not a lawyer, Hetty.

"Don't need 'em. There's two of us, ain't there? Two women...fixin' on a thing?—That there's more power than a whole wagon load 'o lawyers."

"Hetty, we have to be smart about this!"

"Trust yourself, Missy! You got power you don't even know about. Power no man has. Between the two 'o us... they ain't doin' nothing! Marlin' and his cronies, they can't shift me. Nobody'll shift me from my land. That's certain!"

"...All right, Hetty...but just to be on the safe side, I'm going to talk to Robinson and Grinnell. My firm has a pretty long reach."

"...Mostly men?—in that firm o' yours?"

"Mostly."

"...You oughta watch yourself, Missy! Men go the way the wind blows. On your side one day—for themselves the next. You never know when they might turn back on ya."

"I'm a partner, Hetty. My firm's resources are mine to use, and I'm going to use them!"

"...If that's what you think...You feelin' all right, Missy?"

"....The edge of headache, that's all."

"I sent ya a cure. Shoulda taken it!...I reckon we both had a bit too much, didn't we?..."

"The meal was...excellent—I remember that!..."

"...That's somethin'...."

Eve couldn't avoid the question any longer. "...Hetty..."

"...Eyah..."

"...Mirabel, where is she now?"

"Off...doin' chores..."

"Will she be back later?"

"...Gotta come back... don't she." The old woman was being careful now.

"Mirabel's mother—"

Eve saw Hetty flinch slightly "...Say what?...

"Mirabel's mother. You never mention her."

"Gone. I don't think on her." The old woman's tone was flat and final.

"Of course. I heard that she...died. I'm sorry—" The two women were now in the cottage garden.

"...Nothin' for you to be sorry for. You done nothin'." Hetty picked up a hoe and was weeding mercilessly.

"What was her name?"

"...Name?..."

"Mirabel's mother...What was her name?" Eve sensed that she was pushing into some place that Hetty had guarded.

"...Ain't important..." Hetty stopped only briefly in her work and then continued.

"Doesn't she ever ask you about her?"

"No reason for her ta. She's gone...that's all."

"But what about—"

"Becka."

"What...?"

"Becka! That's what I called her. Now, you gonna go after them damn men tryin' ta take my farm like you said, or are you gonna stand around here and stop me from workin'?" Hetty stood leaning on her rake staring at Eve.

The challenge was final and unmistakable. It left Eve with little to say. She turned and left the little garden. She was several steps away when she heard—

"Missy!" The old woman called to her without looking up from her chore.

Eve turned back to see her still laboring.

"...I owe ya..."

"...You're welcome, Hetty..." Eve turned back. There was still that troubling feeling at the back of her mind, that unresolved drunken image from their dinner that gnawed at her memory. Something had changed between them. That uneasy feeling kept her company the whole way home.

***

CHAPTER 51

"When did it happen!" Eve was standing there in the lobby and the receptionist was crying hysterically.

The girl was trying to pull herself together...."Last night....we think. I came in...put on the coffee—I'm always here first...and...and I walked by his office...and he was there! On the desk...like he was asleep. I called nine, one, one...but he was already cold! I knew he was dead. They just now took him away! Oh!—Poor Mr. Gardner!...He was such a nice man!..." The girl dissolved into tears again.

The arriving staff were in clutches around the office hunched in hushed conversation. The whole office was at a standstill. Eve knew that something had to be done quickly or the entire office would descend into confusion and instability. That couldn't be allowed to happen.

"I'll be in my office. Call his home and patch me in—do we know where they took him?"

"They said to the morgue at Bellevue." The girl was trying to keep her composure.

"Fine...then I want you to call Allen Novus. He's the other senior partner. He needs to know. Tell the other second-tier partners who are here that there will be a meeting at 10:00 a.m. to discuss operations. The rest of you need to get on with the work. Novus and Gardner is still open for business. Mr. Gardner would not appreciate our letting everything go. This firm has to function! Please! Do not tell clients about this and do not discuss it with outsiders. We have to make sure the public knows that Novus and Gardner is still up and running in spite of this...tragedy." The staff was stunned by her sudden command and stood immobilized for the moment. "Go! This is no time to stand around!"

On her order the staff began to move again. It was just a few minutes before regular hours; the phones would be ringing, then the markets would open. Novus and Gardner had to be working.

Eve turned back to the girl, "Tell Jace Brillig I want to see him as soon as he comes in."

"Yes, Ms. Truesdale." The girl had regained her self-control. She went to her desk and placed the calls Eve had ordered.

It was all happening so fast! Eve talked to Muriel Gardner, Harold's wife. She was as gentle as possible and asked if she wanted the office to arrange to have the body transported to a particular funeral home. Muriel was not as shocked as Eve would have guessed. She thanked Eve and informed her that she would make the arrangements herself and then notify the office.

Next, Allan Novus was on the phone. He was more upset than Muriel. Novus had been retired for some time, and it was clear why. He was no longer the sharp business mind that Harold had been. He seemed befuddled and confused. Eve told him about the meeting at ten and had a car sent to pick him up. As the only remaining senior partner, he had to be there to make decisions.

The office set into gear. Except for Gardner's empty office, nothing seemed different. The phones rang, clients called. Trades were made...the office was running. That was something.

As Eve walked into the conference room, all the partners available had convened. Allan Novus sat at the head of the table looking stricken and distraught. Several of the partners were catering to the old man, offering him coffee and condolences. She took her seat at the opposite end of the table and waited for a moment. When it appeared that no one was stepping in, Eve stood,

"Would everyone please take a seat?...Allan, thank you for coming on such short notice, but you can understand the urgency of this meeting. Mr. Gardner...is gone. We still have a business to run. It falls to us to decide how to proceed going forward."

"Isn't there some procedure laid out already?" That was George Costa. He was always for 'procedure.' Eve knew him as a 'letter of the law' type. Not creative, but exact. As a second-tier partner, he was good at his job.

"There is, George. I did some checking. It appears that our charter places Mr. Novus in the head chair as the surviving senior man." Eve knew this would cause a stir, and it did. There was an instant worried buzz around the table.

Novus looked out at the assembled group, and he was still sharp enough to realize that he was not equal to running the firm. "Listen, you people. An old fart like me can't keep up with you young wolves! I haven't conducted a deal in ten years! That was Harold's passion. He wouldn't quit...and now he's gone! You're going to have to run the place yourselves, or we're going to have to look for some group to take us over!"

There was another worried buzz. Finally, George rose, "I move we vote for a managing partner to run the business for a period of...one year. At the end of that time, we can vote again."

"You're gonna have a rough time! Once word gets out about Harold. You're going to lose some business without him at the helm. People knew him. You people ready for a rough ride?" Novus spoke what was on every partner's mind. How much could they afford to lose? How bad would it get? Would they be dismembered by the competition?

Eve could feel the room draining of confidence. She stood. "*We've* been running this business for a long time! Harold was important, of course. Yes, people knew him—depended on him, but who did Harold depend on? Us! Each one of us runs a department in this firm. George, didn't Harold defer to you when it came to SEC and taxes?"

"Yes. I always advised."

"Right! Harold trusted us to do our jobs, and we've been doing them. There's no reason we shouldn't keep on doing them. All we need is a C.O.O. and we can keep going. Business as usual."

The partners seemed to relax a little.

George Costa stood again, "I nominate Eve Truesdale for temporary C.O.O."

"Now, wait—I—" Eve was about to object.

"All those in favor?"

The entire Board table voiced, "Aye!"

Eve stopped for a moment to think. Then she spoke. "I've been trying to take a little more time lately. I don't know that I want to take on the workload. Why not you, George?"

"You've already been voted in, Eve!...Mr. Novus, do you approve the vote."

"You got me, fellas. You think she's the one...then she's it!"

It was just that quick. By 10:30 a.m. Eve Truesdale was running Novus and Gardner.

It was as if she were on a run-away freight train! The press was calling. She had the PR department craft a dignified press release indicating that the firm was on solid ground and would continue as usual. The phones began ringing. She spent a good portion of the first day reassuring clients that nothing would change in either the firm's style or its service to clients. She thought she was managing to hold everything steady. What she wanted to know was where the hell was Jace! Now was when she could use him! He was the most creative trader and analyst they had. She had her secretary calling everywhere for him. This wasn't like him. Business was the one thing Jace held sacred, so where was he?

By Tuesday Muriel had planned the funeral service. It was held after business hours. There was no wake. The office sent an elaborate floral arrangement. Allen Novus attended and the entire second-tier. By Wednesday the firm had consolidated itself and everyone was beginning to get back into stride. Everyone, that is, except Eve. She had almost no time for her own department. Jace was still missing. Dick Waring was keeping things moving, but he didn't have the same eye; she had to review everything he did. Jace had a lot of explaining to do, but she was too overwhelmed to try to track him down.

On Thursday morning, she got the call. Jace's car had been found by the Holmsford police, abandoned in the parking lot of the Sleepy Hollow Motel. His luggage was still in the room he had rented. Nothing had been touched. There was no trace of him.

A search was made. His personal effects were held at the police station along with the car which had been towed. The only number they had was Novus and Gardner, which was on the paperwork in the briefcase.

Eve drove in on Friday morning to pick up his effects; she was exhausted and stunned. Harold's death was a shock but not totally unexpected. He was an old man. Old men die. But Jace!...What had happened? Where did he go? He wasn't into solitary adventures—hiking, rock climbing— none of that! Young ambitious business men like Jace Brillig do not just disappear!

"...Well, if it ain't Kenny's Tierney's old girlfriend!..." The desk sergeant smiled broadly as Eve entered the station house. It was a small-town station. The desk was close to the front door in a rear section of the town hall.

"...I beg your pardon—oh." Eve recognized the cop from the wreck that had killed the moving man who attacked her just after she had moved into her house. "I'm Eve Truesdale, Novus and Gardner. I came for Jace Brillig's things." Eve did her best not to react to the leering cop.

"...No can do...Ms.—Truesdale! Personal effects can only be given to the next of kin."

"Are you telling me he's dead?" A new wave of shock coursed through her.

"...Nope. But until we know otherwise, we can only turn over personal effects to the next of kin...father...mother...brother. Guys don't do well around you, do they?"

Eve swallowed back the urge to hit the man, "Mr. Brillig had no next of kin. His parents are dead. There are no siblings.—Can I have them, please."

"What about...cousins....uncles—that sort of thing?" The cop was enjoying her distress.

"I...I don't know..." Eve realized that she didn't know very much about Jace's family connections, but, then, why would she? "Can I at least see them?"

"Sure...why not?..." The cop reached behind the desk to a table which contained a number of items. One of them was Jace's briefcase. "The luggage is in the trunk of the car. That's been impounded...out back. He didn't pay his bill at the Sleepy Hollow."

"My company will...settle with the motel...May I open this?"

"It's locked."

"I...know the combination. Mr. Brillig was my employee." Eve quickly opened the case and looked inside. There were a few loose papers...and there was a thick manila envelope marked 'Eve Truesdale' with her address. She pulled it out of the case.

"Hey, hey, hey, lady! I can't let you take nothin'! Lookin's fine, but you can't take nothin'"

Eve showed him the envelope. "This is addressed to me. Whatever is in this envelope clearly was intended for me."

"How do I know that? There's no stamp on that. That could be anything." The cop was still trying to exercise his authority, and Eve was losing her patience.

"...All right, Look, Sergeant..." Eve looked at the man's name tag, "Michaud...you've had your fun, now I'm calling a halt to it....This envelope is *my* property. I'm entitled to take mail addressed to me. If you have a question about that, you can look it up in the Federal Code. If you try to prevent me, I will have a case with the Town of Holmsford for illegal seizure of personal property, which I will eagerly pursue. I head a large and...influential investment firm. We have lawyers—many lawyers! Once my firm's lawyers are done, I think it's safe to say, you will not be sitting behind that desk or in any kind of a uniform. I will pursue you—very personally. You will not have a pot to piss in by the time I'm done...Now...do you want that?" Eve had no idea what the "Federal Codes" were, but she was reasonably certain the fat sergeant didn't know them either. She considered that like most bullies he wouldn't expect the victim to hit back.

"...Look...Miss...I'm not supposed to release nothin' to nobody unless they're related. That's the law!" Eve stood her ground and stared at him.

"...OK, OK! Take the envelope! It's got your name on it, but I ain't givin' you nothin' else. Not until I get a court order to release the property!"

"I'll get one! For now, this is mine!"

"Are...are you filin' a report?...Missing person?..."

Eve spent the next hour filling out the report. She phoned back to New York to research Jace's family to see if there was anyone to claim his car and bags...It was all so unreal to her! She could still see him in her mind's eye helping himself to breakfast in her kitchen on Saturday. When she sent him away, she had no idea this would happen!

It was nearly nine o'clock when she pulled up to her dark house. There was no moon. Except for the streetlights, the neighborhood was quiet. Marian hadn't been around much at all—not since Nelson. She didn't know where Libby or Donna might be, and she was dead tired.

She nearly collapsed into her front door. She tossed her carry-bag to the floor next to the hall tree and placed her keys in the bowl. She had set her sights on a sandwich and an early bed. She was about to head into the kitchen when she looked down and saw her bag had fallen over and the envelope she had seized from Jace's briefcase had slipped out. She picked it up and absently broke the seal.

Inside was a stapled set of documents with a note paper-clipped to them. The note was in Harold Gardner's handwriting:

> *"Tell her she doesn't have a choice. It's in clause 6. She's being bought out at the current share price as of Friday close. She has to sign it. Once she does, you lead the department. Say nothing of this to anyone until it's done....Gardner."*

251

"...You old son-of-a-bitch, Harold! You couldn't handle a little push-back from a woman, could you?...Jace!" Eve realized what had been going on. It stung her that Jace was slipping her the knife. She thought about how she had pushed him away. Could she really blame him? He wanted to 'own' Novus and Gardner.—With Harold dead...where did that leave him now? For that matter...where did it leave her?

She took the envelope and its contents to the fireplace and burned them. No one needed to see this. No one needed to know about this. When Jace returned—she would have a lot to talk to him about!—Where was he?

***

She slept long. It was past nine when she came to. Half-asleep, she nearly crawled to the kitchen and put on the coffee. She had just taken her first sip when the front doorbell rang.

"Jesus Christ!..." Eve made herself go to the door. The bell sounded again before she got there.

"Coming!..." She opened the door and Mirabel stood there, holding a paper bag and smiling.

"I brung ya a cake..." The girl walked right in, and after a brief moment, Eve closed the door.

"Uh...a cake...Mira, where have you been?"

"I...been around. It's a honey cake—from Hetty—to celebrate."

"Celebrate?...What...what do you mean?" Eve was still not fully awake. "What are we celebrating?"

"...Dominion..." Mira went right into the kitchen.

Curious and confused, Eve followed the girl, "...Dom—...What...?"

She poured herself a coffee and extracting the cake from the bag, cut two large pieces and put them on plates. She handed one to Eve. "...You know...takin' control."

That uneasy feeling began to form in Eve's gut again as she looked at Mirabel.

"You know...two women...workin' together—to keep the farm? Hetty told me."

"Oh...It's a little early to celebrate! All we can do right now is maybe slow them down...try to stop this eminent domain thing from happening..."

"You've got more power than you know...Hetty says." The girl concentrated on her cake.

"...I don't feel so powerful this morning. Not with the week I've had! Our working Senior Partner died on Monday!"

The girl kept munching on the cake, "...That...bad?..."

"He wasn't a young man, but it was...a complete shock! Nobody expected it. Everything was in chaos! Nobody knew what to do..."

"...Nobody?..."

"...What?"

"How 'bout you? I bet you knew what to do!..." She sipped her coffee keeping her eyes on Eve.

"...I...I just did...what made sense. Got everybody to keep moving. Called people together...to talk..."

"...Uh huh..." The girl cut herself another piece of cake.

"They...they made me temporary C.O.O.—just for a year."

"...C. O.O.?...What's that?"

"Chief Operating Officer. They voted me in on the spot...I didn't...expect that..." Eve began to think again about what had happened.

"...That...like bein' in control?..." Mirabel asked the question simply.

"...Temporarily..." Eve was trying to put things in to perspective.

"...I reckon you do good—they'll keep ya!"

"...Mira....Jace is missing!"

Mirabel looked at Eve and took another sip of her coffee..."Where?"

"I don't know! I said, he's missing, Mira. He's gone! They found his car at the motel. His things...I don't know where he is!...No one does."

"...Did ya...still want him?..." The question was quiet...measured.

"No!..but—Mira, you met him! You knew him!—Jace and I were...business associates...." Eve had started to say "friends" but she stopped herself. "We worked together!"

"...I don't think so." Mirabel put her cup down and looked straight at Eve.

"...What?" Eve could feel that anxiety in her gut beginning to gnaw again.

"He...come to me. Last Saturday...after he left you...while I was fixin' to make cheese. He weren't no 'associate' then."

"Mira,...what are you talking about?"

"He was after me...to bed me. He done it that first night I stayed here."

"...You're mistaken."

"I ain't!..He weren't shy about it! Put it right out there, and I turned him down. He come again on Saturday sayin' as how he'd 'own ya' and you'd be workin' for him, if you worked at all...He didn't sound like no 'associate.'"

"...That bastard!"

"I reckon...."

"...Jace...liked women. I knew that! He never tried to hide that from me. He was honest about it; it was part of his charm..."

"...I reckon..."

"I didn't think he'd...What did you say to him?" Eve looked at the beautiful girl who stood sipping her coffee calmly.

"...What do you think?...I don't turn on a friend....Maybe it's good he's gone."

"Mira! Even if Jace...was planning something...I wouldn't wish him any harm!"

"...You didn't have to wish nothin'...It just happened...terrible thing."

"I...I think I need more coffee." Eve went to the pot and refilled her cup. The anxiety was tingling through her whole body now.

"...Don't think on it...You done nothin' wrong,...Let me cut ya some more cake..." the girl took the knife and sliced cleanly through the loaf.

***

CHAPTER 52

"Motion passed! The Town Clerk will draw up the writ, and I'll bring it out to her this afternoon." The vote was four to two. Marlin, Wally Fry, Curtis Bolling, and Esau Carter voted for eminent domain. Only Singleton and Charlie Metcalf voted against.

"I want it in the record that two of us voted against! Jack, this is a dirty, underhanded thing to do to that woman! I'm ashamed we let it pass."

"Duly noted, Charlie. Let it be entered into the minutes that Selectmen Metcalf and Singleton voted against the writ.

"You sure you don't want a police escort, Jack?" Wally Fry laughed uproariously at his own joke.

"I can handle her! She's gonna pay for that new mirror too. I'm deducting it from the check we're giving her for the land...and anything else she costs us!"

"Mr. Chairman...are we sure that we can't just ask Ms. Livesey to sell? Do we really need to force her hand in this?"

"Reverend!...Didn't you hear how she took a swing at him? Old Jack's lucky to escape with his headlights! Ha. Ha. Ha....!" Wally Fry couldn't contain himself.

"I'm afraid she's not much for it, Reverend Singleton. I went there with all good intentions! I tried to reason with the woman, but she got violent! I don't think she's going to agree willingly to anything we propose. No, this writ is the only way, I'm afraid. It's for the good of the town."

"Just how long are you gonna hide behind that idea, Jack! You been doin' that your whole life, meanwhile you do pretty much what you damn please! Taking that farm—the last original homestead in this part of Massachusetts and handing to a real estate company for a goddamn Industrial Park—that's a crime in my book!"

"The chair notes the objections of Selectman Metcalf...Now shall we get on to other business?..."

***

CHAPTER 53

"That's tragic, honey—just tragic! What a terrible thing—dying at his desk like that. How was his wife, honey? I bet she was a wreck!"

"Muriel was...surprisingly composed. She handled the arrangements...notified everyone...She was...fine."

"Uh, huh...you know what that means!..." Libby was stabbing at her cake with a fork.

"Oh, well, honey...what man doesn't? It's still hard to go through it. I feel sorry for her!"

"...She's probably Goddamned relieved! The old fucker probably had half-a-dozen chippies stored away!—With his money?..."

"I don't think Harold—" Eve started to defend Gardner.

"It's a tragic thing, but I always say there's a gift in every bad thing that happens! I mean Chief Operating Office of Novus and—"

"Gardner. Novus and Gardner..."

"Novus and Gardner! Big-time investment company.—I've been telling Nelson that he needs to cut down on his practice a little. Spend a little more time with me..."

"...Well...at least that'll make his life *seem* longer!..."

"You are not going to make me mad! Not today. I'm hosting this time, and I will not let you get to me! Besides, Nelson *loves* spending time with me. He can't keep his hands off me...Especially since I've lost all this weight." Marian stood up from the table and modeled her slimmed down figure in a new brightly patterned sheath dress she had just bought.

"...Have you been running?" Donna was impressed.

"Fifteen pounds! I just don't have the appetite I had before I met Nelson. He seems to...fulfill my needs!"

"Now you're taking away my Goddamn appetite! By the way, this is good cake...Not as good as the one I made with Jonas, though."

"Ugh! That....boy you let into your home?"

"He likes to cook. Baking is his favorite. You're losing weight? I'm finding it! Christ, that kid is so compulsive. Cakes, brownies, cookies...anything sweet!"

"That's an addict, for you! I read about that!" Marian was adamant.

"Now look, you—"Libby was rising to the defense of Jonas when Marian cut in.

"Where's Mira?" Marian was looking at Eve.

"...Huh?...I don't know. She's at the farm, I guess. Hetty has a lot for her to do..."

"I invited her! Didn't you tell her she was invited?

"I haven't seen her!...She hasn't stayed with me at all....And I've been a little distracted..."

"...Well, of course you have! With the new position and—"

"Jace is missing....My 'employee' has disappeared! They found his car and luggage left at the Motel out of town...apparently he came to give me....some documents...and now he's gone."

"...Oh, honey! I had no idea—none of us did! When did this happen?"

"Sometime last weekend apparently. The Holmsford police called me on Thursday at the office. They have his car...his luggage...no sign of him."

"Like Junie Hildebrande?" Marian sat at her chair looking at the other two women.

"Oh, for Christ's sake, Marian. That's stupid! The two things aren't even connected!"

"They both happened here!"

"I found out that he was here to fire me..."

"How do you know that?" Donna suddenly focused on Eve.

"...There was an envelope in his briefcase...I was able to get that; it was addressed to me—a buyout. There was a note from my boss instructing him to make me sign, but...but Harold...died and then...Jace...vanished."

"And now you run the place! Serves 'em both Goddamn right!" I propose a toast!" Libby lifted her lemonade. "To Eve, screw the boss!"

"Screw the boss!" They all toasted her, but Eve sat a little stunned at what she was turning over in her mind...

"...Do you think...somehow...*I* did this?.."

"You!? Unless you shot the old fucker and carried the young one out to the swamp somewhere and drowned him—which none of us would mind—how could *you* have caused any of this?"

"...Hetty says women have power...if they know how to use it..."

"You've been spending way too much time with that Goddamn old Goat Woman! How the hell could you have caused anything?"

"...I don't know...the timing is so...particular..."

"All right, honey! Now, this isn't you! You're exhausted. If *I* said any of this—well, that would just be me—but you! You, Eve Truesdale, the perfect business woman? No nonsense. This is nothing but the extra stress talking!" Marian reached across the table and took Eve's hand.

"...I guess I'm being...I don't know...." Eve looked at the concerned faces around her and tried to pull herself back from the sick feeling in her gut.

"It's fucking ridiculous! Marian's right, and you don't know how much I hate saying that! You need to focus on being the new boss."

Eve suddenly came back to herself. She pulled the anxiety in and smiled. "You're right. It's...it's been—quite a week!"

"...Well, have some more cake, honey. It'll help relieve the stress."

As she watched Marian cut another slice of cake, Eve felt another wave of anxiety begin to rise.

***

CHAPTER 54

There was satisfaction in it, Marlin had to admit to himself. Serving Hetty Livesey with the writ of eminent domain. She wasn't getting away with attacking John Marlin, Chairman of the Board of Selectmen! Who did she think she was? Holding up the town's development?—Pure selfishness! He'd serve her with the writ and that would show *her* who was in charge!

As he pulled up the farm road, he caught sight of the old woman in the goat pen beside the barn. Suddenly he remembered how volatile she could become, and he was having second thoughts about coming out here alone. No!—He would do it. If the old woman got violent again...this time he'd have her arrested! That would show her. Nobody has a right to molest a town official on town business!

Marlin pulled his car gently up toward the barn and turned off the engine. He reaching down on the seat of the car where the writ sat in a white envelope with the town seal on it. He carried it out in front of him as he approached the pens.

"...I see ya fixed ya car!...You need me to take off t'other one this time?"

"Miss Livesey, I don't want there to be any unpleasantness between us..." He stopped by the fence. The old woman was on the other side feeding and watering her goats. The smell was strong in his nostrils.

"I don't reckon this is no social call. What's ya business, Marlin?" The old woman came right up to the fence, but this time he didn't see the staff she had carried on his last visit.

"All right....my business...is this, Miss Livesey." Marlin handed her the writ and took one step back.

Hetty took the envelope and looked at it without opening it. "What is it?"

"It's a writ of eminent domain. The Board of Selectmen has determined that it's necessary for the betterment of the Town of Holmsford to purchase your property for the purpose of the creation of an industrial park. You will be paid a fair market value for the acreage and personal property, as well as the moving of your—home—in consideration of its age and its historic significance—to a location on the remaining land not purchased by the town. All expenses for the home's removal and restoration will, of course, be paid for by the Town. We will also include the addition of amenities, if you so desire."

"Hold on there, Mr. Marlin!" Eve had walked into the barnyard just as Marlin had begun his explanation.

"Ms. Truesdale!—I didn't see you standing there!"

"I'm sure. This writ you're serving, has it been discussed at the Town Meeting?"

"...It will be, Ms. Truesdale."

"Aren't all matters regarding the town voted on in open forum at the Town Meeting?"

"...Well, now, Ms. Truesdale...in the old days...certainly. But these days matters of significance are decided by the Board. Town Meeting is...more of a place to have a street light fixed or pothole filled. Important things...like this...we take care of as part of the 'public trust.'" Marlin wasn't counting on a witness.

"Mr. Marlin, how do you think it'll play...when the people of this town get wind of your maneuvering to move an old woman off her land just so your cronies can make a few bucks?—I wonder how many votes you'll get in the next election. As the head of an influential investment firm, I have access...to some interesting resources. Legal counsel...public relations expertise...." Eve walked toward Marlin and faced him squarely.

"This is a local matter! This is all perfectly legal and above board! We're talking about jobs here, Ms. Truesdale. That industrial park will provide many, many jobs for our citizens. It will reinvigorate the local economy...which is badly deteriorated—and which you are probably not aware of as a newcomer!"

"That's the spin, is it? Jobs? Development? You know, it's been my experience that so many business dealings really can't stand up to close scrutiny. There's always something...questionable."

"...Really, Ms. Truesdale? Well, I suppose that's true. For instance, the Chief of Police informed me this morning that a colleague of yours has gone missing in our town. In fact, we have his car and belongings at the back of the Town Hall....I understand...that you were the last person to see him...I also understand that you have just recently acceded to, shall we say, a position of prominence in your firm in New York. Now, I'm sure everything is fine, but....I wonder how that position would be influenced by the 'close scrutiny' of our police department into the disappearance of your friend. Things can spin in any direction, Ms. Truesdale..."

"You're a real son-of-a-bitch, aren't you!"

"Bitch...son-of-a-bitch...some words just shouldn't be thrown around; don't you agree?"

"You're going to choke on this if you try to go through with it. I can promise you that. You and anyone who voted for this will fall in the public eye. Your little political machine is about to hit the wall, Mr. Marlin!" Eve was trying not to let her anger get the best of her.

"Miss Livesey, I've served you with due notice. In thirty days you will receive compensation for your property and we will arrange for the moving of your home and belongings....Good day....ladies." Marlin nearly strutted back to his car. As he drove off, he reflected on just how satisfying this entire experience was. He had accomplished...what he set out to do. The Goat Woman was put in her place, and that uppity bitch, Eve Truesdale, found out that he didn't back down so easily. Just let her try to make trouble! Just let her try!

"...Ya told him, Missy!" Hetty still stood behind the fence, clutching the white envelope as they watched Marlin drive out of sight.

"I'm afraid I didn't do you much good, Hetty. This is moving too fast. I haven't heard a word from Robinson and Grinnell....I don't know what to tell you."

"You don't hafta tell me nothin', Missy. Ya told him!...That's good enough for me! It's on his head now..."

"Hetty, if we don't find something about Innovative—"

"Don't matter!—I ain't goin' nowhere. I been here and I'm stayin'. There ain't no power on earth can move me...they'll find that out!"

"...He could do harm..." Eve was thinking about Marlin's threat.

"He can't hurt me, Missy. Nobody can!...You warned him what would happen...didn'tcha?"

***

CHAPTER 55

"...You burned it?—The envelope?" Dilla had set out a plate of pastry and she and Eve were sitting at the back of her store sharing an impromptu breakfast.

"I'm not going to show it to anyone. I'm not going to give any of the other partners any reason to doubt my...authority. Besides, it no longer has any weight. Harold is...dead, I'm...in charge! It was a business decision."

"And the only other person who knew about the documents is...missing..." Dilla sipped her coffee.

"I know!—Now, when I think about it, it was probably stupid! When Marlin mentioned my being the 'last person' to see Jace...It felt like I was caught in some ridiculous 'Movie of the Week!' I called him a son-of-a-bitch!" Eve was sipping on her coffee.

"I guess just about everybody's called him that...to his face, behind his back...in print, even," Dilla sighed, "But they keep on electing him!"

"Why's that?" Eve listened as she drew inside herself looking for some kind of solace.

"Well, he's 'their' son-of-a-bitch, dear. When it comes to politics, folks tend to vote for the biggest son-of-a-bitch they can find, as long as they think he's on *their* side!"

"...I can't stop thinking about Jace..." Eve looked up at Dilla.

"...How long were you sleeping with him?..." Dilla met her eyes and didn't look away.

"...Two years...give or take."

"...But then you met Adam."

"Stupid me, eh! You'd think with all my business experience, I'd make better decisions about...Life."

"You're awfully hard on yourself, dear! The world's very different from when I was young. But I don't guess that those feelings are much different. You're only human, dear."

262

"I didn't...commit. Jace was...Jace! Too ambitious, too cock-sure, too...young...He had lots of women; I knew about it. I guess I didn't care!"

"But you did care, dear. Otherwise you wouldn't be feeling this way."

"...Do you think...maybe I caused this?"

"...What are you doing, Eve?...Why are you thinking this way?"

"...Harold's death...Jace's...vanishing like that...They were both planning to oust me from the firm..."

"Eve—That's not even close to possible! You didn't even know what they were doing? Both those men...you had a relationship with them. They betrayed you. I think maybe you've got your grief and anger all mixed up."

"...It just...hangs in my mind...Adam..."

"Adam didn't betray you, dear; You let him go."

"I didn't! I didn't let him go; he rejected me!"

"He rejected himself. You showed him how...complete you were. How self-sufficient. How could he fit in with that?..."

"That's not fair!"

"No, it isn't...but somehow it's what happened. Men aren't as stupid as we like to think they are. They need to know there's a space in you for them."

"...What do I do?..." Eve sat back in her chair.

"What do you want?..." Dilla sat straight in her chair.

"...I don't want to be alone anymore..."

"No, dear, that's what you *don't* want. Every fool knows what they don't want—'I don't want to be poor; I don't want to be sick; I don't want to be alone.' You gotta know what you *do* want. That's the trick. When I was young, you got married. That was...the main choice. Marriage, a husband, children. It was even respected! Having a career—some did it—not many, and they paid a price. Nowadays women can do anything. They're even super-heroes now! But there's still a price, dear. Man or woman, you have to decide what you want."

"I spent my whole career getting to be where I am right now..." Eve spoke slowly as she thought about what Dilla was saying.

"...It's a big thing, dear. Something to be proud of..." Dilla let her think.

"There are only a handful of women right now who have this kind of position...I don't even know why I came to Holmsford. Actually, that's a lie. I was...having some kind of...panic attacks...losing control. I didn't want anyone to see. I thought if I came here, I could get my balance. Get back to my center."

"Has it helped, dear?"

Eve got up from her chair and walked toward the window, "What do you think, Dilla? I'm...a mess! Look at me! I can't make up my mind about...anything! Do you know I got blind drunk at that dinner I had at Hetty's? I've never done anything like that! Never! I even...imagined Hetty turned herself into Mirabel! I looked up, and, in my drunken stupor, I saw Mira sitting in the chair dressed in Hetty's clothes. Scared the shit out of me!—that I could be so...out of control!"

"Is that what you really want, dear? Control?...Control of what?" Dilla could see how distraught Eve was.

"I used to be so sure—of everything. Day to day...I made decisions...ran things...

"Sounds like you still are, dear...Eve, you've been running back and forth between New York and Holmsford...a lot has happened, you're just tired, dear. Worn out."

"No! I'm not! That's just it. I'm...full of pent up energy! I want answers! I want things to...I want to make everything...right!"

Eve had been pacing, working herself up. Dilla watched her, concerned about the manic energy she was showing. She was standing by the window, breathing like she had run a marathon, gripping her coffee cup with both hands. The old woman got up and touched Eve's arm. She could see her jaw, tense and working...

"...All right, dear. Come and sit...Let's figure out exactly what that means for you..."

***

264

CHAPTER 56

Wally Fry had a good morning. The bottle of Jack Daniels he had stowed away the night before had made a good breakfast. Jack had been generous. He had given Wally five hundred dollars cash! Imagine—being paid under the table to make a decision he already agreed with—and Jack had promised 'more to come!'

It was a good morning, but now it was time to re-stock. He bought his supplies at Cardoza's, out of town, on the highway. Nobody needed to know. His daughter Kelly watched him like a hawk, so he made the trip to Cardoza's, where nobody knew him. He bought his supplies a bottle at a time and hid them where his daughter's prying eyes would never find them...in the drop ceiling in his bedroom.

Ssh!...nobody knew! Nobody had to know!...He would just slip out and drive over and be back with his contraband before she came over for lunch. That was their routine. Lunch every day—so she could check on him! It only took twenty-minutes—the roundtrip journey. He could be back, make a couple of sandwiches for the two of them, and she would never be the wiser!

He pulled on his baseball cap, and went out the front door of his 'mezzanine' apartment at The Breakers, an over-priced converted motel that afforded 'luxury' accommodation in the form of two-bedroom apartments with 'complete kitchens and all amenities.'

He had moved there after Lila died. That had been rough. The heart attack was massive. She was dead by the time the ambulance arrived.

He sold the house. Too many memories. He had moved to The Breakers as a way to start over, and he had...started over...with the alcoholism he had conquered twenty years before. It had come back like an old friend, and stayed on like a guest that wouldn't leave. Never mind that now. Get the car keys, get the stuff, and get back—that was the agenda.

The 'amenities' of The Breakers included private entrances that consisted of staircases to the mezzanine. Wally didn't mind, but during the winter it was a blustery walk from the parking lot to the front door. Today, however, it was clear sailing: 75 degrees, light breeze...full sunshine!

He was so intent on his mission that Wally never noticed the loose tread cover on the second stair. He stepped out on it and tumbled 'arse over teacups' to the cement landing below. It was two hours before anyone found him sprawled on the landing with his head twisted at a sickening angle.

John Marlin made sure the coroner reported the alcohol content in his blood. 'Accidental fall, caused by heavy alcohol ingestion.' What a shame!

***

CHAPTER 57

"They're not a publicly held company, Ms. Truesdale."

"Yes, I know Mr. Gottlieb, but Novus and Gardner has expanded our client base in the Boston Area as you know, and we're considering perhaps approaching them with a buyout. However, before we do that, we need to know much more about them...the kind of business they do...their leadership. I understand they're run by Jim Reedy. Find out what you can about him as well. We want to be well-informed before we make an offer."

"All right. How soon do you need the information?"

"I want you to be thorough...but there is some need for expedience..."

"I'll see what I can do...say—end of the week?"

"Thank you, Mr. Gottlieb. I appreciate it, but, of course, I want this kept strictly confidential. I don't want anyone to get wind of our interest."

"Yes, Ma'am. We understand..." Gottlieb hung up.

It was fine; she was fine! She couldn't bring herself to change her office yet, and she still hadn't managed to divert more of her attention to her own department. She still thought of it as 'hers' even though now the entire company was her concern. She had been having meetings with each of the second-tier partners to find out just where they were, what they needed, how they were doing. She had been careful to sound interested rather than critical. She had to enlist them all in the work to be done. The firm not only had to function as before, it had to move ahead, show growth...be a player! She was determined that her new position as C.O.O. should be seen as a new direction for the Company. On the outside, they had to know that the 'Dragon Lady' was in charge, but inside...it was more delicate. Egos had to be stroked. It seemed that everyone was watching her, waiting for her to slip, looking for a weakness. After all, wasn't she a 'woman'?

Eve wouldn't let herself miss anything. Each day she hopped from department to department, partner to partner, joking, cajoling, conferring, confiding, collaborating—checking everything! She left nothing to chance. At night she reviewed the day's results to be prepared for the next day. It was like being at Stanford all over again. All those long nights preparing for exams, studying...preparing for intern interviews, writing papers—and she could never look tired. She couldn't flag, and she wouldn't let herself falter, not for a minute, not for a second. She let the business completely consume her. She invited it!

It was better than feeling. All the activity, the decision-making, the gut-busting work kept her mind away from the disturbing guilt she still held from Harold's death and Jace's...she didn't know what to call it. Still no word of him! It had blocked any thoughts of Holmsford...Adam. For two weeks, for the most part, she had managed to drive that out.

Gottlieb had called her at the end of the week and requested an extension on the time to report on Innovative. He had said that they were still checking into some of their assets.

"Mr. Gottlieb, I'm running a business here. If you can't deliver a simple analysis of a company—"

"Some of their transactions need to be checked, Ms. Truesdale. They're not a public company. I'm having to use...some rather clandestine approaches to get the information. Please, I'm very sorry it's taking a little longer, but you did say you wanted a thorough analysis."

"...All right. I need that analysis by the twentieth. I have...an interested client...who has to make some major changes by the end of the month."

"I will work on it myself, Ms. Truesdale."

This was the first time she had thought about Hetty. That jolt of fear came flooding back. Why? Why did she feel this way? She shook her head trying to shake the feeling out. It was Friday. She gave her administrative assistant instructions that she would be away for the next four days...In Holmsford, Massachusetts. She could be reached by landline, cellphone, and computer. She duly surrendered all the numbers, email addresses—everything that could possibly connect her to the company. The cloak and dagger routine was over. With Harold gone, there was no longer any reason to hide her second residence. There was no one to question her dedication to the company. She didn't have to justify her actions to anyone!

For the first time since she had bought the house in Holmsford, there was no anxious thrill in pulling away from her condo garage to go to her 'secret hideaway.' She was just another New York executive headed for a weekend house. She missed the feeling of rebellion, but there was a greater satisfaction in knowing she didn't have to answer for leaving town. No one would try to guilt her for leaving...mostly because everyone knew where she was. She *wasn't* leaving. The Holmsford house was now just another part of the office...."Yea," she said to herself flatly as she pointed her car up I-95 toward Massachusetts.

***

CHAPTER 58

The night was perfect...cool with clear skies. There were stars everywhere. The trip had taken a flat three hours. As she got out of her car, Eve could smell the sweet scent of honeysuckle wafting on a light breeze. Crickets sang in the grass, and the darkened house glowed in the moonlight, perfect and empty.

As she got out of the car Eve inhaled deeply. Somehow she didn't feel the same freedom she had when she had come home before. She knew she *wasn't* free! The past two weeks had changed her connection here in some way. It wasn't just the removal of the veil from the office. It was deeper, subtler than that, but she couldn't quite articulate it.

Everything in the house was exactly as she had left it. She went to the kitchen for a snack before she went to bed. On the counter was a small honeycake left with a note:

"From Hetty," was all it said.

It was still warm!

"How did she know...?" Eve thought to herself as she cut a slice and bit into it. The honey and spices filled her head, and for a moment she was back at Hetty's table on that night. Reflexively she put the slice down on the counter as if *it* had bitten *her.* The image of Mira sitting in Hetty's clothes at the table returned, and it shocked her! *"Stupid!...Stupid, drunken...idiot!"* She thought as she left the cake with the slice cut from it on the counter and got away from it altogether. She went upstairs and showered and got into bed, but the image kept haunting her, shaming her. It was at least an hour before she could escape into sleep.

She slept in. It was a deep and dreamless sleep. When the phone rang, it was nearly 10:00 a.m. Eve was totally discombobulated as she answered.

"Eve, honey?..."

"...Uh...Marian...Hi..."

"Where have you been? It's been two weeks! I saw your car in the driveway."

270

"...Working, Marian. I do have to do that, you know. My new position...I had to sort things out...be hands on—"

"Well, we're at the Puritan, Honey! The girls and me, and we're taking you to brunch! So, you get your executive self together and come on down here! A lot's been going on—for Holmsford, anyway! You come on down and we'll fill you in! How soon can you get here?"

"Uh....all right. Give me twenty minutes. I'll meet you there. Brunch, huh—what's been going on?"

"Oh, honey, you get yourself down here, and then we'll tell you. Very exciting!"

Eve hung up. Marian! She loved her drama! Eve quickly pulled herself together. She scrubbed her face, brushed her teeth and put on her most comfortable jeans. She wanted to be as far from 'executive' looking as possible. She tied her hair back and applied a little makeup. When she checked her look in the mirror, she decided she looked like a farm wife...maybe with a little New York twist—perhaps the Gucci sandals *were* a bit much.

***

CHAPTER 59

"...on the overpass to 95! Both gone in a fireball! Just like that!"

"When did this happen?" Eve was thunderstruck by the news. She was having a hard time absorbing what Marian was telling her.

"Oh, Honey—last night sometime! I'm surprised you didn't see some of it when you were coming in! They were both just at Fry's funeral, then boom! Gone!"

"Hold on! 'Fry's funeral'—Do you mean Wally Fry, one of the Town Selectmen?"

"Oh...He died a few days ago. Fell down the stairs or something. But those two men! What a horrible way to go!..."

Esau Carter and Curtis Bolling had hit the underpass to the highway to Boston. The whole diner was buzzing about it. At the booths all around them the locals were quietly shaking their heads and muttering phrases like, "You never know!" and "S'pose they were drunk or somethin'?" There was that group mock sorrow when some unexplainable tragedy happens to somebody else. And this was dramatic and exciting! Everyone mouthed the usual sympathetic philosophies and clichés, but really enjoyed the diversion from the normal, day-to-day boredom of small-town living.

Eve could hear snatches of the conversations around her, people going over each horrific detail, extracting the maximum amount of titillation and survivor triumph from it.

"Now, honey, I talked to one of the cops at the scene. Those two men hit that abutment going at least seventy! Can you imagine? What were they doing, having a drag race? If it were two young guys—nobody would think twice! We all know how young guys are! But two older men like that! The car exploded! The two of them were just...incinerated!—It was the exact same place that guy died in his truck, Eve! You know! The one who gave you all that trouble when you first came! The exact same place! They oughta put a light out there or something! It's not safe out there!"

"I'm not taking that fucking road until they do put a light there! I'll go around to the other ramp! Jonas and I used that road just the day before! Jesus Christ! Heat this up, will you, kiddo?" Libby held her cup out to the passing waitress.

"Lenny says it's always been a bad place..." Even Donna added a little absently.

"Well, honey, the 'truck driver' should know!" Marian couldn't resist taking another shot at the man.

"—Eve...what's the matter?" Donna noticed her sitting back looking dazed.

"...Huh?...What...happened to Fry?" Eve could barely get the words out.

"Broke his Goddamn neck! Drunk as a lord, walked out of his house and fell down the fucking stairs! There but for the fucking Grace of God, go I!" Libby inhaled and looked inside as she said it.

"...Do you always have to talk like that? I mean...do you *always*?" It was Marian's turn to ambush Libby.

Eve had to stand up to catch her breath. Three!—She knew they were three of the selectmen who voted for the eminent domain. She knew that from Adam. That was...ridiculous! It couldn't be! And, yes, that was where the moving man had been killed—What was his name?—Kenney...Kenny Tierney. Someone else she had...contended with in some way.

"Eve?...What's the matter, honey?...Sit down, we're going to order!" Marian was pulling at her blouse. "Eve?..."

She was beginning to hyper-ventilate. The diner was turning around, and Eve couldn't seem to catch her breath."

"....Give me a minute!...I have to....step outside. I'll....just step outside for a minute!..." Eve moved quickly to the glass doors at the entrance and pushed them open. She stepped out into the late morning air. It was beginning to get warmer, but the temperature was still cool enough to be pleasant. She collapsed onto one of the green park benches that stretched at regular intervals all around the Common.

Marian followed her out of the Diner, "Eve!...What's the matter, honey? Are you sick?"

"....No...Marian...I'll be fine. It was just too close in there...all the cooking smells. Just give me a moment..."

Marian sat down beside her not sure what to do. "...You know, I wonder sometimes..."

Eve sat trying to clear her head of the panic she was feeling, "...What...?"

"Well, if it's Fate, or God...or, I don't know, the Devil that pushes us the way we go. I mean, when things are good, we 'Praise the Lord,' and when they're bad, we blame Fate or the Devil. People die and we say, 'Their number came up'—like those two poor guys. It all seems so...random! I mean, what's the purpose of it all? Don't you wonder sometimes if it's all just chance, or if there's there some plan—some agenda."

Eve lifted her head and turned to Marian, "...Y-yes!...It does make me wonder."

***

CHAPTER 60

"Hetty done it. I just brought it over. You give me the key!" Mira stood in the kitchen looking at the cake with the half-eaten slice sitting on the counter. "...Ain't it good?"

"It's fine. Very good....Mira, it was still warm when I got here!"

"...Better when it's fresh..." The girl seemed confused by Eve's questions. She had come over as soon as Eve returned from her brunch with the girls.

"Mira, where's Hetty now?" Eve had an edge in her voice.

"...Home...I guess." Mirabel seemed cautious.

"Right now...as we speak—she's home? At the farm?" Eve pushed at the girl.

"...I guess..."

"No, Mira. I mean right now. Where is she right now?"

"I told ya. Home! At the farm!...What's the matter?" Mira was beginning to pull back slightly from Eve.

"Let's go see her!" Eve moved toward the door, but the girl hung back.

"...Why?"

"Let's go see her together. I want to tell her about my progress with the lawyer!" Eve reached out to lead Mirabel by the arm, but the girl pulled her arm away.

"No!....She's...she's doin' a load of work. Ya can tell me, an' I'll tell her."

"I want to see her, Mira. As you said when you came in—it's been two weeks!"

"Eyah...She'll come later. I know she'll want to talk with ya."

"Why not now?...Let's go together."

"I...I ain't s'pose ta be here! She sent me to do some chores. She won't like it. I come 'cause I know you was worried by Jace's goin' away."

"Did he 'go away,' Mira? Is that what happened? Did Jace Brillig just...walk away from his job—especially his new job—replacing me? Did he just walk away from that, and from his brand new BMW...and whatever else he might have had going on? Does that sound right to you?"

"...Don't know...What are ya sayin'? You called him a bastard! He was plannin' to hurt ya! Why do ya care?" The girl seemed genuinely confused by Eve's emotional state.

"Because I don't like the way I feel, Mira! I don't want to be the cause of anyone's...hurt!" Eve was looking at the girl half pleading for some logical idea that would take her away from the direction her mind was taking her.

"...*You* didn't cause nothin'. It weren't you; *you* done nothin'!..." The girl stood back looking at Eve confused.

"I found out three of the town fathers died while I was gone—one in a fall and two...in a crash." Eve turned away and then turned back to Mirabel. "Do you know about that?"

"...I heard...shame..." Mira kept a little distance between them. Her answer was flat and wary.

"Does Hetty know?" Eve was searching the girl's eyes for some flicker of doubt or softness, but all she saw was avoidance.

"...She knows...I gotta go now." Mirabel moved toward the back door.

"I thought we were going to see Hetty together." Eve pressed again.

"I gotta go...chores...She don't like it if they ain't done!" The girl opened the door, and then she turned back to Eve. For just a moment, Eve thought she detected a glimmer of softness in her eyes, "...You didn't...You done nothin'." And she was gone.

***

CHAPTER 61

"...We were all in high school together, Esau, Wally, Curtis....stayed here. Made a life. Wally's wife, Lila?—she was a peach! We all loved her—even Jack. She was just about the cutest thing you'd ever see!...Cheerleader. Wally was the football team's quarterback...way back when. Fast as they come!...I just...can't believe they're gone!" Charlie Metcalf sat with Adam in the empty church. He had come looking for...something—someone he could share his thoughts with. Adam found him sitting there alone.

"...It's hard to let go. When someone passes, it's a little like a chapter being ripped from your book." Adam was trying to allow the man a chance to purge his grief.

"That's it, Adam!—That's just it! I just had three chapters ripped from my book. Doesn't feel like there's much left to read!" Metcalf looked up at Adam with a sad smile verging on tears.

"Well, Charlie, I guess you have to write some new ones. That's what we all have to do—keep writing new ones." Adam couldn't help thinking about Caroline.

"...I know you know how it feels...losing your wife so early. Must have hurt."

"...Yeah...it did. But I'm still here, Charlie. Still trying to write new ones. So are you."

"Don't pay any attention to me, Adam. Old men get maudlin. It's part of the playbook, I think." Metcalf looked at the younger man. "How's the chapter on Eve Truesdale going?"

Singleton's face dropped a little, and Charlie Metcalf realized he probably shouldn't have said anything.

"Sorry, Adam...I thought you were—well, I'm sorry!"

"That's OK, Charlie. I guess that's a chapter that'll have to be considered a rough draft...not to be finished. We haven't been seeing each other for a little while now."

"That's too bad. She's quite a lady from what I've seen. Rich too!—Not a bad catch for a poor country minister!"

277

"The gigolo preacher? Is that how you see me? Really, Charlie?"

"Time moves along faster as you get older, Adam. Don't let your chances slip away!...That's a good-looking woman!"

"I appreciate the advice, Charlie, but I'm not what she needs. She's got a whole sleek, modern, up-tempo life in New York. She doesn't need—what did you call me?—'a poor country minister,' slowing her down."

"...Maybe you need a sleek, modern, up-tempo woman speeding you up! Ever think of that?"

"...Just about every day, Charlie. Just about every day..."

***

CHAPTER 62

"Medium rare—make sure! I don't like it too done!...Baked potato—extra sour cream. Blue cheese on the salad...and broccoli—I won't eat it, but it looks good on the plate. You got that, sweetie?" Marlin had taken himself to 'Esther Louise' on 95 just outside of town. It was pricey, but he decided he needed to treat himself, especially since losing three of his most useful colleagues. Damn shame! He could always rely on Curtis, Esau, and Wally. For a few bucks those three would pretty much give him whatever he wanted—as long as he made it look good.

This deal with Reedy was good! This was the 'big one' he was waiting for. He even thought of retiring on this one! Sell his house in town; get a nice condo in Boca or maybe the Islands! He had to admit he was beginning to feel the New England winter. He was tired of shoveling snow...and he was really tired of trying to pull Holmsford up from its crumbling past! Maybe this was it.

As he waited for his meal, he busied himself calculating just how much he was expecting from Reedy. The Goat Woman's property was valuated at five grand an acre. Reedy had slipped him the cash to give to the appraiser for a 'fair' evaluation. It had come to about a third of the property's real value. The town would buy it for $250,000, then they would sell it to Reedy for $500,000. Marlin would get the quarter mil difference as a 'finder's fee.' When the project was completed, he'd get another one million in consultation fees. Hell, he didn't care what Reedy called them as long as the money came in cash.

What with the money he'd already gotten from Reedy for their other ventures, Marlin was ready. Whatever he decided to do...he could do it! He was feeling pretty much like a king.

Finally, the meal arrived. They always served their steaks sizzling on a heated plate. Marlin loved that—a huge hunk of sizzling meat arriving at the table bubbling and spitting. The potato was massive and the waitress had brought him enough sour cream to slather four potatoes. The salad was huge, with lumps of blue cheese poking through the cream dressing. It was a meal fit for a king.

Marlin tucked in his napkin, contemplating just what he really wanted to do. As he cut a huge piece of meat from the steak, he couldn't help wondering what he'd do by himself in Boca or on the Islands. What was there to do? He'd be by himself. Nobody would know him! No one would wave to him and greet him as 'Selectman Marlin'. He'd be just another well-heeled retiree floating around in shorts the color of ice-cream.

"Don't want that!" He said to himself as he poked the huge piece of steak into his mouth. "Uh uh!—No fun in—that!" As he swallowed he could feel the huge chunk of steak lodge itself in his windpipe. His gag reflex kicked in as his body tried to expel the plug of meat in his throat, but as it did so, the piece of steak slipped further down and packed in more tightly.

Marlin tried to push it out with the muscles in the esophagus, but nothing happened. Cold panic was beginning to take hold.. Marlin leaned down and tried again. Black spots were beginning to appear around his eyes, and he realized he wasn't able to breathe. He stood clutching his throat and the woman at the next table cried out for the waitress.

The girl came immediately and realized what was happening.

"Take it easy, sir. I'm going to perform the Heimlich maneuver. Now just relax and lean forward and we'll get that out for you! Relax!" The girl got behind Marlin and tried to get her fist tight up against his diaphragm so that she could give him the push to force out the blockage.

By now the patrons at the surrounding tables had stood up and were watching, dumbfounded and a little disgusted at the purple-faced man leaning over the adjacent table.

Try as she might the young waitress couldn't get her arms properly around Marlin. He was too fat for that. By now the maître d' was there, and had relieved the girl of her efforts.

Marlin could feel himself beginning to lose consciousness. He was getting angry at the ineptitude of the waitress, and it even crossed his mind that he wasn't going to tip her. At last, he could feel a pair of strong arms gripped around his middle. The maître d' expertly applied the Heimlich several times. Each time Marlin could feel the pressure build behind the blockage, but it wouldn't move! The chunk of meat seemed to slip further in rather than loosen.

The maître d' was beginning to panic now. He shouted to the waitress, "Call 911!" Repeatedly, the man pumped his fist into Marlin's diaphragm. Marlin's ribs were sore now. He was beginning to enter that twilight space between consciousness and unconsciousness. He was trying to stay awake. He was trying to help, but his lungs were bursting.

Just as he slipped into blackness, Marlin thought he saw a face. It was the old Goat Woman, Hetty Livesey, standing by her pens just looking at him. She didn't smile or speak; she just looked on as he blacked out completely.

***

CHAPTER 63

"...So as we think about the time we have...let us all remember that each day is a gift to be fully enjoyed. Young or old, we can never take our time for granted. Savor every moment...use every opportunity to tell those we love how we feel..."

Adam saw Eve immediately as she slipped into the back of the church. She sat in the last pew as unobtrusively as possible. He fought the distraction, but he couldn't help focusing on her.

"They need to know—those that we love, that they *are* loved, that they give added meaning to our lives...That we need them. We need to tell them now...while we can. Life is now. This moment is the only one we *know* we have.

Our sympathies go out to the families of Esau Carter and Curtis Bolling. They were long time public servants of this town, and their service will be held in respect and honor. Thank you all, and God bless. Fellowship will be held in the lower hall..."

Adam blushed as he strode away from the pulpit. He was excited to see her and dreaded it at the same time. During communion he tried to block her out; he knew he still wanted her. He couldn't put her out of his mind, and now here she was. What was he going to do? What could he say? What did he want?

He did his best at Fellowship to greet the congregants. This Sunday almost everyone wanted to talk about the accident. It was the topic of everyone's conversation. Everyone knew Carter and Bolling. Many had voted for them. Whether they liked them or not, everyone was horrified at the violence of their deaths. Some who lived on that side of town had heard the explosion.

Adam let them talk through their shock or sadness, or, in many cases, fear of their own mortality. It was normal...natural. All the while he knew she was waiting to talk to him. She stood in her usual spot, waiting patiently, and he knew he would have to face his own conflicted feelings.

"Hi..." Eve greeted him a little guardedly, but the look on her face was...searching...hopeful.

"Hi...You look good...uh...I heard about your...colleague. Any word of him?" It jumped out of his mouth before he could stop it.

"Uh...no. No, there's no sign of him anywhere. It's all very strange. How have you been?" Eve tried to avoid his eyes. She didn't think she could stand up to his direct stare.

"...Busy. You know...there's always something I have to—"

"Adam, I need to talk to you! I have to talk to somebody!...You are my pastor...right?" She looked up at him, and there was something at the back of her eyes that made him realize that this was not about the two of them."

"Yes...of course!...What is it?"

"I...I don't know where to begin. All right...I think I might be involved in the deaths of Curtis Bolling and Esau Carter."

"What?...Eve, how could you be involved? It was an accident."

"I know—I know that! Just hear me out...because...there's a lot more than Carter and Bolling. I need you to listen to me." She turned away from him for a moment trying to sort out the string of connections she had been pulling on since her brunch the previous day with the girls at the diner. One by one the congregants had left seeing that their minister was in deep conversation with Eve. Although no one listened in, everyone knew that something was 'going on' between the two of them. After all he was still a young man. He was a widower...after all! Let them work out...whatever it was they had to do.

"...Directly or indirectly every one of them had something to do with either me or Hetty Livesey, or both of us...."

Adam had listened hiding his alarm while Eve laid out the 'connections' she had seen between the deaths of Bolling, Carter, Fry, her boss, the rapist-moving man, and her employee's (fiancé's) disappearance. She even brought in the disappearance of the Hildebrand woman several years ago. She was manic, reaching...trying not to think this way, but at the same time giving in to it.

After she stopped, he looked at her. This was not the Eve he knew!

"...What do you want me to say, Eve?"

"Adam, I know on the surface it sounds crazy! It doesn't make complete sense to me,—but, in a way, it does! There's an...intelligence in all this—a pattern! Don't you see it?"

"Pattern...where do you see a pattern, Eve?"

"Somehow it's her! Hetty! She's—engineering all this. That first one—the moving guy? She appeared out of nowhere, and she clubbed him! That's how we met! Somehow we became friends—that was me, I think, and she's got some idea that I'm like her or in some way bonded with her. She said we were 'two women working together' She-she cursed him! I saw it!—I didn't realize it at the time, but she did! And then he died...on the same spot as Carter and Bolling!"

"...Esau Carter and Curtis Bolling didn't do anything to you."

"Not to me—to her, but I've been helping her! Didn't you tell me that they voted for eminent domain? Now they're dead! And Wally Fry! That's three out of the four who voted for it!"

"He had a fall, Eve. He was drunk."

"And now he's dead!—Harold and Jace were plotting to buy me out of the firm. Harold's dead and I'm in charge! Jace is...gone!"

"They didn't have anything to do with voting for eminent domain."

"No! But they were *against* me! Don't you see?—In some twisted way, she's got my back! She wouldn't let them get to me! And there's more!..and...and..." Eve looked up and saw herself in Adam's eyes. What she read in his expression stopped her. She fell silent for a moment and then in a small voice, "...You don't see it..."

"...Eve—"

"No!...I don't blame you... I wouldn't believe it either. Why would you?" Eve sank into herself with the realization that he couldn't believe her.

"You're stressed out..."

"...How could she cause...any of this, right? Curses?...How could I think that?...I should go." Eve turned to leave, avoiding his eyes altogether.

"Eve!..Stay—please. Just talk to me."

"I have to go, Adam. I'm embarrassed enough already."

***

CHAPTER 64

She sat in the huge living room with the lights turned off. In the twilight, the shadows grew out of the furniture and filled the corners of the house. She had been sitting there for hours searching her memory. Seeking that image of Mirabel sitting at the table in Hetty's clothes. Why did that haunt her? Thank God she hadn't told that to Adam! What was happening to her? She had sounded like a lunatic to the one man she needed to believe her.

Why should he believe her? She didn't believe herself—not when she heard herself voice all the suspicions and anxieties she had revealed. She sounded crazy! Maybe she was. Maybe this was her rational mind giving her a wake-up call. Nothing—nothing she was thinking was rational!

There was a resounding knocking at the door. It made Eve jump in her seat.

"Honey! Eve!...It's us! Honey!—we know you're in there! EVE!"

She turned on the hall light and dragged herself to the front door. She snapped the lock and opened the door. Immediately Marian pushed in with Libby and Donna right behind.

"We were so worried about you, honey! You looked terrible at the diner yesterday and..." Marian turned and at looked at Eve, "and you still look terrible! What is the matter, honey?"

"Nothing, Marian! I'm just...exhausted. I got caught up at work, and I overdid it. I guess it's catching up with me."

"Well, we're going to fix that. I brought cake. Let's put on the coffee! C'mon! C'mon, Eve. We're just going to eat cake and gab and have a good time! Let's go girls!"

"You didn't bring the fucking cake, Marian. Jonas baked that cake!..." The girls disappeared into the kitchen, leaving Eve in the hallway. They didn't notice for a moment, and Eve took a deep breath. Maybe she needed company. Maybe....She pushed through the swinging door and joined them.

"All right, now I know we always talk about ourselves—"

"Oh, Jesus Christ, Marian!" Libby rolled her eyes.

"All right! I admit it. I have a slight tendency to talk about myself, but this is Eve's night! We're here for you, honey. We want to hear all about your...your...business and...whatever! You go on, Honey and tell us all about it!"

"There's nothing to tell, Marian. It's all pretty dull. Just a lot of meetings and wrangling—there's nothing you'd find interesting about it."

"All right, then—What about Adam Singleton? I bet there's a lot to talk about in that department!" Marian smiled and winked at the other two women who looked on.

"Adam..." Eve was quiet for a moment before she spoke, "I hate to disappoint you, Marian, but Adam and I aren't seeing each other anymore."

"What! Eve! You and Adam Singleton? You're the perfect couple! Anyone could see that!...What happened?"

"...His choice, really. He...he didn't think we could...make it work. I'm afraid I have to agree with him."

"Well that's a bloodless breakup, if I ever heard of one! Did you have a fight? Did he cheat on you? Did you cheat on him? Give us something we can hate him for, honey!"

"...Adam is...the best man I've ever known. I don't blame him for...for...deciding what he did..."

"No. No, that's not fucking right! You're a Goddamn perfect woman. You're smart. You're beautiful, and you've got enough money to screw anyone you want—and you've never been married! You're the only one I know who's been smart enough to stay out of that mess! Christ, look at us three!"

"Maybe...he knew..." Eve could feel herself weakening.

"Knew what, honey? That man's a fool letting you slip through his fingers! He wants a little chippie, doesn't he! Some simple-minded young thing with a body and no brain?—That's what most men want! I can tell you that!"

"No, Marian. That wasn't it. That's not it at all. I think maybe he sensed that...I was...a little crazy." She couldn't hold it in any longer.

"What! Oh, honey, if *you're* crazy, I'm Lizzie Borden with a hatchet! You are the most sane woman I know! A little obsessed maybe with all that...business you do, but you, darlin,' are not crazy!"

"No fucking way!" Libby chimed in for emphasis. The three women stood there sipping on their coffee looking at her. Eve could feel her reserve crumbling.

"Well...if he didn't think so before, he does now. I really hung out the wash this time..."

She couldn't seem to help it; she let it all out—her ridiculous ideas about the selectmen, the moving man, Harold...Jace...June Hildebrand! She told them about her meeting with Adam—how he looked at her with concern mixed with...pity. That was it! He saw her as...something broken! The realization made her angry, and she began to re-build her entire rationale. She knew what she knew! She revealed Hetty's strange...attitudes about things. In the back of her mind she knew she was being disloyal, but she was defending herself against that...pathetic image of herself she had seen in Adam's eyes.

The girls listened. They let her tell it all. They didn't judge, and most important, they didn't look at her the way Adam did. When she was finished, she stopped. Marian poured her another cup of coffee.

"...I can see it!...Oh, honey, there's some kind of Karma at work here. Don't' you think so, girls?"

"It's Goddamn scary, if you ask me!...You say the old bitch cursed him?"

"...It was...something. When I look back at it—you could call it that. I don't really know that, but...but it looked like it."

"Well, honey, I told you she was dangerous! Junie knew it! She had us all sign that petition. All those...goats! Oh, my God! Poor Junie! What do you suppose she did to her? Oh, my God!"

"No, Marian, I'm just suggesting that there's...there's some connection between all these things. I can't say that Hetty's actually done anything to anyone...I told you, she's been...very good to me..." Eve was beginning to worry that she had gone too far in her explanation. She hadn't counted on this strong...corroboration of her fears.

"...In some places...people believe that evil spirits can be sent...to take revenge. People have seen it..." Donna quietly added her view with the others.

"You mean like voodoo, or something, honey?"

"...That's one. There are others..." Donna drifted off letting the idea sink in.

"Oh, my God—poor Mirabel! Living with that old...harridan! We've gotta help that poor girl out!"

"Can you imagine living in a Goddamn shack with...that? Having to work with goats your whole life! That poor kid. And she's so beautiful!"

Eve got up from her chair and walked to the far side of the kitchen where the light was dim.

"Eve, honey, what is it?..." All three women were glued on her as she walked away.

Eve turned to look at them. "...I...I didn't mention this to Adam...but I went to Hetty's one night for dinner. It was her invitation. I got very drunk on some home brew she served. At one point she touched herself—she said some...words and ran her hand over her arm...and it looked as if her skin turned young and fresh. I don't remember everything, but I remember thinking that it was just some kind of a trick of the mind. Then she...did the same to her face...and—just for a moment—I saw Mira sitting there. It's all confused in my mind, but I know I saw it!..."

"Been there!" Libby shot back. "Homemade liquor will fuck you up real bad! The alcohol content in some of that stuff is through the roof!—You're lucky you didn't have Goddamn alcohol poisoning from that stuff. Hell! Maybe you did! Doesn't sound to me like that old Goat Woman is too damn careful about what she does to people!"

"...I don't know. I don't have a complete memory of it. I know I woke up back here with brier scratches all over my arms, and I was still in my clothes. I had a head like a watermelon!" Eve was still trying to piece that evening together in her mind.

"Yeah—that's it! You had a Goddamn blackout!"

"Whatever it was, I still say we should try to help poor Mirabel. That girl isn't responsible for her crazy grandmother! Something ought to be done!" The girls voiced their agreement with Marion.

There it was—'backup'—support, but when she heard the girls going on about the 'Goat Woman' and all the local slanders about her they had heard, Eve began to get the sickening feeling that she had done something very wrong to tell them. She almost felt better about Adam's pitying view of her than this mindless acceptance of her...unsettling ideas. Eve was beginning to wonder deeply about herself.

***

CHAPTER 65

"St. Barnabas. Reverend Singleton here." It was late Sunday night, and Adam was getting ready to turn in when the phone rang.

"Reverend Adam Singleton?" the voice on the other end asked.

"Yes. Who's calling, please?"

"Reverend Singleton, this is Nurse Howley at Charlton Memorial Hospital. Do you know a Mr. John Marlin?"

"Yes! Mr. Marlin is...is a colleague of mine. What's the matter?" Adam gripped the phone tighter.

"We found this number in his wallet, so we called you. Mr. Marlin has had a mishap. Do you know if there's a responsible family member who can come to the hospital?"

"...Uh...Mr. Marlin doesn't have any family as far as I know. What's happened to him?"

"...Well then, would you be willing to come over? We need to make some decisions. Even though you're not family, it might be good to have his minister here."

Adam didn't bother to say that Marlin didn't attend church. "I'll come right away..."

Even though it was raining, Singleton pushed to make the thirty mile trip in under forty minutes. He raced to the reception desk and asked where Marlin was. The receptionist gave him a room number, "Howland 4 West." He sprang to the elevators, and as he approached the nurse's desk, a large woman in a white uniform stood up. On her uniform was a name plate that read 'Howley.'

"Nurse Howley! I'm Adam Singleton. We just spoke."

"Reverend Singleton?..." the nurse looked at him in his jeans and light jacket. He realized he didn't look much like a 'Reverend' at that moment.

"I'm afraid you got me at an 'unofficial' moment. I'm the pastor of St. Barnabas in Holmsford."

"I see. He's in Room Four, but before you go in, I should tell you. It's not good."

"Is he dead?"

"Clinically—yes. We have him on a ventilator, but we just did a brain scan, and I'm afraid it's flat—no activity."

"...He's...brain-dead?" Adam was trying to absorb the reality of it.

"Yes. We tried to resuscitate, but he was probably gone before he got here."

"What happened?"

"Apparently, he was having dinner. Food lodged in his windpipe. We didn't get to him soon enough. There's nothing we can do for him. I'm sorry to call you so late."

"No, that's all right. It's my job. May I see him?"

"Of course, Reverend. You might want to administer a blessing. If there's no next of kin, we're going to have to disconnect him."

"That quickly? I mean, there's nothing—?"

"I'm afraid not. The machine is keeping his body breathing, but he's not there, Reverend. I'm sorry"

Adam couldn't believe how simple and final it was...not to mention how sudden. Another one of Charlie's friends. Suddenly he remembered Eve's strange relating of recent events, and it made him uneasy. He knew it was just a bizarre coincidence—Marlin was the fourth Selectman to vote for the eminent domain sale of the Livesey property, but...that was just...not possible. He put it immediately from his mind. He had a job to do, and he wanted to give Marlin as much dignity as he could.

He said the prayers, and he held Marlin's hand as the medical staff turned off the ventilator and removed the breathing tubes. He heard Marlin take two or three shallow breaths on his own...and then he just stopped. The attending physician pronounced him dead, and they pulled the sheet up over his head. Adam told them that he would make arrangements for the funeral parlor in town to call for the body in the morning.

On his way home, he kept turning it over in his mind. He would have to make the arrangements through the town. Knowing Marlin, there must be some final 'wishes' to be considered. He doubted John Marlin would depart quietly. There would definitely be some fanfare. What really worried him was what Eve would make of Marlin's death. .What did *he* make of it?

***

CHAPTER 66

"Ms. Truesdale? Phil Gottlieb. I hope I'm not calling you too early, but you did want me to get back to you as quickly as possible."

"It's fine, Mr. Gottlieb. I'm...I'm working from home this morning. You caught me at a good time. What did you find out?"

Eve used her professional voice, but she was feeling anything but professional at the moment. After the girls had left last night, she hardly slept. Maybe it was the coffee, but she was betting that it was her conscience. She had let herself violate a confidence she had made. She had put her own...insecurities before an unspoken compact she had with Hetty. What kind of a woman was she becoming? How had she let herself slip this far into...madness? That was the only word she could think of—to tell all of that lunatic nonsense to the girls? And she had told Adam as well! The remorse sat thick in her throat as she tried to talk with Gottlieb.

"You don't want to invest in Innovative, Ms. Truesdale. They're about to be indicted. Well, Jim Reedy is."

"What? How do you know this?" Eve leaned into her cell phone.

"I know it...because it was my investigation for you that led our firm to turn over evidence regarding Reedy's shady dealings at the state and local level...."

Eve rested her head on her hand and couldn't talk.

"He's been bribing local politicians for years and buying up land all up and down a proposed high-speed rail line route to New Bedford and beyond. I believe he was just negotiating to buy a substantial tract of land in Holmsford. That just happens to be where the line will hub to Providence and New York. Nobody was privy to this information except the Governor and a few of his closest associates. One of them is also implicated. He was on Reedy's payroll too, apparently....Ms. Truesdale? Ms. Truesdale, are you there?"

"...Uh...yes. Mr. Gottlieb, I'm here. You say it was my inquiry that...sparked all this?"

"...We have to report this sort of thing, Ms. Truesdale, or we would be considered collusive...This is all confidential right now. Please say nothing to anyone. The indictment should be public in a couple of days."

"No, no, I understand. I'm just...surprised." Eve was having trouble speaking. "Thank you for the heads-up. I'm sure....my client...will be relieved...uh, not to be investing with them..."

After she hung up, Eve sat there for several minutes, staring into space. The deal—the eminent domain sale of Hetty's property was killed.

Eve could feel herself coming to one inescapable conclusion. This couldn't go on any longer: It was time to take this whole tangle of anxieties, suspicions, and questions to the source...

***

CHAPTER 67

"You can't tell anyone...Not until it's in the news." Eve stood in the pen watching as Hetty went about the ritual of feeding and watering her herd. Once again she felt a punch to her leg. It was the little black buck butting her.

"Get off, there, Pretty Boy!" Hetty pushed the buck back away with her powerful hands, "I warned ya! Do that again and I'll make a stew of ya! Sorry, Missy. He likes ya."

The little buck ran off and stood there glaring at her defiantly as Eve rubbed her thigh.

"...So the eminent domain sale is killed."

Hetty went back to filling her buckets from the well pump. "...Knew it would be...with *you* workin' on it!" She didn't look up as she went about the work. Eve wouldn't take her eyes away from the old woman.

"Was it me, Hetty?" Eve pointed her tone.

The old woman looked up at her for a moment, "...You feelin' all right, Missy? Ya seem...outa sorts."

"Should I be?"...Eve was waiting for some flicker from the old woman.

"Mirabel told me ya was worryin' about...things" Hetty went back to her chore.

"Where is Mirabel, Hetty?" Again Eve pointed her tone.

"Don't know. She comes and goes. I don't watch her."

"But she's always there when you need her, isn't she?"

"Eyah....She better be. When I'm gone, she'll be next here."

"And everybody in town has seen her, haven't they? They know she's your granddaughter...your heir..."

"...Can't say. Don't know what other folks think." The old woman halted momentarily as if she was focusing on something but still kept working. "Been good of ya to take her 'round like you done...I'm thankful."

"...I owed you. Didn't I?...You saved my life..."

Again, the old woman looked up from her work to see her, "Missy, you done more for me than anyone. Nobody much cares—but you do. That's *somethin'* to me."

"...Hetty, tell me about June Hildebrande."

The old woman's eyes clouded and she went back to her work, "...Who?..."

"June Hildebrande, the woman who owned my house before me."

"...Don't have nothin' to tell. Didn't know her."

"She was the one who filed a complaint against you for keeping your goat pens next to her—my property."

"Them pens been there all along. She was a mite too fussy 'bout it."

"She went missing, didn't she?"

"I heard. Shame..."

"Did you know that Esau Carter and Curtis Bolling were killed in a crash."

"...Eyah...I heard."

"It was in the exact same place that man—the one you saved me from—the same place he crashed."

"...That so?..."

"And Wally Fry...another one of the men who voted to sell your land...He died just few days before."

"...People die, Missy..."

"My boss, Harold Garner, died just before he could push me out of the firm, and now *I* have *his* job. Jace Brillig, who was helping him do this...is missing."

"So then...Ya safe!...What are you on about? What are you after, Missy?"

"I have to know, Hetty...Did *I* do...any of this. Did *we*?"

Hetty went back to pouring water into the goat troughs. "...Ya need a physic, Missy!...Ya worryin' 'bout nothin'"

"Am I?"

"You are!" Hetty looked up and nailed Eve with her eyes. "Ya..stewin' and broodin' and what's it got ya? Some graspin,' greedy men got what was comin'—How'd *you* do any 'o that? Ya oughta be dancin' a jig! You and me—we didn't ask for no trouble! It come...and now it's gone! Let it go!"

Now that Hetty was looking at her, she could see the ferocity behind her eyes. It was almost burning in her stare..."I know, Hetty! I know!"

"You know? What do ya know?"

"It took me a while, but...I remember! I saw you! You showed me that night at supper! You showed me!"

"...What are you talkin' about?..."

"I saw! You and Mira! I know!"

"Missy, I don't know what you're sayin'! Ya don't make no sense!—All I showed ya was a paste I make. Good for the skin..."

"It isn't right, Hetty! I don't understand it, but it isn't right!"

The old woman put down her bucket and took a firm step toward Eve. "What are you sayin'?" Hetty's tone changed again. She seemed confused..alarmed.

"I can't keep this to myself! There's more going on here than meets the eye. You-you've done things, things I can't imagine. It was you, wasn't it! Somehow you...caused all this!"

"You want to be careful, Missy...talkin' like that...it ain't good..."

"The Girls know! I told them. I had to tell someone. They know! You've got to be stopped!"

"Missy! Come now, you don't know what you're sayin'. You gotta git right! You're bringin' a pile 'o trouble on yourself..."

"I don't care! People have to know. This is wrong!"

"C'mon, now, Missy...come into the house. I'll make ya a tea."

"No! I don't want anything! You—you want to do something to me!" Eve was backing out of the pen slowly as the old woman came toward her.

"I ain't gonna hurt *you*, Missy! You're my friend! Only one I got. Don't talk like that!"

Hetty kept walking toward her slowly with her hands out pleading as Eve backed away. Finally, Eve could feel the gate at her back. She turned suddenly and pulled it opened and dashed away to the woods.

"Missy! Don't go like that! Don't bring trouble on yourself!" The old woman called after her, but Eve couldn't hear. She was crashing through the woods to the safety of her own home.

***

CHAPTER 68

"I can't say I'll miss him exactly. Even as a kid, he was a spoiled brat." Dilla stood straight and firm as Adam told her about John Marlin. "I expect before long it'll be my turn.—I remember when Johnny Marlin was a baby! His mother and I were friends. She always gave him whatever he wanted!"

"There's a four-day wake...at Latham's funeral home"

"Four days? I guess he was expecting a turnout, hmm?"

"I guess. He had everything planned. Casket, music...no church service and, believe it or not, the monument is already in place at the cemetery. He bought it years ago. Quite a thing...obelisk on a large base. Quite...substantial!"

"Paid for, no doubt, by the town! Do folks know already?"

"It'll be in *The Holmsford Times* this morning. The body's already at Latham's. We're going to have to have a special election. There are only two Selectmen left, Charlie Metcalf and me."

"Call a Town Meeting—for after the funeral."

"Charlie ought to be the Chairman. As pastor as St. Barnabas, I don't think I should be the one. Dilla, I didn't just come here about Marlin. I'm worried about Eve. I know she thinks a lot of you..."

"Esther, her grandmother, and I were real good friends. Eve's a lot like her. She's quite a girl, Adam." Dilla was clear in her implication.

"I know! Believe me, Dilla, I—I know, but I think she's in trouble."

"Trouble? What do you mean?" The old woman moved closer to be sure she understood.

"She told me the wildest...story. Something's not right with her!"

"Story?...What do you mean, Adam?..."

The little bell to the shop door rang furiously as Eve rushed in, slamming the door behind her. She had a copy of the *Times* clutched in her hand.

"Dilla! Dilla, I need to talk to you—Adam! You're here!" She waved the paper as she talked. "Do you believe me now? Marlin is dead too! All four of them! And the eminent domain? Finished! What about that?"

"What? Eve, it's been voted. Even with Marlin gone, the sale will go through. Now, please, calm down!"

"I know....I sounded...weird on Sunday, Adam. I had to work some things out in my own mind." Eve looked at Adam straight on. "But this! Adam, you can't just call this a coincidence!...And there are other things!"

"What other things?"

"I'll—I'll get us some iced tea. I just made it. Sit down, you two. I'll be right back...." Dilla scuttled back to the little kitchen hoping that between the two of them, they could calm Eve's mania.

"There's part of it I can't talk about right now. Not until it hits the papers. I was told in confidence. You'll see then."

"The papers? Really? Then it's something...major?" Adam couldn't help being drawn in for the moment.

"I went there...to Hetty's. To confront her."

"What did she say?" Adam sat at the table listening, trying to understand.

"What was she going to say? 'Right! I did it! I caused all those people to die.' She...pretended not to know. For a moment she seemed almost—sad. The way she looked at me—like I had done something to *her*...but this proves it! This and what will come out in the papers in a few days. It's too much! Too many unlikely things happening in a small town!"

"Eve, Marlin died of asphyxiation. He choked on a piece of meat! There was no foul play!"

Eve looked at him horrified for a moment and inhaled. "...Did you say he choked?..." Eve got up from her seat and walked to the counter.

"Here we are. I made it just before you got here, Adam. It should be good and cold!" Dilla handed Adam a glass and held one out to Eve who didn't turn around. Dilla put the sweating glass on the tray.

Eve turned back to Adam, looking deeply worried, "Adam...when he came—Marlin—when he came out to give Hetty the notice, I was there. We had words. I told him he'd choke on this deal!"

"Eve…"

"I said that anyone who voted for it would pay the price! It was *me*! *I* cursed them!" As the realization set in, Eve could feel herself going weak in the knees. Dilla went to her with Adam right behind. They supported her and took her back to the chair.

"Eve, sit down, dear! Now what is all this about cursing people? What is going on here?" Dilla demanded to be let in on their conversation.

"I'm the one who said it! Somehow, she did what I said! Adam, she's got to be stopped!"

"Eve, dear, slow down! You're not making any sense at all! Adam?" Dilla looked to him. Singleton could hardly maintain his composure. He couldn't bear to see Eve so distraught.

"She…believes that Hetty Livesey caused the deaths of the four Selectmen—because of the eminent domain sale. She thinks that Hetty is able to…to cause things—"

"Dilla, she can! I know she can! It isn't just those four! She made June Hildebrande disappear because she complained about the goats! And Jace! She—she killed Harold Gardner so that I could head the company!"

Singleton got up from the table and walked a few feet away trying to keep himself calm.

"Eve, dear, think! Does that make sense to you?

"No! None of it does…but I know it happened! There is a pattern; you've just got to step back to see it!"

"Hetty Livesey is a lonely old recluse. She's odd—I guess we all are! Think, dear. How could she cause people to die? It—It's all a…construction you've put together. None of it is real!"

"You think I didn't tell myself that? When I hear myself say it out loud—I don't believe it either!…You're the two people…I love most in the world!…"

Adam turned to look at her. He was fighting back his emotions.

"If you don't believe me…all right. Wait. In a few days, it'll be in the paper. The information I can't tell you now. Will you promise me, that when it does, you'll listen to me—really listen to me?"

"We're listening now, dear!"

"No, Dilla. I mean we'll sit down and look at everything. I'll go over everything with both of you. Promise me that!"

"Yes!" Adam's voice was hoarse. He was desperate to pull her back from this thing—whatever it was.

"All right, I won't talk about this with anyone until then. I will...show you that I am in perfect control of myself."

"You don't have to prove anything to us, dear!"

"Oh, Dilla, I do!—Just give me the chance to...draw all the lines for you. In the meantime...I'm going home."

"I'll drive you!" Adam was ready.

"No, Adam! You won't. I'll take myself home just like I brought myself here. I don't need a keeper, and I don't want your...concern. I'll be fine. I'm sorry, Dilla. I didn't mean to upset you.

Eve was calm now. She had made a deal, and she would keep it. She hoped they would.

***

CHAPTER 69

"He wouldn't like it! Jack was a big man with big ideas! He wouldn't like a small turnout for his funeral." Charlie Metcalf was looking down at the body in the casket. It seemed to him that Marlin looked somehow bloated and gray, like a beached whale.

Few came the first day—Adam and Charlie were there. Dilla came and a handful of townies, perhaps twenty in all, but only Adam, Charlie, and Dilla stayed the whole time.

Marlin lay in the huge mahogany casket with silver-plated handles. Around the casket was an opulent display of floral grandeur—all of it pre-ordered by the deceased. The music was nondescript classical, and there was a repeating slide show of pictures of John Marlin at various public functions. There were pictures of his last campaign, a supermarket opening, the opening of the mall. There were pictures of him with several state dignitaries—all designed to create the image of a distinguished and vigorous 'servant of the people.'

"C'mon, Charlie, I'll take you two fellows to the Puritan. You earned it." Dilla looked around the empty chapel and sighed. "Poor Johnny! All that...ambition—for this..."

***

CHAPTER 70

Even though she still had two days before she had to be in New York, Eve concentrated on work. She checked and re-checked the day's activity. She furiously answered every email, every communication. She had called Waring four times regarding the trading for the day, and she had been on the phone extensively with half-a-dozen clients.

They had to know! She was watching—she was in control. There could be no question about her attention to the business or her ability on the job. As she worked, she could feel herself focusing, gaining strength. Adam and Dilla had to believe her! They had to see!

The time had flown. It was nearly five in the afternoon when the phone rang.

"Honey, he did it! He really did it to her!—I tried to tell her!" It was Marian. She sounded hysterical.

"Marian, what are you saying? What's the matter?

"It's Donna!....That son-of-a-bitch beat her up! It's bad, Eve. It's really bad. Libby 's with me; can you come down. We're at Charlton. Please come!"

Eve felt that sick feeling in her gut again. "A-All right, Marian; I'm on my way! Just stay calm. I'll be there!"

Eve put down the phone and the sick feeling rose up and grabbed her, "No...don't you do this! Hetty, don't you hurt them!..."

***

"That fucking asshole! Stupid motherfucker!" Libby was holding Marian and ranting as Eve was trying to piece together exactly what had happened. Marian was too hysterical to talk.

"Libby—please! Why did Dennis do this? What happened?"

"Not Dennis!—Christ, that little faggot couldn't fight his way out of a paper bag! It was him—Lenny! That truck-driver beat her up. He thought she was seeing somebody else!"

"I tried to tell her—a truck driver! Oh, my God, Eve, he beat her so bad! Her pretty face—it was just a bloody pulp! She told me it was him. Oh, my God!"

"They got the bastard! Arrested him. I hope he rots in jail!"

A doctor entered the waiting room and approached the three women, "Are you Mrs. Fletcher's friends?"

"Yes. Is she going to be all right?" Eve spoke for the three of them.

"...We've called her husband—"

"Ex-husband—they were divorced. Is she all right?"

"...She's taken quite a beating. There's been some brain trauma. She's lapsed into coma."

"Oh, my God!" Marian began to weep while Libby held her looking grim.

"There been some swelling. We're trying to minimize that. We just have to wait and see. I've moved her up to the ICU. She'll get the best of care. Try not to imagine the worst. Very often a patient will show dramatic improvement after a few days."

"Can we see her?..." Eve was fighting the anxiety she was feeling. Again it wasn't clear...that this was Hetty. It wasn't clear, and, yet...

"I'm afraid it's only family in I.C.U."

"She doesn't have a family, doctor. She has no children, and her husband—is less than involved. We're her closest friends."

"I understand that, but I can't allow it. You can call. When she's out of I.C.U....then you can come and see her. She wouldn't know if you were there right now anyway.

"*We* would fucking know!" Libby couldn't restrain her anger.

"I'm sorry. Just call, and we'll hope that in a few days...you can see her..."

The Doctor left and the three of them sat in the waiting room trying to understand why this had happened.

Eve was afraid she understood all too well...

***

CHAPTER 71

Even fewer came on the second day of John Marlin's wake. It was Tuesday. People worked. In the evening the last thing they wanted to do was to attend a wake...especially a wake for him. Once again Dilla, Charlie Metcalf, and Adam attended and were ready to greet anyone who did come. They talked about the special election and the Town Meeting that would have to be held. They tried their best to distract each other from the huge, morbid centerpiece in the room. The floral smell was overpowering, and the vast, fancy coffin—like most of the things Marlin had ordered—was too much to face head-on.

About an hour into the wake, Eve arrived. She wore a modest lavender dress and matching shoes, and she did her best to appear calm and respectful.

"Eve, dear! What a lovely dress!"

"Thank you, Dilla...Adam..." She quickly kissed Adam on the cheek, and he blushed. She tried to avoid his searching eyes. "Mr. Metcalf. I'm so sorry. I know you were an old friend of Mr. Marlin's."

"Thank you. It's hard seeing him there. We went to high school together...he was...something!"

"Yes, he was! I met him a few times..." Eve looked around at the empty chapel. "I thought...there would be more people."

"So did he, dear. Eve, you look...tired." Dilla gripped her hand gently.

"I...had a long day yesterday. Technically I'm still at work. And...there were...other things I had to...handle..." She wanted to shout to them about Donna! She wanted to tell them that it was happening again, but she couldn't say that. It was too subtle—Donna's...experience. She wasn't dead—at least not yet! She certainly hadn't disappeared. It could be just...something that happened, but she didn't think so!

"You really need to take some time dear! It's too much!" Dilla looked pleadingly at her.

"Dilla, I can't! I have too many responsibilities to give in to ...fatigue! I have to be in New York tomorrow."

"Can't you...let somebody else take over...just till next week?" Adam was looking at her in his penetrating, earnest way.

She wanted so much to do that! She wanted to walk away from the whole thing, and just let him hold her forever, but the look in Adam's eyes burned her!....If she gave in, if she allowed herself to...falter, who would she be? She'd be some weak, pathetic woman depending on him. She'd be poor, 'crazy' Eve. That was not going to happen! She wouldn't let it. She was right; she knew she was. All their concern and...pity was misplaced! When the story broke in the papers about Innovative. Then they would know!

"...I'll come back. It's only three hours. A pleasant drive!...Adam, I'm fine!"

At that moment the cell phone in her purse rang.

"I'm sorry—I should have left that at home! Excuse me..." Eve took the phone out of her purse and retreated the rear of the chapel.

"Eve Truesdale....."

"Eve!"

"Marian!—I'm at John Marlin's wake right now!"

"I'm sorry, honey, calling you again, but I didn't know what else to do!"

"What is it? Is it Donna?" Eve turned away from the watching eyes at the front of the chapel.

"It's Libby...She—she called me...she's drunk again..."

"...Oh, no..." Eve's shoulders slumped as though she'd been hit.

"It's bad, Eve! There's something really wrong, but I can't understand her!...Can..can you go over there with me. I'm—I need the help. Will you?..."

"Marian...can't you handle this? You've done it before..."

"Just—Please, Eve. I...just can't alone."

"All right, Marian. I'll be right there." Eve ended the call. She didn't know what to say to the waiting trio of people. "Um...it was Marian...She needs my help with something."

"You want me to come with you?" Adam stepped forward.

"No!—" Her tone was harsh and she saw Adam's anxiety rise. "Adam, you're already doing something. *I* can...take care of this. Besides, there may be people coming. You stay here with Dilla. I should go."

"Are you sure, dear? Charlie and I can stay. Let Adam go with you."

"No!...It's...it's personal. Marian would be embarrassed! I can do this. Thank you." Eve turned and walked out of the chapel.

As she drove back home she felt a little relief to be away from Adam's and Dilla's worried looks. She had gone mostly for them. As far as she was concerned, Marlin wouldn't be missed.

***

CHAPTER 72

"Why? What did I do? They all go; they all leave you!—I can't...I don't want to anymore!"

Libby was in a heap on the floor of her bedroom. It looked as though the room had been ransacked. Clothing was everywhere, and she was bleeding heavily from deep cuts on her forearms.

"Help me hold her down! Marian, wake up! We've got to stop the bleeding! Jesus! This is awful!" Eve straddled Libby, gripping both her arms and applying pressure.

Marian stood frozen in the doorway of the upstairs bedroom. The sight of so much blood seemed to mesmerize her. At the sound of her name she came back to herself.

"Libby! Libby, My God, what have you gone and done! I'll get towels. Just—just hold her, Eve!"

Marian ran into the bathroom. It had been turned up as well. The medicine cabinet was open and its contents all over the floor. A cold fear swept through her. She found two clean towels and brought them to Eve, who pushed them against Libby's arms where deep vertical cuts were gouting blood.

"Oh, my God—Libby! Did you take anything? Libby! Did you take any pills?—the medicine cabinet was empty. There are things all over the floor in the bathroom! Oh, Eve—your dress!"

"Forget that now, Marian. We got to stop this bleeding and call 911! Put some pressure on her arms! We need something to tie off the bleeding! Here!" Eve reached for a pair of stockings. She tied each one tightly below the elbow just above the cuts. The blood slowed almost immediately and then stopped. Eve went to her purse which she had dropped in the hallway as soon as she had seen Libby.

"I need an ambulance! Please—right away! There a woman with deep cuts. 24 Cloven Terrace. Yes....Yes....I don't know—I think it might be a suicide attempt. Please hurry!..."

"He fucking left me! Marian, he's gone! Why? What did I do to deserve this? Brad! Brad!"

"Libby, Bradley has been gone for a long time! You know that, Libby! Bradley is dead."

"What...what are you taking about, Marian? He's fucking gone! That goddamn kid left! Why'd he do that, Marian. I was good to him!" Libby was drunker than Marian had ever seen her. She was raving drunk and barely coherent.

"Libby! Bradley is gone! He's dead! You know that!" Marian was shouting at her trying to get her attention.

"What! I know that! Stupid! You are so fucking stupid! Jonas...That Goddamn kid is gone!" Suddenly her face contorted and she began to sob..."Oh, Jesus Christ! Brad! Leave me alone!"

Eve ended her call and came back in, kneeling next to Libby. "They're coming. Libby....Libby! Stay awake!"

"I...think that kid...Jonas? I think he robbed her. It must have been while we were in the hospital with Donna." Marian looked at Eve and then indicated the dressing table. Libby's jewelry case was empty. "I think he took whatever he could find and whatever was in the medicine cabinet and left."

"Goddamn...Goddamn kid! What'd I do to you, Huh....oh, God...let me die! I just want to die..."

"Can you watch her? I want to check something, honey...." Marian got up suddenly and Eve could hear her in the next room rummaging around.

"Libby, do you hear me? Just stay awake. Help is coming. C'mon now! Tell me if you hear me."

"I don't want to live! What's the point...why?..."

Marian came back in the room carrying an open cookie tin, "This is it. Libby had cash in here. She always kept cash around. Wait a minute!" Marian went to the purse hung on the closet door. She pulled out the wallet..."No cash...no credit cards! That little bastard cleaned her out!"

In the distance they could hear the siren. Libby still lay on the floor, drunk, covered in blood, and raving. They set up an IV and loaded her into the ambulance—the EMS squad. They tied her down so that she couldn't hurt herself again.

"You go, Marian—I'll follow in the car."

"...No..." Marian looked up at Eve. Her voice was small and definite.

"I won't be long—"

"I can't, Eve...not anymore....I'm...sick."

"What? What do you mean, Marian?" Eve was struggling to understand.

"Nelson called me this morning....cancer!...I have cancer, Eve. You remember how I was losing all that weight? That was why. Nelson...detected a lump...the left breast. He did all the tests. It's fourth stage..."

"Marian—"

"He's very encouraging...new treatments and all that...but I know; I can feel it coming. You have to take care of her, Eve. They'll put her in the psych ward, you know. They do that with suicides. Maybe that's good. Maybe it's what should have happened a long time ago. I don't know. It's ironic. I finally get a doctor...an oncologist, no less. Go figure!"

"Marian— "

"I'm going home. I bought a cake. I thought I'd bring it with us when we went to see Donna after she woke up. I think I'm going to eat it myself..." Marian seemed drained of all color as she walked away.

As she stood by Libby's front door, Eve began to shake. This was punishment! Retribution! For telling the girls about her. The old woman was exacting a price—warning her!

"No!..No, you won't!..."

Eve closed the front door of Libby's house and walked the two blocks to her own. She let herself in, but she didn't go upstairs to change her bloody dress. Instead she went to her briefcase. She reached in and folded her hand around the familiar shape of her gun. She pulled it out and checked the chamber. It was full. She walked to the back of the house and through the back door toward the goat pens and the woods beyond. It had to stop; she had to stop it!

***

CHAPTER 73

"You wanna watch where your step, Reverend." Hetty was opening a sack of feed as the herd crowded in anticipating the morning feeding. Singleton stood in the pen rumpled and unshaven.

"Did you see her? Did she come here, Ms. Livesey?"

"Eyah, She come. A while ago. She was...outa sorts..."

A small doe had put itself between the two of them. It stood there bleating loudly at Adam.

"Out of sorts?—In what way?"

"...Don't know...She wasn't makin' much sense. Hush you! Move off now. Sorry, Reverend. That one likes ya. Goats is like that. Pained me to see her that way. She done me a good turn."

"No one has seen her. Not for four days. Her car is parked in the driveway. Her house was unlocked—nothing taken...I thought...she might have come here."

The old woman stopped for a moment, and Adam thought he saw her wipe her eyes. She was silent and seemed to need a moment to gather her feelings.

"...She...ain't like other women. She has somethin'!"

Singleton was fighting to keep himself together, "Yes. She does..."

"She weren't no helpless thing. She didn't hang on no man!"

"No...she didn't..." Singleton choked back the catch in his throat.

"...She was findin' her power...Takes a strong hand to master it."

"The police have combed the area."

"Eyah...they was here too. Didn't find nothin'. Too much for her, I guess....Too many pullin' on her. Wantin' from her. She give too much! She give herself away...lost herself...Comes down to it, a woman's got to decide for herself first. I shoulda seen it comin'...stopped it."

"I should have seen it too, Ms. Livesey." As Adam turned to go, the little doe grabbed his pant-leg in its mouth.

"Here you, Missy! You let the minister go now. You gotta let go!" The old women grabbed the little doe by the nape of the neck and held it back, trying to soothe it while it twisted and bleated in her hands.

"Reverend!"

"Yes, Ms. Livesey?..."

"You find her—you tell her for me...how sorry I am she lost her way. I thought the world of her..."

"I'll tell her..." Adam turned again to leave. As he did so, the little doe bleated louder and struggled to kick loose from the old woman as she tried to quiet it.

Adam could hear its cries all the way to his car.

End

ABOUT THE AUTHOR

In addition to <u>The Goat Woman</u>, Mike Champagne is the author of <u>Brother to the Blood</u> also available on Amazon. He is also an actor/director and playwright whose work has been critically acclaimed and seen across the country and internationally. His song cycle, <u>Bittersuite: Songs of Experience</u> ran over a year Off-Broadway in New York City followed by a two-year run in Los Angeles. He lives in New York City with his wife and children.

www.ingramcontent.com/pod-product-compliance
Lightning Source LLC
Chambersburg PA
CBHW020248200626
46816CB00001BA/194